P9-CKS-808

She's No Angel

She's No Angel

E.N. Joy and Nikita Lynette Nichols

www.urbanbooks.net

Urban Books, LLC
300 Farmingdale Road, NY-Route 109
Farmingdale, NY 11735

She's No Angel
Copyright © 2016 E.N. Joy and Nikita Lynette Nichols

All rights reserved. No part of this book may be reproduced in any form or by any means without prior consent of the Publisher, except brief quotes used in reviews.

ISBN 13: 978-1-62286-531-4
ISBN 10: 1-62286-531-6

First Mass Market Printing September 2017
First Trade Paperback Printing December 2016
Printed in the United States of America

10 9 8 7 6 5 4 3 2 1

This is a work of fiction. Any references or similarities to actual events, real people, living or dead, or to real locales are intended to give the novel a sense of reality. Any similarity in other names, characters, places, and incidents is entirely coincidental.

Distributed by Kensington Publishing Corp.
Submit orders to:
Customer Service
400 Hahn Road
Westminster, MD 21157-4627
Phone: 1-800-733-3000
Fax: 1-800-659-2436

She's No Angel

by

E.N. Joy and Nikita Lynette Nichols

Part I

"She's No Angel"

Angel

Chapter 1

"Child, you ain't a madam up in a whorehouse. You are the first lady of Savior Manger Baptist Church. So if you think you're gonna come up in here with your hooker stilettos, skirt above the knees, and blouses with short sleeves so that your bare arms are hanging out, you've got another think coming!" Mother Calloway was furious as she stood in the office of the new first lady of only two months, giving this young'un a scolding, like a mother would a child. Mother Calloway had sworn that if her hair hadn't already been gray for some years now, in just the past few months of dealing with her church's first lady, almost every strand would have been white by now. Still, Mother Calloway woke up every morning, checking for hair on her pillow. This young heifer was bound and determined to make her silky silver mane a thing of the past. The stress the first lady was bringing to the church mother with her hoochie antics was going to make Mother Calloway's hair eventually fall out for sure.

Although biologically Mother Calloway wasn't anybody's mother, having never married or had children of her own, spiritually, she was the mother of every member of that church. Mother Calloway had been a member of Savior Manger since her grandmother led her by the hand through those church doors seventy years ago, when Mother Calloway was just three years old. The building itself hadn't even been as old as Mother Calloway at the time. Ever since then, she'd been committed and dedicated to the goings-on of the church and its members.

Mother Calloway had been there longer than any of the five pastors they'd voted in over the years. She had served as secretary for the last two pastors and now served in that role for their current pastor, Pastor Harrison—the recently married Pastor Harrison. Recently married to the one and only Angel Redford-Harrison, making her the youngest first lady in the church's history, not to mention one of the most attractive as well. Standing five feet even, wearing a size four, with a figure yet to have been disturbed by childbirth, thirty-year-old Angel could pass for the captain of the local high school cheerleading team.

Her dark brown skin was just as smooth as warm chocolate pouring from a fondue fountain.

She kept a nice natural fade, causing her to go to the barbershop instead of the beauty parlor in order to keep her hair looking sharp. Voted best dressed in high school, Angel was a born fashionista who had been sewing since her father, who had raised her by himself, taught her how to. To this day, Angel handcrafted the majority of her own clothing, of which clearly Mother Calloway didn't approve.

Mother Calloway had watched Angel sashay up into Savior Manger like she was going to New York Fashion Week instead of the house of the Lord. The mother had made little comments—which were helpful, of course, done in the spirit of love—here and there to Pastor Harrison, the head of the house himself, about how she felt regarding his wife's attire. But he always seemed to take it as a compliment, instead of as the constructive criticism that Mother Calloway had intended.

"Those pants First Lady wore to Bible study last night sure was fitting around her hips good and tight," Mother Calloway had once told her pastor as she was bringing him his morning coffee.

He'd simply gazed off, with a smile on his face, like he was in la-la land, imagining his wife all over again in those butter-cream high-waist sailor-cut dress pants. "Yes, they were. Praise the Lord," he'd replied, a grin spreading across his lips.

Another time Mother Calloway had said to him, "I saw that skirt First Lady wore today. That must be one she made herself, because the ones in the department stores don't be having slits cut that high."

"As a matter of fact, I think she *did* make it herself. Thank you," Pastor Harrison had replied without even looking up from the sermon he had been working on at his desk.

Mother Calloway had let out a harrumph and had stomped off. She didn't know if her pastor was being ornery or just plain blinded by the young Jezebel who was six years his junior, so much so that he failed even to recognize that Angel's wardrobe was over the top. Mother Calloway figured she'd give him some time to make mention of the issue to his wife and then see if Angel's choice in clothing would change any.

It changed, all right. In Mother Calloway's eyes, it got ten times worse. Obviously, her pastor wasn't thinking with the right head and wasn't going to say anything to his wife. So Mother Calloway felt she had to, especially when, this morning, Angel wore a satin red pencil skirt that showed her knees and that had the nerve to have had a little split up the back, as if enough of her legs hadn't been showing. Sure the weather in Bexley, Ohio, was warming up due to it being mid-May, but she didn't have to wear that white shirt with them li'l ole wee bitty sleeves. Heck, she might as well be wearing a spaghetti-strap tank top. And since when did women wear to church the same shoes strippers wore to the club? Mother Calloway didn't know about other churches and what the mothers allowed their first ladies to wear, but there was zero tolerance for stripper heels at Savior Manger.

During service Mother Calloway had been so distracted by Angel's appearance that she could barely focus on the Word that was being preached. Being the true and dedicated saint that she was, if she was being distracted from God's message, then she could only imagine how many of the other members were—namely, the menfolk. Nope, she couldn't let this go on one more Sunday. She'd made it up in her mind that as soon as service was over, she'd follow First Lady Angel to her office and tell her about herself. She'd do it her own self, instead of trying to throw subliminal messages and hints at the pastor, hoping he would address the matter. By the time that man said anything to his wife, First Lady would be showing up dressed for the cover of the *Sports Illustrated* swimsuit issue.

"I know you are unchurched," Mother Calloway said, continuing her conversation with her first lady, "but if you hear from God at all, then surely He's told you Himself you dress like you're going over to the corner on Main Street to do more than just pass out scripture tracts to the nonbelievers." Mother Calloway shook her head.

Angel had never been one who was easily offended. She took everything in life with a grain of salt, brushing her shoulders off whenever anyone sprinkled a little on them. Other people's actions almost never dictated her own. Even being the unchurched heathen she was—according to Mother Calloway—Angel knew how to turn the other cheek. She'd learned that from her father, who was a very passive, kind, and gentle man. Ever since she was a baby and her mother abandoned them both, her father had raised her to do what he said to do without ever having to yell, cuss, and fuss at her. He had ruled with an iron fist that he'd never had to hit her with. He exuded so much respect that he attracted the same.

Right about now, Mother Calloway should have been very thankful for that. Surely she'd seen enough reality shows to know that not many women were going to stand around and allow themselves to be referred to as a whore and a prostitute without at least throwing a glass of wine on the offender. Or, in this case, a glass of holy water.

"Look, Sister Calloway . . . ," Angel began in her small, respectful tone.

Mother Calloway snapped her head back. "That's *Mother* Calloway to you," she said, taking offense.

"Pardon me, Mother Calloway," Angel said, correcting herself, keeping a genuinely pleasant smile on her face the entire time. "No, I haven't been in the church all my life, but it just so happens that when I first walked through these church doors, it felt like home. When I'm at home, I'd like to think I can dress however I feel comfortable doing."

"I bet you did feel at home when you walked through these church doors," Mother Calloway replied, "and then you had no problem making yourself right at home in our pastor's bed."

Angel kept her spiritual composure, but Mother Calloway was pressing her buttons. "Your pastor, *not* your husband," she said. "My pastor *and* my husband. So what goes on in his bed is only my concern, and I'd appreciate you not even alluding to it."

It wasn't easy, but Mother Calloway had to admit Angel was right. She didn't mind sticking her nose in a lot of places, but in a married couple's bed, it did not belong. Of course, she'd never voice her wrongness to Angel in a million years, but her silence said it all . . . as brief as the silence was.

"Listen here, I have been in church all my life," Mother Calloway snapped back.

"Yes, I know that. You seem to remind me every time you and I have a discussion."

"I was practically born out there on the church pew." Mother Calloway pointed sharply, seemingly toward the sanctuary.

Angel nodded her head. "And you constantly remind me of that as well, Mother Calloway."

"So it's safe to say that I'm saved for real and am much better tuned in to God than you'll ever be."

Angel cocked her head to the side and slightly raised her eyebrows at Mother Calloway. *Are you really?* she thought to herself.

"So it would behoove you to take my advice and put on some decent clothes for Christ's sake. Not only are you representing your husband, a wholesome man of God, but you are also representing God and His Kingdom." Mother Calloway was getting all worked up. She put her hand on her chest and took a breather.

"Are you okay, Mother Calloway?" Angel asked with concern. She extended her hands to try to comfort the older woman.

Mother Calloway jumped back from Angel's touch. "I'm just fine. The Lord is faithful to His own. God will take care of His own. You best believe that!" She rolled her eyes, drained and disgusted that her conversation with Angel seemed to be going nowhere. "Here." She dug down into the Bible bag she was toting and pulled out a catalog and extended it to Angel.

"What's this?" Angel asked, puzzled.

"Here. Just take it." Mother Calloway shoved it into Angel's hand. "It's a catalog called Ashro. It's filled with outfits suitable for first ladies. You can even go to their Web site to see what they have there as well."

Angel flipped through the catalog. It was full of nice, colorful, and beautiful suits and dresses, most with hats to match. There were coordinated footwear and handbags as well.

"They have some nice, classy outfits in there. Things a *real, respectable* first lady should be wearing. Now, if you'd order from there instead of the Victoria's Secret catalog, you won't have a problem with me. Good day!" Mother Calloway turned to exit Angel's office.

"But, Mother Calloway, I don't have a problem with you now."

Mother Calloway turned and shot Angel a stern look. "Oh, Miss Thing, but you do." And with that, she walked out the door, slamming it behind her.

Chapter 2

It was eighteen months ago when Angel first entered Savior Manger Baptist Church. It wasn't because it was Friends and Family Day and someone had invited her. She'd actually been there on a business call. Running a seamstress business from her home, Angel had been there to do some last-minute alterations for a bride who was her client and for her bridal party. It was the day of the wedding ceremony, which was taking place at Savior Manger.

Pastor Isaiah Harrison was officiating the ceremony. Angel hadn't planned on staying to witness the exchange of wedding vows. After making sure all was well with the gowns before all the ladies walked down the aisle, Angel had packed up her things and had left the church dressing room. As she'd headed toward the exit doors, with her sewing cases in tow, the voice of Pastor Harrison, whom Angel had never met, halted her footsteps before she could make it to the doors. He was speaking about how he who found a wife found a good thing. He was reminding everyone in the sanctuary that the bride, Angel's client, was an unashamed forty-year-old virgin. She had spent her years waiting to be found by her husband, since, after all, the scripture didn't say, "She who finds a husband." He reiterated to the women in the sanctuary that they needed to wait on God and not try to help Him out with booty shorts and breast implants. Angel let out a laugh, right along with everyone inside the sanctuary.

At the time, Angel started feeling some kind of way, which she didn't know to describe as conviction. She was guilty of trolling the malls for men. She wasn't a gold digger who was looking for these men to buy her anything at the mall. She wanted to be in a genuine give-and-take relationship. Was it so wrong that she desperately wanted to find her Mr. Right, buy a house on the hill with a white picket fence, have two kids—no pets because of her allergies—and live happily ever after?

She'd been a daddy's girl for years. She didn't know anything else in life other than to be taken care of by a man. A good man at that, because her daddy had set the bar high for any other man to be able to jump over. But after listening to this pastor preach, Angel couldn't help but wonder if she'd been going about it all wrong. Had she been looking for a husband, instead of waiting to be found by one? In just ten minutes she was convinced that going to the clubs, the gym, and Home Depot, looking for a man, had been a waste of her time, which was why it had never panned out and she was still single and was not dating. She was never going to find her husband at the rate she was going. She had to be found *by* him instead, at least that was what Pastor Harrison was saying that God Himself had said.

This whole "God's Word thing" was all new to Angel, who had been inside of a church only if her job required her to be. Her father was a good man and had raised her the best he knew how, but church, prayer, and God just weren't something he'd focused on in raising her. He'd done all the right things by making sure Angel knew who she was: a strong, smart, independent woman. He had not, though, made sure she knew who God was. But like the comedian Chris Rock had said in one of his stand-ups, Angel's father had done his job of keeping her off the stripper pole. Of course, Mother Calloway would beg to differ.

People always made comments that life came without instructions. Well, if what this preacher man was preaching was, in fact, true, there *was* a book with instructions, and it was called the Bible.

And God actually talked to people in the Bible, told them what to do and how to live.

Angel had stood in the church vestibule, taking in all that voice in the microphone had to say. It seeped out of the church sanctuary and into her ears. Before she knew it, the bride and groom had been pronounced man and wife and were barging through the doors and out into the vestibule, followed by the bridal party. Angel, still mesmerized by the words the pastor had spoken, stood there watching as the guests exited the sanctuary, shook hands, and gave their congratulations to the happy couple.

"You did a fine job, Pastor," Angel heard someone say to the tall, medium-brown-complexioned man who was wearing a minister's collar and carrying a Bible. Angel knew that had to be him. That had to be the man who had joined the couple in holy matrimony while giving everyone else within earshot a message about finding themselves in that same position. That had to be the man who'd just unknowingly fed Angel the Word of God, her first spiritual meal ever.

Angel felt compelled to thank him, and perhaps even ask for a second helping. She wanted to know more and fast. Her life's playbook had always had her married by the age of twenty-five, with two kids by thirty. That hadn't even almost happened.

It was better late than never, though, as far as Angel was concerned. So she patiently waited over to the side until the good pastor had excused himself and stepped out of the receiving line.

The man behind the words that had moved Angel headed away from her and down the hall. She struggled to catch up with his long strides. Angel stopped him as he was headed into his office.

"Excuse me, sir . . . Pastor," Angel said, her heels clicking on the floor as she did a light jog to catch up with the man before he disappeared behind the door to his office.

With his hand on the doorknob of the dark mahogany door with a gold-plate sign that read PASTOR HARRISON on it, he turned to face the young, timid woman. "Yes? May I help you?"

"Hi. Yes. I just wanted to . . ." At this point, Angel was a little out of breath and was struggling to juggle her sewing items.

"Here. Let me help you." He opened his office door, then turned and took a couple of items from Angel's hands. "Come in. Have a seat."

"Thank you," Angel said, happy to be relieved of some of the items she'd been carrying.

He walked over to his desk and sat down.

"I don't need to sit. I won't be long, Pastor. . . ." Angel tried to think of the name she'd briefly glanced at on the nameplate. Just that quickly it had escaped her.

"Pastor Harrison," he said. He'd already watched the poor girl struggle physically. He couldn't bear to watch her struggle mentally. "I'm Pastor Harrison."

In Angel's opinion, his voice sounded deeper and rougher in person than it had on the microphone. Perhaps it was a little scratchy after giving that mini-sermon.

"Nice to meet you." Angel smiled. "I just wanted to tell you that all that stuff you said about a woman not out trying to find a man and stuff, it really registered with me. I honestly had no idea that God actually tells us what we need to do, or should I say, not do, in order to become a bride."

"Correction. A wife," Pastor Harrison said.

Angel looked confused.

"Any woman can be a bride. That's easy. All you have to do is go out and buy a wedding gown and pick up a bouquet of flowers at the local grocer. But to be a wife, now, *that's* work."

Angel still looked a little puzzled.

"You ever read about the Proverbs woman?" Pastor Harrison asked her.

"I don't think so." Angel shook her head. "Was that one of Oprah's books of the month?"

Pastor Harrison let out a slight chuckle. "No." He stifled his laugh, seeing that this young woman was dead serious. He looked into her eyes and saw a hunger that every pastor loved in a human's soul: a hunger for the wisdom and knowledge of God and His Word. "Do you have a home church?"

Angel shook her head. "I honestly really don't do church."

"I see." Pastor Harrison opened his desk drawer. He pulled out a church program and handed it to Angel. "This is one of our recent church programs. It lists the days and times of our services. It also lists Bible study and some of our other ministries. How about you join us this week for Bible study, and I'll seek God about what He'd like me to share to the body about men, women, brides, grooms, husbands, and wives?"

Angel nodded, with excitement in her eyes. She absolutely did want to know more. "I am so there," Angel told him. "Can I bring a couple of my girlfriends? I mean, when we're trying to find a man, I have no problem asking them to come to the club with me. So what's the difference? I should be able to ask them to come to church to find a man too, right?"

Pastor Harrison did not want to continue laughing in this young lady's face, but he couldn't help it. "You can most definitely invite them." He leaned in, cupped his hand around his mouth, and whispered, "But can you leave out the part about them coming here to find a man, since that's not necessarily the case?"

"I don't want to lie in church and say I won't mention that, but I will tell you that I'll use it as a last resort to try to persuade them to come. If all else fails, that will definitely do the trick."

The corners of his lips rose into a smile, and he nodded. "Fine." He'd been doing quite a bit of smiling in the past few minutes.

Angel looked down at the program. "Okay, then, I guess I'll see you. . . ." She scanned it briefly. "Wednesday at seven p.m." She looked back up at Pastor Harrison and smiled.

"I'll see you Wednesday," he confirmed.

Angel began to gather her things.

"Let me help you." Pastor Harrison stood. "Are you parked out front or on the side street?"

"Out front," Angel informed him.

"I'll walk you to your car."

On the brief walk to her car, Angel shared with Pastor Harrison why she'd been at the church that day. She gave him a little background information on her father and how he was the one who had taught her how to sew. She found it so easy just to talk to the pastor. He was so relaxed and seemed to laugh at almost everything she said. His laughter became contagious and eventually made her laugh too. For some reason, she'd been under the impression that pastors were all stiff, serious, and thought laughing was a sin.

"This is me right here." Angel pointed to her white Hyundai Sonata as they approached it. She popped the trunk, and they started to load her things in it. "Thank you so much, Pastor Harrison," Angel said, closing her trunk when they were finished. "I can't wait until Wednesday. Will your wife be there to help teach too?"

Pastor Harrison put his head down. "I'm not married," he confessed.

Angel was a little stumped. Why was it she had been led to believe that all pastors were married and had wives in big hats who sat on the front pew? She was a little disappointed as well.

He looked back up at Angel. Reading the look of disappointment on her face, Pastor Harrison asked, "Is everything okay?" It wasn't unusual for nonbelievers to be under the impression that a pastor had to have lived and gone through everything they taught about to be qualified to speak on it. They didn't understand that God could use any living vessel to reach and teach His people regarding any situation.

Angel thought for a moment. "Well, yeah, everything is okay." Not even sounding convincing to herself, Angel pondered her reply as she slowly walked over to the driver's side of her car.

"Wednesday, right?" Pastor Harrison made a stern yet playful pointing gesture at Angel to confirm. In just seconds he had begun to feel some doubt about whether Angel would be at Bible study or not.

"Yeah, right," Angel sighed. She opened her car door and took a moment to watch as Pastor Harrison turned around to head back to the church. "Pastor?"

He turned and faced her.

"I don't want to lie, especially to a pastor. There must be something in the Bible that sends you straight to hell for doing that."

"No . . . well, yes, lying is a sin, but not just to a pastor—to anybody," he explained.

"You asked me if everything was okay. I said yeah, but really, it's not."

"Then what is it?" His voice expressed concern. He took a step back in Angel's direction.

"You're not married."

Pastor Harrison nodded and waited for Angel to continue voicing her concerns.

"So how do you expect me and my girls to come listen to you about wives, and you don't even have one? How can you tell us about husbands when you're not one?"

"Ahhh, I see." Pastor Harrison nodded, understanding. "My intentions are never to tell anyone what I think about anything. My goal is always to share with you what God says about everything. That's where a lot of us make mistakes in life. We always concern ourselves with what man thinks. Who cares what man thinks?" he shouted into the atmosphere, raising his arms and then allowing them to drop down to his sides. "If we all simply lived by what God says, then we wouldn't have any problems."

"Well then, if that's true, and if God said that a man should find a wife, why haven't you found one? I mean, are you even looking for a wife?"

"Constantly."

Angel shrugged her shoulders. "Well, then, what's the problem? Are you psychotic or a procrastinator? What's the deal with you?"

Pastor Harrison chuckled. He liked Angel. She made him smile. "I am neither of those things, but I am cautious. Being a pastor puts me in the spotlight. Women throw themselves at me all the time. And truth be told, that's a turnoff for me. But I have no doubt that in God's perfect timing, He'll place the woman who is destined to be my wife right in front of me."

Hearing those words was refreshing to Angel. Her spirits were instantly brought back up. "And I think that's where an amen goes, right?" Angel questioned.

He smiled. "You can put it right there."

"Amen!" Angel said, laughing.

Pastor Harrison joined in on the laughter. Once it died down, he spoke. "I'm pretty excited about what God will have to say on Wednesday. After all, the message is always for the messenger first."

"Oh, so that means you want to know about finding a wife and what to do as well," Angel said.

"Oh no. I know how to find a wife," he said, and then he got real serious. "I just need God to show me the one He wants for me, but I'll know exactly what to do with her."

"Oh, okay." Angel nodded at his confidence. "So the whole 'hearing from God' thing . . . You actually hear His voice?"

"Something like that," Pastor Harrison said.

"Well, I'm *definitely* going to clean out my ears, because I don't want to miss what He might have to say about my husband." Of course, they laughed again. "Has He ever said anything to you about your wife?"

"Just that she'll be like an angel from heaven, appearing out of nowhere."

"Awww, I think I like God already. He sounds so romantic." Angel looked all starry eyed.

Pastor Harrison held in his laughter, despite a small chuckle slipping out. The entire time they'd been standing outside, guests had been leaving the church, heading over to the reception. The parking lot was now practically empty. There were just a few cars, in addition to the limos transporting the bridal party. Members of the bridal party had remained inside to take wedding photos.

"I better head back in, because they'll be locking up. It was good talking to you, Sister. . . ." Pastor Harrison realized the woman he'd spent the last half hour with hadn't given him her name.

"Oh, my apologies for being rude. It's Angel. My name is Angel Redford." Angel placed one foot in her car. "And you'll definitely see me Wednesday, Pastor. Even if I can't get my girls to come, I'll be here. You never know. God may not just have a message for me about my husband. He could actually make it so that my husband is here in the flesh." Angel gave one last laugh for the road, got in her car, then drove off.

For the last few seconds before her departure, Pastor Harrison had just stood there, almost in a trance. He watched as Angel pulled out of the church parking lot and out of view. He stared until her license plate, which read ANGEL, was out of sight. "See you Wednesday, wife," he said before finding his bearings and walking back inside the church.

Chapter 3

There was a knock at Angel's office door. She exhaled and said a quick prayer. She just knew Mother Calloway was coming back to give her yet another piece of her mind. She'd need the strength to be true to herself, to maintain her integrity as a person, and not be brought out of character. It hadn't been but a minute since the older woman had slammed Angel's office door after calling her a whore and a prostitute for the way she dressed. Angel couldn't understand why Mother Calloway was back already to test her. *Nonetheless, here goes.*

"Come in," Angel said. She inhaled deeply.

Just then the door cracked open, and Pastor Harrison stuck his head in. "Hey, you about ready to head home?"

Upon seeing her handsome husband with those inviting dark brown eyes—it had taken being in his presence at least three times for her to realize his eyes had been inviting her into his life—Angel exhaled. She stood up from her desk and walked over to her husband of two months. She didn't say a word. She just hugged him.

Angel wondered if her husband could feel the tension in her trembling body. He put his arms around her and nuzzled his face in the crook of her neck. As he spoke, she could feel his warm breath hitting her neck. "Baby, are you all right?" He'd picked up on her emotions.

"Don't talk. Just hold me," was all Angel could get out before her voice cracked. She sucked in the tears, though. The last thing she wanted to be able to admit was that Mother Calloway had brought her to tears. No matter how many times Angel brushed her shoulders off, remnants of Mother Calloway's harsh words remained for her to inhale like poison.

For the next minute Pastor Harrison did exactly what his wife had asked of him. He held her. No words were spoken; there was just a silent internal cry on Angel's part. Eventually, she regained her composure enough to pull away. She quickly turned, wiping her eyes just in case a stray tear had escaped, and then walked back over to her desk and sat down.

Still without saying a word, Pastor Harrison walked over and took a seat in the chair on the opposite side of his wife's desk from where she was sitting. He reached his strong hand out to her.

Angel looked down at his hand. A smile teased the corners of her mouth as she thought back to the day he'd extended his hand to her and asked for hers in marriage. It was actually right there in that office. They'd been sitting in the exact same spots as they were sitting now.

It had been a year to the day almost after the two had met. After having attended six Sundays straight at Savior Manger, on the evening of Angel's seventh consecutive Bible study, Pastor Harrison had finally gotten the nerve to ask her out for coffee afterward. It was then when he had expressed his feelings for her verbally, and no longer just with his eyes. The two became inseparable after that. Several months passed, and one evening, Pastor Harrison picked Angel up at her house to take her out to dinner. A few minutes later, when they pulled up in the church parking lot, Angel became somewhat confused. They were supposed to be heading out to dinner. She wondered why Pastor Harrison had brought her to church.

"I just need to go inside and grab something real quick," Pastor Harrison told her. "Come with me. It's dark out here, and I don't want to leave you alone."

He escorted Angel into the church and down the hall, toward his office. She just assumed they were headed to his office, so she automatically headed to his door on the left once they got to where all the church offices were. However, Pastor Harrison went right.

"No. Over here," he said to Angel, flagging her over to the office across the hall from her.

Without a question, Angel followed him into the office. When the door opened, so did her mouth, but nothing came out. The words were stuck in her throat.

Pastor Harrison turned to see the look in her eyes, which reflected the flickering, dancing candlelight. The look of both surprise and amazement on Angel's face let him know that he'd done good. He turned and looked at the setup he'd arranged. There were candles about the office. On the desk was a spread for two, with a single rose in a vase in between the place settings. There was a tray of fruit, cheeses, and meats. There were chocolate-covered strawberries and mini cupcakes.

"You like it?" Pastor Harrison asked, even though he could tell by Angel's facial expression that she more than just liked it.

Angel was finally able to speak. "I love it. Is all this for me?" She took a step closer to the setup, admiring it all.

"It's for us." He continued to speak as he led her over to the chair behind the desk. "I don't want there to be a 'you' anymore." He pulled out the chair and allowed her to sit. "I don't want there to be a 'me' anymore." He walked around to the chair on the other side of the desk and sat. "From here on out, I want it to be us—'we.'"

Angel's eyes glimmered not only from the candlelight, but also from the moisture that was now filling her eyes. "Wh-what are you saying?"

"Angel, I'm saying exactly what that sign on the door says." He turned to the door and pointed.

It was then that Angel noticed a gold plate on the door that read FIRST LADY HARRISON. She gasped and put her hands over her mouth.

Pastor Harrison turned back around. "I want you to be my lady. I want you to be Savior Manger's first lady." He extended his hand out to her. "I'm asking you to be my wife." He dug into his pocket with his free hand and pulled out a small red-leather box. He used his thumb to flip the lid of the box open; then he brought the box over to Angel so that she could see the sparkling three-carat, pear-shaped stone. "Do you want to be all those things for the rest of your life?" Pastor Harrison held his breath and waited for Angel to answer him. He prayed that she wasn't upset that he'd proposed to her at the church, instead of at a restaurant or anyplace else. He wanted to do it on holy ground.

Angel looked at the beautiful ring. She then looked down at the strong hand that he was extending to her. She slowly slid her hand into his.

"I do," Angel said as she now sat in her office as his official first lady after only two months of marriage. "I do want to talk," she told her husband, her mind totally back in the present.

He squeezed her hand gently. "Go ahead. Talk."

But Angel couldn't talk. Not right away. As all those nasty words Mother Calloway had just spoken to her flooded her head, tears flooded her eyes and her throat, and Angel just exploded into a cry. It was the infamous ugly cry.

Still holding his wife's hand, Pastor Harrison made his way to the other side of the desk to join her. He lifted her up into his arms and held her tightly. He gave her one last tight squeeze for reassurance before letting her go.

She ran her hands over her bottom and down the back of her skirt before sitting back down. It had felt good to get that long overdue cry out. She grabbed a couple of tissues from the box on her desk and dabbed the tears away, sniffed, then nodded to her husband that she was okay, that it was okay for him to go sit back down.

Pastor Harrison went and took his seat.

"I don't know how to do this," Angel confessed. "I can't do this. I didn't ask to do this. You might have wanted to be a preacher. God might have told you that He wanted you to be a preacher, but never once when I was growing up did I ever want to be a first lady. Even more so, not once did God ever tell me He wanted me to be a first lady. Because I fell in love with a man who just happens to be a pastor, I have to be a first lady, whether I want to or not. It's not fair." The tears came back with a vengeance. "Why would God put me in a position to be something that I don't know how to be?"

Pastor Harrison looked at his wife and smiled. From the first moments she'd met him, he'd worn that same adoring smile, a smile that usually comforted her, but not that day. Not right then. At that moment Angel didn't want just comfort. She wanted answers. So his smile was close to annoying. "What's so funny?" she asked, her face not reflecting any emotion at all.

"Nothing is funny. You are just so cute."

"Come on, Isaiah. Compliments about my features aren't going to help me right now."

"I'm not saying that you are cute, as in your face."

Angel raised an inquiring eyebrow.

Pastor Harrison put his hands up in surrender. "I didn't mean it like that. We all know that you are a very beautiful woman. When I say you are just so cute, I mean your actions. You're still such a babe in Christ, but that's a good thing." he began to explain. "Because, you see, people who think they are grown and mature in Christ, you can't half tell them nothing. But a babe is always so willing to learn. There's far less to unteach the babe than with the grown folks that may not have been taught the right thing."

Angel looked at her husband as if he were speaking German. "Say that again, but in English this time."

"Never mind," he said, realizing that Angel, not quite two years in her Christian walk, still didn't pick up easily on some spiritual things. He tried going another route. "Do you trust God?"

"What kind of question is that? Of course I do," Angel said emphatically.

"Do you think God would ever put you in a position that He wouldn't equip you to handle? Do you think God would ever place you before man just so they could watch you fall on your face?"

Angel shook her head. "No, but—"

"There are no 'buts.' Either you're going to trust Him or you're not."

"I do trust Him, and I know He wouldn't have me fail, but what about the people who might try to drag me down onto my face?" Angel was thinking of none other than Mother Calloway.

"That's when you lean on the strength of Jesus and your church family. And me. I've got your back, for sure. There's nothing you can't ask any one of us here at Savior Manger and we won't do it, show you how to do it, or at least tell you how to do it."

Angel looked away from her husband. She already knew at least one member of Savior Manger who didn't have a problem telling her anything.

"What's wrong? Why did you look away like that?" Angel's change in facial expressions didn't go unnoticed by Pastor Harrison.

Angel kept her eyes planted on the sign on her door, which read FIRST LADY HARRISON. Across the hall was a door that had a sign that read PASTOR HARRISON. Next to that door was the one that read CHURCH SECRETARY. No way did Angel want to come between, not her husband, but her pastor and the woman who had been a permanent fixture in that church and who was also his secretary. Apparently, no other first lady had had a problem with Mother Calloway. Had that been the case, certainly her husband would have given her a heads-up. So maybe it was Angel who was the problem. Perhaps what Mother Calloway was telling her was right, but she just had a brusque way of saying it. Sometimes older people were just like that. Felt they'd lived a long and hard enough life to be able to say whatever they so pleased.

Taking all these thoughts into consideration, Angel decided not to mention her conversation with Mother Calloway to her husband. Certainly she could handle the senior citizen with the fly mouth. Like Pastor Harrison had said, God would equip her. She trusted that God would help her to deal effectively with Mother Calloway. If not, perhaps God would deal with Mother Calloway Himself.

Chapter 4

"First Lady Conference in Dallas, Texas," Angel said out loud as she read the postcard that had come to the church addressed to her, or rather to the first lady of Savior Manger Baptist Church. Angel always went to her office and went through her mail every Wednesday before Bible study. She was now only three months into her role as first lady, so not much mail came addressed to her personally; there were certainly no invitations to speak at conferences or anything. Even though her invitation to attend the First Lady Conference in Dallas, Texas, wasn't a speaking engagement, it was an invitation all the same.

Curious as to exactly what all a First Lady Conference entailed, Angel quickly powered up her computer. After about forty-five seconds she was logging on and visiting the Web site listed in the brochure. She was amazed to find that the conference was the entire weekend long. There were workshops, luncheons, opportunities to receive spa treatments, and some well-known keynote speakers. The ones Angel hadn't heard of, she Googled and found them to be interesting, powerful women of God. There was one keynote speaker in particular who was somewhat of a new first lady herself. Angel actually watched a couple of her speeches that had been posted on YouTube. She was a firecracker indeed, not exactly what would have come to Angel's mind when she thought of a first lady. But what did Angel know? That was why she had been curious about the conference in the first place. If it could enlighten her at all, then she'd be better off after the conference than she was before.

"Your place in the church. Your place in His Kingdom." Angel read this year's conference theme out loud. If that didn't sound like God had designed this particular message just for her, then she didn't know who else it could be for.

Her eyes widened with excitement as she viewed some photos from previous years' conferences. Her eyes watered at some of the powerful testimonies first ladies had left on the testimonial page. Two hours later, Angel had read every word on every page of that Web site. Not only that, but she'd registered to attend, putting the full payment on her credit card. She was just about to book her flight and hotel when her spirit became a little vexed. She hadn't run this by her husband at all. The fire inside of her had just erupted like a volcano, and she hadn't thought twice about it.

Being a newlywed after being single for so many years, she knew it was going to take some getting used to, to realize that she owed her mate the respect of getting his input on trips that would call for her to be gone overnight and to be absent from the front pew on a Sunday morning.

"First Lady, is everything all right?"

Angel's heart nearly jumped out of her chest; and her bottom, out of her seat. She had been so engrossed in her thoughts about the conference, she hadn't even seen Carmen stick her head through the cracked door.

"Did I scare you?" Carmen asked, now stepping inside the office.

"Oh no, Carmen. You're fine," Angel said, relaxing. She could relax even more knowing that it was friend instead of foe who'd come to see about her.

Carmen was Angel's assistant. The church had hired her part-time for now since Angel herself was just getting settled in as first lady. Angel didn't have many duties as of yet, so she didn't need anyone working with her full-time. In addition to that, unlike the first lady of the White House, Angel hadn't yet decided what her "thing" would be that would ultimately comprise the majority of her duties as first lady. Michelle Obama's was keeping kids healthy. Angel was still playing with a few ideas.

Carmen was a thirty-five-year-old, recently divorced mother of one. The divorce had affected her financially, so the church thought it would be perfect for Carmen to pick up some extra money as Angel's assistant, to complement her pay from her regular nine-to-five job. Not only that, but Mother Calloway had mentioned how it would keep her from sticking her hand in the benevolent fund every month as well.

"Bible study is over," Carmen said. "Pastor is talking with a couple of people as everyone clears out. He asked me to come check on you. I didn't even know you were here."

"My goodness," Angel said, throwing her head back and then smacking herself on the forehead. She'd gotten so caught up in the whole First Lady Conference thing that she hadn't given Bible study a second thought. "I can't believe I got distracted where I let time get away from me like that."

"I think Pastor was a little worried, wanted to make sure you weren't in here sick or something."

"Please tell him I'm just fine, Carmen, and that I didn't mean to worry him." Angel glanced down at her computer. "I'm going to log off. Tell him I'll be down and ready to go in a minute."

"No problem, First Lady. Is there anything you need for me to do?"

Angel smiled at Carmen's sincerity. "No, Carmen. I'm good. You have a blessed evening."

"You too, First Lady. God bless." Carmen exited, and Angel could hear the sound of her footsteps getting farther and farther away.

Angel shut down her computer. She grabbed the conference postcard and placed it in her Bible bag. She'd be sure to talk with her husband about it tonight. Hopefully, he'd approve of the idea. That registration fee was nonrefundable.

After locking up her office, Angel headed to the church classroom where Bible study was held. Mostly everyone had already departed. Pastor Harrison was standing in the rear of the room, speaking with a couple of members. Angel decided she would wait until she made eye contact with him. If it was okay to interrupt, he would wave her over. It was just a matter of seconds before Pastor Harrison spotted his lovely wife standing at the door. A huge smile covered his face, and he waved her over.

His contagious smile jumped onto Angel's face. With a smile as wide as a football field, she took a step toward her husband.

"Fine time for you to show up."

Mother Calloway's words halted Angel's steps and wiped that smile right off of her face.

Angel swallowed. She caught her breath. She hadn't braced herself for the impact of the hard tone Mother Calloway always threw her way. "Mother Calloway. A good evening to you."

"Uh-huh—" Mother Calloway had a couple of pieces of trash in her hand as she'd been picking up the classroom.

"First Lady," a male parishioner interrupted, stepping in between Mother Calloway and Angel, whom he faced. Now it was Mother Calloway's steps that were halted.

"Hi, uhhh . . ." Angel recognized the nice-looking young gentleman's face but couldn't put a name with it.

"Gregory," he said, smiling all up in her face while taking her palm into his own. He kissed the back of Angel's hand.

He'd planted a wet kiss on her, and Angel slowly pulled her hand back and discreetly wiped it down her skirt. She didn't want to offend the man, especially if he meant no harm or disrespect. When she was coming up,

Angel had had an auntie who always planted the "yuckiest, most wettest" kisses all over her face, so perhaps the same went with *Uncle* Gregory. The verdict was still out on that right about now, though, and Angel wasn't about to let the remnants of his wet kiss rest on her hand and cause a breath funk on her skin.

"I sure did miss you." Gregory grinned.

Mother Calloway cleared her throat.

The young man did a double take, as if he himself had to remember where he was, and that there were more people in the room besides him and his married first lady.

"At Bible study. I missed you at Bible study," Gregory said.

Mother Calloway cleared her throat once again, only louder this time.

"*We* missed you at Bible study," he said, smiling a nervous smile as he looked back and forth between Angel and Mother Calloway.

"Well, I'm sorry I missed Bible study," Angel replied, apologizing. "But I'll see you bright and early Sunday morning, Brother Gregory. You have a good evening."

Gregory nodded, looked at Mother Calloway again, then hurried out like he'd been caught doing something wrong.

Angel nodded and smiled. Mother Calloway was sure to wipe that smile off of her face in record time. She was becoming a master at that.

The church mother couldn't approach Angel fast enough. She got so close to Angel that when she spoke, no one else could hear. Through gritted teeth, she said, "Not only do you, as the first lady of Savior Manger, not show up for Bible study, but then you flaunt all up in here and flirt with a boy who is probably still in college. You're acting like a desperate cougar. And right in front of your husband." Mother Calloway was teed off.

Angel just stood there and looked at her for a minute. There was no way Mother Calloway could be serious. Something truly had to be going on with the old lady, so Angel asked her, "Mother Calloway, are you feeling all right?" Angel truly considered that the woman, who was getting up there in age, could perhaps be suffering from the early stages of dementia or maybe even Alzheimer's disease. She was talking real crazy. "Are you serious right now?"

"Don't you try to do that hip talk with me. I'm your elder. Show some respect. Forget about just respecting me. Respect your husband, for God's sake, and if nothing else, respect the Lord's house."

"I mean no disrespect, Mother Calloway. There is just no way you could seriously think I was flirting with Gregory."

"Gregory? So you *do* know his name. Tried to stand there and play stupid, like you didn't know that boy's name. Not only do you know his name, but all of a sudden it's personal too. No longer is it Brother Gregory. Now it's just plain old Gregory. You ain't foolin' nobody, especially me. When you gliding around on thin ice, you bound to get caught slipping. And before you know it, you're gonna fall right through the ice. You won't be able to say I didn't try to save you from drowning."

Angel put her hand up and shook her head. "I can't right now." Angel half understood Jesus' parables. She wasn't about to try to figure out Mother Calloway's.

Mother Calloway's mouth flung open wide. Had this hoochie mama just given her "the hand"? She grabbed her heart and started her rendition of Fred Sanford. She, too, was going to join Elizabeth in heaven.

"Mother Calloway, are you all right?" one of the men who had been speaking to Pastor Harrison said from across the room. He made his way toward the elderly woman and Angel, as did Pastor Harrison and the other gentleman who had been speaking with the men. Everyone else had left the premises.

"Go grab her some water," Pastor Harrison ordered the second gentleman.

"Right away, Pastor," he said, then rushed over to the water cooler and filled a cup with water.

"Mother Calloway, have a seat." Pastor Harrison helped the first gentleman sit Mother Calloway down in a chair. Within seconds, the other man brought the water over and placed the cup to Mother Calloway's quivering lips.

Mother Calloway, shaking, took several sips of water with assistance from the gentleman. She let out an "Ahhh" and then relaxed back in the chair.

"Are you okay, Mother?" Both fear and concern filled Pastor Harrison's eyes.

"Yes, son, I am." Mother Calloway brushed her hand down her pastor's cheek. She did it with such pity. "You are such a good man, Pastor. It's such an honor looking out for your affairs." She turned and shot Angel the look of death. "Speaking of affairs . . ."

Angel swallowed hard nervously. Was Mother Calloway really about to bring this nonsense up with the pastor? In front of these parishioners? Surely underneath Angel's dark shade of brown skin, her cheeks were as red as a devil's horns with the embarrassment of possibly having to defend herself. Speaking of devil's horns, Angel could have sworn there was a pair of horns right before her, attached to the devil himself—disguised as a little, helpless old lady.

"No, no, we are not going to talk about my business affairs right now," Pastor Harrison said. "You need to rest."

"I don't mean *your* business affairs," Mother Calloway objected. "I mean *her* affair." She pointed vigorously toward Angel.

Angel's mouth flew open, but no words came out. Only her husband was able to speak.

"What did I just say, Mother Calloway?" Pastor Harrison said sternly. "We're not going to talk about my business affairs, first lady's, or anyone else's, for that matter." He looked up at the gentleman who had helped him seat Mother Calloway on the chair. "Did Mother ride with you this evening? Can you see to it that she gets back home okay?"

He nodded.

Pastor Harrison turned back to Mother Calloway. "Mother, Elder Paul is going to see to it that you get home safely. We want you to rest. Like I said, don't worry about my affairs or anyone else's. You promise?"

"But—" Mother Calloway began, looking from Angel to Pastor Harrison with much desperation.

"No buts," Pastor Harrison said, cutting her off. He looked at his wife. "Angel, honey, will you carry Mother's purse for her? Deacon Gene and I are going to lock up." Pastor Harrison was referring to the second man. "I'll meet you out at the car."

"Yes, dear," Angel said. Angel scanned the room and spotted Mother Calloway's purse sitting atop one of the desks. She went over and grabbed it while Elder Paul helped Mother Calloway to her feet. Angel walked over and tried to assist by grabbing Mother Calloway's free arm, but the older woman quickly snatched it away, then snatched her purse from Angel, looking at Angel like she'd been trying to steal her purse.

Angel walked beside Mother Calloway out of the church and through the parking lot. She waited as Elder Paul helped Mother Calloway into the passenger's seat of his car. Elder Paul walked around to the driver's side and got into the car.

Mother Calloway sat looking straight ahead, clenching her purse tightly to her chest.

"I hope you're feeling better, Mother Calloway," Angel said sincerely. Angel didn't like to see anyone in distress, even if they'd brought it upon themselves. "Like Pastor said, please let either one of us know if there is anything we can do for you, okay?"

Mother Calloway turned and glared at Angel. "I know something you can do for me right now."

Angel was afraid to ask, but she did, anyway. "And what's that, Mother Calloway?"

"Trash," she spat.

"Pardon me?" Angel was taken aback.

"Trash." Mother Calloway held her hand out. Balled up inside her hand remained the couple of pieces of trash she'd gathered when picking up the Bible study classroom. Apparently, she'd been clutching it as well as her heart and her purse.

Angel opened her palm out flat for Mother Calloway to drop the trash into it.

"Thank you," Mother Calloway said. She shot the evilest glare ever at Angel. With her eyes closed to a squint, she said, "And don't worry about the rest of the trash." She looked Angel up and down. "I'm going to make sure I do everything in my power to rid the church of it." On that note, Mother Calloway snatched the door closed, almost slamming Angel with it.

Angel stepped away as she watched Elder Paul drive off. In a matter of ten seconds she had been convicted, and she repented for thinking, *If that woman is going to be in heaven when I die, send me to hell in a handbag. Just make it a Michael Kors.*

Chapter 5

"Don't forget, you have to try the restaurant Pappadeaux while in Dallas," Carmen said as she helped Angel unload her luggage from the trunk of her Toyota Camry.

Pastor Harrison would have driven Angel to the airport if he could have. He was out of town, on a speaking engagement of his own. He wasn't too keen on leaving his wife behind, and home alone, while he went on out-of-town speaking engagements, which was why he felt it was a divine order that Angel attend the First Lady Conference. He was more comfortable knowing that she was off doing ministry as well. In addition to that, Pastor Harrison was excited for his wife and prayed that God would send her a message to encourage her to be more secure in her role as first lady.

"The Galleria is a must!" Carmen added. "They have an Ann Taylor store, a BCBG—"

"Hold up," Angel said, interrupting Carmen so that she couldn't rattle off more retailers.

"You trying to have me come back fat and broke so you can try to steal my man or something?" Angel said, placing her carry-on strap over her shoulder.

"Oh no, First Lady." Carmen got serious, and her eyes bucked. "I would never do such a thing. You and Pastor are—"

"Relax, Carmen," Angel told her, lowering her hands, signaling for Carmen to drop her tone of anxiety. "It was a joke. Ha-ha." Angel feigned laughter.

Carmen's face remained stoic. First ladies always suspected that women in the church were trying to get their husbands on the low-low. Carmen apparently didn't see anything funny about her first lady's joke.

"Oh, just forget it." Angel shooed her hand. "Anyway, do I have everything?" Angel gave the trunk one last once-over. She then went and double-checked the passenger seat and the floor. She looked down around her at all her belongings. *Purse, check. Carry-on, check. Tablet, check. Suitcase, check.* "Looks like I'm all set."

Carmen closed the trunk. "First Lady, you have an awesome time in the Lord." Carmen hugged her. "I've prayed for your travel mercies, so I know you are going to have a wonderfully relaxing, safe flight."

"Thank you so much, Carmen, for all you do." Angel hugged her assistant back. "Kiss Candace for me," Angel said in reference to Carmen's ten-year-old daughter.

"I will. Pastor told me he is going to be able to pick you back up from the airport Monday morning."

The First Lady Conference went from Friday all the way through to Sunday afternoon. Angel didn't know how spiritually full or exhausted she would be from the conference, so she had decided not to risk running out of gas by trying to catch a flight out immediately afterward. She would stay Sunday night in the comfort of her hotel room and then would fly out first thing Monday morning.

"Yes, that's right," Angel confirmed. "Pastor's flight gets in Sunday night. Minister Johnston is going to preach for him on Sunday."

"Then I guess I won't see you until Bible study on Wednesday."

"Yep," Angel said. "Well, let me get going. I'm not trying to miss this flight. The devil is a liar." Angel waved as best she could, being that her hands were full, and then she headed inside the airport, where she checked in at the Delta kiosk. She received her boarding pass and then took her suitcase over to the luggage check-in station. After verifying for the attendant that her suitcase was unlocked, she headed toward the security gate. She knew better than to put the lock on her suitcase. After 9/11, airlines would pop those locks right off suitcases to see what was inside for the sake of the country's safety.

Angel spent only fifteen minutes in the security clearance line and then made a mad dash for Starbucks. She wished she'd worn flats instead of the four-inch-heel "stripper shoes" that dressed her feet. What had she been thinking when picking out those shoes? Well, she'd been thinking that she'd dress up her casually dressed-down ensemble with the shoes. *Bad idea.*

Juggling a hot cup of coffee as she walked to her departure gate only made her trek that much more uncomfortable. By the time she finished her coffee, she heard the announcement that they would begin to board her flight.

"Just great." Angel frowned, not because she wasn't excited to be heading to Dallas for what she knew was going to be a wonderful experience, but because she now had to use the bathroom. No way was she going to try to lug all her stuff to the bathroom, then into a bathroom stall. She decided to hold it until she boarded the plane and to use the lavatory then, not that stuffing herself into that small space without items in tow was that much better.

"Please have your boarding passes ready," the flight attendant announced as zone two boarded, which was Angel's zone.

Angel couldn't get on that plane fast enough. She found her seat, which was a window seat. That only confirmed that she needed to make it to the bathroom immediately. She didn't want to have to scoot past the people in the middle and aisle seats to get to the bathroom.

She placed her carry-on in the overhead compartment; then she stuffed her large purse, which she'd tucked her tablet inside of, under the seat in front of her. After that, she went and relieved herself. Twenty minutes later, she was saying a prayer to God for a safe flight as the plane took off into the clear blue sky.

Angel was so anxious as she sat on the plane, looking out at the fluffy white clouds. She felt in her spirit that she was going to get exactly what she needed from this conference, which was instructions on how to be a first lady. She wondered if there would be any other new first ladies in the audience who were trying to figure out how to fit in. She wondered if every first lady had a Mother Calloway to deal with. Perhaps Mother Calloways weren't Satan's imps, but tests from God instead.

It would be a blessing on top of a blessing if Angel could get some ideas from the other first ladies on what her "thing" should be. She had a couple of ideas of her own she wanted to run by them as well. Because Angel was so big on fashion, she was considering starting some kind of ministry where she could help the young girls, and the women of the church, to be fashionable without doling out hundreds of dollars that they really didn't have on labels. Her giving fashion advice? *That would give Mother Calloway a heart attack for real*, she thought, then smiled, now strongly considering the ministry.

"Stop it in the name of Jesus," Angel scolded herself under her breath. She leaned back in her seat and closed her eyes. By the time she opened them again, the plane was preparing for landing.

Angel looked at her watch. The plane was right on schedule. It was 10:00 a.m., and her flight had been scheduled to land at DFW at 10:11 a.m. A few minutes later, the sound of seat belts unclicking was like music to the passengers' ears. The flight attendant thanked them for choosing Delta as some of the passengers were exiting the plane and heading toward the baggage claim, while others went to the gates of their connecting flights, headed to their final destinations.

After retrieving her luggage, Angel found the area where the hotel shuttles transported their guests. She located the van with the logo of the hotel she was staying at and headed that way. The driver was at the rear of the van, loading luggage. Angel set hers down next to that of the other hotel guests' and boarded the van.

The drive from the airport to the hotel was short. It didn't take long at all. As the driver pulled up to the front of the hotel, Angel's eyes lit up like a streetlight at dusk. She saw women of all shapes, sizes, ages, and colors. They were dressed and done up, their makeup flawless. Angel figured it was safe to guess that the majority of them were there for the First Lady Conference. As she got out of the van, took her luggage from the driver, and tipped him, she began to notice several women carrying Mary Kay cosmetic totes. Once she entered the hotel, she saw signs welcoming both the First Lady Conference attendees and the Mary Kay Conference. That explained the droves of beautiful women. Combine hundreds of first ladies and Mary Kay consultants, and one couldn't expect anything other than beauty and excellence.

Angel checked into her room and left her luggage to be brought up by the bellhop. She then headed over to the elevator bank. There were smiling women waiting for the elevator to pick them up and deliver them to their respective floors.

"Good morning, Sister," said a fair-skinned woman who looked to be around Angel's age, greeting Angel.

"Good morning to you," Angel greeted in return. "You here for the First Lady Conference?"

"No, I'm a Mary Kay consultant. One of the top sellers in my state," the woman said, smiling.

"Well, you go, girl," Angel said proudly. "I like to see young women doing their thing."

"Thank you. I appreciate that."

"I'm here for the First Lady Conference, but since we'll be at the same hotel, who knows? Maybe we can meet up. My assistant told me I have to go to Pappadeaux to eat and I must shop at the Galleria."

"Well, in addition to Mary Kay, I do catering, so I'm kind of like a food connoisseur, and I will say that Pappadeaux is the truth, honey."

"Then I have to make sure I go," Angel said as the elevator arrived. The two women, along with the other guests that were waiting, climbed onto the elevator. "Five, please," Angel said to the person standing by the buttons.

"Six," the woman she'd been talking with called out.

The door closed, and all the necessary buttons were pushed.

"Do you have a card or something?" Angel asked the woman. "I've never been to one of these conferences before, so I'm not sure how jam-packed it will be. But if I do get a chance to get away, I'd love the company. I'll call you, and if you're available, perhaps we can take a break from here and go check out Dallas."

"That sounds great," the woman said as she reached into her bag. She pulled out a card and handed it to Angel.

"Unique. What a unique name," Angel joked. She scanned the card a little more. "You live in Atlanta?"

"I do now," Unique said. "With all the parties those Georgia peaches be throwin' down there, and with all the fashion shows everyone wants to look good at, even if they aren't the model, I'm in the best of both worlds as far as my catering and cosmetics."

"You are right about that," Angel said. "I've watched an episode or two of *The Real Housewives of Atlanta* and *Married to Medicine*. Them Atlanta chicks be doin' it up."

"Yes. Nothing like where I used to live, which is Malvonia, Ohio."

"Malvonia? My goodness! I live in Bexley, Ohio. We're practically neighbors. Well, we were, anyway."

Unique's face lit up. "We were only what? About a thirty-minute drive from each other?"

"Forty minutes if you go straight down Broad Street." Angel made reference to the busy, congested street that ran through several suburbs of Columbus, Ohio, which was the capital city of the state.

"You got that right," Unique agreed.

The elevator had already stopped on one floor, and now it was at Angel's.

"Well, this is me," Angel said. "It was nice meeting you, Unique."

"You too . . ." Unique's words trailed off because she hadn't gotten Angel's name.

"It's Angel," she said, getting off the elevator. "Enjoy your conference."

"You too," Unique was able to say right before the elevator doors closed, separating the two women.

Angel pulled out the little cardboard envelope her electronic keycards were located in. She opened it to double-check her room number, which the hotel clerk had written on the inside. She followed the signs to her room. After letting herself into her room, she checked out the two queen beds. They didn't have any king beds available, although she'd requested one at the time of her reservation. The fine print didn't guarantee that particular special request, though. She wasn't complaining, especially since check-in officially wasn't until 3:00 p.m., but since they had a room ready, they'd allowed her to check in much earlier than that. Favor!

Angel put her purse down on the desk, which was next to the matching shelf that served as a television stand, a dresser, as well as a secured mini-refrigerator. She walked over to the window and drew the curtain back, then smiled at the sight of the hustle and bustle of the big D. It just looked so busy, like there was so much going on and the folks were happy to be doing whatever it was they were doing. There seemed to be so much to do in Dallas and so much to eat. A knock on the door interrupted Angel's mental affair with the streets of Dallas.

She peeked out the peephole, saw the bellhop, and opened the door.

"Your luggage, ma'am," was his greeting.

"You can put it right there." Angel pointed to the locked door that separated her room from the one next door. While he followed her directions, she went over to her purse and pulled out a couple of ones. She handed them to him, thanked him, and then saw him out.

Registration for the First Lady Conference was from noon to 2:00 p.m. It was now 11:35 a.m. Angel decided she would unpack and relax for a little bit before heading down. She used the bathroom and then slipped into a tee and some warm-ups she planned on wearing when she decided to utilize the hotel workout room. She unpacked her things, placing her undergarments in the drawers, matching her outfits up on hangers in the closet, and placing the shoes she'd wear with each outfit underneath that particular outfit. Next, she placed all her cosmetics and toiletries near the sink. After she did all that, the clock was striking noon.

Lying back on the bed, in the spot closest to the window, Angel retrieved the remote and turned on the television. It was automatically tuned in to the hotel information channel. She watched that for a minute or so and then found one of those *Law & Order* shows to watch. Fifteen minutes into the show, Angel could hardly hear the actors' voices over her grumbling belly. The hunger pangs were not going to let her rest.

"So much for that," Angel said, climbing out of bed and back into the clothes she'd just taken off.

She brushed her teeth, freshened up her lip gloss, and after picking her hair, she sprayed just a tad of olive oil sheen on it to give it a shine.

She checked out her profile and, once satisfied, grabbed her purse and headed for the registration for the conference, which, according to the hotel information channel, was being held in a ballroom on the second floor.

When Angel got off of the elevator on the second floor, she hit an entirely new scene. The silence of the elevator was now replaced with chattering women and laughter. She saw women smiling and shaking hands, as if meeting one another for the first time. For the most part, everyone was dressed casually, which Angel appreciated, considering she had on a pair of black khakis with a three-quarter-length baby blue shirt. Instead of putting her heels back on, she'd opted for a pair of leather baby doll flats that had a single strap going around her ankle. The black, baby blue, and white fashion scarf she wore tied around her neck jazzed the ensemble up just slightly. Angel did notice some of the older women were suited up with matching hats and pearls, but it looked as if the majority of women had taken into consideration their comfort level when traveling when they'd picked out their clothes.

Angel inhaled a lovely scent, which was a mixture of some fine perfumes, body sprays, and colognes. The scent of a first lady indeed.

Angel walked over to the long set of tables where several lines had formed. One woman happened to be walking away, leaving no one else behind her in the line. Angel hurried over so that she could be served next.

"Hi. Welcome to the First Lady Conference," said the woman behind the table, greeting Angel with a smile.

"Hi," Angel replied. "I'm Angel Redford-Harrison."

The woman immediately began to flip through pages on the clipboard she had in her hand. "Are you full-weekend registration?"

At first Angel wasn't sure what the woman was asking, but then she recalled that online there were various options. One could register for a single day, two days, a luncheon only, a dinner only, or the full weekend. Angel had done the latter. "Yes." Angel nodded.

The woman continued her search. "Ahhh, here you are. It was just under Harrison." She checked off Angel's name. She then turned around and grabbed a tote bag. "Inside this bag is all the information you'll need for the weekend. Your agenda is in there, as well as some suggestions for extracurricular activities and things that will be taking place in the city, off-site." She pointed to an area where there were some name badges and Sharpies laid out.

"If you would please, at the end of the table down there, there are name badges for each attendee to write their name on. You just write your name on the white card stock, and inside your bag you will find a clear plastic tab on a lanyard to attach it to. If you have any questions at all during the conference, you can come back down and see any one of us here at the table. There is also a phone number listed on the program agenda that you can call as well."

"You said a mouthful," Angel said, smiling. "Thank you so much."

The woman smiled back. "Thank you, First Lady Harrison. I do hope you enjoy the conference."

"I'm sure I will." Now with her purse and tote bag in hand, Angel headed over to make her badge. After finding the lanyard inside her tote, she put the badge together and placed it around her neck.

She pulled out the agenda to see what all the day entailed. At two o'clock, once registration had ended, there would be the kickoff luncheon with the first keynote speaker in the main ballroom. After that, the women could branch off into their choice of two different workshops. For dinner, the women were on their own, but then at 8:00 p.m., there was an evening mixer put on by one of the conference's sponsors.

Angel looked at her watch. It was an hour before lunch. She figured she'd wait it out and eat the food she'd paid for as part of the conference fee, instead of going down to the hotel restaurant to spend money on food.

Looking around, Angel spotted vendors up and down the hallway. There had to be at least twenty vendors in all. She decided she could easily kill an hour of time by checking out each vendor. There were authors selling books; hat designers; and vendors selling jewelry, oils, prayer cloths, and other unique and original items, all proudly displayed. Angel spent time talking to a woman who designed liturgical dance garments. Angel was so inspired. She was awesome with some good fabric, a needle, and thread but had never thought twice about starting her own clothing line. The seed had definitely been planted.

By two o'clock, Angel couldn't get into that ballroom and get seated for the luncheon fast enough. That little complimentary beverage and snack service on the flight over hadn't done her the least bit of justice. Peanuts and soda could go only so far. With her small waist and frame, she could easily be mistaken for a salad girl, but she could throw down on some meat and potatoes just as freely as the next. A daily trip to the gym, sometimes two, kept her physique on point. But Angel had never let the fear of gaining a pound or two keep her from indulging in her favorite foods.

Angel entered the huge ballroom, which was large enough to house all 357 registrants, and was happy to see that the salads, dressing, rolls, butter, ice water, and tea had already been set out at each round table. The tables were covered with white linen tablecloths and could seat eight women each. Typically, these types of tables seated ten tightly, but these first ladies were given plenty of space to eat and to turn their chairs toward the stage comfortably.

Behind the stage was a gold crushed-velvet curtain that looked like it was for royalty. To the left and the right of the podium, which stood at center stage, was a screen that had the conference title and theme on it. Underneath the screen, on the left, was an area that was encased by a thick plastic partition and that had a drum set. A keyboard sat next to that. Under the other screen were three microphones that had been lined up. Angel's spirit leaped in advance of the anticipated praise and worship that would go forth through the music ministry at this weekend's conference. For now, though, her stomach was leaping in anticipation of some tasty morsels.

One of the few to enter the ballroom thus far, Angel sat at a table where no one else had yet to be seated. Word that lunch was now served soon spread like wildfire, and the women began to enter the ballroom in droves. Within minutes, Angel's table was full, with seven other first ladies seated around it.

For the most part, these women had just met that day. Even if a first lady's armor bearer had traveled with her, the armor bearers were not permitted to attend any portion of the conference. It was strictly for first ladies only. The women needed the comfort of knowing that every other woman in the room had been where they had been or was sitting where they sat. The conference organizers felt the first ladies would be more willing to open up and share if they knew that the women among them had an understanding of what they were going through. Inviting outsiders would have been like the wives in the neighborhood setting up a couples' retreat yet inviting the sexy single woman next door.

There were several women in the room who knew each other from past conferences, had met through ministry, or had become acquainted because they lived in the same city. Angel didn't know a single soul at her table, but she took the liberty of introducing herself to each woman.

The other women began to introduce themselves as well.

"I'm First Lady Chapman of Good Faith Apostolic in St. Louis," a woman said from across the table. She reached into her clutch, pulled out a few business cards, and placed them next to the small floral centerpiece in the middle of the table. The other women partook of the cards, sliding them to one another, then passed out their own cards as well.

Angel was surprised that so many of the women had business cards with First Lady So-and-So of So-and-So Church printed on them. She made a mental note to suggest to the church board and finance committee that she get some printed up to represent herself as first lady of Savior Manger.

"Do you have a card?" one of the women asked Angel.

"No. I was just telling myself that I have to get some when I get back home. I had never thought of getting business cards made up. I had just never looked at it that way, like a business."

"Honey," the woman went on, "just like at home, how the man is the head of the family, but the woman is the head of the home—same goes with the church. Yes, the pastor may be the shepherd leading the sheep, but who do you think has the task of cleaning up after the sheep?"

The women laughed, and one even gave out an "I know that's right."

Angel wanted more of an explanation. "What do you mean by that? I was always taught that the man was the head."

"He is," the woman confirmed, "like I said, of the family. But the wives, we have to run that house like a business. When you're a first lady, you got two houses to run like a business."

"And a lot of these young women nowadays don't see it that way," an older woman said, jumping in. She looked at Angel and another pastor's wife who was sitting at the table and who looked to be around Angel's age. "No offense, but you younger gals done jacked up the whole family balance that we elders spent so many years putting in place."

"No offense taken," Angel said, not the slight bit offended, because in all actuality, she had no idea what balance the woman was talking about and what role she'd played in jacking it up. Angel urged the woman with her eyes to continue. She had no problem being the student, and from the sounds of it, this woman was about to teach.

"See, I'm old school," the older woman continued. "My husband is the provider. He's the head of the family, and I'm the head of the house. We don't do none of that fifty-fifty stuff your generation goes for," she said to Angel. "I don't pay half the mortgage, half the bills, half the car note, and so on."

"And why should you?" added the lady who had started the conversation in the first place. "The men don't do half the cleaning, half the laundry, half the cooking, half the running the kids around to ball practice, PTA meetings, and whatnot."

The woman next to her gave her a high five.

"That's what I'm saying right there," the older woman continued. "If you gon' be the man and provide, then provide one hundred in such a way where the woman isn't fifty percent of the provider yet one hundred percent the keeper. That ain't fair at all." She shook her head. "Marriages are not fifty-fifty. They are one hundred–one hundred. So if the wife is going to do one hundred percent of minding the house, then the husband should do one hundred percent of minding the family."

"I hear what you're saying," the other young pastor's wife said. "But that was a long time ago, way back in the day." She eyed the older woman. "No offense." Clearly, she was throwing shade, though. The poking out of her lips and the wobble of her head indicated such.

The older woman raised an eyebrow, sensing the young lady was trying to get fresh at the mouth with her.

The younger pastor's wife continued. "Nowadays, we have bigger homes and more expensive cars. Most of the time it's the wife who wants the forty-five-hundred-square-foot house, so she should help pay for it."

"Well, as the head of the family," the older woman shot back, "the husband should use wisdom in his role as the leader and should say, 'Baby, now you know my paycheck can only afford us twenty-five hundred square feet, so we can't be neighbors with the Joneses, at least not right now.'"

"Amen!" several of the women said.

Angel just sat back, taking in each woman's valid opinions and points as their discussion continued even after the food and the conference itself was prayed over and the main lunch dish was served. Angel and her husband didn't split the bills fifty-fifty, because for one, the church owned the home they lived in. It wasn't new or in a gated community or anything like that. It was nowhere near close to forty-five hundred square feet, either. It was an older home that at least two previous pastors had lived in before. Over the years it had been upgraded, and it just had a nice, homey feel to it. The church covered the utility bills and the property taxes as well. All of this was part of Pastor Harrison's salary, in addition to a monetary stipend he received. Of course, with the stipend they had to purchase their own food, personal items, and so forth, but that didn't come to even half of the amount a mortgage would have.

Angel kept up the home, cooked, and cleaned. As of yet, there were no little ones to chase around, but when that time did come, Angel was certain she'd do the majority of the child rearing as well. One thing she did understand about being a pastor's wife was that ministry took up a great deal of her man's time.

Although Angel knew her husband loved her dearly, more than anyone besides God, she was willing to take a backseat when it came to sharing his time. But she was riding shotgun when it came to matters of his heart.

There would always be a baby for him to christen, a wedding to officiate, a funeral to preside over, or a sick and shut-in member to visit. Although several of the half dozen ministers under Pastor Harrison would volunteer to

visit the sick and shut-in members to take a load
off for their pastor, Pastor Harrison refused. He
·felt that the church paid his salary and that was
part of his duties. Part of the people's tithes and
offerings went into his pocket as his salary, so
he felt they at least deserved to see his face at
their bedside and not some assistant minister. It
was his hand the members came to shake after
service was over. It would be his hand that was
available to them in their times of need. Angel
was blessed indeed, though, that all her needs
were covered by her husband as a result of his
position in the church.

So, no, Angel didn't have to worry about the
whole fifty-fifty issue in a marriage. That didn't
mean there weren't issues that needed to be
addressed, though, and as the host of the conference walked onto the stage and up to the
clear glass podium to welcome the attendees
and introduce the luncheon's keynote speaker,
prayerfully Angel would get a resolution to at
least some of her issues.

"I'm First Lady Adams, and I want to thank
you for joining me at this year's First Lady
Conference. Are you all enjoying yourselves so
far?" the host asked. She was wearing a shim-
mering, iridescent-like rose-colored capri pants
suit. The jacket had three-quarter-length sleeves.

She had on some strappy silver sandals, but they were closed toe. Angel found those to be very cute and unique. The medium-brown-complexioned woman with a haircut that tapered to her neck also wore a corsage pinned to her lapel. She had on a pair of diamond cross earrings that matched the pendant that hung from her silver neck chain. This first lady exuded class.

Angel took mental notes of the way in which almost all the women were dressed. Since that was Mother Calloway's biggest problem with her, she figured that might be an easy fix. But while Angel would resolve one issue with the older woman who was set in her ways, there was sure to be another. Angel's gut feeling told her so. That was another reason why Angel felt it was important she attend this conference. If she could nip certain situations in the bud before they bloomed, that would save her a great deal of grief.

The ladies in the room clapped and cheered in response to the host's introduction and query. Most had finished eating lunch, while others finished up what little they had left on their plates.

"I *said*, are you enjoying yourselves so far?" the host repeated, and the applause grew louder, which was exactly what she had been going for. "Good, good. Well, ladies, like I said, I'm First

Lady Adams, and I want to welcome you to this year's First Lady Conference. It is truly an honor to be in the presence of you blessed women of the Lord, who came today from all over the map and from different walks of life and from different denominations. This weekend we are not Baptist, Christian, Apostolic, Seventh Day, Lutheran, or what have you. And if we got some Muslims up in here, that don't matter, either. We are simply queens in His Kingdom. In the Book of Revelation, when the angels were flying around God, crying, 'Holy, holy,' because every time they circled Him, they saw a different side of Him, who is to say what each side represented? No one can say. But what if . . ." She wagged a finger and squinted her eyes in thought. "Just what if there was a different side of God to represent every religion and denomination man would be able to come up with? 'Cause, see, God ain't no fool. He already knows what we're gonna do before we even think to do it, let alone go through with doing it. Amen?"

She received several amens from the women.

"So do we really believe for one second God would allow man to do anything without Him being a part of it? Even the so-called atheist and devil worshippers . . . Did God not say, 'I created all things; both good and evil'? In other words,

'Yeah, I created Satan's dirty behind, so I know him better than he thinks he knows you.'"

"You preach!" someone shouted, and others clapped.

"No, no, I don't preach. That's my husband's job," she replied and smiled. "I know some of you have been called to preach beside your husbands, but I'm a teacher, not a preacher, and there is a difference."

"Amen!" several women shouted out.

"That's right," said others.

Angel looked around in complete awe, feeling the warmth in the room. Some of the women might have been strangers in the natural, but in the spirit, everybody seemed to know everybody and didn't respond to each other like strangers. Angel could feel the love and desire among these women to want to help and lift each other up. The feeling was so heavy that Angel's eyes filled with tears. She quickly used her lunch napkin to wipe them away. Nothing would blur her vision and prevent her from seeing from what God wanted her to see and take away from this conference.

First Lady Adams continued. "This weekend we are all like-minded, with one goal. That goal is to learn how to better serve in the church and in the Kingdom, period." She paused for the women to agree verbally or with nods. "And I'm sure our keynote speaker for the afternoon is going to bring forth a Word that is going to help you if not get a little closer than you are now to that goal, then to reach it."

The excitement and anticipation could be felt in the room by all. These women were definitely on a mission.

"So without further ado, I'm going to introduce this powerful woman of God. Now, you might have read a little bit about her in your program, but trust me . . ." She put her head down and laughed while shaking her head from side to side. "There truly are no words to describe this woman. Hello!" She waved her hand and stomped her foot.

Those familiar with the keynote speaker chuckled. Angel looked in the program. She recognized the name and remembered having Googled the woman and watching a couple of her other speaking engagements on YouTube. Angel sat straight up in her chair and was equally as excited for the keynote speaker, whose reputation preceded her, to take the stage.

"Let me just say that when I threw this woman's name in the hat to be a keynote speaker, not all immediately jumped on board. Some folks had this to say, and some folks had that to say. I even had something to say to my own self. But then I had to stop and ask, 'What does God say?' And that shut everybody up."

"I know that's right!" someone shouted out, and laughter reverberated throughout the room.

"Let me just tell you this," First Lady Adams continued. She took her time as she spoke to scan the room and make eye contact with as many of the women as she could. This was ministry, but it was also personal. She wanted to try her best to let each and every woman know that she was talking to her and that God's Word was specifically for each of them. "Whatever God has to say this afternoon, He's going to say it through lady elect Lady Arykah."

Clearly, Angel was in store for a treat by the way the women roared before First Lady Adams could even finish the introduction. First Lady Adams had to lower her hands to get the women quieted down. Once the noise settled, she continued speaking.

"I said Lady Arykah, and if you're waiting on a last name, it's in the program. You don't need to mention a last name when someone says Beyoncé, and you sure don't need one when someone says Lady Arykah. Beyoncé has that kind of status in the world. Well, Lady Arykah has that kind of status in the Kingdom."

Once again, the women went crazy with applause and shouts.

Seeing that they were not going to settle down until the woman of the hour was at the mic, First Lady Adams did her best to finish the introduction over the women's cheers. "Ladies, Sisters, women of God, I present to some and introduce to others Lady Arykah, first lady of Freedom Temple Church of God in Christ in Chicago, Illinois. Chi-Town in the house!"

Applause filled the atmosphere. Those women who had actually traveled from Chicago let out a couple of extra whoops for their hometown girl.

Lady Arykah stood from one of the two reserved tables that sat closest to the stage. The applause did not die down as she climbed the four steps up to the stage, which was skirted with the same material as the curtains hanging in the background. She made her way over to the podium. As she strutted like a true queen of the throne indeed, the silver silk two-piece suit she wore glimmered with every move she made. Her silver, wide-brimmed hat was tilted on the right side of her head, and it almost covered her right eye.

Being a plus-size woman, weighing over two hundred fifty pounds, Lady Arykah was confident in her own skin. Vanity was her middle name. She never stepped one foot out of her home until her hair and makeup were perfect. Her pointed nose and full lips complemented her mocha-colored complexion. Someone would have a better chance at convincing Lady Arykah that the sky wasn't blue before she believed she wasn't the most beautiful woman God had ever created.

Although she looked like the most confident woman in the world to the other women in the room, Lady Arykah's heart was beating out of her chest at a rapid speed. Don't get it twisted. Lady Arykah couldn't get any more confident in herself when it came to her appearance and all that she had accomplished in life thus far, with God's help, of course. God had brought her a mighty long way indeed. But even though she delivered every time, she still got a little nervous when she was about to come forth with God's Word. Well aware of the fact that God could use, would use, and had used anybody to do His will, she was still in awe of the fact that He would choose to use her.

That powerful introduction that First Lady Adams had just given her had only put that much more pressure on Lady Arykah. She had to bring it. She couldn't let God down. She couldn't let these women down. She had to teach like she'd never taught before. The ladies who had gathered for the conference weren't just any typical group of women. Lady Arykah stood in the presence of ministers' wives, women who were on her level, women that knew God's Word and could try the spirit by the spirit. But anybody who knew Lady Arykah knew that she was always up for a challenge and would always meet it, by any means necessary.

Clearly, the attendees had no doubt that Lady Arykah would be bringing forth nothing but God's holy Word. They could feel it. The God inside of Lady Arykah shined way brighter than her suit on the outside. Lady Arykah hadn't been married to her husband, Bishop Lance Howell, a full year. Most of the women who attended the conference were vested in their marriages, and some had married long before Lady Arykah had even been born. Then there was the minority: women who had been married to pastors for only a short period of time. Of course, Angel fell right into that category. As a matter of fact, she was the newest pastor's wife among all the women in the room.

Knowing that Lady Arykah too was still in the honeymoon stage made Angel that much more eager to hear what the woman of God had to say. Because not only did the two women have that in common, but both had been unchurched, never imagining in a million years they'd end up being the first lady of a church. There were times in Lady Arykah's past when others hadn't even been willing to refer to her as a lady in general, let alone respect her as a first lady. But that had not kept Lady Arykah from ministering in whichever capacity she was called to.

Even though Lady Arykah had been validated by God, as she stood before these pastors' wives, fear still began to creep into her spirit. Would she be able to live up to that introduction and what these women now expected of her? Was she *really* good enough or even knowledgeable enough to teach these women, some of whom were decades older than she was? Was there anything she could possibly share with them that they didn't already know? Would they accept her? Would they take her seriously? There was only one way to find out.

Once positioned behind the podium, Lady Arykah looked out at the women in the ball-room. Even though one of the first things she'd learned when it came to ministry was not to look into people's faces, she did it every time. Yes, sometimes, some of the women's faces would be twisted up with that "Who does she think she is?" expression. But even that never deterred her. It only made her want to show them exactly who she was just that much more.

She scanned the room, taking in the many faces. Lady Arykah didn't know how many there were in attendance, but if she had to guess, she'd say three hundred–plus pairs of eyes were staring back at her. They were filled with such anticipation. Those eyes looked more confident in her than she felt about herself. Their eyes were hungry and thirsty for direction. She was there to deliver a message and had to trust that God knew what His people needed and when they needed it.

Finally, Lady Arykah took a breath and exhaled. Even though a prayer had gone forth covering the food as well as the conference just an hour or so ago, the luncheon keynote speaker was still in need of one last prayer. So with her eyes open, Lady Arykah silently prayed, *Lord, please write on my tongue.* She glanced down at her notes, which had been placed on the podium ahead of time, and then she looked out at the women again. By now, the women were dead silent. All applause had ceased as the willing vessels, open to receive, waited to hear a Word from the Lord.

"Who can find a virtuous woman? For her price is far above rubies." Lady Arykah opened with Proverbs 31. Surely that was to be expected by some. Women's conferences almost always focused on the whole Proverbs woman thing. But Lady Arykah was about to put a different kind of twist on it.

Lady Arykah didn't get a response from the women. She was confident all the first ladies were well aware of the scripture. Then she rephrased it. "Are your husbands worthy of you?" she asked the women. "What was your price?"

"All right now," Lady Arykah heard First Lady Adams say.

"You're already preachin', Lady Arykah," an unknown woman from the audience yelled out.

A few more amens and heads that nodded in agreement encouraged her.

"Some of y'all were cheap, while some of y'all just gave it away for free," Lady Arykah said with a straight face.

"Ouch. You steppin'. You steppin'," could be heard.

"Some of y'all shouldn't have worn those cute li'l open-toe shoes," Lady Arykah warned. "Because I will be steppin' on toes this afternoon, so you best hide yours under a nice pair of loafers if you don't want to give your true self away."

"Ha!" First Lady Adams uttered, then high-fived her neighbor.

"But for those of you who wanna get set free, go on and kick your shoes off, because we're gonna tell the truth and shame the devil at this conference. Is that okay?" Lady Arykah challenged the women.

"Yes, ma'am," the women responded in unison. Some even kicked off their shoes, ready to receive any help that cometh from the Lord.

Lady Arykah turned toward the table she'd been sitting at. First Lady Adams now occupied the seat that Lady Arykah had vacated to come to the stage. "Lady Adams, I ain't come here to play."

Lady Adams stood up. "Oh, we already know. Go ahead and do your thang."

"If I say something that convicts anybody's spirit in this room, take it up with the Holy Ghost, 'cause I ain't got that kind of power on my own."

"Say that!" First Lady Adams waved her hand and then sat back down in her seat.

Lady Arykah turned straight ahead and spoke to the women. "I bring you greetings from Freedom Temple Church of God in Christ in Chicago, Illinois, where my husband, Bishop Lance Howell, is the pastor."

"All right" and "Amen" could be heard throughout the room as the women gave a hand praise.

Lady Arykah glanced over her left shoulder at the screen. She read to herself the theme of the First Lady Conference.

"Your place in the church, your place in His Kingdom," she said, reading the words out loud. "Do you know your places, ladies?" she asked the women. It was a rhetorical question; she didn't expect anyone to answer. "How many of you *really* know what your role in God's Kingdom is? Your role in the church that your husband pastors?"

Still no response from the women. They just sat attentively.

Lady Arykah kept on. "How many of you *really* know what it means to be a preacher's wife?"

"Teach this afternoon," someone yelled.

"Talk about it," another woman called, encouraging Lady Arykah. "Tell us what it means."

"It's pretty much a no-brainer when it comes to doing the work of our Lord," Lady Arykah said. "Everyone's assignment in the Kingdom of God is the same. Live a sin-free life, treat our neighbors right, feed the hungry, clothe the naked, fund the poor, obey the laws of the Ten Commandments, and win souls for Christ. That is our day-to-day operation."

"Well?" some women offered in unison.

"But being married to ministers makes our places in the church a little challenging," Lady Arykah said.

"*A little*?" First Lady Adams asked out loud and chuckled.

Most of the women joined in on the laughter.

Lady Arykah also chuckled and turned to face First Lady Adams. "I think I'll say that in another way." She faced the audience. "Being ministers' wives makes it difficult to keep our places in the church."

A woman jumped up from her seat and yelled out, "*Now* you're sayin' something."

Angel sat in amazement at the back-and-forth banter between the women and the keynote speaker. It wasn't all stiff and uptight, like some might think a First Lady Conference would be. These women were like girlfriends sitting around in a living room, having a sista-to-sista conversation.

"We don't get the privilege of taking our hats off." Lady Arykah stroked the brim of her hat to make sure the women got a good look at it. It had been custom-made to go with her outfit just for the conference. Some chuckled at the keynote speaker's playful show of vanity. Lady Arykah went back into serious mode. "We don't get to take a vacation, not really, anyway, because the cell phone is still going to go off like crazy even when we're on the beach, trying to catch some sun."

"Tell me about it," someone hollered.

"Been there, prayed that," called another.

"We can't say that we don't wanna be bothered when someone comes to us for help," Lady Arykah preached. "We always carry the burdens of the congregation on our shoulders."

"That's the truth, Lady Arykah," Angel heard someone at her table say. Angel was too engrossed in the speaker's words to turn and see who it was.

"We have to smile, we have to nod our heads, and we have to hug and encourage those that are troubled, even when we are troubled ourselves. I can't tell you how many times I've had to counsel women to hang in there when it comes to their marriages and to support their husbands, even when I threw a cast-iron skillet at my own husband that very morning."

The room erupted in laughter. A few of the women even jumped to their feet. "Come on, Lady Arykah. Come on, girrrl. You already know."

First Lady Adams stood again. "You better tell the truth in here."

"I have to minister to the next wife about how to please and keep her husband happy so he won't stray *again*, when I'm still learning how to meet my own man's needs." Lady Arykah rolled her eyes. "Come on, First Ladies. Y'all know what I'm talking about in here. It's frustrating sometimes when my husband wants to make love, and I wanna just go to sleep. But I gotta do what I gotta do to keep him true and faithful to me." She suddenly broke out in song. "My mind's telling me nooo. . . ."

Some of the women stood to their feet in laughter as Lady Arykah did her own take of an old classic R. Kelly song.

"But his body, his body wants me to say yesss."

One of the women, who had been fanning herself with a handmade fan she'd purchased from one of the vendors, jumped up from her table and began to wave the fan in Lady Arykah's direction.

That room was in an uproar. The women were high-fiving each other and laughing until tears ran down their faces.

"Come on now," Lady Arykah said. "I love me some Mary Mary and Marvin Sapp, but that ain't what's playing on my MP3 player when I'm ministering to my husband in the bed."

"Say that! Say that!" one woman shouted as the other women hooted and high-fived each other.

Lady Arykah loved the fact that she wasn't preaching to the walls. These women were feeling her. It was clear by their responses that they could relate. She continued. "Ain't no shame in my game. I'm the freakiest woman in my church. I have ninety-nine problems, but sexing my man ain't one of 'em."

First Lady Adams, without getting on the stage, stomped over to where Lady Arykah stood and threw her terry-cloth towel at the speaker. It landed on Lady Arykah's silver Christian Louboutin stilettos. Lady Arykah's red bottoms were adorned with Swarovski crystals, and the six-and-a-half-inch heels raised her heavy frame. "Girl, you better keep on preaching up in here."

The women couldn't believe what Lady Arykah had just said, but they applauded her. They were already learning something about her and about themselves. They were not alone in their struggle to keep their husbands happy in the bedroom so that the next chick didn't do it in a hotel room.

Lady Arykah bent over and picked up the towel from off her shoes and dabbed the beads of sweat that were starting to form on her forehead. "How many of you know that the way you say hello to your husband in the morning determines the way things go down in the bedroom when the light goes out at night? There are no rules or restrictions when it comes to the activities in your bedrooms. Some minsters' wives are too stuffy. Yeah, I said it. You don't wanna do this, and you don't wanna do that. Some of you been married over twenty-five years and don't even know where your husband's birthmarks are. But I bet Sister So-and-So knows where they are."

Not a single chair held a butt. All three hundred fifty or so women were standing and screaming.

Lady Arykah felt her help coming on. "Each and every one of you in this room has had a disrespectful tramp grin in your man's face. Humph. Y'all better learn how to drop it like it's hot and pick it up like it's low." Lady Arykah did this little dip move, which made the women in the room weak.

The ladies couldn't contain themselves. They roared. The room sounded like a basketball arena!

"I just got out of jail for beating a tramp down," Lady Arykah confessed.

First Lady Adams had not yet returned to her seat. She stood in front of Lady Arykah in surprise. Clearly, this was not something she had uncovered when she investigated Lady

Arykah as a speaking candidate at this year's conference. The look on First Lady Adams's face said as much. She was in complete awe.

"It's true," Lady Arykah said and nodded her head. "I'm not proud to say that I brought shame to my husband and our church. I had a weak moment when his ex-girlfriend got in my face. She had the gall to tell me that she wanted her man back and that she was willing to do what she had to do to get him. Well, before I knew it, the devil took control of me, and I took control of that chick's neck when I wrapped my hands around it. A tramp ain't gotta like me, but she will, for sure, respect me and mine."

Some women came and stood right before Lady Arykah on the main floor. It looked like an altar call had been made. It was obvious Lady Arykah wasn't alone in her conflict with disrespectful women when it came to being a first lady.

"Go 'head. Preach. You're telling the truth," one of the women down front shouted. Tears were streaming down this woman's face. "You're talking to me right now."

Another sister placed her arm around the woman in support. Another handed her a tissue.

"Hide your feet now, because I'm about to come down your aisle," Lady Arykah warned.

"Some of you used to be the tramp some of us first ladies had to look out for. Watch it now!" Lady Arykah began to do a two-step as some of the women moaned. "I know I used to be." She laughed. "But for God's amazing grace . . . He did it for me. I said, He did it for me, y'all!"

The women cheered for Lady Arykah's deliverance.

"But, anyway, like I was about to say, I know there are probably some of you out there that didn't read the Book of Ruth. Take a minute to read it before the weekend is over. It's only four chapters," Lady Arykah said. "Ruth was a hardworking, morally chaste woman who waited patiently for God to send Boaz to her. Boaz treated Ruth with respect, while fulfilling his lawful responsibility. He and Ruth obeyed God's laws."

"Come on. Teach it," some of the women shouted at Lady Arykah.

"I always encourage the single women at my church never to marry the man you can live with, but instead, marry the man you can't live without."

"You sho 'nuff telling the truth," First Lady Adams offered.

"Some of y'all in here knew you weren't in love with that preacher when he wined and dined you, but you were in love with the possibility of becoming a first lady. Y'all wanted that title. And because you didn't follow in Ruth's footsteps and wait on the Lord to send you your very own Boaz, you settled for Lazyaz, Drunkaz, and Goodfornothingaz."

The women screamed again. Angel high-fived the young sister at her table. "I have never heard it put quite like that before," Angel said and laughed.

First Lady Adams raised her hand, with one finger up, in the air. She shook her head as she walked back over to her seat. Lady Arykah's bluntness was making her too weak to stand any longer. "Oh my God, I can't take it."

The other women who stood on the main floor made their way back to their seats as well.

Lady Arykah started up again. "Then there are those of you who were so eager to become a pastor's wife and claim your spot on the front pew, you made a deal with Poaz, Dumbaz, Crackheadaz, Lyingaz, Cheapaz, and Brokeaz."

"Shame the devil and tell the truth, Lady Arykah!" one of the women shouted out.

"Just because he's got a collar around his neck don't mean nothing," Lady Arykah announced.

"That's right," someone called out.

"Anybody can preach and teach the Word, but can they *live* it?"

"Say it again," First Lady Adams requested.

Lady Arykah obliged. "Can they live the Word of God?"

There was a hand praise.

"Your so-called Mister Right was only two days out of being a Lockedupaz when you met him. And now you wanna play the victim when he beats . . ."

Lady Arykah extended the microphone to the ladies in the audience, and they all shouted, "Yoaz," as the room erupted in praise.

Some women were those women Lady Arykah had spoken about. Some had been delivered from their situations, while others were praying to be delivered from them. Yes, there were some pastors' wives who were dealing with ungodly situations with their mates. Some women were in tears, while others comforted them. True deliverance was taking place in that room. The Holy Spirit was having His way as women cried out, some falling to their knees in prayer, and others on their knees in praise.

All Lady Arykah could do at that point was lay the microphone on the podium and go take her seat. Had she been at an awards show, she would have thrown the mic down like the rock stars did. Their way of saying "'Nuff said!"

Some women were still yelling out for Lady Arykah to preach, to go forth with more Word, and to come back to the podium. They wanted more. God was speaking their language through this woman of God. He was using her to touch their lives and their situations. He was using her to confirm some things in their spirits.

First Lady Adams had been hunched over, with her hand on her womb. Lady Arykah had hit on some things in her own life as well. Once she was able to, First Lady Adams rose up, left her seat, and made her way back up onto the stage. She passed Lady Arykah on the steps of the stage and grabbed her hand, letting her know it was a job well done.

First Lady Adams walked over to the podium. Initially, she reached for the mic, but then she dared not touch it. She felt a strong pull. God wasn't through with these women yet. There was more He wanted his daughters to be told, but not through her. Not through First Lady Adams. Not at this very moment. There was, indeed, a great deal of information she planned on sharing with these women throughout the conference weekend, but right now it was not her time.

She stood at the podium and looked over at Lady Arykah while shaking her head from side to side, in disbelief at how God had just used

her sister in Christ. "My God, my God," First
Lady Adams mumbled. She waited to see if Lady
Arykah was going to come forth again with the
Word and give the women what they wanted,
what they apparently needed.

Lady Arykah looked around the filled room at
all the women calling for her. Vain in the flesh
but humble in the spirit, Lady Arykah was well
aware that all glory belonged to God. These
women weren't cheering and calling for her, but
for the God *in* her. They didn't want anything
from her but what God had for them by using
her. Feeling the pull of the Holy Spirit, Lady
Arykah stood and walked back onstage and over
to the podium. She and First Lady Adams locked
eyes. First Lady Adams smiled, nodded, and
stepped aside. She did not return to her seat,
for the anointing and the power in the room
wouldn't allow her to sit still. She took several
steps back toward the curtain. She remained
on the stage, with her hands lifted as she spoke
in tongues, praying that God would continue to
have His way with Lady Arykah, to have His way
up in that place this afternoon.

Lady Arykah picked up the microphone. She
once again looked among the faces in the room.
"You being here today was no accident. God is
using this conference to shape you and prepare

you for the place He wants to bring you to tomorrow. You gotta trust His plan, even if you don't understand it. If you can't trace God's hand, just trust His heart. Remember that whatever you give in the name of Jesus will be given back to you in good measure. . . ."

The women joined in with Lady Arykah to finish the sentence. "Pressed down, and shaken together, and running over."

Lady Arykah gave a final sweep of the room and observed the many women who had been touched today. "You're gonna leave this conference like fine wine, aged to perfection," Lady Arykah told the women. "Today you graduate from knowing your places in the church to knowing your places in God's Kingdom. Today you are transformed. Today you are blessed and highly favored, and today you will claim your title as queen."

The women who had returned to their seats were back at Lady Arykah's feet, right below the podium. Tears had caused their eyeliner and mascara to smudge. Some of the ladies looked like raccoons, but they didn't care. They were being delivered and set free.

"The pastor's wife is the anchor of the church," Lady Arykah said to the women. "She's the backbone. She's the link that holds the chain together. The pastor's wife is the glue that keeps the church walls intact."

The women were delirious, crying and shouting out at the same time.

Lady Arykah sashayed across the stage with the mic in her hand. "She glides. She holds her chin up, and her head is held high. Her back is straight. Her torso is long. She is the first lady of the church. It's time to take your places in the church, ladies, and to know that is where you belong. Don't take it personal when other women of God challenge you and make you feel unlikeable. God didn't put you in the church to get other women to like you. He placed you there to minister to women who are like you. And it's time to be about the work in God's Kingdom. In Jesus' name!"

Lady Arykah laid the microphone down on the podium and took her seat again. She was done. Her assignment at the First Lady Conference had been completed. Unbeknownst to both her and Angel, though, her assignment in Angel's life was just about to begin.

Chapter 6

"I'm glad to see that you all have stood to your feet, but I hope that wasn't for me, but for the God in me. Hey!" said the keynote speaker at the final session of the First Lady Conference.

The attendees had been getting blessed from Friday to Saturday, and the same had just occurred on Sunday.

Sunday's luncheon keynote speaker had just brought forth a Word for the ladies, comparing their roles both in the church and in the Kingdom to that of Esther's role in the palace. She'd had the women on their feet from her opening line of "Who does hell think you are?" She'd said it with her hands on her hips and with her head tilted to the side. The words had erupted with such power, vengeance, and force. It was like God Himself had sent her there personally to let the devil know exactly who these women of God were and to tell him to keep his hands off of them, off of their life, off of their gifts, off of their talents, and the hands of the Jezebel spirit off of their men.

The final keynote speaker was now closing out her speech, and her speech was closing out the conference itself. The musicians were taking their places behind their respective instruments on cue, just like in a church service, when the pastor began to wind down his or her sermon.

"Ladies, before I go, I just have one more thing to say to you," said the petite brunette of medium height. Her pale face was now red from all the tears she'd wiped away from her own eyes and face during her speech, which included her own personal testimony of struggling to accept her calling as a first lady.

The musicians began to play a soft melody.

"Even though you may not even feel as if you deserve to be sitting on that first pew in the church, supporting your man, especially when once a upon a time you used to be sitting on the first bar stool in the club trying to find a man."

Several women stood to their feet, and those that had already been on their feet clapped and shouted.

"You right about it," Angel admitted. She could recall many a time when she and her girlfriends had gone to the club in their Saturday night best, scouring the place for a potential husband. That wasn't who Angel was anymore, though, but she could certainly attest to it. Unfortunately, that was where most of her girlfriends still were.

That first time she'd called each of them up and invited them to Bible study with her, they'd laughed her right off the phone. By the third and fourth time she'd invited them to Bible study and church, they'd started hitting the IGNORE button on their cell phones. They didn't even call her up to invite her to their club outings anymore, because they didn't want to risk having to go to church with her in return. At first, feeling shunned by her friends, Angel had felt somewhat hurt. Eventually, though, Angel had got so consumed by the Word of God and by following the instructions on life that she had no time to follow her girlfriends to the club, and she no longer wanted to. The phone calls to and from her girlfriends became far and few between. Two months into church Angel got saved, two months after that she was baptized, and now she was a first lady. Her girlfriends did finally come to church, but only to attend her small, intimate wedding.

They'd parted by saying such things as "I miss you" and "We have to start hanging out again," but those were just words that none of the girls had put into action.

Angel's life had changed. Her walk and talk had changed. Even though she had good times and good memories with her girlfriends, that season of her life was over. She still called them up every now and then, not to invite them to church, but just to check in on them. It wasn't an easy feat for Angel to keep from telling her friends about the goodness of the Lord. She loved them so much that she wanted them to know that her chances of seeing them again in heaven were greater if their souls were saved. But Pastor Harrison had told her that just because a person was saved didn't mean they had to preach to everybody all the time or quote scripture. He said that sometimes they got a better result when they just sat back and let their walk do all the talking.

With that said, Angel had decided she'd just walk it out. She prayed daily that her friends would see what God was doing in her life and would want to serve the God she served. She was happy with the man of God sent to her by God Himself, and she wanted for nothing and chose happiness daily. Prayerfully, she hoped that they would see that if He did this for her, He would do this for them too.

"Some of your friends are still on that bar stool," the keynote speaker continued.

Angel's mouth dropped. That woman was all up in her head.

"But you just keep praying for them, not shaking your head in disgust at them, because how easy and quickly we forget that *we* used to be right next to them. You might be doing the Holy Ghost dance now, but y'all was twerking before Miley Cyrus even got slapped on the booty by the doctor, let alone was shaking her booty."

The women laughed.

The speaker herself even had to laugh at that one. "But seriously, ladies, I'm about to get out of here. So let me close by saying this." She looked as many women dead in the eyes as she could. "You are not on that bar stool anymore, looking for a husband. You're here today because you have been found. You have been wifed. He put a ring on it."

The women began shouting.

"I'm just trying to speak everybody's language," the speaker said. "But you are in a position where you are called by God to serve many. Many lives depend on you. I once heard Author Colette Harrell say that somebody else's blessing is waiting on the other side of your obedience. So see, you are in a life-or-death situation as first lady."

"Amen!" shouted First Lady Adams from her amen corner.

"You are right where you are supposed to be, both in the church and in the Kingdom . . . and in your home and in that bed, lying next to your husband. Don't let anyone try to tell you otherwise. I know it gets hard and rough sometimes. Some of you have gone through hell and high water, and some of you are just pulling out your umbrellas and heading through the storm. But you are the ark, and y'all do know what happened to the ark during the storm."

First Lady Adams jumped to her feet and shouted, "It rose above everything!"

"There you go!" the keynote speaker shouted, pointing to First Lady Adams, who began dancing in the spirit.

Shouts of "Hallelujah" and "Glory" filled the sanctuary as the musicians began to play a more upbeat tune that lined up with the Holy Ghost–anointed dance of First Lady Adams.

"The more it rained and stormed, the higher the ark rose," the keynote speaker said. "The storms cometh to take you where?"

She cupped her hand around her ear while all the women yelled out, "To higher ground!"

"Yes. To the mountaintop," the keynote speaker confirmed. "That storm is not to drown you, but to take you to higher ground." She reached her fist out and clenched it tight, as if she was holding on to something for dear life.

With conviction she said, "So, hold on, ladies. You're right at God's promise. Don't jump ship now. Don't let the riptide pull you under. But hold on! He's taking you higher, He's taking you higher, He's taking you higherrr." She held on to that last note until every woman in the room was on her feet.

The musicians sent up praise with their instruments as the women praised God with their mouths and hands.

"Hold on!" the keynote speaker said. "Just hold on." She put the mic down and allowed the women to bless God, to praise Him, and to worship Him. Her work was done. The conference was done, but the work God had for these women was nowhere near done.

On her knees, Angel lifted holy hands and cried out to God. She had truly been blessed and schooled at this conference. She now had more confidence than ever in her role as first lady of Savior Manger Baptist Church. Something was being birthed inside of her at this very moment; she could feel it. Even though she'd once felt like nothing more than the preacher's wife, just sitting on the pew for show, that was no longer her mind-set. The church needed her. God needed her. His people outside of the church needed her. The Kingdom needed all the gifts, talents, and ministry that God had instilled in her and that He was birthing in her and unearthing in her. Just like the keynote speaker had said at the beginning of her speech, God had created her for such a time as this. This was a new season for Angel, but it was her season. Her role in the church and in the Kingdom was important, and Angel would refuse to allow anyone to tell her different, and that included Mother Calloway.

Chapter 7

"Oh, honey, I missed you so much." By the time Angel got off the plane, waited in the long line to use the ladies' room, then made it to the baggage claim, her husband was already waiting by the luggage carousel, with Angel's suitcase at his feet. She threw herself right into his waiting arms. She then pulled away, looked him in the eyes, and planted a delicious kiss on his lips. "Mmm," she said as she pulled away, her eyes closed. She kept them closed for a few seconds after she'd pulled away from the kiss. A smile spread on her lips. When she opened them, Pastor Harrison was staring at her with a dumbfounded look on his face. "What?" Angel asked.

He smiled and let out a slight chuckle. "*You* tell me what. Like what did they *really* teach y'all at that First Lady Conference?"

"I can show you better than I can tell you." Angel gave him a naughty yet desiring look.

"Well, I'm watching." He raised his eyebrows. "Show a brotha something," he said, challenging her.

Angel hit him playfully on the arm. "Come on. Let's get out of here before we end up victims of a sex tape leak."

Pastor Harrison laughed, picked up his wife's suitcase, and took her carry-on from her hands. He then escorted her to where their vehicle was parked in the airport garage. On the way home, all Angel could talk about was how priceless what had been imparted to her at the First Lady Conference was.

"Well, it sounds like your spirit is definitely renewed," he told her once they pulled up into their two-car garage. "I'm glad God sent what you needed."

"I can say that there were some very powerful and wise women of God there who absolutely spoke to my spiritman."

"Good." Pastor Harrison turned the car off and looked at his wife. "Any live in Ohio who you can perhaps stay connected with? I think it would be great for you to have some women in your circle who understand your position in the church and what you are going through."

"None from Ohio," Angel told him. "But there was this one keynote speaker, Lady Arykah. She's from Chicago. I did get a minute to speak with her. I happened to run into her in the hotel lobby later on the same day she spoke. I could not let that woman pass me by without telling her how her words touched me."

Angel shifted her body in his direction. "Husband, when I tell you that message she gave was through her from God and just for me, I'm not exaggerating. She is pretty much a newlywed and is new to this first lady thing too, but no one would be able to tell. She's just so comfortable and confident in the role she's been placed in. And you wouldn't believe what some of the women at her church have put her through. Church folks can be a trip!" Angel shook her head as she recalled and then relayed to her husband some of the vicious things Lady Arykah had shared with her that the women at her church had done to her. "She actually beat down her husband's ex-girlfriend, who had tried to creep back in his life. And Lady Arykah went to jail for it too."

Pastor Harrison looked at Angel and frowned. "Say what?"

Angel chuckled. "I'm telling you, Lady Arykah ain't no joke. She didn't sugarcoat anything. Straight talk," Angel said. "That's what she's all about."

"Well, thank God you don't have to deal with anyone as callous as that at Savior Manger. Everyone there loves you and respects you as first lady." Pastor Harrison opened his car door and got out to go around and open Angel's for her. Even after he walked around the car and opened her door, Angel's body was *still* facing where he had sat. It was like she was frozen and couldn't move. With her mouth still hanging low after dropping open when she heard the words he'd just spoken, she didn't move.

"Did he *really* just say that?" Angel said softly to herself. Her eyes were blinking with confusion.

"Wife, what's wrong?" Pastor Harrison asked once he saw Angel wasn't moving.

Angel slowly shifted her body toward her husband. Now she sat frozen, looking at him, still questioning in her mind if he'd really just said those words. Now it was time to be certain. "Did you really just say that *everyone* at Savior Manger respects me?"

"Well, yes." He shrugged. "They do, or at least I've never seen or heard anyone disrespect you."

"Then clearly you need glasses and to get your ears checked." Angel got out of the car, almost pushing her husband out of her way.

Stunned wasn't the word to describe the way Pastor Harrison looked. His eyes bucked, and he spread his hands out in a questioning manner. "Hey, what's going on here?" He closed the car door, and then quickly, before she could get away, he grabbed Angel gently by her arm to stop her from storming off. She halted but stood facing the door, not him. He turned her to him and put his hands on both her arms. He stared at her in order to try to read her face before he spoke.

"Has something been going on at church that you haven't told me about? Something must be going on, because, Angel, honey, I've never experienced this type of attitude from you before."

Always the cool, calm, collected, "brush her shoulders off" type of gal, Angel rarely let anything get to her to the point where she was visibly angry. She always just swept everything under the rug and kept it moving. People would be who they were. All she could do was pray for them. After that, either one of two things were going to happen: either the person was going to change or she was going to stop caring. But how much longer did she have to pray in order for Mother Calloway to see that all Angel wanted to do up in Savior Manger was to serve God, now more than ever? She didn't want to worry about how she dressed or how she interacted with the men in the church. She wanted to operate with a free spirit, not an uptight one. She wanted to know that she was not being hovered over and monitored by the church mother.

"If something was going on, you would have told me, wouldn't you?" Pastor Harrison asked his wife. "I hope we have the kind of marriage where we can talk as husband and wife about anything. I mean, sure, I understand there will be some confidential matters that members may share with just one of us through counseling or whatnot, but when something is affecting us individually—in our own personal lives—we need to be able to open up to each other about it. Yes?" Pastor was nodding, as if he was trying to pull a confirmation out of his wife.

Angel just stood there, her eyes watering and her bottom lip trembling. She was overcome with emotions. Thoughts of the way Mother Calloway had policed her and the way she'd been treating her were stirring up some things, as was the fact that Angel had kept it all from her husband. She'd practically lied to him by omission, and that didn't make her feel like a good wife. Pastor Harrison was right; he deserved to have comfort in knowing that if something was going on in his wife's life, she would come to him. Angel expected the same in return. Yet she'd kept him in the dark. Not only that, but she'd had the nerve to give him attitude about something he was none the wise to.

She had no right to be upset with her husband. He had asked her on many occasions if she was all right, if she needed to talk. Not wanting to make waves in the church, Angel had always declined the offer to talk and had kept things to herself. But she'd learned at the conference that sometimes a person had to make waves in order for things to keep flowing along. Waves carried the unnecessary things, the things that didn't really belong in the water, to shore, where everyone could see them. Often, making waves was the only way to keep the water clean. Well, for the first time, Angel was about to make some waves. Angel just prayed she wouldn't need a life jacket to stay afloat in the turbulent waters.

"Have a good day," Angel told Pastor Harrison the next morning. She kissed him good-bye before he headed to the church to work. He also had some church-related things off-site that he needed to take care of, such as visiting a few members who were in a nursing home. Last on his agenda for the day was the church finance meeting.

The fact that he had a finance meeting made Angel feel a little anxious. Mother Calloway would be there. She sat on almost every committee at the church. Last night, after Angel had shared with Pastor Harrison the way the church mother had been treating her, he'd told her that he was definitely going to have a word with Mother Calloway. No telling how the old lady was going to react. She was either going to snap at Pastor Harrison or hold her fury in and take it all out on Angel for ratting her out to the pastor.

Angel prayed this didn't make things worse between her and Mother Calloway. Angel going to their pastor might make her look weak in Mother Calloway's eyes. Make Mother Calloway think she could run over Angel even more so now. That was one of the reasons why Angel had wanted to handle it herself. Her initial plan had been basically to ignore Mother Calloway to the point where the old lady would eventually see that her digs at Angel were useless and ineffective and would lay off of her. On second thought, she considered that Mother Calloway was getting up there in age. Maybe she'd die first, and then Angel wouldn't have to worry about her at all. Angel had repented after that second thought, which was a useless thought, anyway. Angel knew Mother Calloway would put heaven on hold just so her spirit could hang around and haunt her.

Even though Angel was a little concerned about any backlash from the entire situation, she had to admit that sharing everything with her husband last night had felt like a weight being lifted off her shoulders. Holding it in hadn't felt healthy. Releasing it had been refreshing. Angel felt like she hadn't exposed Mother Calloway in a vindictive way. She had simply let Pastor know how his secretary was treating his wife. It hadn't been fair that she was feeling a certain kind of way and he had no idea why. Well, now he knew, and now he was going to do something about it.

"I'll take care of this, wife," Pastor Harrison had promised Angel last night, before they turned in for bed. "You won't have to tolerate this kind of behavior for one more day. That I can assure you."

Angel felt assured, all right. She felt assured that either Mother Calloway would receive her pastor's words and do better or she would rebuke him, forming a wedge between them in what had been a wonderful relationship. The latter was what Angel had feared all along.

After Angel closed the door behind her husband, she immediately dropped to her knees in prayer. She had work to do today herself. She wasn't about to let her nerves and the spirit of anxiety keep her from doing her best. She needed to pray those negative emotions away.

"Lord, please soften Mother Calloway's heart to receive with understanding the words my husband is going to place on her today. Season his tongue with the heart of Jesus when he speaks with Mother Calloway, removing all his fleshly emotions as my husband."

It was Angel's prayer that her husband would go to Mother Calloway only as her pastor. He'd been quite upset after hearing some of the things Angel had shared with him. No man would want someone dogging his wife out, so it was only natural for him to have those feelings. But those weren't the feelings Angel wanted to be in her husband's heart when he approached Mother Calloway. She wanted genuine love for both the church secretary and the first lady to be in his heart.

"I pray that after today I will have a loving relationship with the church mother, who I know has positively affected many lives at Savior Manger," Angel continued to pray. Other members had spoken openly about the positive role Mother Calloway had played in their lives. "I would like to reap the good fruit of her labor in your Kingdom and be affected positively by this woman as well. I thank you in advance, Lord, for being in the midst of this situation and for being in the midst of it all. In Jesus' name, I pray. Amen!"

Angel got up from her knees, having meant every single word of her prayer. She absolutely did wish for a positive relationship with Mother Calloway. Angel thought that initially, when she first started attending the church as just a new member, she'd had a good relationship with Mother Calloway. Mother Calloway had always spoken to Angel whenever she saw her. Now she rolled her eyes and let out a huff that was like a gust of arctic wind meant to topple Angel over in the deep freeze. At first, Mother Calloway would sit next to Angel in Bible study to help her find the chapters that were being referenced by the pastor so that she could read along. Now Mother Calloway sat across the room, glaring at her, as if she wanted to throw her Bible at Angel and hit her upside the head with it.

Angel had racked her brain many a time, trying to figure out where things had gone wrong. Was it something Angel had said or done that had offended Mother Calloway, something that she didn't realize she'd said or done? After all, she'd been a new saint. Any old thing could have flown out of her mouth, and while Pastor Harrison might have thought it was funny and might have laughed at Angel, perhaps Mother Calloway had been offended.

No closer to figuring out where things had gone wrong between her and the church mother, Angel decided that she would offer Mother Calloway an apology for anything she might have done to offend her. It wasn't about being right. It was about being righteous.

Now, with renewed hope and a prayer, Angel headed to her workroom to get her own day started. She had some robes she had to fix for a few members of the church choir. God would fix everything else.

Chapter 8

Angel was a tad nervous about heading down to Bible study. She'd sat at her desk and opened every single piece of mail and read every single word multiple times; even the junk mail was thoroughly devoured.

Pastor Harrison had returned home yesterday evening and had shared with Angel that he'd indeed spoken with Mother Calloway. He'd asked her to stay a few minutes after the finance meeting and had the conversation with her about her treatment of Angel.

"I could tell by Mother Calloway's reaction to my concerns that she had no idea she was coming at you so disrespectfully," Pastor Harrison had shared with Angel. "She agreed to do better now that she knows better. Her only thing was that she wished you'd come to her first and given her the opportunity to apologize and correct things."

She had no idea? Angel had thought, doubting this was the case. But the same way Angel had no idea whether she'd said or done anything to offend Mother Calloway, it could very well be vice versa . . . maybe.

A knock on her office door tore Angel's thoughts away from the conversation she'd had with her husband last night. She looked up at the clock on the wall. Bible study was about to start in two minutes. It was probably Carmen coming up to get her so that she wouldn't lose track of time and miss Bible study, like she'd done before. Although on this particular evening, Angel really wouldn't mind missing Bible study if it meant avoiding Mother Calloway. But she was the church secretary. It was inevitable that Angel would ultimately run into the woman. She might as well get it over with sooner rather than later. Plus, she'd feel better confronting the woman in front of a room full of people versus one-on-one.

"I might as well go face the demon now," Angel said, then immediately looked up to heaven. "I mean, my demons." She straightened her shoulders. "Sorry, God. I'm trying."

Angel stood from her desk as a second knock fell upon her door. "I'm ready, Carmen. Here I come." Angel grabbed her Bible bag and walked over to the door. When she flung the door open,

Angel thought the blood might have drained from her body. The person standing on the other side of the door was not who she was expecting.

"No, it's not Carmen. I thought I'd come up and let you know that Bible study is about to start. Wouldn't want you to miss it again. God always has an on time word for everybody." Mother Calloway smiled at Angel, as if the two had been best friends their entire lives.

Angel remembered this side of Mother Calloway. She remembered this smile. It was the way she used to smile at her when she first started attending the church. It was just so welcoming, made Angel feel right at home. Angel's lips spread into a smile as well. She was glad at the thought that she and Mother Calloway could go back to the good footing they'd started off on.

"Well, thank you for coming to see about me, Mother," Angel said. "I appreciate that."

"No problem," Mother Calloway said as sweet as peach cobbler. "But that's not the only reason I came up. I wanted to talk with you. I had a conversation with Pastor Harrison last evening, which I'm sure you're aware of."

Angel swallowed. *Here it goes.* "Yes, yes, I am aware."

"I thought about everything my pastor said to me last night about what *you* told him." She emphasized the word *you*.

Angel's smile was slowly but surely fading on her face, just like the sweet tone Mother Calloway had initially used.

"I slept on it, and I prayed on it," Mother Calloway said, "and so I wanted to come up to your office today to tell you that I'm sorry."

Angel exhaled. She wanted to kick herself for just seconds ago thinking the conversation between her and Mother Calloway was going in another direction. After all, this was what she'd prayed for, and prayer still worked. "Oh, Mother Calloway—" Angel began, the smile returning to her face right before Mother Calloway cut her off.

"I'm sorry for the day you ever stepped foot in this church," Mother Calloway spat out with venom.

Angel immediately began to step back as Mother Calloway took steps to close in on her as she continued to speak.

"All was well up in Savior Manger until you came in here, pretending you were here to find Jesus when you were really on the hunt for a husband." She nodded her head knowingly. "Uh-huh. Didn't know I knew that about you, did you?"

Angel was at a loss for words. She was still stuck on the evil look plastered across Mother Calloway's face.

"And, oh, you went straight for the top. A deacon or an elder wasn't good enough. No, you had to stick your claws into the head of the house. Well, you got him, all right, and now you're trying to turn him against me. And before you know it, you'll have him turning against the entire congregation. Maybe even God Himself!" Mother Calloway was now practically yelling at Angel as she pointed an accusing finger in Angel's face.

By now Angel had a look of horror on her face. Mother Calloway had backed her up against her desk and was up in her face.

"But as God is my witness, before I let you do that—"

"What in the world is going on in here? I can hear voices all the way down the hall."

Both Angel and Mother Calloway looked toward the doorway, where Carmen was standing.

"Oh, dear, thank goodness you are here." Mother Calloway grabbed her chest and fell into the chair by Angel's desk.

Carmen immediately ran over to assist the elderly woman. "Mother, are you all right?" She looked up at Angel with questioning eyes. "What was going on up here?"

"This so-called first lady is not who everyone thinks she is," Mother Calloway began. "You should have heard the way she was talking to me." She looked at Carmen sympathetically. "Well, you *did* hear her, didn't you? Loud talking me, like she's crazy." Mother Calloway shook her head. "I've been the church mother around here long enough to deserve at least a little respect. No first lady has ever treated me this way."

Angel thought she might die when she saw tears forming in Mother Calloway's eyes. Enough was enough. Mother Calloway was no test. Angel had it right the first time, when just moments ago she'd thought of her as the devil. Well, maybe being a demon slayer was part of the calling God had on Angel's life, because she wasn't about to let this woman run this type of shenanigans up in Savior Manger, no more than Esther was about to allow Haman to run amuck in the palace.

Angel had to find the strength within to stand up to this woman. She thought back to everything that had been ministered and instilled in her at the First Lady Conference. She had felt so equipped and powerful upon the closing of the conference. She wasn't about to cower down in fear now. What would she look like, allowing a little old lady to strip her of her power? But, on second thought, maybe this *was* a test from God.

If she couldn't stand up to Mother Calloway, what good would she be to the army of the Lord in a battle with Satan? She might have failed the test before, but this time, she was bound and determined to pass it with flying colors.

"Angel," Carmen said as she looked at her first lady, "what's really going on?" Carmen's eyes pleaded with Angel to tell her that it wasn't so. To tell her that no way had the first lady she looked up to with such respect verbally assaulted the church mother behind closed doors.

Before Angel could respond, Mother Calloway jumped in. "It's absolutely true. She talked to me from out of the side of her neck. Shocked me so bad, almost gave me a heart attack. That's no way to talk to the church mother."

Angel had to put a stop to this nonsense and right now. "You might be the church mother, but you are not *my* mother," Angel told her unapologetically. She'd had enough of this old bat, and if Pastor Harrison couldn't handle Mother Calloway, clearly, she would have to. And she felt well equipped and within her rights to do so.

"What did you say?" The expression on her face showed that Mother Calloway was in shock that the young first lady had spoken to her that way. She was used to Angel being coy, quiet, meek, and docile. Had this little gal finally found her voice, and in front of company?

"You heard me," Angel said, raising her shoulders and straightening her back. She was displaying her newfound confidence, or as one of the women at the conference had referred to it, power. "You are *not* my mother. As a matter of fact, you're *nobody's* mother." Angel folded her arms and let out a harrumph. "Well, maybe you are a mother, all right, but not the kind everybody thinks you are."

Mother Calloway gasped and clutched her chest even tighter. Her eyes just about popped out of their sockets.

Any other time Angel might have given a rat's behind about the older woman's aging heart, but not today. She wasn't about to play Mother Calloway's games. God didn't play, and neither did Angel, not from this day forward. "I'm not about to stand here and play these games with you, Mother Calloway. I'm going to Bible study." She shot a look at Mother Calloway. "You might want to head down as well. Surely God has an on time word for you too." Angel headed for the door.

Mother Calloway moaned and groaned, as if Angel's words were sending her to an early grave. "Oh, my stomach." Mother Calloway placed her hand on her belly. "I think I need one of my special peppermints to help settle it down."

Carmen's face was covered with fear, but Angel couldn't have cared less and proceeded with her exit.

"Angel, wait!" Carmen called out. "What about Mother Calloway?"

"Oh, God will take care of His own. You best believe that," Angel said over her shoulder and then kept on stepping until she was in the doorway.

"Angel!" Carmen called again, in disbelief that the first lady would turn her back on them.

"Angel, humph," Mother Calloway spat. "She's no angel."

Upon hearing Mother Calloway's words, Angel stopped dead in her tracks and turned around to face the women. "You're right. I'm not Angel. To you, I'm First Lady Harrison, first lady of Savior Manger Baptist Church." Angel lifted her shoulders proudly, no longer wanting to hide behind the title but claiming it and wearing it like a badge of honor instead. It was almost as if a fresh wind had blown through that office. Perhaps that had been God's sign that the old timid, quiet, and submissive Angel was all right in the home, but not in the church—and definitely not always in the Kingdom. Life was a constant war between good and evil. God needed some soldiers in His army, not someone who was going to let the devil run right over them. And only God had the power to shift a person's life instantaneously to change them.

Angel thought it ironic that she'd been doing all this praying for God to change Mother Calloway, and here God had chosen to change her instead. She could only smile inside, because on the outside she had a stern face, which let these women know that she meant business.

"Carmen, Mother Calloway will be fine," Angel told her assistant. "There are some notes that, as my assistant, I need you to take. I'll see you downstairs at Bible study. Lock up my office behind you please." After turning on her heels, Angel walked out of the office, proud of herself for standing her ground. Hopefully, she'd shut Mother Calloway up once and for all.

But that wasn't nearly the case. Angel was no longer in earshot when Mother Calloway managed to spit out the words "First Lady of Savior Manger Baptist Church, huh? Well, not for long. Not if *I* have anything to do with it."

Part II

"Angel on the Front Pew"

Lady Arykah

Chapter 9

"I'm going to get rid of that so-called first lady if it's the last thing I do!" Mother Calloway spat, breathing in and out heavily.

"She's our pastor's wife," Carmen reminded the church mother.

"She may be his wife, and who knows? Maybe she's a good wife at that. But she is not the proper first lady for this here church!"

Mother Calloway's argument with Angel, the first lady of Savior Manger Baptist Church, really had her fired up. "Just wait until I tell all the other church leaders how that wench just talked to me. They'll see her for exactly who she is by the time I finish painting a picture of the heifer. Just like me, they'll be questioning why the pastor ever married that heifer in the first place." Mother Calloway shook her head. "God knows I love Pastor Harrison to life, but if it means he has to be voted up out of here to get rid of that siddity broad, then so be it."

Mother Calloway was so riled up that sweat had formed across her forehead. She was heated. She tightened her lips and wiped the sweat away with the back of her hand. Then she looked down at the moisture on her fingers. "Got me sweating." Mother Calloway massaged her scalp and felt dampness. "If that witch makes me sweat out my fresh perm, I swear to God!" Her hand was now balled into a fist.

"Mother Calloway, just relax," Carmen said. She placed her hand on Mother Calloway's back.

The two women were right where Angel had left them when she stormed out of her own office just a moment ago. Mother Calloway was sitting in the chair, feigning a heart attack. Ever since she found out that Angel and the pastor were engaged, Mother Calloway, the church mother, had been tongue-lashing Angel into a corner. But today Angel had stood up to her. Mother Calloway wasn't used to that. Clearly, Carmen, Angel's assistant, had been caught off guard by Angel's stance as well, never having seen that side of her first lady before. Carmen stood over Mother Calloway, trying to get her to relax before her heart really did give out on her. She began rubbing her hand up and down Mother Calloway's back.

"Stop it already!" Mother Calloway snapped. "What are you trying to do? Burp me? Do I look like an infant to you?" Mother Calloway shooed

Carmen's hand off her back. "Don't go babying me. Keep it up and you'll be next."

"Please, Mother," Carmen continued to plead, not paying much attention to the words Mother Calloway was saying. It wasn't hard to determine that Mother Calloway was in her flesh right now and didn't mean half the things she was saying. "Just calm down."

"Calm down? *Calm down*?" the church mother shouted. "Did you just hear how that young hussy talked to me?" Mother Calloway glared at the office door of First Lady Angel Redford-Harrison. She read the doorplate out loud. "First Lady." Mother Calloway let out a huff, then mumbled the first lady's name. "Angel." She shook her head in disagreement. "Well, she's no lady, and she sure as hell ain't no angel."

"Mother!" Carmen threw her hand over her mouth and had a true look of horror in her eyes.

"What?" Mother Calloway spat in response to Carmen's dramatic antics. She looked around on the floor, thinking the poor girl must have seen a mouse or something.

"What do you mean, what? Didn't you just *hear* yourself?" Carmen then said in a whisper, "You cussed."

Mother Calloway shot straight up in her chair. "The devil is a liar. I would never," Mother Calloway said, begging to differ.

"Mother, I promise you that you just said the *H* word," Carmen said.

Mother Calloway paused and replayed the last few words of her rant in her head. Within seconds, she too had the same shocked expression on her own face that Carmen had just worn. Mother Calloway placed her diamond ring–covered fingers over her mouth. "Oh, dear Lord, I did, didn't I?"

Carmen nodded.

Mother Calloway's eyes filled with tears. Her hand began to shake.

"Mother, it's okay," Carmen said, trying to assure her.

Mother Calloway shook her head as tears fell. "You know, I ain't never said a cussword since high school." She looked at Carmen with sincerity in her eyes. "I don't listen to music with cussing. I don't even read books with cussing, which is why the only fiction authors I read are the ones who write for that Urban Christian book company. They ain't allowed to cuss in their books. I don't care nothing about that 'keepin' it real' crap. That's for the world. I'm all about the Kingdom, which means I'm just trying to keep it righteous." She shook her head again as more tears fell.

Carmen grabbed a tissue for Mother Calloway from off their first lady's credenza. She began wiping Mother Calloway's tears for her. "I understand how devastated you must feel. To an outsider, it might not be that serious, but I know that feeling of backsliding and feeling as though you've grieved the Holy Spirit. But I know your heart, Mother. Never in my five years of membership at the church have I ever heard you even almost cuss, let alone allow an expletive to come out of your mouth right here in the house of the Lord."

Mother Calloway fell quickly out of her crying mode and looked up at Carmen, poking her lips out and cutting her eyes. "Was that last comment your way of trying to make me feel better?"

Carmen thought for a moment. Perhaps she could have left that part out about Mother Calloway not only having cussed, but also having done it in the church house, no less. That was kind of like pouring salt into an open wound.

"Just forget it!" Mother Calloway snatched the tissues from out of Carmen's hands and wiped her own tears away as she reflected upon the past ten minutes.

It was ten minutes ago when Mother Calloway had come up to Angel's office to give her a piece of her mind. Angel had told their pastor about the disrespectful way Mother Calloway had been coming at her. Pastor, in turn, had had a little talk with Mother Calloway about it. In all her years at Savior Manger, Mother Calloway had never been called to the proverbial principal's office. Angel was blemishing the church mother's record as a flawless saint.

Surprisingly to Mother Calloway, the usually timid Angel, fed up with Mother Calloway's constant bullying, had turned the tables and had read the old woman like a chick on the street. Angel had said what she had to say, and then she had left Mother Calloway sitting in her office to lick her wounds. At least Carmen was there to help bandage them up.

By now, surely, Angel was down in Bible study, getting a new revelation on the Word of God, while Mother Calloway was calling her everything *but* a child of God. In those past few seconds of thought, Mother Calloway figured she'd already cussed. Later on this evening, when she got on her knees to repent, it might as well be worth it, so she let it rip.

"That low-life whore!" Mother Calloway said. "Came up into this church like some young, gold-diggin' hoochie just to try to snatch up our pastor. Why couldn't she go after a rapper or a ballplayer, like a normal ho?"

"Mother Calloway!" Carmen's eyes bucked out of her head. She resembled a deer that had been caught in headlights. She just couldn't believe the words that were coming out of the mouth of the church mother, who she knew to be a sweet old lady. The same woman who was a pillar in the church and who served as a leader to all the members. "I've never heard you talk like this," Carmen said. "Just a second ago your spirit was in mourning for letting a cussword slip, and now you're talking about First Lady Angel like this. The devil must be a liar."

"No, the devil must be alive and well," Mother Calloway retorted. "And Satan himself is disguised as a nice-looking young gal in pumps, who just happens to be the first lady of Savior Manger Baptist Church. The irony of it all is that she goes by the name of Angel. But she's definitely no angel. She's the devil, if I ever—"

"I can't listen to any more of this," Carmen said. She put her hands over her ears. "Mother Calloway, I love you—God knows I do. But I can't stand here and allow you to talk about my first lady like that."

"Then sit down." Mother Calloway nodded at the chair opposite the side of the desk where Mother Calloway was sitting, which was Angel's chair. "Because I'm just getting started."

Carmen exhaled and put her hands down. "I'm not sure what exactly is going on between the two of you, but, Mother, I have not witnessed our first lady to be any of those names you are accusing her of being. She's been nothing but kind and respectful since she stepped foot in this church a little over two years ago."

Mother Calloway shook her head. "If only you all could see the side of her that I do." Mother Calloway shook a stern finger at Carmen. "She's got you all fooled." Mother Calloway poked herself in the chest. "But not this old lady right here. No siree. I got a discernment about these kinds of things. I know a devil when I see one."

"As you should, considering you have to face one every time you get up in the morning and look in the mirror."

Both Mother Calloway and Carmen gasped when they heard the very person they'd just been speaking about say those words. Neither of them knew that Angel had appeared a few minutes ago and had heard every word they said.

Mother Calloway looked at Carmen and said in an "I told you so" manner, "You see that? You see what I'm talking about now, don't ya?"

Angel stood in the doorway with her hands on her hips. She looked at Mother Calloway. "Still talking trash about me, huh?" Angel then looked at Carmen. "And why are you standing there and even entertaining the trash she's talking? It makes you just as bad, Carmen."

"First Lady, I—" Carmen began to explain.

Angel put her hand up. "I understand you've known Mother Calloway much longer than you've known me. Certainly, your loyalty lies with her."

"You're wrong, First Lady," Carmen replied, correcting Angel and taking a step toward her.

Mother Calloway threw her head back at what Carmen had said. "*What*?" She was shocked to hear Carmen's lack of support.

Carmen looked over her shoulder at Mother Calloway. "I'm sorry, Mother, but my loyalty is and always has been with God."

Angel nodded her head in agreement with Carmen. "I can respect that." Angel walked behind her desk. "I came back up because I left my Bible bag." She reached under her desk and pulled out her tote that housed her Bible. "Unless there is some unfinished business we need to attend to, shouldn't we all head down to Bible study? Our pastor has opened with prayer and has already started tonight's lesson." She looked from Mother Calloway to Carmen. Angel knew the hatred that Mother Calloway felt toward her, and after hearing what she'd said to Carmen, Angel didn't want to leave the bitter old woman in her office a second time. For all Angel knew, Mother Calloway might plant a bomb beneath her desk.

At first they didn't budge. Mother Calloway was the first to let Angel's words kick in.

"Oh, so now you're stooping to putting me out of your office," Mother Calloway said. She shook her head as her eyes filled with tears. "I honestly can't believe this. Been a member of this church almost my entire life, and never have I been talked to and treated in such a manner by any member, let alone a first lady."

Carmen hustled back over to Mother Calloway to comfort her. She put her arm around her. "Mother Calloway, First Lady isn't putting us out. She just cares enough about us that she wants to make sure we don't miss getting blessed by Pastor Harrison's message." Carmen looked at Angel. Trying to be the peacemaker, she begged with her eyes for Angel to agree. "Right, First Lady?"

"Yeah. That's it," Angel said sarcastically. She was, in fact, kicking them out of her office diplomatically. And even though Carmen meant well, Angel did not want to join her in trying to appease Mother Calloway. If anybody needed to extend an olive branch, it was Mother Calloway, at least as far as Angel was concerned, anyway.

"*Right*, First Lady?" Carmen repeated.

"I already answered you, Carmen," Angel said through clenched teeth, trying her best to keep imprisoned the words that truly wanted to escape her mouth. In spite of the hard look on her face, the real words Angel wanted to speak were soft and kind. But Mother Calloway had taken her kindness for weakness one too many times and had bulldozed right over the petite, five-foot-tall, even size four first lady. This evening Mother Calloway's sharp tongue and nasty remarks to Angel had been too much. They'd brought out a side of Angel that Angel didn't even know had been lying dormant in her like a virus.

Carmen looked at Angel with pity, silently begging her to say the right words. "*Right*, First Lady?" she asked a third time.

At first, Angel had been proud of standing up for herself and to Mother Calloway, but as she'd made her way to Bible study earlier, her spirit had felt so convicted for the way she'd snapped at Mother Calloway. It hadn't all been the Holy Ghost ordering her words and steps, as her flesh had had a say-so as well. She'd ended up behaving just as badly as the church mother. It didn't matter that Mother Calloway was over forty years older than Angel. Like Angel had learned at the First Lady Conference, the man—typically the pastor—was the head of the church home, but the woman—the first lady—was the head of the church family. Angel needed to be an example and rise above the drama, not squat down in a two-piece bikini, showing her butt and diving right into it. That wasn't who Angel was, and she could have kicked herself for having allowed Mother Calloway to take her out of character.

So as much as Angel wanted to stand her ground and remain hard, that just wasn't who she was. Yes, five minutes ago she'd been fed up with Mother Calloway's bullying and name-calling. That old woman had had her seeing red, had brought her to her boiling point, so she had to let out a little steam. But the last thing Angel wanted was for anybody to think she was a bad person. It bothered Angel that Carmen might even be persuaded to see her in a negative light. Even though Angel felt that she was right in how she'd handled Mother Calloway, giving her an eye for an eye, and that it had possibly been a long time coming to the church mother, Angel was more concerned with being righteous than being right. So with that final thought, Angel took two deep breaths, counted to three, and then spoke.

"Right, Carmen." Angel smiled. "No way would I ever put you and especially Mother Calloway out of my office. After all, my name might be on the door, but this is the Lord's house. The last thing I ever want to do is disrespect the Lord's house." She looked at Mother Calloway. "Or His saints."

Carmen was glad to hear Angel say that. She tapped Mother Calloway. "See, Mother, I told you. We have a fine first lady."

Mother Calloway rolled her eyes and chose not to agree.

"Mother Calloway, I'm so sorry for the way I spoke to you a few minutes ago," Angel said, apologizing. "It might have been a little abrasive."

"A *little*?" Mother Calloway let out a harrumph.

"I never meant to offend you," Angel continued. "I never desire to return an offense for an offense."

"Are you sitting here, trying to say that I offended you?" Mother Calloway said, taken aback.

"Well, yes, you have. Plenty of times," Angel said. This was where Angel's flesh wanted her to remind Mother Calloway that even their pastor had had to meet with her in private to confront her about the situation. Until Angel had mentioned Mother Calloway's treatment of her, her husband had been none the wiser. That alone had upset Angel. She felt that as her pastor and especially as her husband, he should have made it more of a priority to be aware of the situation, and perhaps he should have even discerned it. But Angel didn't hold his past actions against him. She was just glad that once he'd been put on notice, he'd taken immediate action in confronting Mother Calloway.

Obviously, though, not even the head of the house had gotten through to Mother Calloway.

In Angel's opinion, Mother Calloway was now ten times worse as a result of her conversation with Pastor Harrison. So what good would it do to remind the older woman about a conversation that clearly had had no effect on her behavior?

"The devil is a liar!" Mother Calloway said. "I have *never* offended you." She struggled to get up from the chair, until Carmen finally assisted her to her feet. Mother Calloway brushed her hands down her lavender skirt suit. "I will not stay in here and be lied on." She looked at Carmen. "You can be influenced by this heifer all you want, but not me. I'm too strong in the Lord to be fooled by this wolf in sheep's clothing."

"I can't even believe you're serious right now, Mother Calloway," Angel said. "You've called me all kinds of whores and gold diggers to my face. Just now a heifer. Did you not think that would offend me?"

Carmen cleared her throat. She had, not less than two minutes ago, heard Mother Calloway call Angel out of her name. She used the clearing of her throat to remind Mother Calloway of this.

Mother Calloway snapped her neck around to shoot Carmen a look. "It's the truth," Mother Calloway said. She then turned her attention back to Angel. "And if the truth offends you, then that just means that you walk in offense."

Looking at Mother Calloway was like looking at an evil presence. Angel couldn't do it right now. She closed her eyes. Angel didn't know how Mother Calloway could sleep at night. Did this woman really not realize that she was tormenting Angel? *Give me strength*, Angel prayed silently and then opened her eyes. She shook her head as she stared at Mother Calloway. "I'm truly going to pray for you, Mother Calloway."

Mother Calloway glared at her. "I hope you mean that, First Lady, because you best believe that I'm going to pray for you too."

"I don't doubt for a minute that you will," Angel said. "It's just what you're going to pray that worries me."

"As you should be," Mother Calloway said coldly. "Because the prayers of the righteous availeth much." Mother Calloway looked at Carmen. "Help me on to Bible study, child. I'm not feeling well. Think I'm gonna have pastor lay hands on me afterward."

On any given day Mother Calloway was normally good and capable at maneuvering about the church without any help at all. But today she wanted Carmen to escort her to the Bible study classroom. It didn't take a rocket scientist to realize it was her way of getting Carmen to leave Angel's side and stand by hers. Now that Angel thought about it, there had been a couple of

Sundays when Mother Calloway requested that Carmen assist her into the sanctuary for service.

Carmen looked at Angel. She was torn, and it could be seen in her eyes. Carmen wanted to help the church mother, but at the same time, she wanted to remain by her first lady's side.

No longer able to take the distress Carmen was clearly enduring, Angel nodded for her to go ahead and walk Mother Calloway out. "I'll lock up my office, and then I'll see you in Bible study," Angel told Carmen.

Carmen nodded, cast her eyes downward, clearly feeling like a traitor, then obliged Mother Calloway by looping her arm through hers and escorting her out of the office. As the two crossed the doorway, Mother Calloway looked over her shoulder at Angel and gave her a wicked grin. It went unnoticed by Carmen.

Angel watched the doorway until both women were no longer in sight. She stood there for a moment, feeling frustrated and drained. The next thing she knew, tears were falling from her eyes. She loved her husband. She loved her church. All she wanted to do was be a good wife, a good first lady, a servant of God, and make it into heaven. It all sounded easy enough. Unfortunately, though, it appeared as if in order to get into heaven, she was going to have to go through hell with Mother Calloway first.

Chapter 10

Angel and Isaiah were sitting at their dining-room table when he noticed that Angel's mind was preoccupied. Isaiah watched as his wife twirled her spaghetti with her fork but did not eat.

"There seemed to be quite a bit of tension between you and Mother Calloway in the classroom during Bible study tonight," Angel's husband said to her.

Angel dropped her forkful of spaghetti. When the metal hit her glass plate, it rang loudly. "For *real*, husband? *Now* you notice tension?" Angel shook her head, then picked up her fork again.

Had her husband of going on four months just had the nerve to make that comment? There had been nothing *but* tension between the church's first lady and the church mother ever since Angel officially became first lady of Savior Manger Baptist Church. All Mother Calloway's eye rolling, eye cutting, head snapping, and digs had gone unnoticed by him up to this point.

Angel ate the spaghetti. With her mouth full, she mumbled, "Really? Tension? You think?"

"Whoa." Isaiah held his hands up in his defense as he leaned his body back away from his plate and against his chair. "Don't forget you just told me a few days ago how badly you felt Mother Calloway was treating you. Now that you've told me, I guess I'm aware and pretty much on the lookout for it. I was hoping that I was wrong in my observation tonight. Considering I had a talk with Mother, I was certain things between the two of you would improve."

Once again Angel dropped her fork. This time not as hard. She exhaled. "I'm so sorry, honey. I didn't mean to snap at you like that. You know that's not how I normally communicate, especially with my husband."

He nodded his acceptance of his wife's apology. He had to admit, though, that he had been a little thrown off by Angel's attitude and sharpness. At one point in their relationship he'd called her slicker. When Angel had asked him why, he told her because like a rain slicker, even in the biggest of storms, Angel managed to allow things just to roll right off of her. She was nonconfrontational and knew how to listen to other people speak without interrupting or getting fired up. She never sweated the small stuff.

In his heart he felt that even though Angel didn't know it, God had given her the exact qualities a first lady needed.

"I appreciate you talking to Mother Calloway on my behalf," Angel said. "A part of me wanted to believe that after your talk with her, things would be all right. But I guess it was wishful thinking on both our parts."

"You want to tell me what happened?" Isaiah said as he continued eating.

Angel thought for a moment. From the jump she'd wanted to handle her situation with Mother Calloway on her own. But since she'd already brought their pastor into it, why not share with him all the details? "Let's just say that the church mother pretty much thinks that I'm a snitch, that I ratted her out to you. That I'm trying to wreak havoc between the two of you and will eventually do the same with you and all the church members."

Isaiah stopped chewing. He squinted his eyes and, in disbelief, said, "No way. Mother said *that*?"

Angel's neck became stiff and straight. Her bucked eyes stared at her husband. "Are you saying you *don't* believe me?"

"No, not at all." He chuckled. "It's just that . . ." His words trailed off. He set his fork down this time, picked up the cloth napkin on his lap, wiped his mouth, and then placed the napkin on the table. He looked his wife in the eye, took a deep breath, all the while gathering the correct words to say and determining how to say them, then spoke. "Look, honey, Mother Calloway has been my secretary for all the years I've been pastoring at Savior Manger. Even before I began pastoring, I was a member of the church for ten years. During those ten years I served on several auxiliaries, ministries, or what have you. I've served side by side with Mother Calloway. I've watched her interact with members and past first ladies. I've seen a lot, Angel. And I can honestly say that I've never seen out of her what you are describing. I'm just saying." He shrugged.

As she listened to her husband speak, Angel's eyes welled up. From the sound of things, no matter what kind of spin he was trying to put on it, her pastor—her husband—didn't believe that what she was saying about Mother Calloway was true.

Isaiah continued. "When I see wrong taking place, folks doing the wrong thing or treating people wrong, I shut it down. You see how quick I was to move when you told me how you felt Mother Calloway was treating you. But I must say, Angel, no one besides yourself has ever had a bad word to say about Mother."

"And maybe that's because Mother Calloway hasn't had anyone to treat badly but me. But then again, you know how folks allow old people to do and say whatever they feel like saying or doing. They just brush it off. I, too, brushed it all off at first. But the more I brushed it off, the more she brought it on. Maybe everyone else can continue brushing off that woman's actions, but not me, Isaiah, and I hope you're not asking me to."

"No, I'm not," he said. "I'm just suggesting that maybe you think back to the incidents in which you were offended by Mother Calloway, replay them in your head, and reevaluate whether or not she was really trying to be cruel. Or like you said, just being an older person getting up there in age."

"I don't think I misunderstood Mother Calloway calling me a gold-digging preacher chaser."

"*What*? She said those exact words?" Isaiah was on the edge of his seat.

"Well, not exactly," Angel said.

He rested back into his chair.

"But she has a strong opinion about me, and I didn't want to bring this up, but . . ." Angel's words trailed off as she thought about whether she should open the can of worms she was gripping under the electric can opener.

"Please, go on," her husband insisted.

"I think it might be because of you."

He raised an eyebrow. "Come again." No way had he heard his wife insinuate that he was somehow behind Mother Calloway's actions.

"You have a great deal to do with the way Mother Calloway feels about me."

"What do you mean?" He leaned in with curiosity.

"During one of my little run-ins with Mother Calloway, she made a comment about me coming to Savior Manger, pretending I was there to find Jesus when I was really on the hunt for a husband. She then gave me this knowing look and said, 'Uh-huh. Didn't know I knew that about you, did you?'" Angel said. "It was something about the way she said it and the look she gave me that had me pondering what she'd said and what exactly she meant by it. Then it hit me—the first conversation I'd ever had with you."

Isaiah furrowed his eyebrows, trying to recall the conversation in question.

"I'd made a comment to you about me bringing my girlfriends to church so we could find a man."

He thought again and then laughed. "Oh yes, I remember that. Actually, your entire reason for wanting to come to church was to find a husband. Well, not like that, but you know, to learn what

God had to say about the whole 'husband finding a wife thing' biblically." He smiled, thinking about that first time he met the woman who he knew would be his future wife. "Oh, you sure did have me cracking up."

Angel didn't even crack a smile as she watched her husband. Once he realized she was not amused in any way, form, shape, or fashion, he coughed his laughter away and got serious.

"Yeah, I remember that conversation between the two of us, but what does it have to do with what Mother sa . . ." His words trailed off as he got what Angel was alluding to. "Ohhh."

Angel allowed her husband a moment for it to begin to sink in before she spoke again. "Well, did you tell Mother Calloway I came to church looking for a husband?"

He looked at his wife. "Well, yeah, but not like that."

"Thanks a lot, husband." Angel pushed herself away from the table and headed for the steps.

"Whoa. Wait, Angel. Hold up." Isaiah got up from the table and went after his wife. He caught her at the foot of the staircase. He grabbed her from behind and pulled her against his chest as he hugged her. They didn't speak for a few seconds; he just held his wife, who was visibly upset.

"You thought I was a joke, and now so does Mother Calloway," Angel finally said.

Isaiah continued to hold his wife. He didn't say a word. He needed his actions to speak for him for a moment. He needed his wife to feel the love and loyalty he had for her. He kissed her on the back of the head. After a few more moments he turned Angel to face him. "Baby, I don't know what the devil is trying to do right now, but I rebuke him in the name of Jesus. I will not have you believe that I hurtfully went behind your back and told Mother Calloway, or anyone else in the church, for that matter, that the only reason you came to church was to find a husband. You and I both know those were not the exact circumstances."

"Exact circumstances," Angel said. "That wasn't the circumstance at all. Yeah, I had been looking for love in all the wrong places—clubs and Home Depot. No, I didn't want any ole man. I'm not the kind of girl who just needs a warm body next to her. I had dreams and goals that included a husband, children, a real family. When I overheard your preaching that day at my client's wedding ceremony and you mentioned something about the Bible saying 'He who finds a wife,' and not 'She who finds a husband,' I was intrigued. I wanted to do things the right way. So, no, maybe I didn't come to church to find a husband per se. But I did start coming to church to learn how one could perhaps find me. I'm just a little disappointed that a conversation that I thought was between you and me Mother Calloway somehow found out about. And *I* didn't tell her." Angel crossed her arms and waited for her husband to reply.

Isaiah could see in her eyes the hurt and pain of what Angel considered to be a betrayal. "Baby, I'm sorry. There was no malicious intent. I just thought you were so darn cute. You made me laugh. You made me laugh more in that one conversation than I had laughed that entire month." He chuckled again at just the thought. "For days after meeting you, every time I thought about our first conversation, I laughed. Mother Calloway finally threw her fists on her hips and told me that I needed to let her in on the joke. So that's when I told her. We both got a good laugh."

"At me, *huh*?" Angel asked. "Like I said, you thought I was a joke. Eventually, you realized that I'm a serious and smart girl. But unfortunately, Mother Calloway has not changed her first impression of me, which you gave her." She shot him a harsh look. "Now I wonder how many other conversations of ours you've shared with Mother Calloway." Angel turned to go up the steps, but her husband rushed around and took two steps at a time to get ahead of her and stop her.

"What goes on between us as husband and wife stays that way." He was adamant in his tone. "One thing you never have to worry about is me ever allowing anyone else into our relationship."

"But don't you see, honey?" Angel said with such desperation. "You already have. Maybe you didn't mean any harm by it, but—"

"I didn't," he assured her, taking her hands into his.

Angel looked down at her hands, which felt so warm and safe in her husband's. But even though her hands were safe with him, she still wasn't totally convinced her words were. "Nonetheless, it's coming back to bite us."

Isaiah exhaled. "Then I guess since I'm the one who unknowingly planted the seed in Mother Calloway's mind about your intentions, I should be the one to change her mind. I'll address that matter with her."

"Oh, Lord," Angel said, removing her hands from her husband's. "I better make a doctor's appointment then, because let Mother Calloway tell it, snitches get stitches. I'll be needing to get stitched up real good. That woman was furious that I so-called ratted her out to you. She cut me up a good one with her tongue today, before we came to Bible study."

"Ah, so I was correct in my assessment that there was tension between the two of you?"

"Tension? You should have heard the things Mother Calloway *said* to me," Angel replied, letting loose. Her frustration became even more evident as she stood there on the steps and went on and on about the names Mother Calloway had called her, the things she'd done, and how she'd even tried to pull Carmen into it.

"So Carmen witnessed Mother Calloway saying these things?" Isaiah said. He lit up at the thought that there'd been an eyewitness. It would no longer be his wife's word against Mother Calloway's. No one would be able to accuse him of taking his wife's side simply because she was his wife. That was something pastors had to be mindful of.

"If Carmen hadn't been there, Mother Calloway probably would have removed her earrings, kicked her shoes off, and clocked me. I would have been getting stitches for real," Angel said, as serious as all get-out. "I bet that woman carries a jar of Vaseline in that Bible bag of hers. Probably passing it off as some anointed cream," Angel huffed.

"Hmmm," Isaiah said, deep in thought. "Before I speak with Mother Calloway again, do you mind if we get together with Carmen first? Carmen has known Mother for several years. Maybe she's noticed a change in her. Something really could be going on with Mother Calloway. She could be going through dementia or something. You might remind her of an old college friend from the past who did something bad to her. I don't know. It could be anything."

"I said the same thing myself at first," Angel said, "which is another reason why I continued to give her the benefit of the doubt. But something tells me she's just being downright evil." Angel shrugged. "But like you said, Carmen has been around her longer than I have. You've been around her the longest, of course, but you've seen only one side of her. Carmen has now been privy to both. I'm willing to get Carmen's take on it, if that's the route you want to go. But like I said, in my gut I feel Mother Calloway knows exactly what she's doing and when to do it. Carmen had a front-row seat to see Mother Calloway's ugly side."

"If you don't mind, I would really like to give Mother the benefit of the doubt," he said. "I think I owe the woman that much."

What about what you owe me? Angel thought, then quickly removed the words from her mind.

She knew that her husband was a fair man and that he needed to take the necessary steps to deal with Mother Calloway. "Whatever it takes to get to the bottom of things, because, Isaiah, I won't take but so much of her. I've been kind, forgiving, and apologetic to her, but enough is enough, and tonight I had enough."

"I hear you, baby, loud and clear." He rubbed Angel's cheek. "I'm going to take care of it. I'm going to take care of you, always."

Looking into her husband's eyes, she could see his sincerity. "Good," Angel said. "Now that we have all that cleared up, I'm going back to finish my spaghetti." She put her hand on her stomach. "I'm starved, and I'm not trying to miss no meals over that woman." She turned to head back down the steps.

Isaiah grabbed her hand and stopped her.

"What?" She looked at him.

"But I'm finished with my dinner," he said.

"Okay, and . . . ? You can go on up and get ready for bed. I'll be up after I finish down here." She went to walk away again, but he hadn't released her hand, so she was jerked back. "Honey, what is it?" she asked irritably, looking down at her hand, still clasped in his.

"I'm not sleepy," was all he said.

"Okay, so come down and help me with the dishes, then," Angel suggested.

"I was kind of thinking more like I wanted dessert."

"Well, I really didn't make anything sweet for tonight, but I can whip up—" Angel stopped mid-sentence when she saw the sensual look her husband was giving her. He clarified it by raising his eyebrows. "Ooh. *That* kind of dessert." Angel licked her lips. "Well, I usually like to have dinner before dessert, but in this case, I'm willing to throw caution to the wind."

"That's exactly what I'm trying to hear," Isaiah said excitedly, pulling Angel tightly against him and planting a kiss on her lips and savoring her taste. "Sweet. Just how I like my dessert."

Angel kissed him this time. "Well, let's head up these steps, because there is nothing I like more than watching a man eat his dessert." Angel winked and then led the way up to their bedroom.

Chapter 11

"Go ahead, Carmen. You were there. You heard everything that was said. Tell my hus—" Angel stopped to correct herself, knowing it was imperative that she to refer to her husband according to the capacity in which he was now serving. "Tell Pastor Harrison what took place in my office prior to Bible study this past week."

Angel was filled with so much anxiety. If only she'd had a camera in her office to record everything that had gone down. But then again, there'd been a camera when Solange went Karate Kid on Jay Z, yet there was nothing audible to confirm exactly what had gone on. That bodyguard in the elevator might not have spilled the beans to TMZ, but since there wasn't a "billion dollars" at stake in the office, like there had been on that elevator, perhaps Carmen would talk.

All eyes were on Carmen as she sat in the chair on the opposite side of Pastor Harrison's desk.

He sat in his cranberry leather chair, while Angel, too anxious to sit, stood next to his desk. Pastor Harrison had called Carmen that morning, asking if she could stop by the church when she got off work to talk for a second. Just as Pastor Harrison had mentioned to Angel last evening, he wanted to get the opinion of someone who had a longer history with Mother Calloway regarding the church mother's behavior.

Carmen squirmed a little, feeling like she was definitely in the hot seat. Angel's eyes were burning a hole through her as she waited for Carmen to tell their pastor all the names Mother Calloway had called her. A ball of nerves, Carmen looked downward and swallowed hard.

"Carmen!" Angel said, not realizing she'd stomped her foot.

Carmen snapped her head up and jumped at the sound of Angel's foot hitting the floor.

"First Lady," Pastor Harrison said, putting up his hand to calm her down. He then looked at Carmen. "Carmen, I understand if this is a little uncomfortable for you. That you feel as though you are being put in between—"

"That's *exactly* how I feel, Pastor," Carmen was quick to say, cutting her pastor off. "I love both your wife—First Lady—and Mother. And it pains me that the two women I adore and look up to aren't getting along."

"It's not due to a lack of my trying, that's for sure," Angel said. "I tried to be apologetic to the woman the other day, but—"

"Apologetic for what?" Pastor Harrison asked Angel curiously. According to his own understanding, which was based on what Angel had been telling him, it was Mother Calloway who should have been apologetic. What did Angel have to apologize for?

"Well," Angel began, then suddenly got fidgety and quiet. She was embarrassed to tell him how Mother Calloway had taken her out of character.

Carmen spoke up. "Well, when I came up to First Lady's office, looking for her to come down to Bible study . . ." Carmen paused. She quickly shot Angel a look and then looked past her, not really making eye contact. "I heard lots of yelling, even before I made it to the door." She repeated her previous action of looking at Angel, then looking past her.

"Go ahead, Carmen," Pastor Harrison urged her in a calming tone, even though inside he was eager for her to get to the meat of it. He all of a sudden had a strong suspicion that his wife had fed him only the bare bones.

"Well, when I came into the office," Carmen continued, "Mother Calloway was gripping her chest. She fell into the chair."

Pastor Harrison perked up. A look of concern covered his face.

"I ran over to her side to comfort her," Carmen continued. "Apparently, the shouting match with First Lady had just been too much for her heart."

"Shouting match?" Pastor Harrison looked at Angel with questioning eyes. A shouting match usually took two people. From all that Angel had relayed to him, Mother Calloway had been the only one out of order.

"Well, yeah," Carmen said. "Like I said, I could hear them yelling from all the way down the hall. Mother Calloway said that First Lady had been loud, talking to her like she was crazy. She also said that no first lady had ever treated her that way. And I don't think she meant that in a good way."

Pastor Harrison tucked his lips in tightly. Angel could tell that he was discomfited that the first time he was hearing of her stooping to Mother Calloway's level was right now, and from someone other than Angel herself. He wore the exact expression that defense attorneys wore when the prosecution hit them with something big during cross-examination that their client had failed to mention to them.

Now it was Angel who looked downward as Carmen continued to do what Angel now wished she wouldn't, which was talk.

"I remember First Lady telling Mother Calloway that she wasn't her mother." Carmen looked at Angel apologetically. But by the same token she shrugged, as if to say, "Well, you're the one who wanted me to tell him what I heard."

At this point, Angel sat down in a chair. She took off her proverbial seat belt. Her bus ride was about to end. The six-ton vehicle was coming to a complete stop so that Angel could step off and get under it. Why wait for Carmen to throw her under it? Might as well crawl under the bus herself.

"First Lady told her that she was a mother," Carmen continued, "but not the kind everybody around here thinks she is."

Angel buried her forehead in her hand and shook her head. Yep, that bus was about to roll right over her.

"Carmen, if you don't mind," Pastor Harrison said, "can you please excuse me so that I can have a moment alone with the first lady, please?" Pastor Harrison stood.

"Sure, Pastor. I don't mind at all." Carmen couldn't get out of there fast enough. She shot up from her chair. "Have a blessed day," she said once she was in the doorway. She looked at Angel. "You too, First Lady."

Angel shooed Carmen off with the hand that wasn't cradling her forehead. The office door closed, and now that Angel was alone with her pastor, she could feel his eyes burning a hole through her. She did nothing. Just sat there wishing everything hadn't come out the way it had. She could only imagine how things might look to him. It probably appeared as though Angel had been so quick to come tell him about how Mother Calloway had acted a fool, yet she'd failed to share any of her own negative behavior. Well, Carmen had gotten a start on it, Angel figured, so she might as well finish.

"I know what you're thinking," Angel said as she looked up at her husband. "It's not what it looks like. Yes, I did say some not so kind things to Mother Calloway, but only after she started it."

He clasped his hands together, then looked at Angel. "She started it," he repeated. "Sounds like something one of the kids in youth church would say."

"Are you calling me a child?" Angel asked with a slight attitude. Clearly, she was no longer addressing him as her pastor, but as her husband.

Isaiah looked at Angel while moving his head from left to right, as if trying to figure something out. "What's going on with you?" he asked with much sincerity and concern. "Since when do you act like this? Talk like this? I don't understand.

Is it the title of first lady? I understand that sometimes titles can go to people's heads, but—"

"Don't," Angel said, putting her hand up and shaking her head. She was becoming emotional as her eyes filled with tears. "I understand that I've been on edge lately. I've allowed that woman to bring out the worst in me. I can feel the change. I just didn't want to allow her to run all over me anymore. So maybe I've confused standing my ground and standing up to her with coming down to her level. With acting just as mean and nasty as she is. And not only does Mother Calloway deserve not to be treated that way, but definitely neither does my husband." A tear fell from Angel's eye. "I'm not that girl who cops an attitude, who rolls her eyes, who snaps her neck, who claps her hands at every syllable being enunciated when she's reading someone. I don't even read people. I'm usually the one who gets read and doesn't even realize I'm being read, because it's just not that big of a deal to me." Angel had said a mouthful. She let out a deep breath.

Her husband waited for her to take a breather so that she could continue.

"Having the title of first lady could never go to my head," Angel said, "because it's not something I asked for or want. If I could have that title removed from that door across the hall, as well as from my life, I would."

Isaiah winced slightly. He knew Angel hadn't planned to fall in love, marry a pastor, and become a first lady, especially considering she had been unchurched her entire life and had had no idea what it all would entail. Angel had mentioned to him that being a first lady was a struggle, but her comment about removing the title made it sound to him like she was contemplating removing him from her life. After all, that was the only way she could no longer possess the title of first lady of Savior Manger Baptist. As long as he was the church's pastor and she was his wife, she'd be the first lady.

"Well, honey, I don't know what to say to that," he said. There was a lot he could say, but he was afraid it would all be coming from the place of a fleshly vessel. Then again, maybe that was what Angel needed right now, for him to be her husband, to remove his role as pastor completely. This whole thing was starting to get a little confusing for him as well. He'd have to decide when she was his wife and when she was the first lady. When she needed a husband and when she needed a pastor. Now it was he who was questioning his role.

"Right now, honestly, I don't want you to say anything," Angel stated. "You've said enough. It's clear that you are on Mother Calloway's side, both you and Carmen."

"Now wait a minute," he began.

"It's true, Isaiah. You have a longer history with Mother Calloway than you have with me. I've been in your life for only what? Two years?" Angel raised her hands and then let them fall to her sides, as if two years was a mere drop in the bucket.

"I'm not even going to allow you to go there," Isaiah said. "You are my rib, which means you've been with me all my life. We are one, Angel. I'll always be with you and never against you. Even if you're wrong, I'll do what I have to do as a husband to get you right."

"Aha! So you think I'm wrong," Angel said.

"No, no, no." He put his hands on each side of his head in confusion. He then cupped them around his mouth and breathed into them. After taking a few seconds to gather his thoughts, he spoke again. "Let's just table this for now. I think we both need to pray on some things in order to get clarity on the situation. All of this coming together to talk is useless without a resolution. And in order to find a resolution, we need to get to the root of the problem."

The root of the problem is Mother Calloway. Angel stared at her husband for a moment to make sure he was finished speaking before she spoke. "Pray, huh? I'm not trying to be funny or disrespectful in any way, but is that going to be your answer for everything, to pray?"

Isaiah stood, walked over to his wife, and put his hands on each of her shoulders. "Actually, yes, that will always be my answer."

"Well, when will your answers ever involve action, actually *doing* something?" Angel asked.

"The first thing, regardless, will always be to pray. When it comes to things like this, you should never act without first praying. Jesus is the answer, Angel. Our help always cometh from the Lord." With that said, he kissed his wife on the forehead and rubbed her chin with his thumb. He then walked over and grabbed his suit jacket from the coatrack. "I have to drive up to Westerville, to the manor, to visit Sister Josie's mother. I'll be home a tad late. Are you cooking, or would you like me to bring something home?"

"Cooking," Angel said unenthusiastically.

Isaiah hated seeing his wife so down. "Don't worry, honey. God's got this," he assured her as he put on his jacket. "Be sure to close and lock my office door when you leave. I love you."

"I love you too," Angel said to her husband as he closed the door behind him.

The moment that door closed, Angel broke into tears. There was a whirlwind of emotions tearing through her body. She was angry, disappointed, frustrated, hurt, and confused and was feeling betrayed, and the emotions were scattered between Mother Calloway, Pastor Harrison, and Carmen. Angel felt as if Carmen could have just simply agreed that Mother Calloway had been talking to Angel out of the side of her neck. And their pastor, her own husband, in spite of what anyone said, should have been on her side regardless. Her word should have been enough. At least that was how Angel felt, anyway.

After a couple of minutes had passed, Angel was still sitting and bawling her eyes out. She felt like a fool, like a big old baby. She wiped her tears away, gathered herself, then stood, and exited the office. She locked up as instructed and then headed over to her own office.

Once in her office, Angel closed the door and went and sat down in her chair. She aimlessly stared down at her desk calendar. "Pray. Oh, I can pray about Mother Calloway, all right, but you might not like what I pray for when it comes to that woman," Angel said, as if she were speaking to her husband.

She shook her head. Her eyes landed on her calendar, on the days of the First Lady Conference, which she'd attended earlier that month. She'd penned in "First Lady Conference, Dallas, TX" for those dates she'd attended. She thought back to how excited she'd been about attending the conference. She'd been struggling with her role as first lady, so when she got a flyer inviting her to the conference, she'd thought that it was the answer to her prayers, that whatever she learned at the conference would help her navigate in her role in the church better. The weekend-long conference, which had included workshops, had been very helpful. Angel had come back with a fire lit underneath her. It hadn't taken long for the waters from Mother Calloway's raging storm to put that fire out, though.

Feeling that maybe she could at least try to ignite a spark and light things back up, she pulled out the notebook she'd used to take notes during some of the workshops that had been offered at the conference. She began flipping through the pages. The more she digested, the more she felt her strength renewed. After about a half hour of reviewing her notes, she closed the notebook.

"Well, Lord, I do feel a fresh wind, that's for sure," Angel said. She tried to maintain her positivity, but within moments, reality set in. No matter what, she'd still have Mother Calloway to contend with, and the church mother had seemed to pull Carmen over to her side. The two of them together had Angel's own husband doubting her. "God, why don't you have anybody to back me up?" Angel moped. Refusing to sit there all evening and sulk, Angel decided to close shop and head home. She had a couple of sewing projects for clients that she needed to complete.

When Angel went to put the notebook away, a card fell from it and landed on the floor. She stretched to pick it up so that she could place it back within the pages of the notebook from which it had fallen. But after retrieving the card, she stopped in her tracks and read it. All of a sudden Angel's entire being just lit up. After staring at the card for several moments, with a huge smile on her face, Angel shouted out, "Yes!"

She stood up, with the card still clenched tightly between her fingers. "Isaiah can pray all he wants to. Yes, our help may cometh from the Lord, but it comes from man also. And have I got the perfect man from whom my earthly help will come." Angel kissed the card. "Or should I say woman?" Angel looked up to the heavens. "God, I knew you wouldn't send me off to the wolves"—she looked down at the card—"without the ammunition to take 'em all down with me."

Chapter 12

On the South Side of Chicago, Lady Arykah Miles-Howell sat behind her desk in her office at Freedom Temple Church of God in Christ. She looked toward her office door and yelled, "Did you send it to me?"

"Yes, I did," Myrtle Cortland, the church secretary, yelled back. Myrtle's desk was just outside of First Lady Arykah's office and that of her husband, Bishop Lance Howell.

Though church etiquette would have been displayed if they'd simply used the intercoms on their desks or dialed each other's extensions to converse, Arykah and Myrtle often chose to yell back and forth to communicate instead.

Arykah logged into her e-mail on her desktop computer. She saw the e-mail that Myrtle had sent and read the subject line: *Women's Retreat—Paid*. Arykah double-clicked on the attachment and waited for the document to open. She was anxious to see how many women had paid to attend the very first women's retreat, which she had organized for the upcoming Fourth of July weekend.

Arykah had been the first lady of Freedom Temple for only six months, but she had hit the ground running as soon as Lance introduced her to the congregation as his wife. In that short period of time, Arykah had managed to eliminate the then church mothers Gussie Hughes and Pansie Bowak. The two elderly women hadn't liked Arykah from the moment they met her. Arykah had thrown the strict Church of God in Christ's traditional dress code way off when she appeared as lady elect dressed in six-and-a-half-inch stilettos. The mothers had sat on the second row, directly behind Arykah, turning their noses up at her tight crimson dress, the hemline of which had stopped just above her knees. That was a no-no for those old-school saints.

And if Arykah's dress hadn't been enough to send the mothers over the edge, when they got a good look at her thick false eyelashes and her lip color to match her dress, the mothers had clutched their hearts as if they were going to have a heart attack. It had been all they could do to keep from passing out in the sanctuary.

Since the mothers had no choice but to accept that their pastor had gone outside of the church to marry, rather than sticking with tradition and marrying a woman within the immediate church family, they had plotted and schemed to oust Arykah by any means necessary. From putting red ink on Arykah's chair to taking a photograph of her having lunch with a potential male client and sending it anonymously to her husband—their pastor—Lance. Their hope had been that he would get angry at Arykah for cheating on him and would divorce her, opening the door for a new wife of their picking. The mothers had stopped at nothing to destroy her.

Mother Pansie Bowak had hated Arykah so much that she propositioned her mentally ill nephew, Clyde Trumbull, to go to Arykah's home and beat her. However, Clyde had taken his orders a step further when he raped Arykah and caused her to miscarry. After that, Bishop Lance Howell had cleaned house and had rid Freedom Temple of the evil mothers, as well as Sharonda, Mother Gussie Hughes's granddaughter, who had served as the church's secretary for a short period of time. Sharonda hadn't set out to hurt Arykah in any way, but being the granddaughter of one of Arykah's enemies, Sharonda had been found guilty by association and had been fired from her position.

Myrtle Cortland now served as the church's secretary. She had left her own church, where she had been a member since she was a young girl, when she learned of the devious acts the mothers at Freedom Temple had committed against Arykah. Arykah and Myrtle had met seven years ago, when Arykah's best friend, Monique, dated Myrtle's son, Boris. Monique's relationship with Boris was abusive. He had constantly ridiculed Monique about her plus-size frame. His cocaine addiction had only added fuel to an already burning fire.

Myrtle and Arykah had joined forces and had tried to convince Monique that Boris was toxic and she needed to remove herself from his life. Finally, it had been Adonis Cortland, Boris's cousin and Myrtle's nephew, who stepped in and saved Monique. Adonis had stolen her heart from his cousin and had made Monique his wife. So not only had Freedom Temple gained a first lady, but Monique, Adonis, and Myrtle had joined the church as well.

If Arykah had to guess, she'd say that 250 to 300 women attended morning service each Sunday. But looking at the registration numbers, she was disappointed to see that although 225 women had signed up for the retreat, only 97 women had, in fact, submitted deposits or paid for their retreat in full.

"Wow," she sighed. With the women's retreat only four weeks away, Arykah had hoped that many more women would have committed to going by now. When Stephanie, the church's program director, had announced that Arykah was heading up Freedom Temple's first annual women's retreat, the women in the sanctuary had exploded with applause. And when Stephanie had told the women what the three-day weekend would entail—that it would include facials, massages, manicures and pedicures, shopping, and a gift basket full of treats for each attendee—the women had exploded with applause again. Therefore, Arykah had assumed that she was on the right track when it came to warming the hearts of the women who hadn't necessarily liked her when she joined the church.

"Hello, beautiful."

Arykah looked up from her computer and saw her husband standing in the doorway of her office. She sighed again, "Hey, honey."

Lance entered Arykah's office and sat down in a chair across from her desk. "I get a warmer greeting than that from our little Yorkie, Diva Chanel. At least her tail wags when she sees me."

Arykah forced a smile. "I'm sorry, babe. Of course I'm happy to see you."

"I can't tell," Lance said.

Arykah turned her computer around to show Lance what appeared on her screen.

He looked at it, then asked, "What's that?"

"It's the registration list of all the women who signed up for our upcoming women's retreat at the Swan Lake Hotel in Wisconsin."

Lance looked at the screen again. "That's great, cheeks," Lance said, calling Arykah by the nickname he'd given her. Arykah's wide backside was his favorite part of her body.

"It's not that great," she said, turning the computer back around. "Only ninety-seven women have financially committed in some way to going. I was really hoping that more women would have paid by now."

"Over two hundred women have signed up, though. That's good."

Arykah shrugged her shoulders. "Is it? Only ninety-seven women have paid for the retreat." She didn't even bother to mention that some of those were women who had merely paid a deposit and still had a balance left. "I have rooms reserved at the hotel based on the number of ladies that signed up. I'd hate to have to call up the hotel and cancel all those rooms we've been holding. And Lord have mercy if they make me pay some type of penalty if they can't rebook them."

Lance saw the disappointed look on Arykah's face. Since she had gotten to Freedom Temple, Arykah had gone beyond her call of duty as the first lady. She had done away with the church's rule that single mothers had to stand before the church and confess their sin of fornication and ask for forgiveness. Arykah had convinced Lance to banish the rule that babies of unwed mothers couldn't be christened in the sanctuary.

"Cheeks, don't get discouraged. You have almost a hundred women who have committed to attending. You don't know folks' circumstances. Some of the women may be waiting for their next paycheck to pay their balances. Others may have signed up with high hopes and every intention of attending, but then realized that their financial situations won't allow it. But I do think that putting together a women's conference is just what the ladies of Freedom Temple need. I've heard women talking about it in passing. They're excited. So, don't give up on the women just yet."

"I guess," Arykah commented. "But it's not a conference, honey. It's a retreat. The two are very different."

Lance cocked his head to the side and asked, "How?"

Arykah opened her middle drawer and withdrew a copy of the itinerary that she had printed for the retreat. She held it up for Lance to see. "Have you seen this?"

He shook his head from side to side. "No, I haven't. But Mother Myrtle told me about the conference."

Arykah's eyes grew wide. "For God's sake, it's not a conference! It's a *retreat*. I just told you that."

Lance crossed his left ankle over his right knee. "'Splain the difference, Lucy," he mocked in his Ricky Ricardo voice.

"Well, a conference is formal. Women assemble in a room, like for a church forum. They dress up in their Sunday best and get preached at by women speakers. Then there's a lunch break and more preaching. I just spoke at a first ladies' conference in Dallas two weeks ago. Don't you remember? That's where I met First Lady Angel Harrison, that fairly new first lady I was telling you about." Arykah threw a stare at her husband, urging him to recall their pillow talk.

Lance nodded. "Yeah," he said. "She's the one in a situation that is similar to the one that you were in with Mother Pansie and Mother Gussie, right?"

"Right," Arykah said. "Well, First Lady Angel's nemesis is named Mother Calloway, and she's giving Angel pure hell, Bishop. Like me, she's a newlywed, and she's at her wit's end. I feel really bad for her."

"Hopefully, First Lady Harrison can find a way to win Mother Calloway over."

Arykah didn't respond. It hadn't worked out that way with the mothers of Freedom Temple. Mother Pansie was arrested for soliciting her nephew to rape Arykah. But without any proof that Mother Gussie was involved in the scheme, the police couldn't charge her with anything. Lance had banned her from the church. Since she and Mother Pansie were best friends, Lance didn't believe that Mother Gussie was innocent.

"Anyway, Bishop," she continued, "a retreat is more laid back. It's a weekend of pampering, eating, and massages, topped off by a word from the Lord on Sunday morning, which yours truly will bring."

"Oh, I see," Lance said. "It's more like a weekend getaway."

Arykah smiled. "Now you got it."

"Give me a rundown of the entire weekend." Lance was always genuinely interested in his wife's affairs.

Arykah opened the folded itinerary and looked at the activities that the weekend of the retreat featured. "All the women will meet here at the church at nine a.m. on Friday morning. We'll gather in the sanctuary for a short prayer, then load up on the coach buses. It's about a three-hour drive to the Swan Lake Hotel in Wisconsin.

I estimate that we'll arrive at the hotel at around twelve or twelve thirtyish. The ladies will all check into their suites and relax for a few hours. The pajama bash begins at seven."

Lance chuckled. "Pajama bash, cheeks?"

She smiled. "I reserved the conference room at the hotel for Friday and Saturday evening. The ladies of Freedom Temple will dress in their onesies, twosies, or whatever they wear to bed. I've arranged for a wide spread of appetizers, such as cheeses, fruit, ham, and turkey slices. We'll have cupcakes, frappé, and raspberry tea. With candles being the only light in the room, it'll be a cozy and intimate atmosphere. With their pajamas on, the ladies can just relax and mingle."

"Cheeks, have I ever told you that you're—"

"That I'm so extra?"

Lance laughed out loud.

"Yes, Bishop, you have, and I extra agree with you. You know how I do things. It's either go big or go home. This is my first retreat as lady elect of Freedom Temple Church of God in Christ. I will not have other first ladies around Chicago talking about me, saying that I couldn't pull this off."

Lance had married a plus-size woman with a plus-size vision and a plus-size attitude. "And we can't have that."

"You're doggone right," Arykah insisted. "I gotta always be on top of my game. Humph. If folks are gonna talk about me, they ain't gonna have a choice *but* to say good thangs. You feel me?"

Lance chuckled at his wife's enthusiasm. Arykah's emotions were on level ten and climbing.

"But, anyway, on Saturday," she continued, "we have a prayer breakfast from eight to eleven. After we eat, we'll board the coach buses that'll take us to the new outlet mall that just opened in the Dells. It's only a five-mile drive from the hotel."

"I should have known," Lance said. He knew that Arykah lived to shop, and she shopped to live. There was no way she would plan a women's outing that didn't include shopping.

"When we return from the mall, the ladies will be able to enjoy massages, facials, and manis and pedis at the hotel."

"What happens if some women can't afford to be pampered, cheeks? If some women are struggling to pay for the retreat itself, you already know any type of pampering isn't in their budget. I'd hate for anyone to be left out and made to feel bad."

"No one will be left out, Bishop, 'cause I've taken care of the expense for the spa treatments for every woman who goes on the retreat. That bit of information was included in the church announcements last Sunday."

Lance wasn't surprised to hear that from Arykah. She was very generous. Unbeknownst to Arykah, Lance knew about the private meetings that she had held behind the closed door to her office with members of the church, mainly women, who were struggling financially. Single women with children who couldn't make ends meet, some who faced eviction from their apartments, and others who needed household bills paid. Arykah had written many personal checks to cover expenses for members who were in dire need. And just as the first lady of the church should, Arykah had kept their matters private. She had never revealed to Lance what was told to her in confidence. Lance became privy only to some of these matters when a couple of the women came to him and praised him about his generous wife.

Lance was pleased to see that Arykah had finally settled into her role as lady elect. After her rape and miscarriage five months before, Arykah had shut down mentally, and she had shut Lance out physically. Arykah had blamed Lance for not being home when she answered the doorbell the morning the rapist beat her and forced himself on her. For an entire month Arykah hadn't allowed Lance to touch or even kiss her. It was Myrtle who had counseled

Arykah and snapped her out of the anger she harbored for Lance. Myrtle had been able to convince Arykah that the rape and miscarriage were tragic, but she had assured Arykah that God would use her brokenness for her own good and His.

"On Saturday evening," Arykah said, "after everyone has rested from the trip to the mall and all the pampering, our banquet dinner will be held at the hotel. Elder Dollie Sherman from Progressive Ministries will speak Saturday night."

Lance's eyebrows rose. "You got Dollie to speak? How on earth were you able to pull that off?"

Elder Dollie Sherman, of Chicago, Illinois, was a powerful woman of God and was always on demand to speak at churches and events.

"I called her and begged," Arykah said.

"And that's it?" Lance was surprised to hear that was all it had taken.

Arykah shrugged her shoulders. "Yep. And a nice monetary gift persuaded Dollie to commit."

Lance lowered his head and glared at Arykah. "How much are you paying her?"

It wasn't uncommon for her to overspend for the things she wanted. Being a real estate agent who sold million-dollar homes afforded Arykah all the luxuries of life. If she wanted something, Arykah purchased it, no matter the cost.

"That's for me to know and for you not to worry about. You can't put a price tag on a beautiful weekend, Bishop."

Arykah lay the itinerary on the desk in front of her. Then she turned around in her chair and pulled a folded white T-shirt with red lettering from the credenza behind her. "Look at what the ladies will wear to the banquet. No stuffy suits for us." She unfolded the shirt so that Lance could read the words.

He scanned the front of the T-shirt. "Freedom Temple Church of God in Christ's first annual women's retreat. July third through fifth." Arykah turned the shirt over to reveal the back, and Lance continued to read. "I must work the works of Him that sent me, while it is day; the night cometh, when no man can work." Lance smiled and looked at Arykah. "All right, cheeks. Go ahead with John, chapter nine, verse four."

"That's the theme for the retreat," Arykah said as she folded the T-shirt and placed it back on the credenza. "That scripture is the text for my message on Sunday morning at the retreat."

"Well, it sounds like you have everything under control. I am extremely proud of you."

Arykah looked at her computer again. "With only ninety-seven women having paid money, I'm starting to stress."

Lance stood, leaned over the desk, and kissed Arykah's lips lightly. "You're getting yourself all worked up for nothing. The conference will be a success. The women will come through, everyone will have a blessed time, and your reputation will remain intact, I promise."

"From your lips to God's ears," Arykah responded. "And if you call it a 'conference' one more time, you won't get any nooky for a week."

Lance chuckled and glanced at his wrist-watch. "My bad. It won't happen again." It was six o'clock. "It's getting late. Are you ready to head on home?"

Arykah nodded her head. "Uh-huh. As soon as I finish up a few things. I should be no more than twenty minutes. I was at the realty office all day, but I wanted to stop by the church and check on a few things."

"Okay. Well, I've been here since nine this morning. I didn't have any meetings at the construction company today, so I spent the whole day here at the church." Lance owned Howell Construction Company, which was located on the north side of the city. Often when he didn't have any pressing issues at the company or at construction sites, Lance would spend his days at the church. "I'm going to head over to my office and close down shop," he said while exiting Arykah's office. "I'll wait for you, cheeks," he told her over his shoulder.

No sooner had Lance closed the door behind him than Arykah's cellular phone rang. She glanced at the caller ID but didn't recognize the number. Arykah pressed the TALK button and brought the telephone to her left ear. "Arykah speaking."

"Hello, Lady Arykah. This is First Lady Angel Redford-Harrison of Savior Manger Baptist Church. We met a couple of weeks ago at the First Lady Conference in Dallas."

Arykah smiled into the telephone. "Of course, First Lady. How are you?" Arykah figured she must have talked Angel up.

Angel didn't hide the sigh she released into Arykah's ear. "I wish I could say that all was well, but I can't even lie."

"I'm glad you called, 'cause I can certainly use an angel right now, but from the sound of your voice, I guess you need an angel as well."

"That's the absolute truth, Lady Arykah," Angel said. She sat behind her desk at the church.

"Ooh, child, I know that voice all too well. Means somebody is on your last nerve."

"Humph. You must be psychic," Angel said.

Arykah leaned back in her chair and crossed her ankles beneath her desk. "Nope, I'm not psychic, and I'm no prophet. I just been pissed off enough times by enough people is all. Plus, somebody is always taking up residence on my last nerve, so I know the feeling. But let's start this conversation over. In my Wendy Williams voice, I ask, 'How you doing?'"

Angel laughed. It felt good to laugh, considering everyone on her side of the map wasn't doing anything but bringing her heartache and grief. "Like I said, I would love to say that all is well, but the truth is . . ." Angel's voice cracked as she tried not to become too emotional. "My spirit is broken, and if things don't change around here, I'm afraid that my marriage is going to be broken as well."

Arykah's eyebrows rose, and her back came away from her chair. "Whoa. Hold up. This sounds serious."

"And believe me when I say that I wouldn't be calling you at seven o'clock in the evening if it wasn't."

"I'm on Chi-Town time. It's only six o'clock here."

Angel felt better knowing that it wasn't as late as she thought it was. It was okay to call folks after business hours if you had that kind of relationship with them, but Angel had met Arykah not too long ago. Arykah had been the first keynote speaker of the conference, and Angel had been mesmerized by the words God had given her to speak. The message had resonated with Angel all the more considering that like herself, Arykah was new at this first lady thing as well. When Angel saw Arykah down in the hotel lobby later that evening, she'd had to stop her and let her know how much her words had touched her spiritman. Arykah had taken the time even then to sow into Angel more by sharing some of her own personal testimony: how she had been tried and tested by members of her husband's church. And even though Arykah had come out of the battle with wounds, scabs, and scars, she'd gotten the victory in the battle. So who better for Angel to reach out to than Arykah? Angel was in a battle herself, and if Arykah could serve as her commanding general and help lead her to victory, she was almost certain all would be well.

"Oh, things have changed, all right. They changed for the worst. I wasn't sure if you'd remember exactly who I am, Lady Arykah," Angel continued. "After we talked and shared some things, you gave me your card and told me that if I ever needed anything, I could call you."

"I remember exactly who you are. I'll never forget the little chocolate, petite thing who I could fit in one side of my pants leg. I still have that picture that I had that man who was walking by in the lobby take of us. I didn't post it on Facebook, because standing next to you added ten pounds to my already voluptuous figure. So instead, I just made it as a screen saver on my phone. Every time I go to dial up Giordano's, the pizza place, I see your little self on my screen and go hop on the treadmill instead."

Angel burst out laughing.

"You're laughing, but I'm as serious as a heart attack over here."

"You look good, Lady Arykah."

"Oh, I know I'm fabulous, honey. But you know how folks always say that things could be worse? Well, they could be. I know I'm thick, but at least I ain't ole girl on that segment of *Iyanla: Fix My Life* where the firemen had to come cut the doorway openings of that woman's house just to get her out."

"Yes, I saw that episode," Angel said.

"I don't have diabetes, and I don't huff and puff from just a trip to the mailbox," Arykah added. "So certainly things could be worse. But I'm the kind of person who says, 'Yeah, things could be worse, but they could also be better.' So I at least try to do better. Seeing your little self makes me want to do better. That's all I'm saying. Though you're a dime, honey, I'm fifty cents. That's five dimes, if you aren't good at math. You know what I'm saying?"

Angel laughed out loud again. "I know *exactly* what you're saying." Angel hadn't been on the phone with Arykah a good five minutes, and yet her spirit was already lifted. Even through the phone this woman's confidence and strength were so exuberant that they almost transferred to Angel's bones. But with Angel, all it took was someone like Mother Calloway to make her doubt herself. With Arykah, it was like trying to knock out King Kong. And Denzel said it best in his movie *Training Day*: "King Kong ain't got nothing on me!" In this case, King Kong didn't have nothing on First Lady Arykah Miles-Howell. It would take a lot to knock her down and keep her there.

"I'm really glad you called, First Lady," Arykah said sincerely. "But I'm not glad to hear about the turmoil in your life."

"Trust me when I tell you that I'm not glad to have turmoil in my life. I honestly thought things were going to change once I returned from the First Lady Conference. I just learned so much from the conference. The spirit was so high. I was uplifted and encouraged. I left that place with a newfound strength and a different attitude. I can honestly say that I was not the same person when I left that I was when I arrived. The Word you delivered had a lot to do with that."

"To God be the glory," Arykah said, not taking any credit at all for the Word that had come forth from her belly that afternoon. She was just the vessel God had used to deliver His Word.

"When we spoke in the lobby, I mentioned to you the church mother who was giving me all kinds of issues."

"Uh-huh. I recall," Arykah acknowledged. "Mother Calloway, right?"

Arykah couldn't see Angel nodding her head but felt it. "Right. I was determined to go back home and not allow that woman to get to me. I was going to shut all her shenanigans and nonsense down. I put on the armor of God and was ready to stand my ground."

"Okay," Arykah said, her tone revealing that she presumed things hadn't gone down for Angel as planned.

"And I did stand my ground . . . at first. But then I stooped right down to that old woman's level." Angel sighed.

"What happened?" Arykah asked.

"Lady Arykah, I went in," Angel confessed. "My assistant happened to be there when Mother

Calloway was showing out, so I thought for once I had somebody who had my back. Somebody who witnessed the way Mother Calloway was treating me and could back me up. Long story short, when my husband, Pastor, asked my assistant what she'd witnessed, of course the only thing that came out of her mouth was what I'd said to Mother Calloway."

"Not good," Arykah said. She felt bad that it sounded as if Angel had no one on her side. Arykah, on the other hand, had her best friend, Monique, who always had her back. They had been arrested and had gone to jail together when Lance's ex-girlfriend pushed Arykah too far. Lance had also come to Arykah's rescue when he got rid of his ex-girlfriend and the mothers who tortured Arykah.

"Not good at all," Angel agreed.

"Well, did your husband at least hear you out about why you said what you said to Mother Calloway?"

"He listened, but I don't think he heard me, if you know what I mean. When all was said and done, he suggested we pray on it." Angel sighed. "I'm the first one in line to rely on a wing and a prayer to get me through the day, but I'm tired. All this talking and praying, I can't . . . Something needs to be done. But I feel so alone, like there is no one on my side. Mother Calloway was practically there when they were digging the hole to build the church. She's part of the foundation that has kept the church standing and functioning. No one wants to see her in a bad light. I was just certain my own assistant would come to my defense, because she was there. No, my husband wasn't there, but he's my husband, dang it. He should know me. And he should be . . ." Angel allowed her words to stop. She was never going to bad-mouth her husband to anyone.

"He should have protected you," Arykah said, finishing Angel's thought. "That's what a husband does for his wife."

Angel didn't confirm or deny this. She remained silent.

"Let me tell you something," Arykah added. "You're wrong."

Angel felt as though her heart had slithered out of position and down to her stomach. She grabbed her belly, as if to catch the falling muscle. She couldn't believe that the one person she felt would be on her side, would understand exactly where she was coming from and what she'd been through, would tell her she was wrong. Angel was all in her emotions when Arykah began to speak again.

"Let me clarify what I mean by that," Arykah said. "You were changed as a result of the conference. You hopped on that plane and headed back home, thinking that Mother Calloway had changed too. You were wrong in thinking that the change in *you* would somehow make *her* change. And there is a possibility that it can happen. I hear preachers preaching all the time that the other person begins to change when you do. In some cases, I believe that to be true. In other cases, not so much. Some folks are just hell-bent on being evil. Point-blank. Period. Honey, not even Jesus could change everybody, so what on earth makes you think *you* can? Now I'm going to give you five seconds of silence in order to marinate on that." And Arykah did just that.

Angel could imagine the saucy first lady counting up to five on her freshly manicured acrylic nails.

"Do you catch what I'm throwing at you?" Arykah asked.

After allowing Arykah's words to sink in, Angel realized she had made a mistake in thinking she was going to come back from that conference and watch things change overnight. Yes, God could change things overnight and in the blink of an eye. Heck, God could do every single thing man had ever asked of Him. But He won't. He can, but He's not always going to do it. Angel was not the least bit offended by Arykah for telling her that she was wrong. In fact, the conviction sat well in her spirit. Angel didn't mind being corrected.

"I get exactly what you are saying," Angel said and then sighed.

"Well, how come you don't sound too thrilled about that? I just gave you a revelation from God."

"I know, and I thank you. That Word was both encouraging and discouraging at the same time. How am I supposed to know if God is going to do it or not? If He's going to fix things? I'm just supposed to sit around and wait? To continue to get beat up by Mother Calloway? This can't be what God has for me."

"Why not you?" Arykah asked Angel. "You think that being a pastor's wife should keep you off the devil's list?"

"Well, I—"

Arykah cut Angel's words off. "I'm sorry to drop this bomb on you, but the fact that you *are* a first lady is *exactly* why you're on his list of folks to steal from, kill, and destroy. You see, when God gives you an assignment, the enemy places a target on your back and shoots his bullets for sport."

Arykah's own words hadn't been easy for her to accept herself when Myrtle had spoken them to her just three months before. Myrtle had shared words of wisdom with Arykah in telling her that sometimes God allowed trials and tribulations to occur so that folks could have a testimony. It was when a young lady at Freedom Temple confided in Arykah that she had been raped and was having a difficult time dealing with it that Arykah had understood Myrtle's words. Because Arykah had experienced that type of trauma herself, she'd been able to empathize with the woman. She had brought the woman comfort and had assured her that it might take time for her to understand that all things work together for the good of the Lord.

"Like I said back at the conference," Arykah continued, "if you can't trace God's hand, then you gotta just trust His heart, 'cause He'll never leave you."

Angel was crying openly. Arykah could hear her sniffing through the phone.

"I know He won't," Angel agreed.

"Three months ago, I was raped in my own home," Arykah blurted. She didn't know Angel that well, but Arykah felt that Angel was on the edge of a cliff, ready to leap. She had to save Angel, and that meant sharing her testimony.

"What? Oh my God." Angel immediately forgot about her own issues and began to feel complete compassion for Arykah.

"It nearly destroyed me. I was angry at the world, I was angry at my husband, and I was most certainly angry at God for allowing it to happen. I couldn't go to work, I didn't go to church, and I didn't leave my bedroom for weeks. My mind was so far gone that I shut down completely. I didn't wanna be bothered with nobody and didn't want anyone to say anything to me. I wanted to die."

"Lady Arykah, I can't imagine what you must've gone through. How were you able to bounce back?"

"I had an angel on my shoulder. Her name is Myrtle Cortland. She got me to understand my position as a first lady. She explained to me that when I married a pastor, I had involuntarily become a minister as well. She basically told me to get myself together and stop the pity party, because I had work to do. I needed to be strong for the women who sat in the sanctuary Sunday after Sunday, hurting and suffering. Myrtle told me that I had many crosses to bear. She told me that I was responsible for souls. God had given me an assignment to see about His flock."

"Wow," Angel said, in awe, as she listened intently to the words Arykah was relaying.

"I wouldn't wish what I went through on my worst enemy," Arykah continued. "I thanked God for choosing me, because my suffering surely did not outweigh the glory. My marriage is stronger than ever, I have gained the love and respect of my members, and life is good. And that's what I want you to see. I want you to see that your troubles with Mother Calloway won't last always. There's joy after this."

Once Arykah was finished speaking, there was silence on the line, and then Angel could be heard sobbing.

"I didn't mean to make you cry, but growing pains do hurt. Do you remember what I preached at the First Lady Conference?"

Angel sniffed. "I'll never forget it. You said that God was using the conference to shape us and prepare us for the place He wants to bring us to."

"And?"

"And we had to trust His plan, even if we didn't understand it."

Arykah urged Angel to keep going. "Last but not least . . ."

"That we were blessed and highly favored and needed to claim our titles as queens," Angel said.

"Amen," Arykah said. "I need you to remember, love, that you changing does not mean that you have to change your character. You can win a fight without drawing blood, so put your claws away, because that's not who you are. Don't try to stand toe-to-toe with Mother Calloway's flesh, because like the scripture says, honey, it ain't flesh and blood that we're up against. You might be looking at Mother Calloway, but her old wrinkled self ain't even who you're up against. That's why nobody else sees what you see. So don't think it strange, for it was already written."

"So it's kind of like that movie *The Sixth Sense*, where only that little boy can see all the dead people? I'm the only one who can see this side of Mother Calloway?" Angel got chill bumps on her arms, thinking about that.

Arykah burst out laughing. "Girl, how long you been saved? I thought I was bad." She laughed again. "You're cute, First Lady, but no, that's not really what I'm trying to say." Arykah paused for a minute to think. "Ummm, then again, maybe it is sorta, kinda like that. I mean, you know the devil can't touch you without God's permission, right?"

"I know," Angel acknowledged, then blew her nose and wiped her tears away. Even though the same problems that had existed prior to the phone call still existed, Angel felt better knowing that God would not leave her there. That He was in the midst of it all. She had Arykah to thank for that. "Lady Arykah, I have to say that you have a way of putting things that is just so real," Angel said. "You've helped me so much."

"Good. I'm glad I could be of help."

"So, I guess I better stay covered in the armor of God. Keep my head covered, chest, feet, and all that other good stuff," Angel said. "It all just feels so foreign to me. I'm not a fighter, never have been, yet God puts me in a position where it seems like all I'm going to have to do is fight. I'm used to walking away."

"You never walk away. Never, ever, ever turn your back on the devil," Arykah was quick to say. "You ever noticed that in the scripture, where it's telling you how to gird up with the armor of God, not once does it mention anything about putting something on your back?"

Angel allowed the scripture to flow through her head. "You're right. I never paid much attention to that until you just mentioned it."

"Well, then don't ever turn your back, 'cause it ain't covered. That's just what the devil wants you to do."

"You know, I feel kind of bad that we keep referring to Mother Calloway as the devil," Angel said.

"I'm not referring to Mother Calloway per se as the devil. I'm just referencing the devil's plans.

He can use people, places, and things. In spite of what some folks want to believe, the devil has power. He has never been nor will he ever be as powerful as God and the name of Jesus, but that rascal got some skills. And don't you forget it. He uses . . ."

Angel joined in with Arykah in saying, "People, places and things."

"That's right. You got it," Arykah said. Arykah's eyes were drawn to her doorway. Lance stepped two feet into her office and saw her talking on her phone. He tapped his wristwatch three times. Arykah knew that he was letting her know that it was time to leave the church. She nodded her head at him.

"Well, I guess I've taken up enough of your time," Angel said, trying her best to sound strong. Even though Arykah had at least got the fire up under her—it was not fully lit again but was a spark, nonetheless—she still felt somewhat doubtful. But she was going to push through. "Thank you so much for speaking with me."

"Anytime. I meant what I said when I gave you my number. I've been where you are at, and if there is anything I can do for you, just let me know."

"I wish you could be where I'm at now, literally," Angel said, voicing her wishful thinking out loud. Being able to call up Arykah at will felt like an honor indeed. But having her right there by her side to guide her steps would make Angel feel much more secure. But then again, wasn't that what the Holy Spirit was for?

"You got this," Arykah assured her. "With God for you, who can be against you?"

Angel let out a harrumph. "Where do you want me start?"

Arykah chuckled. "I know the feeling, but trust me, you got this, girl."

"Thank you so much for the vote of confidence. Have a good evening."

"You too," Arykah said. She disconnected the call and laid her phone on the desk. She looked at Lance. "That was First Lady Angel Harrison. She's got troubles."

"That church mother is still giving her the blues?"

Arykah nodded her head. "That wolf is gonna eat that poor little sheep alive."

Chapter 13

"Honey, what colors are you wearing today?" Angel asked her husband as she scanned their walk-in closet for something to wear to Sunday church service.

Angel had to admit that initially after her little meeting with her husband and Carmen, when she'd felt like no one was on her side, she hadn't even wanted to go to church this Sunday, let alone coordinate with the man she felt should have had her back more. But after speaking to Arykah, Angel was convinced that Mother Calloway had some type of stronghold on that church. Dealing with the flesh and blood of a hundred-year-old woman was easy for a young, fit woman like Angel. But Arykah had reminded her that she wasn't dealing with flesh and blood, but with evil principalities instead. This wasn't even a battle for Angel, for the Word said that the battle was not hers. Yet she wanted to make it her own husband's battle. Angel refused to let any woman, no matter her age, think for one minute she could ever come between her and her husband. So today, and every Sunday for the rest of their lives, she was going to walk up in that church with her husband and show that they were color coordinated, so that everyone would know they were on the same page.

Isaiah had just gotten out of the shower. He was still a little damp and had nothing but a towel wrapped around his waist. Even though he was six years Angel's senior, physically, he looked six years her junior. His workout on the gym equipment they kept in the basement, which he hopped on several times a week, really showed in those triceps and biceps.

"It's Communion Sunday. I'm wearing my purple and gold robe today," he replied.

"Purple and gold, huh?" Angel said. Even though purple was one of her favorite colors, Angel realized that she really didn't have many purple garments. If she wanted to coordinate her outfit with her husband's on Communion Sundays, she would have to do something about that. The only purple dress she owned she'd worn the last time her husband had worn his purple and gold robe. "Can't you wear the black-and-white robe?" Angel asked, pulling out a nice black-and-white suit she had purchased last month at a consignment shop but hadn't worn yet.

"Babe, you know I always wear the purple and gold one for Communion. The black-and-white one is the one I wear when I'm doing weddings or christenings."

"All right already," Angel huffed and continued fishing around in her closet. "Aha!" She pulled out a long gold dress that she'd forgotten all about. It was actually a dress a former client had purchased to wear to a charity event. She'd hired Angel to do some alterations on it. When the client's fiancé, the person she was supposed to be going to the event with, left her for her cousin, the client never wanted to see that dress again, so she told Angel she could have it in lieu of the payment Angel was supposed to receive. Angel felt bad enough for the woman. She didn't want to haggle or demand payment, even though the dress really wasn't something Angel would wear. Angel just felt that the color gold never complemented her dark skin. But now she was glad she had bartered. For it was the only other item she had in her closet that would match her husband's attire. It was a little dressy and more formal than she'd like it to be. Her shoulders would even show. But she had a cream garment that resembled a vest that she could wear to tone it down just a bit.

"You found something?" Isaiah asked Angel as he pulled out some slacks and a shirt from his side of the closet.

"Yep. I found a gold dress." Angel examined the dress. "It might be a little too big in some places, but I think I have a few minutes to spare to fix it up."

"Well, you better get to moving. I don't want to be late for corporate prayer. You know all the leaders and I meet in my office for prayer prior to the beginning of every church service."

"Now, you know I know that." Angel sucked her teeth.

"I'm just saying," Isaiah said. "You're about to go down to your workroom and design a dress, so I just wanted you to be mindful of the time."

"I am *not* about to go design no dress." Angel playfully swatted her husband on the butt.

He looked at her seductively. "Oh, now, don't start none, and it won't be none. We may have five minutes to spare, but if you keep playing with me, woman, you only gon' have three left to make that dress."

"I'm not making a whole dress. I'm just taking it in a little bit," Angel said, correcting him. "And why would I have only three minutes left to do it?"

Isaiah allowed his towel to drop. "'Cause, baby, you know all I need is two."

Angel laughed out loud. "Just nasty!" she exclaimed as she brushed by her husband with the gold dress in hand and exited the closet.

"Don't be scurd!" Isaiah called out to his wife as she exited the bedroom. "It won't bite as long as you don't bite it."

"Lord, please don't strike the man of God down before he gets a chance to deliver your Word today," Angel prayed as she made her way down the steps to her workroom. Angel needed to pray, all right, but it should have been for herself.

"I'll see you down at service." Angel kissed her husband on the lips as they stood in the hallway between his office and hers.

"All right," he said and headed in the direction of his office, where some members of the leadership were already waiting for him. He stopped and turned back to his wife. "Angel, a thought just hit me. I was thinking, why don't you start joining us for corporate prayer?"

Angel paused. "It's for leaders. I don't head a ministry right now." Making that statement reminded her of something. "I do have something I want to run past you, though." Angel's eyes lit up, and she got excited. "When I went to the First Lady Conference, they had vendors selling goods. There was this woman who designed liturgical dance garments. She was selling her handmade garments, and they were beautiful."

"So you're thinking about making and selling clothing?" he asked.

Angel shook her head vigorously from side to side. "No, no, no." She thought for a second. "Well, yes, maybe . . . eventually. But it just reminded me of something. You know how much I love fashion, right?"

Googly-eyed, Isaiah stared at his wife, looking her over from head to toe. "Oh yes. Looking like a modern Marilyn McCoo from that show *Solid Gold*."

Angel scrunched up her face. She had no idea who her husband was referring to.

"Come on, now. You're not that much younger than me." He couldn't believe his wife didn't know anything about the eighties music show he was referencing.

"Anyway," Angel continued, "I was thinking about starting a ministry to help the young girls and women of the church to be fashionable without doling out hundreds of dollars that they really don't have to spare for labels."

"So you're going to make them some clothes?"

"No. Well, yes, maybe. Eventually. If any are interested in making their own, I'd be willing to help them. But for starters, I just want to show them how it can be done with articles of clothing they already own, or how to shop at thrift stores, secondhand stores, and consignment shops but look as though they shopped at Macy's, Saks, and Nordstrom."

Isaiah thought for a moment. "Wow. That sounds like a really good idea. Write up a proposal that I can present to the board."

"I've already started drafting notes, scriptures, and ideas," Angel said proudly.

"So you do have a ministry in the works." It was his eyes that lit up this time. "I'm so proud of you, babe. I know it's hard. But thanks for trying to do this."

Angel smiled.

"So, since you'll be heading the . . ." He thought for a minute and then said, "Dressed for the Kingdom Ministry." He winked. "That makes you a leader, so get on in here and pray with the rest of us leaders."

"Dressed for the Kingdom," Angel repeated. "I like that title."

"I love . . . ," Isaiah said.

"Me or the ministry?" Angel stood there with a coy look on her face.

"Both." He grabbed his wife by her hand. "Come on. They're waiting."

As the pastor and first lady headed into his office, the last couple of leaders came up the hallway and followed behind them.

"Good morning, Pastor," everyone greeted.

"Good morning," Pastor Harrison replied. He then stood in silence, with a look of expectancy on his face. Finally he said, "Well?"

The leaders looked among themselves, searching faces for answers. Was there something their pastor had asked them to do that they'd forgotten about?

Finally, one leader spoke up. "What is it, Pastor?"

"Aren't you all going to say good morning to First Lady Angel as well?" Pastor Harrison replied.

Everyone's eyes then fell on Angel. It was almost as if they would never have noticed her if Pastor Harrison had never mentioned her.

"Oh, good morning, First Lady," the leaders chorused.

In Angel's opinion, some of the greetings were genuine. Some seemed forced. As for the ones that seemed forced, she had no idea why. She'd never had any problems with any of the leaders, except for . . .

"Mother Calloway, I almost didn't see you sitting back there," Pastor Harrison said after he spotted her sitting on the couch in his office. Most of the leaders were standing around, since they usually stood in a circle and held hands for morning prayer. They'd been blocking the view of Mother Calloway. "You feeling all right?"

The room fell silent. One would have thought Pastor Harrison had asked the woman for her family's secret recipe for their world-renowned sweet potato pie.

Deacon Gene, who was head of the deacons' board, cleared his throat. "Actually, Pastor, Mother Calloway was just telling us how she hadn't been feeling well."

Pastor Harrison looked concerned as he walked over toward Mother Calloway. "Have you seen a doctor, Mother? It's unusual for you to be under the weather. Heck, you could beat each of us in a relay race on any given day," he joked.

Even though Mother Calloway was one of the oldest members of the church, not even a cold could keep her down. She had so many old-school remedies that she used to keep herself nice and healthy, nipping any ailments in the bud before they had time to take her down. She'd always say that the Lord had too much for her to do to be bedridden even for a day.

"We found it unusual too, Pastor," Deacon Gene said on Mother Calloway's behalf. "But we could tell things weren't right with her from the moment she entered the room. She just looked drained, tired, and worn out. Almost like someone had put a spell on her or something." He cleared his throat again.

Perhaps Pastor Harrison didn't notice, but Angel didn't miss it when the deacon's eyes quickly darted to her and then down to the floor.

Pastor Harrison chuckled at Deacon Gene's reference to a spell being cast on Mother Calloway. He was the only one chuckling, though, taking what Deacon Gene had said as a joke. "What's hurting you?" Pastor Harrison asked Mother Calloway.

"She's not really in much pain. Just weak." This time it was the head of praise and worship who spoke up on Mother Calloway's behalf. "Fighting with the devil can take all the strength out of a person." Her eyes quickly darted to and from Angel.

Angel's eyebrows rose just like the proverbial red flag. Mother Calloway had obviously shared her and Angel's argument with the other leaders. It was clear whose side of the story they were believing and backing.

Mother Calloway sat on the couch, looking like a helpless infant, allowing everyone else to do her bidding.

Angel decided to step in on her husband's behalf. Again, she didn't care for the way the woman treated her or for the fact that she was trying to turn other church leaders against her, but she wouldn't ever want to see anything happen to Mother Calloway healthwise. The argument between the two of them had been weighing heavily on Angel, so she imagined the same went for Mother Calloway. Stress was known to make a person ill.

"Has anyone taken her temperature?" Angel asked, walking toward Mother Calloway. "She could have a fever." Angel raised her hand, as if she was going to put it on Mother Calloway's forehead.

"Nooo!" almost everyone in the room yelled out.

The leader of praise and worship leaped over to the couch and stood in front of Mother Calloway. She held both her hands up, stopping Angel in her tracks. She then began to speak to Angel in a stuttering manner. "She, she, she doesn't have a temperature, First Lady. No need to touch her."

Angel looked down at the leader's hands. They were trembling as they kept Angel at bay. "Well, okay," Angel said. She looked over her shoulder at her husband. She shot him a look, as if to ask, "Do you see the way everyone is acting, or is it just me?" Angel didn't doubt for one second that she might be the only one who sensed that something strange was happening. After all, she was the only one who saw Mother Calloway's actions as unbecoming of a church mother.

Pastor Harrison glared through the slits below his eyelids. "Angel, well, at least go grab Mother a bottle of water. I don't have any cold ones in my refrigerator. You know I like mine at room temperature, and I keep forgetting to refrigerate some for guests."

"No problem. You know I keep plenty of cold ones in my office refrigerator." Angel turned to leave.

Once again, almost everyone in the room spoke at once. "No!" they yelled in unison.

"What is going on here?" Pastor Harrison asked outright. "If I didn't know any better, I'd say none of you want First Lady to aid Mother Calloway at all. You all are acting like she has the cooties, and if she touches Mother Calloway or anything of Mother Calloway's, she might pass the cooties on to her."

"More like *roots*," someone mumbled under their breath.

Pastor Harrison turned around to look for the person who had uttered the words. "Pardon me?" He wasn't able to determine from whom the comment had come, so he waited on the culprit to speak up. No one did. "Am I hearing things, or did someone just allude to the fact that First Lady Angel might put roots on Mother Calloway?"

Angel noticed her husband's jaw tighten. That happened only when he became upset. Secretly, a part of her wanted him to get upset and let Mother Calloway, and anyone who supported her shenanigans, have it. But Angel had allowed Mother Calloway to take her out of character and Angel had shown her tail; the last thing she wanted was for the house shepherd to allow the same thing to happen with him. It was one thing for the first lady to snap off, but for the pastor to do it, and in front of all the leaders, would not be a good look at all.

"See? It's just like I told you." Mother Calloway pointed her usual accusing finger at Angel. "Now you got the pastor talking sharp, something he's never done in his entire history of being a pastor here. I knew it would be only a matter of time before you had our pastor turning against the entire church." She looked over at Pastor Harrison. "Pastor, I hate to say it, but you married a woman with the spirit of Jezebel."

Angel gasped. She wasn't shocked that Mother Calloway was practically calling her a Jezebel; she just couldn't believe she was actually saying it to their pastor. Things were truly about to get real now. Everything Angel had been telling her husband about Mother Calloway—which he didn't want to believe was true—was manifesting itself right before his own eyes. Ironically, Angel couldn't be more elated that Mother Calloway had chosen to show who she really was up underneath that church-mother persona. Angel's gasp wasn't due to shock at all. It was more like an exhale. Finally, the truth would prevail.

"Mother Calloway, woman of God," Pastor Harrison said, as if he wasn't so certain of that last part of his statement, "I respect you. God knows I do. And the same respect I have for you is the respect I expect for you to have for my wife." He looked at the other leaders. "That goes for *all* of you." Pastor Harrison then said with a raised voice, "What's wrong with you people?" He was trying his best to keep his temper in check. He'd never had to raise his voice, not in this manner. By the looks on some of the leaders' faces, they weren't used to their pastor's tone, either. The only times they'd heard him get that loud was when he was in the pulpit, preaching up a storm.

"Pastor, if you don't mind," began Deacon Gene, the unspoken spokesperson, "it's not so much as what's wrong with us as I think it is what's wrong with your wife. Mother Calloway told us about all the horrible things First Lady has said to her. She said if Carmen hadn't come into the room, there was no telling what would have happened."

"What do you mean, would have happened?" Pastor Harrison asked.

"Mother Calloway said that First Lady was just yelling and charging toward her," Deacon Gene continued. "I asked Carmen to confirm that she heard all the yelling, and she did. You can ask her yourself."

"I already did," Pastor Harrison replied.

The leaders appeared to look shocked by this new information. They eyeballed one another, some with furrowed eyebrows.

"So you already knew this?" Deacon Gene asked.

"And you brought her in here to pray with us, anyway?" one of the other leaders said, pointing at Angel.

"Pastor, you're known for sitting folks down when they are out of order," Deacon Gene continued. "Yet instead of sitting her down," he said, also pointing at Angel, "you bring her in here to stand with us. I'm confused."

"Oh, don't find it strange," Mother Calloway said, chiming in. "The works of the devil are something else."

"And you, of all people, should know!" was what Angel wanted to blurt out, but she had promised herself that she would never allow Mother Calloway to make her come out of her face again. Besides, doing it once in front of Carmen had been bad enough. If she did it in front of this entire clan, they'd probably take her out behind the church and stone her to death. After all, they'd already alluded to her being a witch. So maybe they'd burn her at the stake instead.

"Or the works of a witch," said the praise and worship leader, adding to Mother Calloway's last comment.

"Enough!" Pastor Harrison shouted. "I don't like to raise my voice, but this is all a ball of confusion. The God we serve is not a God of confusion, so this must stop now. First Lady Angel is not a Jezebel, and she's not a witch or any other kind of evil, so I'm going to ask all of you

to refrain from referring to her as such either
directly or indirectly. You wanna talk about sitting folks down? Well, let me hear someone else
say it, and I'll sit everybody down. Not one soul
in this room can afford to cast a stone." Pastor
Harrison eyed each and every one of the leaders
to make sure they saw just how serious he was.
His jowls were tight. "Is that understood?"

Although a couple of heads nodded, no one
spoke up.

Pastor Harrison repeated himself. "*Is* that
understood?" He wanted to be certain everyone
had a clear understanding of his intentions.

Although it was all pretty much mumbles,
the leaders acknowledged Pastor Harrison
verbally. He looked at Angel. His heart ached
for his wife. He could see the pain in her eyes.
This whole thing was hurting her, yet she
was letting it roll off her shoulders like the
passive, good-hearted, soft-spoken woman
that he knew her to be. Angel was a champion,
someone who never wanted any trouble.

"Service is about to start," Pastor Harrison
said. "Let us just pray, and then we'll reconvene
in my office after service. All right, everyone?"
He looked sternly at the leaders. Some nodded.
He then looked at Angel. "Because this is something we must resolve, and I will see that it most

definitely gets resolved. Okay?" His eyes held such promise, Angel had no choice but to believe him.

Angel nodded. "Sure."

Pastor Harrison turned back to the leaders. "Now can we all gather hands?"

All the leaders gathered in a circle. The praise and worship leader assisted Mother Calloway over to the circle.

Angel then took a step toward the circle. She was immediately stopped in her tracks by the looks all the leaders gave her. They then shot Pastor Harrison a look. They didn't have to speak; Pastor Harrison knew they were suggesting that until they all did get a chance to talk about and resolve the matter, Angel should not participate in the leaders' corporate prayer.

"First Lady, for now, let's just—" Pastor Harrison began, until Angel cut him off.

"It's okay. I'll just wait for you in the sanctuary, like I usually do," she said. Every Sunday Angel sat on the second pew in the sanctuary. After prayer, the reading of scripture, and announcements, Pastor Harrison, covered by his armor bearers, would enter the sanctuary. The first pew was reserved for the leaders, who followed in behind their pastor.

Pastor Harrison walked over to Angel and took her hands in his and then said in a whisper, "Thank you for understanding, sweetheart." He kissed her on the forehead.

To Angel, it felt like his lips stayed pressed against her skin forever. Forever ended all too soon. When he lifted his lips from her, released her hands, and then walked away and joined the leaders in the prayer circle, Angel never felt more alone in her life.

She stood there, shaking her head, with tears in her eyes. She could not believe this was happening. How in the world could Mother Calloway always manage to fool so many people and get them to side with her? Angel looked at Pastor Harrison, who was among those in the circle. He wasn't siding with Mother Calloway. He was just trying to keep peace and order in the house of the Lord. She understood his calling and is obligation to the people. It didn't mean she liked it, though.

As the leaders, hand in hand, decided who would lead prayer, Angel couldn't stand there and watch any longer. They were all in a circle. She was literally on the outside, looking in. Before now she hadn't really felt like an outsider. But today her husband had had this bright idea that she should join them in prayer. A part of

Angel wanted to blame him for the position she now found herself in. But she quickly shook that thought off. Like she'd told herself before, this thing was not going to affect her marriage. She said a silent prayer.

Dear God, please keep me and my husband joined as one, like-minded in all things concerning you, Lord, and the matters of your business. Let no one separate me from my husband any more than anyone could separate me from you. In Jesus' name. Amen.

Angel turned to exit the room.

"Angel."

Angel stopped in her tracks when she heard her husband. Her spirit leaped for joy. Just that quickly her prayer had been answered. God had touched his heart and soul. He could feel the disappointment and pain within Angel and knew that he had to make it better. She belonged by his side, despite the opinion of anyone in that circle.

"Yes, Pastor?" Angel said without turning around, because she didn't want anyone to see the silly, huge grin on her face.

"Please make sure you close the door behind you," he requested.

Immediately, Angel's face sagged into a frown. The tears that had filled her eyes earlier now slid down her cheeks. She swallowed the wail that almost released itself from her throat. She was able to let out a soft "Yes, Pastor" before exiting the office and closing the door behind her.

Angel shut her eyes and threw her hand over her mouth to suppress the cry that was bound and determined to make its way out. She could hear the praying on the other side of the door. They all seemed to be of one accord. Angel began to doubt herself, thinking that maybe she was the one who was off-key. She just wasn't fit for this role of pastor's wife. She wasn't built to deal with people like Mother Calloway. She felt she couldn't attend enough conferences to help her win this uphill battle. Perhaps life would be easier if she just threw in the towel. If she just went with the flow. If she just took any blows that came her way like a champ and kept it moving. Trying to fight back was too much, especially when she felt as though she didn't have anyone in her corner.

Angel took a deep breath and then opened her eyes. Since her eyes were blurry with tears, she thought she was seeing things. She wiped the tears from her eyes and began to focus. Within seconds it was clear that Angel wasn't seeing things. God had answered her prayer, after all.

Chapter 14

"Jesus!" Angel said, then covered her mouth with her hands. She didn't know how loud she'd said it and didn't want to interrupt the corporate prayer going on behind her, on the other side of the closed door.

"Although I know how to quickly switch up a bottle of water for a bottle of Stella Rosa wine, and if you let my husband tell it, I've made him feel like he was walking on water a time or two, but still, I'm not Jesus. You can simply call me Arykah."

Angel could no longer hold all her emotions in. She burst out crying and threw her arms around Arykah's neck. "Lady Arykah, you have no idea how glad I am to see you." Her shoulders began to heave up and down, she was crying so hard.

"Get ahold of yourself," Arykah said, patting Angel's back. She looked around the hall. "Where's your office, the ladies' room, or something? We need to get you together."

Angel pulled away and pointed to her office, right across the hall.

"Come on." Arykah walked Angel over to the door. She went to turn the knob, but the door was locked.

Angel began digging through her purse for the key. She retrieved the key and unlocked the door. Arykah followed behind Angel as they entered the office of the first lady of Savior Manger Baptist Church. Arykah closed the door behind them both, then walked Angel over to the love seat, which sat by the window in the office.

"Can I get you some water or anything?" Arykah asked Angel.

"No. You being here is enough," Angel said as she sat down, still not truly believing that Lady Arykah was actually there.

Arykah sat down next to Angel. She removed her large pink hat from her head. The hat was decorated with rhinestones, and the brim was trimmed with pearls. The cuffs and the collar of Arykah's pink suit had the same embellishments. She set her hat between them on the love seat. Arykah looked around and then hopped back up to go get Angel a tissue. She returned to her spot on the love seat and handed Angel the tissue, which she had pulled from a box of Kleenex that sat on Angel's desk.

"Thank you." Angel sniffed.

"What's got you doing the ugly cry?" Arykah asked.

Angel wiped her face. "I don't know whether to call it my hope, faith, or what, but it keeps going up and down. One minute I feel like everything is going to be okay. I'm standing on God's Word that He has my back and will catch me if I fall. Then, the next minute I feel like I am in a hopeless situation and am getting knocked to the ground." Angel looked at Arykah. "Like just now. I walked out of my husband's office, ready to just give up and call it quits. Then when I saw you standing there . . ." Angel couldn't even finish her sentence. She buried her face in her hands and wept.

Arykah just sat and waited patiently for Angel to speak again.

Angel wiped her face once more. She then looked Arykah straight in the eyes. It was really starting to sink in that Arykah was right there in the flesh. But what had made her come? "What are you doing here, Lady Arykah?"

Arykah chuckled. "Am I not welcome in the house of the Lord? You don't want me here?"

"No, no, no. Please don't misunderstand me. Of course you're welcome here at Savior Manger.

Truth be told, you couldn't have come at a better time. I need you. I'm just shocked that you're actually here."

Arykah sighed. "Well, I hate to say it, but when I got off the phone with you a couple of days ago, something told me my words were a 'right now' Word for you, but not in a good way."

Angel looked confused. "What do you mean?"

"'Right now' in the sense that they encouraged you and lifted you up at that given moment. But I bet you not even five seconds after we ended that call, you were back to doubting yourself."

Angel didn't disagree, which told Arykah that she was right.

"Uh-huh. I knew it," Arykah said. "I could feel that Wizard of Oz spirit all over you, with you being the Cowardly Lion, thinking Dorothy can lead you to the Wizard so that you can get some courage. In our case, I'm Dorothy."

"It was that obvious, huh?" Angel asked.

"Yep, which is why I clicked my heels three times and got here as fast as I could." Arykah smiled and patted Angel on the hand. "I couldn't sleep, thinking about what my girl must be going through here."

"Your girl?" Angel said with enthusiasm. It had been a while since anyone had referred to her as their girl. Once she got into church, the girlfriends Angel used to roll with slowly but surely began to distance themselves from her. It felt good to Angel for someone to look at her as their buddy, their roll dog—because God knows she needed one right about now.

"Yes, I know we just met, but I like you, First Lady Angel." Arykah tapped Angel on the knee. "I could tell you were good people when we met at the First Lady Conference. You know how they say 'Try the spirit by the spirit.' Besides, I don't hate on other females. I'll give anybody the benefit of the doubt. But I have no doubts when it comes to you. Otherwise, I wouldn't be here. Trust and believe that." Arykah exhaled and allowed her shoulders to loosen and slouch. "Now, tell me what's going on. It doesn't look like you were having a good morning at all." Now that Angel had gotten her emotions under control, and Arykah was good and comfortable, she was ready for Angel to spill the tea.

"I wasn't. As a matter of fact, it was the worst morning ever." Angel proceeded to tell Arykah all the details of the morning, up until she exited her husband's office. When Angel was finished, the room was silent. She waited a few seconds for Arykah to respond, but Arykah remained silent. Tense, but silent. Her knee bounced, but she remained silent. The vein in her right temple was pulsating, but she was quiet.

"Are you okay?" Angel asked her.

Arykah didn't respond. She just stared off into space.

"Is everything okay?" Angel asked it a little louder this time and touched Arykah's shoulder.

"Huh? What?" Arykah said, Angel's touch snapping her out of her daze.

"I was asking you if everything was all right."

"With me? Oh yeah. I was just sitting here thinking about how, since Mother Calloway is so old school, I want to pull out a can of good old-fashioned whupyoaz on her."

Angel waited for Arykah to laugh, but clearly, it was no joke, because she didn't crack a smile. Her knee was still bouncing, but she didn't crack a smile.

"You can't be serious. Mother Calloway is seventy-plus years old."

Arykah's knee stopped bouncing, and she stared Angel right in the face. "I don't care about how old anyone is. If someone is bold and bad enough to be disrespectful toward me, then yeah, I will fight."

Angel's eyebrows rose at the thought of Arykah fighting, and fighting an old lady at that.

Arykah saw that Angel was shocked at her words. "Oh, you didn't know?"

Once again Angel waited on Arykah to laugh, chuckle, snicker, or something, but she'd never looked more sincere about the words she'd just spoken.

Angel stood and began fidgeting, flexing her fingers nervously. "I'm glad you're here, Lady Arykah, but I don't want you to come here to beat up the bully for me. Two wrongs don't make a right."

"Then let me just hide her dentures or something," Arykah begged.

"*Lady Arykah!*" Angel said in a scolding manner.

Arykah waved her hand at Angel. "Okay, forget it," she pouted. "You're no fun. We'll do it the godly way. But if at any time during this process you change your mind, just—"

"I won't," Angel said, cutting her off.

Arykah sighed. "Nope. Not even a little fun."

There was a light tap on Angel's office door. Both she and Arykah turned their attention toward the door.

Angel looked at Arykah. Angel's eyes had a little frightfulness hidden in the background.

"Go ahead. It's okay," Arykah whispered, urging Angel to be brave and face whatever was on the other side of that door. "Remember, you're not alone now. I've got your back."

Angel knew that God had her back in the spirit, but Arykah meant it more in the physical sense. Angel's courage was building and could be seen in the way she lifted her chin and said, "Come in."

The door opened a crack. "First Lady Angel, are you ready to head down to service?" Carmen asked as she peeked in the room.

Angel exhaled. It wasn't Mother Calloway. She was glad of that. Although she knew it was inevitable, she'd rather not deal with that woman at this moment. On the flip side, she couldn't say that she was all too happy to see Carmen, either. She wasn't sure how she felt about Carmen right about now. She still had tire marks on her from the way her assistant had thrown her under the bus and let it run all over her.

Carmen hadn't lied to Pastor about Angel or anything. Angel couldn't deny that Carmen had merely repeated the things she'd heard Angel say to Mother Calloway. It would have helped Angel plead her case a lot better, though, if Carmen had at least confirmed that Angel's actions were only in self-defense, as she had to protect herself from all the daggers Mother Calloway was throwing at her. All of this caused mixed feelings, leaving Angel to wonder whether she could trust Carmen as her assistant.

"You go on ahead of me, Carmen. I'll be there shortly," Angel said.

"Oh." Carmen seemed a little stunned by the fact that Angel was dismissing her. She looked over at the stranger sitting on Angel's love seat. She then looked back at Angel with eyes that asked, "Is that my replacement?"

Angel, sensing Carmen's uneasiness, said, "Carmen, this is Lady Arykah Miles-Howell. I met her at the conference in Dallas. Lady Arykah, this is Carmen." Angel wanted to let Carmen sweat it out by not referring to her as her assistant. In addition to that, she was still on the fence about Carmen's role in her life.

A relieved look rested on Carmen's face. She didn't seem to care that Angel hadn't used her title of assistant. She was just glad it wasn't the title of the woman who was sitting on the love seat. "Oh. Okay. Pleased to meet you." Carmen smiled at Arykah.

"It's nice to meet you as well, Carmen," Arykah greeted.

Angel just sat there and stared at Carmen. She didn't ask her to carry her Bible bag, lock up the office behind them, or anything else.

"Well, I guess I'll see you in the sanctuary, then," Carmen said, realizing she wasn't needed by her first lady.

All Angel did was smile. She had no more words for Carmen.

Carmen finally got the hint, and her head disappeared back through the crack in the door.

"So that's Carmen, huh?" Arykah asked Angel.

"The one and only."

"How did she come to be your assistant?"

Angel thought for a moment. "It was pretty much both my husband's and Mother Calloway's idea. Carmen needed extra money, and I needed a hand, as I was new at these first lady duties and all." Angel shrugged. "I didn't see the need to interview a whole lot of people for the position. She was already a member of the church. Plus, Carmen had welcomed me with open arms when I arrived here at Savior Manger. She seemed nice. Just a single mom trying to raise her daughter up right."

"You two close?" Arykah was trying to get a feel for Angel and Carmen's relationship.

"She's about the closest person I'd even consider calling a friend. At least she was."

"You don't have any friends or family here at this church? Someone who will have your back?"

Angel shook her head. "Nope. Like I said, had you asked me last week, I would have told you Carmen."

Arykah lowered her head and stared at Angel. "First Lady Angel," Arykah explained, "a first lady needs a roll dog, and what I mean by that is someone who'll roll with you no matter what. Someone who's gonna defend you, protect your character, and make sure that nothing or no one can harm you."

Angel shrugged her shoulders. "I can't say that I have any friends like that. Well, I have my husband, of course, but . . ." Angel hated to say it, but the verdict was even still out on him, too, for the moment.

"At my church, I have Team Arykah. My team consists of five women who I know for a fact will kill somebody if they mess with me."

Angel's eyes shot up in the air. "What?"

"Not *kill* as in 'put someone to death,' but *kill* as in 'put folks in their places for coming at me sideways.' Remember at the First Lady Conference when I told the women that I had just gotten out of jail prior to coming to the conference?"

Angel nodded her head.

"Well, that wasn't a lie," Arykah said. "Me and my closest friend, Monique, had jumped a chick for disrespecting me, and we were both arrested for that. I'm not saying that fighting is the only way to get respect. And Monique and I should not have been fighting, especially in the church.

But the point I'm trying to make is you need someone just like my friend Monique. Someone that'll protect you at all costs. It doesn't sound like Carmen does that. And that's why I'm gonna have a little chat with her before I leave here."

Angel became nervous. "What are you going to say to Carmen?"

"Don't worry. By the time I leave this church, Miss Carmen will know that she has to step up and be your ride-or-die chick or step aside and let someone else do it. So I guess we better get this Holy Ghost party started," Arykah said, getting up off the love seat. She put her hat back on her head.

Angel grabbed her purse and her Bible bag. She looked around to make sure she had everything. "Let's do this."

"Wait," Arykah said, stopping Angel. "Where's your hat?" She looked around the office.

Angel frowned. "My hat?"

"Yes," Arykah said. "Your big hat. Don't you own a hat collection?"

Angel shook her head. "No. What's the deal with hats?"

"Honey, first ladies always wear hats. *Big* hats. Your hat tells folks who you are without you having to introduce yourself. You really need to start looking like a first lady. You need a hat collection."

Angel didn't argue the fact. She didn't know what she needed at this point.

Arykah looked at Angel's dress, giving her a complete once-over. There were no diamond studs. There were no pearls. She looked at Angel's feet. Her cream heels weren't stilettos. They seemed to be three inches high at best. Arykah made a mental note that before she returned to Chicago, she would school Angel in detail about first lady attire. But that wasn't the main order of business that needed to be taken care of.

As Angel and Arykah were about to head out of the office, Angel turned to Arykah and said, "Thank you for being obedient to your spirit and coming here to Ohio. I felt so helpless until you showed up."

"Your help cometh from the Lord, but your backup hail from Chi-Town, baby. Now let's go and set some order." Arykah extended her hand outward toward the door. "After you, First Lady."

Angel led the way out of her office, with her head held high and her shoulders squared back.

"That looks good on you," Arykah said as they walked side by side.

"Oh, this dress?" Angel said, looking down at her gold dress.

"No, the confidence you're wearing. I like it."

Angel smiled. "Thank you."

"Just don't let it be temporary, and don't let it be induced by my presence. Remember the lion had it in him all along. I'm just here for support. To sit, watch, listen, offer you advice, and give Mother Calloway what she wants."

Angel nodded. Confusion then took over. "What do you mean, give Mother Calloway what she wants?"

"I know you don't like to say it, but after what you shared with me about the stunt she pulled this morning in getting everyone to be against you, it's clear that's nothing but the work of the devil. So since she wants to play devil's advocate, I'm going to give her what any devil desires."

"What's that?" Angel said.

"A vacation in hell."

Chapter 15

When Angel and Arykah arrived at the entrance to the sanctuary, Arykah stopped in her tracks.

"What is it? What's wrong?" Angel asked, wondering why Arykah was no longer walking beside her, but was behind her, standing still, instead.

"Where's your husband?" Arykah looked around, as if waiting on someone. "Don't you enter the sanctuary with him?"

"Well, no," Angel said with a shrug. She then turned and pointed toward the pulpit.

Arykah looked in the direction in which Angel was pointing. Pastor Harrison was already seated in his chair, fit for a king, off to the left of the podium. There were a couple of other chairs reserved for assistant ministers.

Arykah looked at the shepherd of the house in his gold and purple robe. "He's already in the pulpit?" she questioned.

"Yes. We must be running a little late." Angel didn't realize she and Arykah had been chatting in her office that long. That was probably the only reason why Carmen had come up to get her. It had probably been their pastor who had sent Carmen to fetch the first lady. "I'm usually already seated by the time he comes out."

Arykah watched Pastor Harrison as he sat there and sang along with the choir. She frowned. "He doesn't escort you to your seat every Sunday?"

Angel shook her head. "No." She wasn't under the impression that he should do so. No one else had ever questioned it. Certainly if that was something that should have been taking place, Mother Calloway would have pointed it out. She lived to fuss at Angel and to tell her what she was doing wrong.

"Well, he should. At least that's how we do it at our church," Arykah told her. "I know every church is different, but these folks up in here need to know that you and Pastor Harrison are one. They need to know that he's got you." Arykah shook her head. She could understand why Angel felt so alone.

Arykah couldn't fathom her husband strutting into that sanctuary like a peacock without its beautiful feathers, she being the feathers, of course. She loved when Lance knocked on her office door right before service, poked his head inside, and said, "Cheeks, it's time to head down to service."

It was music to Arykah's ears when she and Lance appeared at the sanctuary doors and the praise and worship leader said to the congregation, "Everyone, please stand and receive our bishop and first lady." Aretha Franklin said it best: r-e-s-p-e-c-t.

Lance would then escort Arykah down the center aisle to her place on the front pew. He always made it a point to kiss her cheek before he took his place in the pulpit. Some of the first ladies, Arykah knew, sat right there in the pulpit with their husbands. Noticing that the only other available seats in the pulpit were occupied, Arykah figured that wasn't the case for Angel.

"Come on. Let's go," Angel said to Arykah and then grabbed hold of Arykah's arm and started to walk.

Arykah didn't budge.

Angel gave her a look that said, "What now?"

"Well, does *anyone* escort you to your seat? Perhaps an usher?" Arykah asked as she dipped her head into the sanctuary and spotted an usher in each of the three aisles in the nice-size sanctuary. They each stood facing the door, with their gloved hands behind their back. Surely one of them had to have seen their first lady coming. Why hadn't one of them made it their business to come see Angel to her seat?

"Nope. No one," Angel replied sadly, knowing that wasn't the answer Arykah wanted to hear. She then thought for a moment and perked up a little bit. "Well, Carmen does sometimes. But lately, Mother Calloway has been needing her assistance in being escorted to the sanctuary."

"So, let me get this straight," Arykah said. "Carmen, *your* assistant, doesn't always escort you to your seat, 'cause she may be with Mother Calloway?"

Everything Arykah was alluding to was starting to sink in for Angel. She nodded her head shamefully. Why hadn't she realized any of this on her own? She had to admit that there had been a time or two when she watched her man enter that sanctuary, looking good with the glory of God all over him. She had imagined being by his side. At one point she had decided to share her feelings with her husband. She had reconsidered, though, and had never made her wishes known, because she didn't want people to think she was just trying to be his trophy, when in fact she was. Angel was his Oscar and his Emmy. She was his gold medal. She was his prize. If only she had opened her mouth up about it, perhaps she wouldn't be standing here now, feeling like a fool next to Arykah. Angel knew that by pointing out all the things that Angel should have been requiring or receiving, Arykah was not trying to make her feel some kind of way. This didn't make it sting any less, though.

"Humph," Arykah said. "If nothing else, at least Miss Carmen should be by your side." She looked down at one of the bags dangling from Angel's arm. "To at least carry your Bible bag." *I really gotta get ahold of Carmen*, she thought to herself. Noticing the solemn look on Angel's face, Arykah decided to let it go for now and move on. She'd try her best to observe in silence, but she couldn't make any promises. "Okay. Let's go."

Angel and Arykah entered the sanctuary and walked down the center aisle. When Angel stopped to take her place in her normal spot on the second pew, Arykah kept walking.

"Right here," Angel called out to Arykah.

Arykah stopped and watched Angel scoot down the pew and sit, leaving a spot for Arykah to the left of her.

Arykah stood there, dumbfounded, for a moment. She looked at where Angel was sitting. She looked at the front pew, where Angel wasn't sitting, then looked back at Angel again. She could almost taste the blood, she was biting her tongue so hard.

Without saying a word about how she felt about Angel not having a spot on the front pew,

Arykah joined Angel on the second pew. In the pew in front of them, some of the other church leaders were seated, including Mother Calloway.

"Is that her?" Arykah pointed to the older woman wearing a purple dress with gold accessories. Her silver hair had fresh, tight curls.

"How'd you guess?" Angel asked in a whisper. "I didn't even have to point her out to you."

"I could smell her," Arykah said, twitching her nose.

Angel giggled. "That lilac spray she uses is pretty strong." Angel didn't know how the other leaders could stand sitting right next to her. Angel was behind her, and the smell was assaulting her nose. And even though in the past Angel had watched a couple of the leaders hold handkerchiefs or tissue over their nostrils until the scent died down, to Angel's knowledge, not one person had ever asked Mother Calloway to go easy on the spray that was causing such a stink.

Arykah wasn't laughing when she said with a straight face, "I wasn't talking about the smell of her perfume. I was talking about the smell of sulfur."

"Well," was all Angel could say as she situated herself next to her Bible bag and purse.

Across the aisle Arykah noticed a row of men seated on the front pew. They were all decked out in black suits. She leaned into Angel. "Who are they? The men in black?"

"The deacons," Angel said. "They all wear black suits on Communion Sunday."

Arykah looked at the leaders on the pew in front of them. She then looked back over at what she referred to as the men in black. For the life of her, she didn't understand why she and Angel were not sitting on one of those front pews. She didn't care how active or inactive the first lady of a church was, it was just an unspoken rule that if her tail wasn't in the pulpit, next to her man, then she better be planted right smack in front of him on the first pew.

Praise and worship began their last selection. It was a beautiful worship song that put most of the congregation on their feet, with hands raised. Angel was one of them. Arykah would have to repent to God later and have her own personal worship with Him in her hotel room, because right now her spirit was vexed by what she was witnessing. She wasn't about to put on a front and pretend to be worshipping. She worshipped only in spirit and in truth. Even if the other members of the congregation didn't know she was faking, God would.

After just sitting back and watching for so long, Arykah couldn't take it anymore. Her tongue was wagging in her mouth like a hyperactive dog's tail. She had to let it loose. Arykah stood to her feet and said in Angel's ear, "Why aren't you sitting on the front pew?" Never mind that she was interrupting Angel's moment of worship. She just had to know.

"Huh? What?" Angel opened her eyes. Her holy hands remained lifted. She kept her eyes on praise and worship and merely leaned her ear toward Arykah.

"Why are you not sitting on the front pew?" Arykah repeated, jabbing her finger toward the pew. She wore a scowl on her face. From the outside looking in, one might have thought she was reading Angel by her gestures and facial expression.

"Because the front pew is reserved for the church leaders. I'm not a head of any ministry at this point."

Just then Carmen entered the sanctuary from a side door to the right of the pulpit. With one hand, she carried a bottle of water. Apologetic, she held up an index finger on her other hand as she walked in front of people. Carmen handed Mother Calloway the bottle of water. Mother Calloway thanked her and then scooted over to make room for Carmen to sit down next to her.

Arykah's eyebrows rose. "*Really*?" She elbowed Angel, who had closed her eyes after answering Arykah in an attempt to go back into worship.

"Well, why is Carmen sitting on the front pew? What ministry is she in charge of?"

Angel opened her eyes and saw Carmen comfortably seated next to Mother Calloway. She shrugged her shoulders. Carmen had never sat on the front pew before. Usually, she was either sitting with Angel or helping out in her daughter's classroom in youth church. Angel had never paid it any mind one way or the other. None of this had ever been a concern to her, but from the way Arykah was acting, it should have been an abomination. Still, Angel tried to appear unaffected. "I really don't mind. Honestly." Angel didn't want Arykah to get all worked up about something she deemed minor.

"Well, you should mind," Arykah couldn't help but snap. When Angel closed her eyes again, Arykah took the hint that the subject was no longer up for discussion. She'd table the conversation . . . for now.

Arykah politely sat back down in her seat while the congregation finished worshipping along with the praise and worship team. She proceeded to observe the morning service at Savior Manger. Right after preaching a lengthy and moving sermon, Pastor Harrison asked if anyone had any praise reports or needed prayer.

This led to him laying holy hands on some people. The moment he signaled for his holy oil, Arykah watched how Mother Calloway took it upon herself to jump up and assist him when it was time for him to lay hands on the women.

In Arykah's mind, that was a definite no-no. Angel should have been the one assisting Pastor Harrison. Lance always had Arykah by his side when he was ministering to and blessing the women. Once again, Arykah had to remind herself that not all churches and pastors were the same in the way they operated. What she did know was that she loved and was so grateful for the way her husband operated. Bishop Lance Howell, aka smooth operator. Arykah loved to assist her husband in ministry whenever the need arose. She felt it was her job as a first lady to support her husband, and not the duty of the mother of the church.

As soon as Pastor Harrison gave the benediction, his armor bearers and the church leaders stood and filled the pulpit. They remained in close proximity while some members of the church made their way to the pulpit to greet him. After this, Pastor Harrison exited the pulpit, surrounded by his armor bearers.

Arykah was fit to be tied. She just knew that eventually the man was going to come take Angel by the hand and that they would leave the sanctuary together. At Freedom Temple Church of God, after her husband gave the benediction, he would grab Arykah's hand and escort her to the sanctuary doors. The two of them would stand and shake the hand of each member as they left the church. As much as Arykah kept telling herself that not everyone did things the way she and Bishop Lance Howell did them, she wished they would, at least in Angel's case, anyway. Angel needed that type of reinforcement. She wasn't the type to bogart and overstep her boundaries, especially when she didn't even know what her boundaries were. Being a seasoned vet and the head of the church, Arykah felt Pastor Harrison should have taken the lead on that and helped guide Angel to some degree.

"Now what?" Arykah asked as she noticed the congregation members exiting the sanctuary. She had to ask, because for all she knew, Angel was the one who stayed and cleaned the church up!

"We can head back up to my office," Angel said. "Then I'll introduce you to Isaiah."

Back upstairs in Angel's office, Arykah took her big pink hat off and sat down on the love seat. Angel grabbed them both a bottle of chilled water from her mini-fridge and then sat next to Arykah.

"So, did you enjoy the service?" Angel asked as she handed Arykah a water.

"I can't say that I did," Arykah answered honestly.

Angel's face nearly hit the floor. In her opinion, Savior Manger had one of the best praise and worship teams in the town. Even though she was biased, if you asked her, her husband could preach a mean sermon.

"I mean, the Word that your husband preached was good, but there were so many things out of order when it came to you that I just couldn't concentrate. From your husband not escorting you to your seat, to Mother Calloway and Carmen sitting on the front pew and you on the second pew, to Pastor Harrison not using you, but Mother Calloway instead, in ministry."

Angel lowered her head. She sighed. She opened her mouth to speak but then closed it before any words could come out.

"Go on. Say what's on your mind," Arykah urged her.

Angel exhaled. "Well, I was going to say my usual 'I am new to all this and really don't know what the correct order is, what my role is, and what I should be doing,' but I'm starting to sound like a broken record to myself." Angel looked at Arykah. "I mean, look at you. It's not like you went and took a crash course in becoming a first lady, yet you just get it."

"And you got *it* too," Arykah assured her. "Baby, just use *it*. Dang."

Angel paused for a minute, then said timidly, "Can I be honest with you?"

"Considering all you're ever going to get from me is honesty, I expect nothing less."

"Well," Angel began apprehensively, "if I'm honest with both you and myself, I feel like if I just sit back and say nothing, then nothing will be expected of me. That way I won't get it wrong. I won't fail because there will be nothing to fail at." She paused for a moment. "The minute I start demanding things and questioning things, then things will be expected of me. And I have no idea what to do. I just . . ." Angel's words trailed off as she became frustrated with herself.

"I really want to sympathize with you," Arykah said, "but ignorance is not bliss. Still, I wouldn't care if you never made a mumbling word like Jesus on the cross. People, everybody, especially leaders, know how to show you respect. Period. That goes without saying."

"But I guess I never demanded it." Angel continued to make excuses.

Arykah threw her hands on her hips. "Well, what have you done to not just receive it? I hear folks all the time yapping about how you have to earn respect. I beg to differ. I'm going to respect everybody I come into contact with, *unless* you give me a reason not to." Arykah pointed to her chest. "I don't care about what so-and-so says about ya. Show me different." Arykah relaxed her arms across her lap and spoke in a calm demeanor. "So I repeat, what have you done in order for them not to respect you?"

Angel didn't have an answer to that. She'd done nothing to harm anyone, at least not to her knowledge. "I know things have to change," Angel admitted.

"Not just things, but *you*," Arykah pointed out. "You are a mighty woman of God. I'ma need you to start using the power vested in you by our Heavenly Father."

Angel nodded. Arykah was right. Again, Angel had no problem accepting corrections from the woman who was becoming a true mentor to her.

There was a knock on the door.

"Come in," Angel called out.

The door opened a crack, and Pastor Harrison entered. "Hey, love," he said to his wife, with a huge smile on his face, as he closed the door behind him.

Angel immediately stood to her feet at the sight of her husband.

Arykah sat back and observed the way husband and wife lit the room up as they gazed into each other's eyes. Angel's entire countenance had changed now that her man was on the scene. Her head was lifted, and her shoulders were steady. Now, this was what Arykah envisioned Angel looking like as she entered and exited the sanctuary on her husband's arm on Sunday mornings. And it didn't go unnoticed how his eyes gazed right past Arykah, as if only his wife was in the room.

"Hey, honey." Angel floated across the room and into her husband's arms.

He looked into his wife's eyes momentarily before planting a kiss on her lips. Even after he lifted his lips away from hers, he took yet another moment to look into his wife's eyes.

Arykah cleared her throat and then stood in the presence of the head of the house.

"Oh," Pastor Harrison said, noticing Arykah near the love seat. "I saw that you had a guest back in the sanctuary," he said to Angel. "I wanted to introduce myself." He stepped around Angel and walked over to Arykah and extended his hand toward her. "I'm Pastor Harrison."

Arykah shook his hand. "I'm Lady Arykah Miles-Howell. I bring you greetings from Freedom Temple Church of God in Christ, where my pastor and husband is Bishop Lance Howell."

"Well, praise God," Pastor Harrison said, genuinely honored to have the wife of Bishop

Howell visit Savior Manger. He'd heard only good things about the bishop and great things about Lady Arykah from Angel.

"Honey, Lady Arykah is from Chicago," Angel said. "She and I met at the First Lady Conference."

"Yes," Pastor Harrison said knowingly. "Angel speaks highly of you. Welcome to Savior Manger."

"It's my pleasure to be here," Arykah said. "You have a lovely church home."

"I was just about to invite my beautiful wife to dinner. Why don't you join us?"

Angel walked over and stood next to her husband. "Yes, Lady Arykah, please come."

Arykah looked at Angel. "You know, since I plan on being here for only a day or so, I was hoping that you and I could spend some first lady time together."

Angel knew what Arykah was getting at. Arykah hadn't hopped on that plane because she and Angel were old college buddies. They hadn't even known each other for a full month and had talked on the phone only once. Angel wasn't even sure if Arykah would label her as a friend. They were definitely sisters in Christ, connected through the blood of Jesus, but it was apparent that Arykah was there on a mission and for a purpose and didn't have time to play around.

"Oh, okay. Absolutely." Angel looked at her husband. "You don't mind, do you, honey?"

"Of course not," Pastor Harrison answered. "I'll take a rain check." He leaned in and whispered something naughty in his wife's ear that only she could hear. "'Cause you know I like to get wet."

As dark as Angel's skin was, she somehow still managed to turn beet red. Her man had a way of making her blush. Arykah knew the feeling all too well as she looked down to give husband and wife a brief moment of not so private privacy.

Pastor Harrison kissed Angel's cheek. "Enjoy your time with your guest. I'll meet you at home." Pastor Harrison looked at Arykah. "Lady Arykah."

Arykah lifted her head and gave him her attention.

He continued. "If I don't see you again, it truly has been a pleasure meeting you. Please don't let this be your only visit to Savior Manger. I'd love for both you and Bishop Howell to return."

Arykah smiled and nodded her head. "It won't be my last visit, I'm sure. And I'll definitely extend the invitation to my husband."

On that note, Pastor Harrison winked at Angel and then turned and exited the room with a smoothness that would give President Obama a run for his money.

The minute that door closed, with Pastor Harrison on the other side, Arykah's pleasant and buttery demeanor evaporated. "Call your assistant and tell her that you wanna see her in your office right now." Arykah was pointing to the phone on Angel's desk.

Knowing that Arykah was ready to get right down to business, Angel hustled over to her desk and picked up the phone. She went to dial Carmen's number but then realized that she didn't know it by heart. She put the phone down and retrieved her cell phone. She had Carmen's number stored in her mobile address book. Angel dialed Carmen's cellular telephone and asked her if she would come to her office.

"I'm actually on my way up," Carmen replied. "I just finished helping Mother Calloway with a couple of things."

Angel thanked God she didn't have the call on speakerphone. That was all Arykah needed to hear. No sooner had Angel ended the call and relayed to Arykah that Carmen was on her way up than there was a knock on the door.

Carmen slowly cracked open the door and poked her head inside. By now Angel and Arykah were sitting on the love seat, taking swigs of their water. "You wanted to see me, First Lady?"

"Yes," both Angel and Arykah said at the same time. The two women then looked at each other. Arykah had a look in her eyes that showed how anxious she was to go in on Carmen. At that moment, Angel and Arykah had a silent conversation with their eyes.

"You all right?" Angel's eyes asked Arykah.

"I'm good," Arykah's eyes replied. "You go first," Arykah's eyes added as her head nodded for Angel to proceed.

Angel turned to look at Carmen. "Yes, Carmen, I did want to see you." She waved Carmen over to them. "Come on in."

Carmen's eyes darted from one woman to the next. It was almost as if she had a feeling that she was about to be ambushed or something. Arykah thought for a minute there that Carmen did a little backpedaling, as if she was reconsidering entering the office.

Carmen entered. She usually closed the door all the way behind her. This time she left a small crack. Angel was looking down, screwing the cap back on her bottle of water, but none of this went unnoticed by Arykah, who chuckled inside at Carmen's actions. She had to admit that she was a little tickled that she could sometimes have this kind of effect on people. Arykah never set out to intimidate anyone. That was not who she was. But who she was, was a woman who was not to be played with, and apparently, Carmen could see that this was true.

"First Lady Angel, your assistant here looks a little parched," Arykah said to Angel while glaring at Carmen the entire time. "Perhaps she could use a bottle of water as well."

"Oh, no. I'm fine," Carmen quickly assured Arykah, raising her hands to decline the offer. She swallowed hard, as if she was trying to force something down. One would have thought that she did, in fact, need a beverage to wash away something that was stuck in her throat.

"I'll give you a bottle, anyway," Angel said after hearing Carmen swallow so hard.

"Umm, I think we got the last ones, First Lady," Arykah said, raising an eyebrow at Angel. "Maybe you all keep more down in the church kitchen or something."

Angel shot Arykah a puzzled stare. She'd just grabbed each of them a bottle of water from her fridge. If she recalled correctly, there were several left.

Her eyebrows still raised, Arykah bucked her eyes at Angel, hoping the first lady could take a hint.

Finally, it registered in Angel's brain that Arykah wanted her to leave the room so that she could have a minute alone with Carmen. "Oh, oh, yes. Sure. Church kitchen. Water," Angel stammered as she made her way over to the door. "I'll go grab you one, Carmen."

"Oh, I can get it myself," Carmen was quick to say, making a sprint for the door.

"Your first lady says she'll get it for you," Arykah said, jumping in, "so let her get it." Arykah smiled at Carmen. It was a cross between a "kill 'em with kindness" smile and an "If only you knew what was really up underneath this smile" kind of smile.

Once again, Carmen swallowed hard. She folded her hands in front of her and began to wring her fingers. "Oh, okay." She gave Angel a nervous smile. "Thank you, First Lady."

Angel nodded and then went to open the door. Before exiting, she gave Arykah a look that said, "Please don't hurt her."

Carmen stood there, still wringing her hands, looking around the office.

"Sit with me, Carmen," Arykah said. She patted the area on the love seat that Angel had vacated. "Let's chat."

Carmen didn't have a clue what Arykah would want to chat with her about, but she didn't want to be disrespectful to her first lady's guest by asking. She just went and sat down next to Arykah.

"Carmen," Arykah began, "who appointed you to be your first lady's assistant?" She got right to the point. She didn't know how long Angel would be gone, and she felt it best to have the conversation with Carmen outside of

Angel's presence. She wanted Angel to have no accountability at all for what might go down in this office.

Carmen frowned and cocked her head to the side. "Um, well, no one appointed me. It sorta just happened. The suggestion was made, and I accepted."

Arykah mimicked Carmen when she frowned and cocked her head to the side. "How so?"

Carmen frowned again, and she fluttered her lashes, as if she was annoyed. "I don't mean to be rude, Lady Arykah," Carmen said with just a pinch of disdain in her voice. The average bear might not detect it, but Arykah wasn't the average bear.

Hmmm. So Miss Thing wanna go toe-to-toe, huh? Arykah thought in her head. She loved it when she was up against someone in her same weight category personality-wise. With Carmen, it seemed like up underneath all that "single mother and assistant to the first lady" crap, there was a hood chick just waiting for a reason to reveal herself. Arykah had her reasons, but she actually hoped this was the case with Carmen.

"Why are you asking me this?" Carmen continued.

Arykah sensed that Carmen was becoming even more uneasy in her presence. Her defenses were up. Although Arykah loved a challenge, she wasn't here to challenge anyone. She just wanted to help the church's first lady out. She decided in that moment that perhaps she could get further along with Carmen if she used honey instead of vinegar. "Perhaps I should have given you the decency of knowing my intentions for being here."

Carmen nodded, all ears.

"I'm here because First Lady Angel is troubled by some of the members at this church," Arykah stated. "I don't like troubled waters, and I'm sure you don't, either. Am I right about that?"

Carmen nodded her head again, still not quite sure about where Arykah was going with all this.

"And we definitely don't want to see our friends in troubled waters, either, right?"

Carmen nodded a third time.

Next, Arykah asked Carmen, "Are the two of you friends? You and your first lady?"

Carmen thought for a moment before she answered. "Well, I can't say that First Lady Angel and I are friends, but we are friendly toward each other. We had seemed to be getting very close until . . ." Carmen wasn't sure how much, if anything, Arykah knew about Angel and Mother Calloway's feud. She didn't want to go blabbing her mouth. She already felt as though she was in the middle of the madness.

"Until what?" Arykah asked. "Mother Calloway got involved?"

Carmen nodded, realizing that Arykah was privy to Mother Calloway and Angel's not so good relationship.

"Well, that's a problem, Carmen," Arykah said. "First Lady Angel has no family here at Savior Manger. She and Pastor Harrison are newlyweds. It's no secret that when a pastor marries, especially someone outside of the church, tension rises."

Carmen nodded respectfully. She'd lost her sassiness, which confirmed Arykah was right about changing her style of delivery when it came to Carmen. "You're right," Carmen agreed. "There is a tremendous amount of tension between First Lady Angel and a few of the members here, especially Mother Calloway."

"I understand that Mother Calloway doesn't like the new first lady."

Carmen chuckled. "That's really putting it mildly. Mother Calloway despises our first lady, but I do manage to keep them in their separate corners."

"And how exactly do you do that, Carmen?"

Carmen shrugged her shoulders. "I mean, when they get into it, I take Mother Calloway in another direction."

"And then what?"

"And then nothing. I just keep them apart, and everything seems to die down, for the time being, anyway."

"And do you return to First Lady Angel and console her after Mother Calloway has ripped her to shreds?"

Carmen looked at Arykah while trying to figure her out. Right when Carmen had thought she knew exactly what road Arykah was heading down, she'd veered off the road most traveled. Carmen decided that riding in the passenger seat might not be the way to go. But if she was going to have a driver, it was fine time she asked the driver just where the heck they were going. "Lady Arykah, I don't know exactly what all First Lady Angel has told you, but—"

Arykah cut off Carmen's words. "She told me that she's being bullied by Mother Calloway, and from what you told me, you go aid the bully after the fight."

Carmen's breath caught in her throat. She really did need that water her first lady had gone to get. Once she was able to speak, with her voice now raised an octave, she said, "Bullied? Really? First Lady used that word?"

"Even if she didn't, I'm using it, because that's *exactly* what Mother Calloway is doing."

Carmen shook her head from side to side vigorously. "I don't know if I would call Mother Calloway a bully. I mean, isn't that a word used only on the playground?"

"Actually, it isn't," Arykah replied, correcting her. "There is bullying in the workplace, in relationships, in the home, and sometimes even in the church," Arykah explained. "Bullying, plain and simply put, involves an imbalance of power. Bullying is not a phase and has nothing to do with age."

Carmen couldn't say much to that. Apparently, Arykah had done her homework and then had taken the liberty to school her. "I guess when you put it like that . . . ," Carmen said, feeling slightly bad that up until now she hadn't realized that what Mother Calloway was doing to Angel had such a name. Carmen had been bullied in school when she was a little girl. It hadn't felt good, so she imagined that it didn't feel good for her first lady, either.

"If you never saw Mother Calloway as a bully, what would you call her? A liar? Would you say that Mother Calloway is a manipulator?"

"Well, I—"

"Or perhaps she's a devil in disguise?" Arykah said.

Arykah saw sweat beads appear on Carmen's forehead. She had the poor doe cornered. Perhaps Miss Assistant wasn't 'bout that life, after all.

Carmen shifted on the love seat. She didn't like being taken back to the painful years in her own life. She shook it off and then straightened her back. "What's going on here?"

Oh, there was that sassiness again. That made Arykah smile inside.

"I feel like I'm being ambushed," Carmen said. "I can't control First Lady's or Mother Calloway's actions. Those two are grown-up women. Why am I being put in the middle of this mess?" Carmen rolled her eyes. This conversation couldn't end soon enough as far as she was concerned. She only wished that her first lady would walk through those doors and rescue her. Then it hit her. Perhaps that was exactly what Angel had wanted her to do that day Mother Calloway had her hemmed in, in the office. Conviction filled Carmen's being.

"Look, Carmen," Arykah stated, "I like the fact that underneath that pretty brown skin of yours is a little fire, because that's exactly what a first lady needs from her assistant. That gives me comfort. What I like even more is that you know how to suppress it and when to let the beast loose once you're backed up in a corner.

That's a good skill to have too," Arykah said, complimenting her.

"Well, thank you," Carmen said, surprised by Arykah's comment.

"But just so you know, God ain't through with me yet. I don't have that type of self-control, so I'ma need you to bring it down just a little bit so that we don't mess up First Lady's office. All right?" Arykah said that as diplomatically as she could while staring right into Carmen's eyes. She had to let Carmen know that if she came out of the side of her face one mo' time, she couldn't promise that she wouldn't mop up the floor with her face.

"I apologize, Lady Arykah," Carmen said in a more respectful tone. "I meant no disrespect."

"Apology accepted," Arykah said and then continued. "As you can see, I'm not one to sugarcoat things, Carmen, so here goes. If you're gonna be First Lady Angel's assistant, then you need to have her back."

"I do have her back," Carmen protested. "I have her back when I keep Mother Calloway away from her. I do that by walking Mother to the sanctuary. I keep Mother Calloway settled by getting her what she needs and keeping her preoccupied so that she lets First Lady be. I walk Mother Calloway to the car. I—"

"And it never once dawned on you that those are the things you are supposed to be doing for your first lady?" Arykah asked. "Isn't *she* the one you should be covering and making sure is all right?"

Carmen sat and thought. Everything Arykah was saying was correct.

"Your first lady told me that Pastor Harrison had a meeting with just the three of you. Mother Calloway was nowhere around, yet you still saved face on her behalf."

Carmen felt bad enough for her lack of support for Angel. She had done some things wrong, but in her own defense, she felt she'd done some things right. "But I told Pastor Harrison the truth in that meeting. Like I told both Mother Calloway and First Lady Angel, I'm not taking either one of their sides. I'm only on God's side."

"So was it God's side you were on when you told Pastor Harrison only what Angel had said to Mother Calloway? Why didn't you reveal Mother Calloway's ugliness as well?"

Carmen leaned back against the love seat and pursed her lips. It seemed like everything she said, Arykah shot down, like she was a self-propelled guided missile. She couldn't win for losing with this woman. She was ready to throw in the towel. But she still had a little fight left in her. "I wanted to."

"Well, why didn't you?" Arykah was like a dog that had latched on to its bone and would not let it go.

Carmen exhaled. "Because Mother Calloway can be . . . she can sometimes be . . ."

"A beeyatch?"

Carmen's eyes bucked out of her head. She covered her gaping mouth. This was the second time in a week someone had cussed in the house of the Lord. First, churches started letting their members bring in beverages and feed their kids snacks in the sanctuary. Now, people couldn't even wait to get out of the church parking lot to let juicy expletives fly. What was the world coming to?

"It's okay, Carmen. You can say it," Arykah said, encouraging her. "Come on and tell the truth and shame the devil. Mother Calloway can be a straight-up biddy at times, *right*?"

Carmen didn't speak. She looked at Arykah and slowly nodded her head. She wasn't about to verbalize it, though, and be just as guilty. No one would ever be able to testify that the words had actually come out of her mouth.

Arykah looked at Carmen for a moment. Just a few moments ago Carmen had had a little fire up under her. Arykah had almost thought she'd about met her match. Seemed like just the mention of Mother Calloway's name had a way of putting fires out. "Are you afraid of her?" Arykah asked Carmen.

Carmen looked at Arykah. "Not afraid of her necessarily. Perhaps afraid of what she can do," she admitted. "Mother Calloway has a great deal of power around here. And she has a way of reminding you of it if you get out of place."

"Kind of like a bully, huh?" Arykah could see the revelation in Carmen's eyes. She'd just realized that she'd indirectly been getting bullied too. "So, you threw your first lady under the bus 'cause you're afraid of what Mother Calloway might do?" Curious, Arykah asked, "What exactly is it Mother Calloway *could* possibly do?"

"I was struggling before Mother Calloway suggested I pick up some extra ends as First Lady's assistant," Carmen said. "I figured the same way she used her authority to give it, she could take it away. And I really need the money. My ex and this child support thing is giving me the blues. It was a blessing for Mother Calloway even to consider me for—"

Arykah had to stop Carmen right there. "Girl, don't you give that old woman that kind of power," Arykah said. "Yes, God uses man to bless His saints, but it is *God* who ultimately gives and takes. Nothing can supersede His divine order, and don't you forget it."

"I hear you," Carmen said.

"I don't need you just to *hear* me. I need you to *believe* me. You got it?"

Carmen looked into Arykah's eyes and nodded with confidence.

Arykah let out a gust of air and stood as she straightened out her outfit. "Lord, I don't know how Iyanla does it," she said under her breath. She then turned to face Carmen. "Look, Carmen, I'm gonna deal with Mother Calloway, but first, I'm gonna deal with you. You need to grow some cojones, okay? You're a grown woman. And there's no reason why you should be intimidated by an old woman. Mother Calloway can't whup your butt. You gotta stand up to her. She pushes you around because she thinks you're weak. The same way you showed me that fiery side of you, burn *her butt* with it. I guarantee you she'll be just like a child who has been warned not to touch fire, because it's hot. Once they see for themselves that they can get burned, they know not to touch it again."

Carmen smiled at Arykah's analogy and agreed with a nod.

"What it boils down to is that First Lady Angel doesn't need any weaklings on her team. If you're not up to play the part of her assistant, then you shouldn't have auditioned for it."

"I know you're right, Lady Arykah, but—"

"There are no buts, Carmen. It's hard out here for a first lady. Your first lady needs someone who's gonna defend her, stand up for her, cover her, and protect her. Now, you're either gonna piss or get off the pot. Time's run out for playin' games. Woman up and get in your position and stay there!"

Carmen was speechless at Arykah's boldness. She gathered her words and stood. "I am going to make a conscious effort. But it is easier said than done."

"No, it ain't," Arykah quickly countered. "That's what I flew to Ohio to do—make it easier to do. See, First Lady Angel is meek and timid, but I'm from the streets. I know how to roll in the mud with the best of them. Like I said, Mother Calloway ain't nothin' but an old-school bully."

"I can't disagree with you, Lady Arykah. You're absolutely right about everything. I was wrong for not standing up for First Lady. She didn't and doesn't deserve to be treated badly by Mother Calloway."

"I'm glad we see things eye to eye, Carmen. Does this mean that you're gonna have her back when she needs you to?"

Without even hesitating, Carmen replied, "Yep. After all, it's two of us and one of her."

"No," Arykah said, correcting Carmen. "It's *three* of you." She pointed up to the heavens. "And with me just being an hour flight away, make that four." Arykah smiled.

"Thank you, Lady Arykah. We may have started off a little on the wrong foot, but I do appreciate what you are doing for my first lady."

"So does this mean that you're gonna set Mother Calloway straight the next time she tries any of her shenanigans? After all, being a bystander and saying and doing nothing are almost as bad as being a bully."

Carmen thought for a minute and then began nodding her head. With confidence, she said, "You know what? I think I just will set that old lady straight." She laughed. "But I wanna see how you do it first."

Arykah screamed out in laughter.

Angel entered the room to see both her assistant and Arykah cracking up. This was a good sign and music to her ears. She'd envisioned entering the room, finding that Arykah had Carmen by the throat, and hearing a muffled squeal coming from Carmen's throat, instead of raucous laughter. This put an automatic smile on her face. Apparently, whatever Arykah had set out to discuss with Carmen had panned out.

"You ladies want to let me in on the joke?" Angel asked as she walked across the room with a bottle of water in hand. She handed it to Carmen, who could hardly take it, as she was laughing so hard.

"I can show you better than I can tell you," Arykah replied. "But things could get messy, so you should probably stay here." She looked at Carmen. "So with that being said, take me to Mother Calloway." Arykah headed to the door without even waiting for Carmen to be her guide. She'd gotten through to Carmen, but there was still plenty of unfinished business with the church mother.

Carmen was right on Arykah's heels. "Thanks for the water, First Lady," she said as she passed Angel, "but, uh, I think I'm going to need some popcorn to go along with it." Carmen let out a mischievous chuckle and followed Arykah out the door.

Angel looked upward and said, "Oh, Lord, I knew this was too good to be true." She walked over to the door and stood in her office doorway, having no idea what lay ahead. But she could only imagine.

Chapter 16

When Carmen and Arykah entered the church vestibule, they found exactly who they were looking for. With her office being closed up and locked, Carmen had suggested that Mother Calloway was either down in the sanctuary or had gone home. From the way Mother Calloway was policing the front doors with her purse and Bible bag in hand, it was obvious that she was watching for her ride to pull up. Her back was to the women while she looked impatiently out the glass church doors, her head turning from left to right.

"That's her," Carmen whispered and pointed.

"I know," Arykah whispered back. Looked like fate was on Arykah's side. Had the old woman gone home, there was no telling how long Arykah would have had to hang out in the city in order to catch up with her.

Arykah scanned the area and took note that no one else was around.

Carmen stepped toward Mother Calloway. "What are you doing, Mother Calloway?" she asked her.

Mother Calloway whipped around sharply, with a mean mug on her face. She saw that the voice belonged to Carmen, and an immediate smile took over her face as she relaxed her shoulders. "Oh, Carmen, honey," Mother Calloway said, "it's you." Mother Calloway looked from Carmen to Arykah and then back to Carmen. She had seen Arykah and Angel come into morning service and sit behind her. Mother Calloway had wondered who Angel's guest was.

She was about to find out.

"I'm waiting on the COTA Mainstream bus service to take me home," Mother Calloway replied. On some Sundays she hitched a ride with a church member. There was a time or two when she'd even utilized the church transportation ministry. But she didn't like having to get ready and head out for church so early so that the driver could make a hundred stops to pick up other members. On days she wanted to ride with just herself and the Lord and not feel obligated to engage in any type of conversation, she utilized the city public transportation service designed to service the elderly and handicapped.

She had to schedule the ride in advance and pay a small round-trip fee, but the peace of mind was worth it, in her opinion.

Arykah looked around again for good measure. Carmen and Mother Calloway were the only other souls in the vestibule. Apparently, all the other members had left the church already.

To God be the glory, Arykah thought in her head. There was a chance she might not want any eyewitnesses around for this. From what she'd been told, Mother Calloway liked to get a little turned up. Well, the only thing Arykah had to say about that was, "Turn down for what?"

Mother Calloway stood staring at Arykah while she said to Carmen, "Aren't you going to introduce me to our visitor? I suppose if our first lady had gotten her down to the sanctuary on time, she could have been introduced along with the other first-time visitors." She looked at Carmen. "But you know our first lady runs on CP time." Mother Calloway sucked her teeth.

Arykah was appalled that Mother Calloway would speak in such a way about her very own first lady, and to someone who was attending the church as a guest of the first lady, no less. That let Arykah know right off the bat the kinds of things Mother Calloway was saying about Angel to people who weren't Angel's friends. It was high time to shut this old woman up for good.

Carmen began the introductions. "Mother Calloway, this is First Lady Arykah." Carmen looked at Arykah, signaling for her to finish the introductions, as she wasn't sure about the name of the church Arykah was visiting from.

Introductions and pleasantries were the last thing on Arykah's mind, though. "Carmen, honey?" Arykah coughed. "I think I'm the one who is a little parched now." She coughed again. "I left my water up in First Lady Angel's office. Do you mind?" She coughed.

"Here. Take mine," Carmen said, shoving her bottle of water toward Arykah. No way was she going to miss this action.

Arykah looked down at Carmen's bottle of water and then back up at Carmen. She raised an eyebrow.

"What?" Carmen asked. "I haven't drunk from it yet."

"You go ahead. That one is *yours*." Arykah tried to speak as calmly as possible while keeping a smile on her face. She couldn't wait to put Mother Calloway in her place, and Carmen was delaying the process.

"Really, I don't mind—" Carmen began.

"Carmen!" Arykah snapped, making her jump. Mother Calloway didn't budge. She was completely unaffected by Arykah's brashness. After all, these days she was the queen of brash.

"Uh, yes, Lady Arykah," Carmen finally agreed. "I'll go get your water." Carmen reluctantly walked away.

As soon as Carmen was out of sight and hearing range, Arykah stepped to Mother Calloway and connected the tips of their shoes. Arykah glared into Mother Calloway's eyes. "Look, you old wrinkled prune, you may have everyone at this church walking on eggshells, but I ain't scared of you."

Needless to say, Mother Calloway was caught off guard by this type of brashness. She didn't know who Arykah was or where she had come from, but she wasn't about to allow her to step up in Savior Manger and speak to her that way. She wouldn't allow her own first lady to get away with that, let alone another church's first lady. "What!" Mother Calloway gasped. She went to point her finger in Arykah's face. "Just who do—"

Arykah balled up her lips and cut off Mother Calloway's words. "I'm not here to have a conversation with you, so shut up and listen." Arykah hated that she had to talk to this little old woman like this, but past experience had proven that it was the only type of language women like her understood. "I'ma tell you this one time, and one time only. Back up off of First Lady Angel."

Mother Calloway went to speak again, but once again, Arykah cut her off.

"Look, I know how you must feel," Arykah said in a more sympathetic tone, but one that still showed that she meant business. "Pastor Harrison is probably like a son to you. Some woman, who wasn't even raised in your church, comes in, and the next thing you know, she's wearing the title of first lady. Trust me, I get it." Now it was Arykah who pointed a finger. "But you're going to get over it. Your first lady ain't going nowhere. So you can pull your fangs out of her and treat her with the respect she deserves as the first lady of this house."

Mother Calloway made sure Arykah was finished with her spiel before she snapped her head back and said, "Who the heck are *you*?"

Arykah spaced her words apart. "I'm . . . your . . . worst . . . freakin' . . . nightmare. I flew all the way from Chicago to tell you that if you don't stop messing with this here church's first lady, you're gonna find yourself in a whole lotta trouble. Or you're gonna find yourself a new church to worship at. And I *dare* you to think that I'm playing with you."

Mother Calloway stepped backward, clutching her chest.

"Go on and clutch your pearls, old lady," Arykah said, "but when they break off the string, be careful not to trip and fall on 'em and break your neck."

"Jesus!" Mother Calloway called out, taking Arykah's comment as a physical threat.

Arykah stepped toward Mother Calloway as the old woman continued to back up.

"Carmen!" was the name Mother Calloway called out next. Jesus, Carmen, anybody . . . She didn't care who at this point.

"You can call on whomever you want to right now. But in the meantime, take a look at this face," Arykah said to her. "If you see it again, I ain't gonna do no talkin'." Arykah raised her eyebrows and gritted her teeth. "You *hear* me? You *don't* want me to come back here, Mother, at least not under these circumstances."

Mother Calloway shivered. Arykah had seen that look before, when she had threatened Mother Gussie back in Chicago, at Freedom Temple. Arykah knew she had made her point with the old lady.

A horn could be heard beeping. Both Arykah and Mother Calloway looked out the church doors to see the COTA transportation vehicle parked outside.

Arykah grabbed ahold of Mother Calloway's arm. Mother Calloway was horrified. Her eyes nearly bucked out of her head. Just then, both Angel and Carmen appeared, their heels clicking quickly on the tiled floor, sounding like a couple of Little Red Riding Hoods in a race to save Grandma from the Big Bad Wolf.

When Mother Calloway noticed the two women, she decided to put on a show. She began yelling. "This woman—she put her hands on me. Do you two see this? *Do* you?" she cried out to Carmen and Angel.

"Why, Mother," Arykah said in a sugary sweet tone, "I was just assisting you to your ride outside." Arykah looked over her shoulder at Angel. "You *did* say that Mother Calloway has been needing quite a bit of help from your assistant, right?"

Angel nodded.

Arykah turned back around and faced Mother Calloway. "Well, I'll be glad to assist you, Mother Calloway. That way, Carmen can tend to the first lady, just as she should be doing, *right*?" Arykah dared Mother Calloway with her eyes to disagree. When Mother Calloway neither agreed nor disagreed, Arykah continued. "Besides, I wouldn't want you to fall down and break your neck, *right*?"

Mother Calloway glared into Arykah's eyes. Arykah glared back with the same intensity. Each woman determined she would not be the first to look away or blink.

Someone had finally stood up to Mother Calloway. That person had communicated with her in her own language, the language she understood well. So with that, she understood that Arykah meant business. Idle threats had not been made on this here day. Today Mother Calloway had met her match. She'd been KO'd, but not by her original opponent, Angel. But it looked as though after getting fed up with the beat down Angel had been receiving from Mother Calloway, the trainer had decided to jump in the ring and finish the fight.

Mother Calloway continued her stare down with Arykah, but she realized Arykah was not going to back down. If Arykah wasn't mistaken, she could see Mother Calloway relent, judging by the look in the old woman's eyes and the slight nod of her head, as if to say, "I guess the best man won the fight."

But with Mother Calloway being who she was, she wasn't about to lie out on the canvas for the full ten count. She snatched her arm away from Arykah. "Thank you, but no thank you. I'll see myself out." With that, Mother Calloway jerked her body around toward the exit doors.

The women watched in silence, wondering what in the world Mother Calloway could be thinking. They were wondering if the first thing she was going to do was hop on the phone with Pastor Harrison and tell him everything that Arykah had said and done, and how Angel had done nothing but stand on the sidelines and allow it to happen.

Angel quickly decided that she better at least try to make nice with the church mother. "I'll see you at Bible study, Mother Calloway," Angel called out in a tone that questioned whether there would be a truce between them.

Mother Calloway stopped in her tracks. She paused for a minute and then slowly turned around. She looked first at Arykah, who was giving her a knowing look and a slightly mean mug. Mother Calloway then looked at her first lady.

Angel stood there, with a tired yet hopeful look on her face. Angel didn't want to fight anymore. She had never wanted to fight in the first place. Her prayer had been that Mother Calloway would be just as tired. She stood silently, hopeful that her prayer had been answered.

The horn outside blew again. Mother Calloway exhaled and then spoke. "I'll see you at Bible study at seven p.m. sharp," she said in an exhausted voice, which signaled that she was indeed tired of fighting. It was barely visible to the naked eye, but the corners of her lips even rose into a slight smile. Even if Angel hadn't stood toe-to-toe and gone the full twelve rounds with Mother Calloway, at least she'd been smart enough to go seek help. For that,

Mother Calloway had a newfound respect for Angel. The last thing she wanted was a first lady who would just lie down and die.

Before turning away and exiting the church, Mother Calloway said to Angel, "And not to worry if you're running a little late on Wednesday. I'll save you a seat."

This put a genuine smile on Angel's face.

And on that note, Mother Calloway turned, winked at Arykah, and then exited the church. "Yep," Mother Calloway said under her breath. "I'll save you a seat. Gotta keep my enemies closer." She then disappeared out of sight.

Angel exhaled as she watched Mother Calloway walk out of view. "Now, that's the old Mother Calloway I know," Angel said, nodding her head. "By leaps and bounds."

Before Mother Calloway could make it outside, the horn beeped one more time. The three women inside could hear Mother Calloway yelling at the driver to hold his britches.

"So she's taking baby steps," Angel said, correcting herself, and the three women burst out laughing.

Angel walked over to Arykah and threw her arms around her. "Thank you so much, Lady Arykah. Thank you." Angel was so emotional that tears began to fall from her eyes. "Lord, I thank you for sending this woman of God on your behalf."

Carmen watched the two women embrace. She, too, was so thankful for Arykah. Now she was no longer in the middle of the first lady–church mother drama. She would be able to sleep much better at night. And that was a good thing too, because it was getting to the point where Carmen didn't even want to come to church anymore so that she wouldn't get caught up. Now the devil was a liar!

Carmen placed her hand on Arykah's back. "Lady Arykah, I have to admit that First Lady Angel and I were around the corner, eavesdropping." She put her hands over her mouth and laughed. "Oh my God, I can't believe you said those words to Mother Calloway."

Arykah pulled out of the hug and glared at both Carmen and Angel. "Y'all didn't hear anything, *did* you?"

Angel was the first to shake her head no vigorously. "Nope, I didn't hear a thing." She looked at her assistant. "Did *you* hear anything?"

Carmen shook her head no as well. "Not a word." She pretended to zip her lips closed.

Arykah gave Carmen a high five. "Now, *that's* what I'm talkin' about, Carmen. Thanks for having my back."

Carmen looked at Arykah, shook her head, and said, "What did you expect? I learned from the best."

Chapter 17

An hour later Arykah and Angel were feasting on steak and lobster at Morton's, the Steakhouse. Arykah couldn't speak for Angel, but she knew *she* had worked up an appetite with all the day's events. It was hard to believe that she hadn't even been in town a full twenty-four hours. When she hopped on that early flight this morning, she honestly had had no idea what it would take, or how long it would take, to address Angel's issues. But what she did know was that God's will would be done.

"Thanks for allowing me to treat you to dinner, Lady Arykah. It's the least I can do after you put the fear of God in Mother Calloway's heart." Angel chuckled. "The look on that old biddy's face when you said to her, 'You don't want me to come back here,' was priceless. You might as well have been balling your fist up, puffing out your chest, and saying, 'You want a piece of me? *Huh*? You want a piece of me?'" Angel held her stomach, she was laughing so hard.

"Oh, you think that's funny, huh?" Arykah smiled. It did her soul good to see Angel smiling, considering that when she first laid eyes on her earlier today, Angel had been crying like a baby. Oh, how God could turn things around in the blink of an eye.

"It was so funny that I regret that I didn't snap a pic with my camera phone."

Arykah swallowed a spoonful of lobster bisque. "Chile, that was nothing. I done dealt with two Mother Calloways of my own . . . at the same time. I knew I could handle one."

Angel drank from her glass of iced tea. "You think she got the message, or could that have been just another one of her fronts?" Angel knew for a fact how good Mother Calloway was at turning on the charm and then turning it off. She'd played a lot of folks. Who was to say she hadn't just played Arykah?

"I know she did," Arykah answered matter-of-factly. "Trust me. Mother Calloway is getting ready to be your best friend."

"I seriously doubt that," Angel said and then took a bite of her steak.

"Trust and believe that your troubles with Mother Calloway are over."

The strange thing was that slowly but surely, Angel was starting to believe. After all, if she were in Mother Calloway's shoes, Angel knew

for a fact she'd be on her best behavior in order
to keep Arykah from coming back.

Angel appreciated the fact that Arykah flew in
from Chicago to create order with both Carmen
and Mother Calloway. Arykah's work might be
done, but Angel's wasn't. There were still some
things she had to address with her husband
regarding the order of service. Angel wasn't
going to address these things just because
Arykah had pointed them out. There were some
things Angel had questioned herself but had
never spoken about. It was high time Angel
found her voice and used it . . . permanently.

As if Angel had spoken her thoughts out loud
for Arykah to hear, Arykah said, "Now that we
have Carmen and Mother Calloway in check,
let's get Pastor Harrison together as well."

"I promise you I was just thinking that very same
thing in my head," Angel said. She placed her fork
down and thought for a moment. "I just don't
know how or where I should start. The last thing
I want to do is to tell the preacher how to preach.
Won't that be out of order? I mean, who am I to—"

"His wife, that's who," Arykah said with a
mouthful of food. She then hurried to finish
chewing and swallow so that she could say what
she was dying to get out. "I'm not here to get into
marital affairs or to stir up any mess between

you and your husband, so stop me if you feel I'm overstepping my boundaries." Arykah pointed her fork at Angel. "But the two of you should be announced and should enter the sanctuary together on Sunday mornings."

"But what do I say when Isaiah asks me why?" Angel said. Once again she was worried about folks mistaking the change for Angel being arm candy.

"Because folks need to know that you two are of one accord, that you're on the same page, and that you're happily married. In other words, girlfriend, tricks need to know that Pastor Harrison is your *husband*, and that you ain't gonna play any games."

Angel laughed out loud. She loved the way Arykah expressed herself. She pulled no punches. "Everyone knows we're married. I'm listed in the church program."

"Only in name, honey. You better make your presence known." Arykah raised her left eyebrow only and glared at Angel. "And on top of that, do they respect your marriage?"

Angel recalled that this morning her husband had ordered the leaders to speak to her, but that had been both men and women. "Lady Arykah, I can honestly say that I haven't had any problems with just women."

"So far," Arykah stated. "I didn't have any problems, either, until my husband's ex-girlfriend wanted him back. Then I had to go to jail. Folks will mistake you and Pastor Harrison as having a spiritual disconnection. Some women think that if you ain't sharing the pulpit together, then you ain't sharing the bed together, either. Like I said, I'm not trying to get all up in your business or your bedroom. But I know how chicks are." Arykah squinted her eyes, as if she was flashing back to her own drama with Lance's ex. "They are so calculating." Realizing she was all up in her own feelings, Arykah recomposed herself. "I really don't like that the first lady has to sit on the second pew."

Angel shrugged her shoulders. "It's been that way since I got to Savior Manger."

"Well, that needs to change, effective immediately. Pastor Harrison should escort you to the front pew every Sunday. If anything, Mother Calloway belongs on the pew behind you. You're the first lady of the church—not her."

Angel nodded her head. "I agree."

"Good. So make it happen. Talk to your husband. He's the head shepherd. Share with him your concerns. Pastor Harrison loves you. I saw the way that man looked at you when he entered your office today. It was like I wasn't even there. And all *this* ain't easy to miss." Arykah twisted her hips.

Angel smiled.

"Just talk to him. He'll listen. And another thing that fried my butt is the fact that Mother Calloway is by your husband's side when he's operating in prayer ministry and laying on hands. When I saw that woman jump up, all coordinated, wearing her own purple and gold to match his robe . . . girl!" Arykah rolled her eyes. "I wanted to lay my own hands on her."

Angel started to laugh, but then Arykah put a sharp end to that.

"It's not funny," Arykah said seriously. "I know I can be larger than life sometimes and have a wit to me, but I'm so serious right now. I noticed how you like to laugh, chuckle, and giggle things off. It's good to always have a joyful spirit. But it's not good to do it as a means of deflecting. I mean, Mother Calloway pounced all up like a cougar today in that sanctuary." Arykah cocked her head to the side, raised her eyebrows, and asked, "Where they do that at? Certainly not at Freedom Temple, honey. I wish a broad *would* try to step in my place. That trick would be snatched bald right there in the sanctuary." Arykah grabbed at the air like she was grabbing someone's weave.

Angel laughed loudly, then quickly looked around the restaurant, hoping that no one had paid much attention to her outburst. There were a couple of eye rolls, so she mouthed an "I'm sorry" to them. She then turned to Arykah to apologize as well. "I'm sorry. I don't mean to keep laughing. I'm not deflecting. It's just that you are too much for me right now."

Arykah drank from a glass of raspberry lemonade and swallowed. "I'm just saying that you gotta use your power to create order. Before you came along, Savior Manger didn't have a first lady in place. But you're there now. Folks need to know their places. You can't continue to be ignored or overlooked. A woman in your position can't afford to be meek and timid all the time. Church folks are rough, and once they see that you're weak, they'll pounce on you like a cat on a ball of yarn."

Angel nodded. "I hear you, and I agree. I'll speak with my husband tonight."

"And do it right," Arykah said. "Don't just get all up in his face and try to lay down the law. He is the head, and don't you ever let him forget it. Chile, you better run his bathwater, then join him in that tub."

Angel's cheeks got heated. "Are you saying I should seduce him?"

"Heck, yeah!" Arykah squealed. "Work what you got to get what you want from your husband." Arykah got deep with Angel. "Girl, you better make that man howl at the moon. Tear that bedroom up."

Had anyone walked by at that moment, they would've been able to see Angel's tonsils. Her mouth had dropped to the floor. A truck could have passed through it.

"And guess what?" Arykah said. "It ain't even a sin, girlfriend, 'cause that's your husband. Ya hear?" Arykah raised her hand for Angel to give her a high five.

Angel became excited and high-fived Arykah. "Okay, I'll do it. You haven't steered me wrong when it comes to advice yet."

"Rock your man's world and watch him give you what you want." Arykah turned her attention to her plate.

Angel just sat there, shaking her head at Arykah while watching her eat.

Feeling Angel's eyes burning through her, Arykah looked up. "What?"

"Girl, I'm just so full right now, and not from this meal." She pointed to Arykah. "You need to teach a class about this. That's all I'm saying, because this is some good stuff you're giving me."

"I'm glad you feel that way, 'cause you got the tab."

"I already told you dinner was on me."

"Oh no, girlfriend," Arykah said. "I'm talking about the thousand-dollar tab."

Angel's eyes bucked.

"I don't preach for free."

***

"Where to now?" Angel asked Arykah once the two of them had buckled their seat belts in Angel's car. Angel and Pastor Harrison always drove separate vehicles to church, just in case he had church business to tend to before or after. He didn't want to inconvenience Angel if there were other things she needed to do.

"You can take me to my hotel. I'm staying at the Hilton Columbus at Easton. I checked in already this morning." Once Arykah's flight landed at the CMH airport, she'd still had time to spare before services started at Savior Manger. She'd taken the liberty of going to the church Web site to check the service times. She'd been pleased to see a beautiful picture of Pastor and First Lady on the home page. That was one less thing she had to point out to Angel. "I dropped off my luggage and had a car take me to the church this morning."

Angel looked at the clock on her dashboard. "It's not even five o'clock yet. You sure you want to head back to your hotel?"

"Ain't you tired of me yet?" Arykah asked her.

Angel vigorously shook her head no. She enjoyed Arykah's company. It reminded her of the old days, of hanging out with her girlfriends. It definitely filled a void. "Don't you wanna see the city? I don't mind being your chauffeur." A sudden thought entered Angel's mind as she started the car. "And why in the world are you staying at a hotel? I have a guest bedroom you can stay in. I redecorated it myself just recently, when I moved in after Isaiah and I got married."

Arykah turned her entire upper torso in her seat and faced Angel. "Lesson number one," Arykah began. "Never invite a woman to stay in your house with you and your man. Not your best girlfriend, not your cousin, not even your sister."

Angel shook her head. "Man, I just can't get it right, can I?"

"Don't worry," Arykah said. "Hang with me, kid, and I'll get you right."

"I know you will," Angel said without a doubt. "You get everybody right."

"Amen!"

Angel started to pull off.

"But seriously, though," Arykah continued, "there can only be one queen in the castle. So, never, I mean neva, eva, eva, allow another female to be in a position where she has to change into pajamas in your home." Arykah couldn't emphasize that piece of advice strong enough. "Marriage is hard enough on its own. You don't need anyone or anything in your house, making trouble."

"But if your husband wants to get with your cousin, sister, or friend, don't you think he's going to do it whether she spends the night or not?" Angel asked.

"Yes," Arykah said. "But why on earth would you want to make it easier for him by handing your man booty on a silver platter?"

Angel thought for a moment. "I guess I would feel just that much worse if I knew I was a contributing factor."

"Right. What woman in her right mind, living holy under the marital laws of God, would want to help her man cheat?"

"Say no more," Angel said as she turned out of the restaurant parking lot. "On that note, I'm taking you back to your hotel quick, fast, and in a hurry!"

Both women laughed.

"You know, Easton is one of the most popular spots to shop at in Columbus," Angel said. "They have Macy's, Michael Kors, Louis Vuitton, and if you're ballin' on a budget, they even have H&M."

Arykah's mouth was watering at the sound of some of her favorite stores.

"Well, what do you say?" Angel asked Arykah as she stopped at a red light.

"Girl, you had me at Macy's."

Chapter 18

In the ladies' department at Macy's, Arykah pulled an emerald-colored, paisley-embroidered two-piece skirt suit from the rack and held it up for Angel to see.

"Oh, that's right up your alley," Angel said, complimenting her.

Arykah smacked her lips and cocked her head to the side. "Girl, this is a size six. Do *I* look like I wear a size six? This is for you, silly girl." Arykah shoved the suit into Angel's arms.

"Oh, okay, well . . ." Angel hesitantly accepted the garment and examined it. "Like I said, I like it, for you. But it's way too fancy for me, don't you think?" Angel scrunched her nose while tilting her head from side to side to better examine the outfit.

"What I think is that you are a pastor's wife, and, honey, you need to start looking like one. Image is everything." Arykah scanned Angel's body. "You *are* about a six, right?" she asked.

"Yeah, but . . . ," Angel said as she held the outfit out as far as her arm would stretch and continued to look at it.

"Go try it on, then." Arykah watched as Angel gave the suit a once-over. "I'm not saying there is anything wrong with what you have on now. Just step it up a notch. Be over the top with it, the way only a first lady can get away with."

Angel shook her head. "I just don't think it's me."

Arykah sucked her teeth. "Then just humor me, please."

Angel sighed. "All right." With the garment in hand, she headed toward the dressing room.

Arykah waited right outside the dressing room for Angel to come out.

When Angel stepped out of the dressing room, dressed to the nines, Arykah squealed, "All right now, First Lady, look at you."

Angel looked in the mirror. She couldn't help but smile. "I *do* like it." She modeled the suit for Arykah by doing a couple of twirls. "Actually, I *love* it." Angel giggled like a high school nerd getting a makeover from the most beautiful girl at school.

"See, I told ya," Arykah said, smiling.

Angel brought the cuff of one the sleeves up to her face and looked at the price tag. Her eyes grew wide. "Oh, heck no." She looked at Arykah with bulging eyes. "I have never spent this much on an outfit before. I'll take a picture of it and make it myself." Angel wanted to start a ministry to help other women dress fabulously without spending an outrageous amount of money, so what would it look like if she didn't take her own advice?

Arykah laughed at Angel's facial expression. She looked like a three-year-old girl who was running to the potty but didn't make it in time. "I ain't askin' you to pay for nothing. This is my treat."

Angel glanced at the price tag again. "Did you *see* how much this suit costs?" She held her arm up to Arykah's face. "It's more than my car note."

Arykah shooed her arm away and, without even looking at the tag, said, "I don't care how much the suit costs. Consider this to be included in that thousand-dollar fee you already owe me." Arykah winked, knowing that Angel knew she'd been kidding about the whole thousand-dollar preaching fee.

Never in Angel's life had she owned a designer suit worth that kind of money. Not even with a Macy's discount shopping pass would she have thought to purchase it. In department stores, Angel headed directly to the sale racks. So Angel found it thrilling that Arykah was the type who didn't care about the price. She thought women did that only on reality shows, to show off. But Arykah was the real deal. Still, she couldn't allow someone else to spend money on an outfit that she wasn't willing to spend herself.

"As good as I look in this suit, I can't let you do this," Angel said. "Besides, it will go against everything I plan to educate women on in a ministry I'm considering heading."

"Oh, so you do have a plan to get your buns seated on that front pew, after all, huh?" Arykah joked.

"Oh, stop it," Angel said, shooing her hand. She then proceeded to tell Arykah exactly what she'd just told her husband earlier that morning about the ministry she was thinking about starting.

"That sounds great," Arykah said. "But in this case," she noted, rubbing the material on the suit, "you wouldn't be spending the money yourself. It would be a gift from me." Arykah leaned in and, with squinted eyes, said, "And you wouldn't want to teach those women to block blessings, now would you?"

Angel hadn't really looked at it that way.

"Well, what do you say?" Arykah said, tapping her foot to show her mounting impatience.

Angel looked at herself in the mirror again and then looked at Arykah. "I say thank you."

"Good. Now, hurry up and get out of that outfit," Arykah ordered. "We still have the hat and shoe department to hit up."

Angel shrieked. "What?"

Arykah threw her hands on her hips. "Well, what the heck you gonna wear with that suit?" She looked down at the heels Angel was wearing. "Those are cute, but they ain't gonna cut it. You need stilettos, at least six inches."

"I've never walked in a pair of heels over three inches," Angel confessed.

"Then you haven't walked at all, honey child." Arykah snapped her fingers and turned to walk away, while throwing over her shoulder, "Meet me at the register."

While Angel retreated to the dressing room to change back into her gold dress, Arykah called up Myrtle, Freedom Temple's secretary, and asked her to book her a flight back out to Chicago for the next day. Just as she ended the call, Angel met her at the nearest counter.

Angel stood to the side and watched Arykah make the purchase with her credit card. When the transaction was complete, Arykah turned and handed Angel the plastic garment bag. She was a little stunned to see Angel standing there with tears in her eyes.

"Why are you crying?" she asked Angel sympathetically.

Angel sniffed. "It's just that I was thinking maybe it's *your* name that should be Angel." Angel started to cry harder. "I mean . . . you . . . don't . . . even . . . really . . . know . . . me."

Arykah put her hand on Angel's shoulder. "Of course I know you. I wouldn't be here if I didn't." Arykah lifted Angel's face by her chin. "Honey, you are me. I've been where you have been. And knowing what I know and how this situation could have ended . . ." Arykah's voice began to crack as she thought about all she'd gone through when dealing with some vicious church mothers. "I wouldn't have been able to live with myself if I hadn't gotten on that plane to come see about you. I know what it feels like to be thrown to the wolves. But now when I leave here, when I get back on that plane to Chicago, I will know one thing for certain and two things for sure."

"What's that?" Angel said, finally able to subdue her tears.

"That you will be thrown to the wolves again . . . That's just life," Arykah said. "But this time when you come back, you'll be leading the pack. Can I get an amen?" she said, lifting her hands to the heavens.

"Amen," Angel said with confidence. "Amen."

***

"What in the world is all this?"

Upon hearing her husband's voice, Angel looked up at the bathroom doorway. She stood from where she'd been sitting on the side of the garden tub. She flapped her hand a little to air-dry it. She'd been using it to generate bubbles after having poured bubble bath under the running water.

Angel lifted her shoulders, put a hand on her hip, and stood in the most seductive stance she could. With the way she looked in her black, silk and lace two-piece lingerie short set, another gift from Macy's that Arykah had insisted on buying, she could have stood any ole way. The lust in her husband's eyes confirmed this.

"Well . . . ," Angel began, taking slow steps toward her husband. She could feel some of the rose petals she'd scattered about sticking to her bare feet. "You said you liked to get wet, so I figured I'd run you a nice, hot bubble bath." She stood on the tips of her toes and planted a soft kiss on Isaiah's lips.

He closed his eyes and licked his lips, as if he could taste Angel on them. "Mmm." He opened his eyes. "I guess the honeymoon ain't over with."

"Baby, it's just getting started," Angel said, then twisted her lips into a crooked smile. "Now, get naked." Angel proceeded to help her husband undress. In less than a minute his clothing was a pile on the bathroom floor, and he had slid into the deep garden tub, covering his body with bubbles.

"Aren't you going to join me?" he asked.

"In a minute," Angel said. "But first I want to serve you."

Isaiah's eyes bucked like never before.

"*Not* like that." Angel play slapped him on the shoulder. "Like this." She walked over to the small wooden table used as decor. It usually housed some artificial flowers in a vase, but today resting on the table was a platter of ripe strawberries with some chocolate dip and some yogurt dip. Angel lifted the platter from the table and carried it over to her husband. "For you." She sat on the edge of the tub, took a strawberry, dipped it in chocolate, and then fed it to her husband.

"Wow." Isaiah chewed after taking a bite, then wiped a little bit of chocolate that had dribbled down his lip. "This is really nice, Angel. Thank you, honey."

"You are so welcome."

"I wasn't expecting this." He swallowed. "Especially after this morning's episode. I thought you'd be a little . . ." He tried to imagine exactly how Angel would feel, but he had no words.

"Never mind this morning, Isaiah," Angel said. She then thought twice about that statement. "Actually, yes. About this morning . . ."

Isaiah gave a look of expectancy mixed with a little repentance. He knew this was a conversation they most certainly had to have. He'd wanted to talk to Angel over dinner. He had even arranged for a brief meeting with some of the church leaders after they talked among themselves first. But Arykah's surprise visit had thrown a monkey wrench into those plans. Right now he simply wanted to indulge in strawberries and his wife's company and save church business for later. But it looked as though the inevitable was about to take place, possibly ruining the mood.

"Don't make that face. This is going to be a good talk," Angel assured him. She took another strawberry, dipped it in the yogurt, and fed it to him. She then stood to go place the platter back on the table, but not before devouring a delicious strawberry herself. Angel went back and sat on the edge of the tub. She was glad to see a more relieved expression on her husband's face. "Is the water okay for you?"

"Perfect," Isaiah replied.

Angel proceeded to cup her hands, fill them with water, and let it trickle down her husband's chest. "You looked real good in that gold and purple robe of yours today," she said, complimenting him as she continued her task at hand.

"Thank you."

"I imagined myself walking arm in arm with you as you entered the sanctuary in all of God's marvelous glory." Angel stared off into space, as if she was reminiscing about the sight of her husband this morning. She then snapped out of it. "But I can't even pray with you in the morning, let alone enter the sanctuary with you."

The words "Here we go" were written all over Isaiah's face. "That's the thing, Angel. I've come to the conclusion that you should and you will be joining us in corporate prayer on Sunday mornings from now on."

"You've come to the conclusion," Angel said. "What about everyone else who adamantly disapproved of that this morning?"

"Well, when you couldn't join me for dinner, I ended up meeting with the co-pastors and a couple of the church leaders."

"And?" Angel decided to allow her husband to do all the talking for the moment.

"And we all agreed that you are my rock, my rib, the other bookend opposite me that keeps the church standing. If anybody is supposed to be in that room, covering me, covering the church, and covering the saints of the church, it better be the first lady."

Angel was a little taken aback that they'd all come to such an agreement, considering the way they'd treated her this morning. "*Everyone* agreed?" What her husband was saying was just too hard for her to believe.

Isaiah paused for a moment. "Perhaps not everyone. But God did, and He has the final say."

Angel nodded. "I get that, but I don't want there to be any type of tension or people feeling a certain kind of way come Sunday morning, when I join in on the prayer circle."

"Look, Angel." Isaiah lifted his sudsy hand out of the water and took Angel's hand in his. "Although in my eyes you are the perfect wife and the perfect first lady, you are not going to have a perfect relationship with everybody. Everyone doesn't have to and won't always agree with the things you do. But when you know it's right in your spirit, you have to have the strength to do it, anyway. If God says something, you don't have to get permission from man. If that was the case, the saints would be running the church instead of me . . . under the guidance of the most superior counsel of all, of course." He looked upward, then back at his wife. "Pastors have to be able to stand with God and not waver from

His instruction." He lifted her hand and kissed the back of it. "First ladies too."

Angel nodded her acknowledgment of the words her husband had just spoken.

"I'm here to support you, and that's not ever going to change. I need you to know that, Angel. But what I need to know is that you can support me as well. How do I know that to be true if you can't stand up for yourself? I need to know that my wife can stand on her own two feet and rule the world, or at least Savior Manger. That's why I . . ." Isaiah paused, as if he was considering whether to finish what he was about to say.

"That's why what?" Angel was curious to know.

"That's why initially I didn't interfere with you and Mother Calloway's little . . . thing."

Angel pulled her hand out of her husband's, and her mouth dropped. "You mean you *knew* how that woman was treating me? *Before* I told you?"

Isaiah shrugged. "Kind of. Mother would drop little hints, or digs, if you will, to me about you. If she was saying that stuff to me, oh, I knew Mother was speaking on it to you."

"Stuff like what?" Angel was trying to remain calm, but she was not too happy about the fact that Isiah had acted none the wiser about Mother Calloway's actions.

"Just stuff about the way you dress." Isaiah thought for a moment and then chuckled. "And that time at Bible study not too long ago, when she tried to insinuate that you were having an affair." Isaiah couldn't help but laugh.

Angel stomped her foot like a two-year-old having a temper tantrum. "This is *not* funny, Mr. Harrison. How *could* you? And when I did mention it to you, you acted like you didn't believe for one minute that Mother Calloway would behave in such a manner." Angel splashed water in her husband's face. She stood up and placed her fist on her small waist. "You knew what that woman was doing, and you just stood there and let it happen?"

"No, *you* stood there and let it happen," Isaiah said, correcting her.

Angel closed her mouth. What could she say? Isaiah had not told an untruth. Even though she'd want her husband to defend her at all cost, it wasn't like she was a helpless child who couldn't speak or fend for herself.

"I thought Mother might have been saying little things to get under your skin. But I admit I was in disbelief when you laid everything out. I just couldn't picture Mother doing and saying some of those things. Things that went way beyond just little digs. And even then, I didn't question how long Mother Calloway would continue on with her antics, but how long *you* would allow it."

"So are you saying this is *my* fault?"

"I'm saying that a person can only continuously do to another person what they allow. And I wanted nothing more than for you to be able to handle the situation on your own, because, trust me, honey, Mother Calloway is the first of many, and *she's* saved," he huffed. "Imagine when you start to encounter the ones that ain't."

Angel allowed Isaiah's words to marinate. "I don't know whether to be mad at you or to thank you."

"Thank me?" Now it was Isaiah who was taken aback.

"Yes. You heard me." Angel rolled her eyes in her head, as if she hated having to admit that her husband was right. "I want to bop you upside the head for not just shutting Mother Calloway down and making my life easier. But I want to thank you for not just shutting Mother Calloway down and making my life easier. I get what you were trying to do. You wanted me to find my own way."

"And did you?"

Angel thought for a second. "Yes, but I have to admit I had a little help . . . well, a lot of help, actually."

"Let me guess. Lady Arykah."

Angel gave a mischievous smile.

"Oh, Lord." Isaiah closed his eyes and rested his head against the tub. "I don't even know if I want to know how Lady Arykah helped you."

"Trust me, you don't. So don't even ask," Angel said. "But let's just say that Mother Calloway and I ended things on good terms. She's even going to save me a seat at Bible study."

Isaiah raised his head, and his eyes lit up. "Praise God! Hallelujah! To God be the glory."

Angel laughed. "See? You can trust me to take care of business."

Isaiah nodded. "I always knew you could. It was just a matter of time. I wanted you to find your own way, to make your own way, to create your own blueprint as first lady. And it sounds like you did just that. I'm proud of you, and I love you."

Her husband's pride and confidence in her made Angel tingle inside. "Thank you, and I love you too." She sat down on the edge of the tub.

"My wife, first lady of Savior Manger Baptist Church, found her voice," Isaiah bragged, grinning from ear to ear.

"I'm glad to see you are so happy about that, because I'm going to start using it. And the first thing I'd like to say with this newfound voice of mine is that when you enter the sanctuary, I don't want to be sitting in there, waiting on you. I'm your wife. You are the pastor, and I'm the first lady. There is no reason why we shouldn't enter the sanctuary together." Just thinking about it got Angel all riled up. She stood and began pacing as she spoke. "And whose idea was it for me to sit on the second pew?"

"Yours," Isaiah said. "When you started attending Savior Manger, you always sat on the second pew. After we got married, you continued to sit on the second pew. Nobody told you that you had to sit on the second pew."

Once again, Isaiah was right. Angel couldn't be mad at anyone but herself for planting her behind on that second pew every Sunday. If she recalled correctly, this morning not one person put up a fuss when Carmen planted her behind on the first pew. So it was safe to say that they wouldn't have fussed if Angel had done the same thing a long time ago.

"Well, I'm no longer choosing to sit on the second pew," Angel said with authority, like a real shot caller.

"Fine with me," Isaiah said. "Anything else?"

Angel thought for a moment. "As a matter of fact, there is something else. That ministry I was thinking about starting . . . Well, it's no longer a thought. It's a vision, and I'm going to see that it manifests. I'm going to work on a mission statement this week. And with your approval, of course, I'd like to submit it to be posted in the church bulletin." Angel looked at her husband, searching for any objections in his eyes. If she wasn't mistaken, there was something she was seeing in his eyes, but it wasn't an objection. "You're enjoying this, aren't you?"

Isaiah licked his lips. "More than you'll ever know."

Angel stared at her husband for a moment. "If I had to guess, I'd say you're turned on by all this."

"If these bubbles weren't blocking your view, you wouldn't have to guess." Isaiah raised his eyebrows up and down a couple of times to make his point.

"You dirty boy," Angel teased.

"I can't help if seeing my wife take charge gets me a little worked up."

Angel shook her head. "You are something else."

"And so are you, my dear wife," Isaiah said. "Are there any other laws you want to lay down, because if all church business is resolved, there's a little husband-and-wife business I'd like to resolve in the bedroom."

Angel gave her husband a sensual look. "I'm just waiting on you."

"Baby, you don't have to tell me twice."

As Isaiah let the water out of the tub, Angel rejoiced inside. She couldn't believe how a day that had appeared to start off as the worst day of her life had ended up as the best.

Arykah was right, Angel thought to herself. All the while she'd had all the answers she needed to make things right within herself, and without having to follow the Yellow Brick Road. All she really had to do was follow the direction of the Holy Spirit. But for now, as she watched her husband, dripping wet, rise from the tub and step out, she knew he was the only thing she was about to follow . . . right to the bedroom.

Chapter 19

"Good morning, Mrs. Miles-Howell." The clerk at the reservations counter greeted Arykah bright and early Monday morning. "We do hope you enjoyed your stay at the Hilton Columbus at Easton."

"Good morning," Arykah replied. "I most certainly did." Arykah proceeded to settle her bill as the bellboy who was carrying her luggage on a cart stood next to her.

"Thank you, Mrs. Miles-Howell," the clerk said after checking Arykah out. "We do hope you will come back and see us again."

Arykah smiled and then turned around to head out the hotel doors. Her eyes immediately lit up when she saw a familiar face. She asked the bellboy to wait a moment while she stepped just a couple of feet away and acknowledged her visitor. "Well, this is certainly a surprise."

"I've come to see you off." Angel stepped to Arykah and hugged her tightly. "Since you wouldn't accept my offer to take you to the airport myself."

"Like I told you last evening, I booked a car for round-trip transportation when I booked the trip here to Ohio. Girl, when I'm read' ta go, I'm read' ta go," Arykah said. "I can't be depending on folks for no ride." She then changed the subject. "But, anyway," she said, "how did it go with Pastor Harrison last night?"

Angel smiled mischievously. "Let's just say that I'm glad we made that pit stop over at the lingerie department."

Arykah gave Angel a high five. "Ha. Won't He do it!"

"Girl, yes, he will do it," Angel said. She then stared off into space, reminiscing about last night. "Over and over and over again."

Arykah elbowed her out of her daze. "I meant won't *God* do it, *not* your man."

"Oh, my bad." Angel laughed. "Anyway, not only did I want to see you off, but . . ." She began digging through her purse. She pulled out her checkbook and a pen. "I do appreciate all that you've done for me, Lady Arykah. I want to at least reimburse you for the cost of your flight and hotel."

"First off, you can put that checkbook right back where you got it," Arykah ordered. "You didn't ask me to come here. I came on my own, remember? And second, know when to drop that whole Lady Arykah mess. We're friends now, Angel."

Angel's heart nearly melted. It was now safe to say that she truly had a girlfriend to look out for her. "Thank you, Arykah. But please allow me to pay for your transportation . . . something."

Arykah shook her head. Her no was emphatic. "Maybe someday you can pay me back with a girlfriend getaway on a beach somewhere. Now, something like *that*, I'll never turn down."

Angel smiled at Arykah's never-ending generosity. "You got that coming."

Arykah turned, remembering she had the bellboy waiting. "Chile, let me get on out of here. I got this poor man waiting." She signaled for the bellboy to continue escorting her out of the hotel.

When they all got outside, Arykah's car and driver were waiting for her. The driver opened the back passenger door for Arykah to climb inside. Arykah hugged Angel one last time and got into the backseat, and the driver closed the door behind her. Arykah rolled the window down as the driver walked around to his seat and got in the car.

"I was right, wasn't I?" Arykah said to Angel.

Angel looked clueless about what Arykah was referring to.

"Just like the lion in *The Wiz*, you had everything in you that you needed all along." Arykah winked her right eye at Angel.

Angel smiled. "Yes, I did, didn't I?" she said proudly.

"I may not be Dorothy, who can lead you down the Yellow Brick Road to the Wiz, but I'm Lady Arykah, hontee, first lady of Freedom Temple Church of God in Christ, and I can take you to the king. The king of kings!" Arykah snapped her fingers four times while zig-zagging them in the shape of the letter *Z*.

Angel waved as the vehicle pulled away. That one day with Arykah had seemed like a lifetime. In just twenty-four hours the two of them had formed a bond, a sisterhood. That, in itself, was priceless to Angel. Angel was going to miss her new friend. But something told her that the two of them would definitely keep in touch and that they'd see each other again. Perhaps it would be sooner than Angel thought.

Chapter 20

On Tuesday morning Myrtle walked into Arykah's office with a coffee mug in her hand. "Good morning, First Lady," Myrtle greeted as she came and stood on the opposite side of Arykah's desk. "We missed you this past Sunday."

Arykah was sitting behind her desk, looking over some files. "I missed my church family too."

Myrtle sat the mug on the desk, in front of Arykah. It was just how Arykah liked it. "Well, did you do what you set out to do in Ohio?"

Arykah nodded her head. "Yep, First Lady Angel is gonna be fine. I made sure of it." Arykah had one thing on her mind. She wanted to know if more ladies had paid for the upcoming women's retreat. She looked up at Myrtle. "Did you send me the updated numbers for the retreat?"

Myrtle nodded her head. "I sure did. It's in your e-mail."

"How are we looking?" Arykah asked.

"See for yourself," Myrtle said snidely and walked away. But Arykah didn't see the slight smile on Myrtle's face as she exited the office.

On her desktop computer, Arykah saw the e-mail from Myrtle. She double-clicked the attachment and silently prayed to God that all the women who had signed up for the retreat had paid their bill in full. As Arykah scanned the e-mail, she picked up the mug and drank the white chocolate mocha drink that Myrtle had prepared for her. Arykah almost choked on the hot liquid easing down her throat as she let out a victory scream. She saw that almost two hundred women had paid in full. "Yes, God!" Arykah sat the mug on her desk, danced in her chair, and began to give God praise. She then looked up to the heavens and said, "Leave it to you, God. While I'm off taking care of somebody else's stuff, all along you were taking care of mine." She shook her head, in complete awe of her Heavenly Father. He was the best daddy ever.

She couldn't wait to dive in and get to work on some unfinished business related to the retreat. She was now more pumped up than ever. She wasn't a good five minutes into working on retreat-related tasks when her phone rang.

She looked at the caller ID and didn't recognize the number. For a moment she was going to let the call go to voice mail so that she could continue with the task at hand, but then she decided to answer the phone instead. "Arykah speaking." She listened for a moment as the caller spoke. "Yes, I do know First Lady Harrison," she said to the caller.

For a few more minutes Arykah listened and nodded. The caller then finally gave her an opportunity to get a word in. "So you would need me to come to California when?" Arykah skimmed her calendar as her jowls filled with air. She let the air out of her mouth when she realized the time the person on the phone needed her in California rolled into the dates of her women's retreat.

Arykah began shaking her head. *Nope.* That weekend had been a long time coming, and she would need that entire week to prepare, to make sure nothing went wrong. "I'm sorry, but—" Arykah began, but the caller, sensing rejection, cut her off. Arykah listened as the caller promised her an all-expense-paid trip to California, including a hotel stay of her choice.

Arykah's lips spread into a slight grin as she thought about a nice hotel on the beach with poolside service. Her smile wasn't long lived, though, as she realized that beaches and fruity drinks with little umbrellas would not be her mission there. The caller on the phone wasn't inviting her there for hors d'oeuvres and cocktails. No, she had something else much more tedious in mind.

"As first lady of God's Saints Chapel, I'm in desperate need of your help," were the first words that had come out of the woman's mouth. No greeting or nice pleasantries. She'd gotten straight to the point, as if she were making a 911 call. Her tone was serious. That was a sign that whatever was going on over there in California was going to require some *serious* attention. Which meant that there would be very little downtime to unwind and enjoy the California sun.

"First Lady, I really would like to help you," Arykah said, "but I'm hosting my church's very first women's retreat July Fourth weekend. So you see, your dates will overlap with my previously scheduled commitment." Arykah tried to let her down as gently as possible.

"Perhaps you can come the week after the retreat?" This woman was not going to take no for an answer.

Arykah scrolled through her calendar, which was practically full. It was possible, though, that she could move some appointments around and make the trip happen. "Well," Arykah said as the caller waited on pins and needles. "You know what? I think I can make it happen."

"Yes!" the woman cried. "Thank you so much for your obedience, Lady Arykah." After promising to call Arykah back to discuss flight details and hotel accommodation options, the woman ended the call.

As Arykah went to move the calendar aside, a sudden thought crossed her mind. There was a phone call in order. She picked up her cell phone, scrolled through her contacts, and dialed. After a couple of rings the caller picked up and gave her usual pleasant greeting.

Arykah returned the greeting. "Good afternoon to you too, First Lady Harrison."

"Arykah!" Angel was ecstatic to hear from her friend. "What are you up to?"

"Oh, nothing. Just thinking about what I'm going to pack for this sudden trip to California I have coming up." Arykah poked out her lips, waiting for Angel to confess.

"Ahhh. So I take it First Lady McKenzie called you."

"She did," Arykah said. "Thanks to a little birdie giving her my phone number."

"I'm sorry. I hope you don't mind. But I met First Lady McKenzie on a prayer line, and she's got troubles. You instantly dropped in my spirit as someone who could possibly help her. I know you helped me."

"I'm always happy to do the Lord's work, but it's no picnic. I mean, yes, it makes your soul feel good to know that God has chosen you to operate on His behalf, but the hits you have to take when trying to do God's work . . . huh!"

"You're a natural at this. It will be fine." Now it was Angel doing the encouraging.

"You know me. I'm a big personality," Arykah said. "I have confidence the size of the moon, but can I tell you something?"

"Sure," Angel said.

"Whenever I'm on assignment, I always get nervous. Sometimes doubt creeps in and makes me question if I'm the right woman for the job. Going to give a Word and speaking at conferences is one thing. But actually going into someone else's church to help them resolve issues . . . Me? Of all the people, me?"

"Why not you?" Angel asked. "Look at what you did for me. I truly see you moving toward not only speaking to other first ladies, but also being a mentor to them in times of real need."

Arykah took in Angel's words, receiving them graciously through her spirit, as Angel continued.

"You are a powerful woman of God. Don't you want to operate in all that power? You may get to the point when all you have to do is walk into a room and demons flee."

"Wow. I never really thought of it like that. Hmm. Look who needs who now." Arykah was truly starting to believe that perhaps her calling was not being met solely by speaking engagements. Maybe she needed to dig them stiletto heels into the dirt and get her acrylic nails a little dirty too.

Angel chuckled. "Girl, we need each other. So the same way you were there for me, you better believe I'm going to be there for you."

Arykah perked up. "I'm so glad you said that. Which brings me to the real reason why I called."

"Whatever it is, you got it," Angel said, feeling totally indebted to Arykah.

"Good. Because who wants to go all the way to sunny California alone?"

Angel paused for a few seconds; then what Arykah was getting to kicked in. "*Really*?" Angel asked excitedly before Arykah could even make it plain.

"Yeah, if I'm going to California on your referral, you're going with me. You're the one who put my name in the hat and had Lady McKenzie call me. I've been back in Chicago for all of one day, and I get an invite to California. What kind of mess is that?"

"A blessed one, that's what kind," Angel replied.

"And it will be even more blessed with my sister girlfriend in Christ right there with me to help me along the way."

"Now you know you don't need any help. Even if you did, what help could I be?"

"The same kind of help you were just a minute ago. You have a power too, Angel. Your compassion, kindness, calmness, and ability to think before you speak are just what I need. I need your spirit there, because I have no idea what I'm going to be up against."

Angel took in her friend's words. She understood exactly what Arykah was saying. When Arykah came to Ohio and the two of them were together, the atmosphere had changed. It had shifted mightily. If it worked in Ohio, why wouldn't it work in California? Besides, how could Angel deny her friend's call for help? Arykah had been there when Angel needed her, so it was only right that Angel returned the favor.

"So how many outfits do I need to pack?" Angel said.

"*Yes!*" Arykah exclaimed, pumping her fist. "I'll give you all the details once First Lady McKenzie gets back with me."

"All right, sis," Angel replied.

"Angel?" Arykah said.

"Yes?"

"Thank you."

"No. Thank you, Arykah. It means a lot to me that you trust me to come along on this endeavor."

"Ummm, I'm kinda thinking God chose us both. Something tells me us bumping into each other in the lobby at that conference was no coincidence. God had a plan for us all along."

"You, know what? I think you're right."

"So on that note," Arykah said, "I'll see you in Cali."

"See you in Cali, girl," Angel said before the two of them ended the call.

A few weeks later they were both on a plane, headed for California. They knew what they were going there to do. They'd packed the two most important necessities: suntan oil and, more importantly, holy oil. They were ready. The question was, was California and God's Saints Chapel ready for them?

Chapter 21

"Mother Calloway, why don't you just go ahead and do us the honors of opening this evening's Bible study up for prayer?" Pastor Harrison suggested.

"Oh, no." Mother Calloway sat in her seat, adamantly shaking her head. "First Lady Angel told me that she would be opening us up for prayer this evening. I'm not going to use my foot to step on First Lady's toes," she said, while thinking, *But I surely wouldn't mind using my foot somewhere else on First Lady.* She struggled to keep from letting out a menacing chuckle.

Mother Calloway had been on her best behavior since her encounter with Arykah a couple of weeks ago. Make no mistake. It wasn't because the visiting first lady had made a threat or two. Mother Calloway had too much invested in her standing in the church. Not only that, but she'd invested too much time and energy in making sure the first lady of Savior Manger Baptist Church met her standards of approval.

She'd definitely met her match in Arykah. But she wasn't about to let some big-boned diva shut her down, not that easily. She'd be lying if she said that Arykah hadn't made her want to pee her Depends, but her spirit had tried Arykah's, and Mother Calloway knew that woman wouldn't have hit her elder. Mother Calloway had, though, been pretty entertained by the verbal combat the first lady had put on. As a matter of fact, Mother Calloway had enjoyed the fight. It had been a long time since anyone'd had enough courage to stand in the ring and go toe-to-toe with her.

"Bunch of wimps," Mother Calloway would call those who cowered in her presence. "Soft, gullible fools," she'd say about the ones who would let her walk all over them simply because she was an old lady. The church leaders weren't exempt from her name-calling, either. When it came to being true soldiers in the army of the Lord, Mother Calloway felt some of the church leaders didn't stand a chance on the front line. The only thing that saved Carmen from Mother Calloway's wrath was the fact that when put in the middle of Mother Calloway and Angel's fight, Carmen had voiced that her loyalty to God over-powered any loyalty she might have toward man. Carmen was a little soft, but she had a flip side to her. Not everybody had to be hard as nails all the time. Balance was definitely needed in the church, and it was that balance that Mother Calloway was hell-bent on bringing out in Angel if she was to be the lady of the house.

"I'm sure First Lady won't mind you taking the liberty of saying prayer to get us started," Pastor Harrison said to the church mother. "How about we let First Lady close us out in prayer?"

"If she even shows up," the head of praise and worship said under her breath. She said it low enough that the pastor didn't hear her, but Mother Calloway did.

Mother Calloway hid her smirk. Getting some of those leaders to turn on Angel had been fairly easy. After all, Mother Calloway was a trusted and loved lifelong member of the church. She was an old-school saint and had practically been born on the church pew. If anyone recognized the devil, it would be her. So convincing the church leaders that Angel had a devilish spirit hadn't been too difficult. Mother Calloway had the power to have folks either for or against someone. Up until Angel became first lady, she'd always used her powers for good and not evil. But her days on earth were numbered, as she was getting up there in age. She needed to feel confident that Angel could pick up in the battle where she would leave off. If ever the time came when Mother Calloway felt Angel had it in her to be that kind of first lady, she was sure it wouldn't be difficult to get the leaders to be 100 percent for Angel, if she didn't die first.

"I'm honored that you'd have me pray in lieu of your wife, Pastor," Mother Calloway said, "but I'd hate for her to walk into Bible study and I'm doing her assignment."

Pastor Harrison exhaled. "I understand," he said, although he was not too thrilled about Mother Calloway declining. But like he'd told Mother Calloway, he understood.

For the past two weeks, things between Mother Calloway and his wife had been drama free, and that was how he wanted to keep it. This past Sunday, when Angel inserted herself in the corporate prayer for leaders, Mother Calloway had been the first to open the circle and take Angel's hand to include her. He didn't know if it was Mother Calloway's willingness finally to accept Angel or if it was the advice from Angel's newfound friend from Chicago, but Angel had been beside her husband in the church services and was becoming a true leader. So, of course, he felt that Mother Calloway didn't want to disrupt what looked to be Angel becoming comfortable in her role as first lady.

The problem Pastor Harrison had now, though, was that it was already five minutes past the time when Bible study should have started. Too bad Carmen was at home, caring for her sick child. She would have prayed. He looked at the clock on the wall. He'd give the first lady five more minutes, and after that, he'd just have to open up in prayer himself if he couldn't get someone else to do it.

"I hope you don't take this the wrong way, Pastor," Mother Calloway said after noticing him staring at the clock, "but you might want to have a little talk with First Lady about time management. If we can be on time for our hair appointments, if we can be on time for our jobs for a boss who didn't hang, bleed, and die for us, then surely we can be on time for the Lord."

"Amen," a couple of folks hollered, which was the type of response Mother Calloway was hoping her words would generate.

"I'm sure she is just running a little behind and will be here any minute," Pastor Harrison said in his wife's defense. "Probably just got caught up in something. Angel is a very busy woman, you know."

Mother Calloway took note that Pastor Harrison had referred to her as Angel, which meant he was referencing her in wife mode and not first lady mode. She grinned and kept pressing. "There is nothing wrong with being busy, as long as you're just as busy for the Lord."

"Welll," someone sang out, their way of agreeing with what Mother Calloway had said.

"There's this thing called balance," Pastor Harrison shot back, his frustration and agitation with Mother Calloway's comments about his wife now evident both on his face and in his tone. "Maybe you should try it sometimes, *Mother*."

There were a couple of gasps in the room. No one had ever heard Pastor Harrison talk to the church mother with such an authoritative tone. But he was the authority in the house, even if he wasn't the oldest.

Mother Calloway wasn't the least bit bothered by her pastor's tone toward her. She felt it was fine time that he threw his weight around when it came to his wife. "I hear you, Pastor. I know about balance, but what I don't know is what could be so important as to keep your wife away from her duties at the church?"

"Mother Calloway, you know very well what could be so important as to keep me away from my duties at the church," Angel said from the doorway. She'd been standing outside the door, off to the side, listening, complete dumbfounded, as the church mother bashed her and questioned her dedication to the church and God. Angel couldn't believe it. A leopard never changed it spots, and neither did an old bitty, apparently,

because Mother Calloway was back to her trifling ways. Only this time she had put the knife
away when she was in Angel's face, but had got it
all nice and sparkly before pulling it out behind
her back. Angel had stood there in pain while
Mother Calloway had rammed the knife into her
spine, but she wasn't about to let her turn it.

"First Lady," Mother Calloway said, surprised
to see Angel. She had been almost certain that
special peppermint run she'd sent Angel on
would take her at least another ten minutes
or so. She had made sure she'd sent her to the
farthest store down the road.

"What?" Angel said, slowly entering the room.
"Didn't expect me back so soon from the errand
that you sent me on?" Angel pointed at Mother
Calloway. Angel had arrived at church a full
half hour prior to Bible study. She'd been in her
office, minding her own business, when Mother
Calloway appeared in her office doorway, holding her stomach. Angel had immediately jumped
to her feet and run to assist her elder.

After Angel asked if she was okay, Mother
Calloway had informed her that she'd been
having stomach issues but that it wasn't anything a peppermint wouldn't cure. Low and
behold, Mother Calloway's purse held none of
the special peppermint candies she preferred

to calm her belly. Mother Calloway had asked Angel if she'd run out and grab her some right quick, and that was when Angel had looked at her watch and had informed Mother Calloway that Bible study was to start in a few and that she'd been asked by Pastor Harrison to open up with prayer this week.

Mother Calloway had keeled over in pain. After that, Angel couldn't refuse. She'd written down the name of the peppermint brand and the store from which Mother Calloway usually purchased the candies. Out the door Angel had gone, only to return and find Mother Calloway acting none the wiser about Angel's whereabouts.

Everyone's attention went toward Mother Calloway. They were waiting for her to address what Angel had said. In their minds, there was no way Mother Calloway had known where Angel was all along. How could she possibly be the one responsible for sending her out yet sit up in that room and try to run her into the ground?

Angel pulled a bag of peppermints out of her purse. "Here, Mother Calloway. Your special peppermints for the stomachache you said you had."

Mother Calloway was so busted. One would have thought she would cower, cast her eyes downward, but instead she graciously accepted the mints from Angel. "Oh yeah. I forgot that's where you were. Thank you, First Lady. You'll have to forgive me. This old mind of mine comes and goes when it feels like it."

There were few things Angel could do right now. She could bury her head in the sand and let Mother Calloway be who Mother Calloway was. She could even call Arykah up and ask her for advice or request that she come kick Mother Calloway's butt for her. She could even fuss Mother Calloway out real good, only to feel bad about it and back down to her again, like she had the last time. But Angel decided she'd do none of those things. With the respect and dignity an elder deserved, she'd shut Mother Calloway down once and for all. Angel wouldn't allow her own flesh to interfere this time.

Angel would demand her own respect. She didn't need her husband to do it for her, and she didn't need Arykah to do it for her. God was no respecter of persons, so if He could give others the power and strength to demand the respect they deserved, then why couldn't He give it to her?

Help me, Holy Ghost, were the words Angel prayed before she began. "Mother Calloway, there is nothing wrong with your mind. I have no doubt that you are of sound mind and body. And in spite of the way some of these church members, who are supposed to be *leaders*, end up being *followers* behind you, I'm sure they know it too. You aren't some weak little old woman who can be bullied. Anybody who knows you can vouch for that."

Angel looked around the room at some of the members, who were, in fact, vouching for her last statement via head nods.

"You are a warrior," Angel said. "And in all honesty, a warrior who I looked up to and wanted to be just like when I first started attending this church."

Mother Calloway nodded slightly. Her eyes filled with hope as Angel spoke.

"Wait. I take that back," Angel said.

Mother Calloway's eyebrows sank in, and her forehead wrinkled.

"I didn't want to be like you. I wanted to be better than you. Because if we're going to win this race, then we have to keep raising up others to be better. We have to continue to be stronger, better, and wiser. That's what I want." Angel stood up straight and stiffened her shoulders while puffing out her chest. "And that's who I'm going to be. I'm going to be better—a better woman, a better saint, and a better first lady of this here church."

Angel pointed to the floor for effect. "While I'm running this race, you can try to stick your foot out all you want to trip me up, but as many times as I may fall, I'm going to rise. I'm going to keep getting up over and over and over again. So instead of being busy making sure you do everything you can to keep me behind you, allow me to race beside you, and then push me along ahead of you. Then, when the next person comes up on my heels, I can do the same for them. And so on." Angel had a pleading and sincere look in her eyes.

Pastor Harrison walked over and placed his hand on the center of his wife's back and began to rub it. "She's right, Mother," he said. "We all can't be at the same level. We have to help one another rise by lending our shoulders for others to climb on, not our foot to kick and hold them down."

"Amen, Pastor," Mother Calloway said, her eyes filling with tears. "Yes, Lord." Mother Calloway lifted her holy hands and shook her head back and forth as she spoke in tongues. She then looked up to the heavens. "Yes, thank you, Jesus. You answered my prayers. Yes, you did. Hallelujah."

Angel and Pastor Harrison looked at one another, a little puzzled, not certain about which prayer God had answered for Mother Calloway. They would soon find out as Mother Calloway continued her prayer of thanks to God.

"All I've ever wanted for this church was a strong first family. A strong pastor and a strong first lady to produce strong children who will follow suit and lead the church. Thank you, God, for I see that's exactly what you have given me in the couple standing before me." She looked around at the other members who were present. "That's what you have given us. Thank you, Lord."

"Amen," a couple of members said.

Mother Calloway pulled a handkerchief from her purse and wiped her tears. She looked up at her pastor and first lady. "I know that tomorrow isn't promised and that I won't always be around to make sure Savior Manger Baptist Church remains a pillar of this community and some place God's people can run to when they're running from the devil. I've spent countless nights praying that God equips this place with true, strong, powerful leaders. That's been my only prayer." She looked at Angel. "When you first started coming here, I thought you were as sweet as caramel corn."

Angel smiled at the compliment.

"You were so kind, gentle, and meek, awesome characteristics indeed. But when I learned that you were going to be the first lady of this church, I hate to admit it, but a fear rose up inside of me."

"Fear?" Pastor Harrison asked.

Mother Calloway nodded. "Yes, Pastor, fear. I feared that First Lady wasn't going to be strong enough to handle the things, people, and situations that come along with running a church." She turned her attention back to Angel again. "And that's when I started operating in fear. I started testing you and challenging you. I felt that if you couldn't stand up to me, then how on God's green earth were you going to stand up against the devil?"

Some eyes landed on Angel to see what her response would be upon learning that Mother Calloway had been purposely taunting her. Of course, this wasn't news to Angel, so hearing Mother Calloway's words didn't anger Angel, but they did give her confirmation of her own thoughts about the situation, as well as a new insight and revelation.

"Thank you, Mother Calloway!" Angel exclaimed, to the surprise of almost everyone in the room. If ever they were willing to give Angel a pass for showing anger toward Mother Calloway, it was now.

No one was more shocked and surprised at Angel's reaction than Mother Calloway. And she would have liked to have a heart attack when Angel bent over and pulled her in for a tight hug. She couldn't believe this was Angel's reaction to her having confessed to the poor girl that she'd knowingly and deliberately put her through hell. Then again, she could, because that was who

Angel was. Those were the characteristics that had made her like the girl in the first place.

"I'm sorry," Mother Calloway said as Angel released her from the hug. "But I'm a strong believer that if you don't go through hell, I mean really get put through some real hell, how are you ever going to be able to recognize the devil when you see him, let alone be able to whup his tail?"

"I appreciate that, Mother Calloway, and in spite of everything I've said in the past, you are no devil."

"Oh, I know. And in spite of everything I just said here a minute ago, I still think you are no angel."

At first Angel smiled, because she had thought Mother Calloway was going to give her a compliment. Once the words settled in, Angel raised an eyebrow at Mother Calloway.

"Oh, I'm still messing with you, child." Mother Calloway shooed her hand.

There were chuckles throughout the room.

Angel smiled. She could tell Mother Calloway was just joking by the little wink she gave her. It was the same wink she'd given Arykah after those two had gotten into it. That made Angel think of something. "Mother Calloway. I want to apologize for the way my friend Lady Arykah treated—"

"Don't you dare apologize for that woman of God!" Mother Calloway said.

Angel was surprised how defensive Mother Calloway was when it came to Arykah. She'd thought for sure that Mother Calloway would request that Angel ban her from ever stepping foot in their church again, or even from the state of Ohio!

"She came at me with the holy boldness that she was supposed to come at me with. She tried the spirit by the spirit without fear. Sometimes that's exactly what you have to do. Sometimes you have to get ugly for things to turn out pretty. You know what I'm saying?"

"I do now," Angel said.

Mother Calloway stared off into space and smiled. "I really like that Arykah girl. She's a demon slayer. That's someone you can send into the devil's camp to get your stuff back, and she will come out unscathed, with yo' stuff and yo' mama's stuff too!"

Both women laughed.

"But don't tell her I like that about her," Mother Calloway said. "She's been validated by God, and that's enough. Sometimes when man gets to validating folks, they get a haughty spirit. She's just fine the way she is."

"Yeah, she is," Angel agreed. "That Lady Arykah is something else." Now it was Angel who was staring off into space, in admiration of her Chicago friend.

Mother Calloway noticed the look on Angel's face. "Don't worry. You'll get there. God done connected you two together for a reason. I think Lady Arykah will be a great mentor for you."

Angel nodded in agreement.

"I do too," Pastor Harrison said, jumping in. He then looked around the room. "Well, saints, I'm sure everyone will agree that what we just witnessed was a Bible lesson in itself. Amen?"

A chorus of amens followed.

"So why don't I just go ahead and pray us out for the evening?" Pastor Harrison said. "But thank you all for coming out and being able to witness this move of God."

"Hallelujah!" Mother Calloway said, raising her right hand.

Pastor Harrison prayed and then dismissed everyone from Bible study. While everyone else filed out of the room, Angel remained with Mother Calloway.

"I just want to thank you again, Mother," Angel said. "Although I might not agree with your tactics, you did help me to find my own strength, in both myself and in the Lord."

"To God be the glory," Mother Calloway said. "I know I operated in fear, and I repent, but if I die and go to hell so that you shall live and go to heaven, so be it."

"Awww, Mother Calloway," Angel said, her eyes filling with tears as she offered another great big Holy Ghost hug to the woman.

"Well, anyway, let me go so Elder Paul can walk me out," Mother Calloway said after a moment.

"All right, Mother." Angel helped her to her feet. "Thank you again for everything." A million thanks weren't enough, as far as Angel was concerned.

Angel escorted Mother Calloway out of the room. Elder Paul was standing outside the door, talking and waiting on Mother Calloway.

"You have a good evening, Mother Calloway." Angel hugged her and then turned to go in the opposite direction.

"Aren't you fixing to head out too?" Mother Calloway asked curious.

Angel paused and then turned back around and faced Mother Calloway. "In a bit. Since Pastor let us out early, I'm going to go do some work on a proposal for a new ministry that Pastor is going to put before the board. It's a clothing ministry called Dressed for the Kingdom. I'm going to be mentoring young ladies and women on how to dress for the Kingdom on a budget."

"That sounds like something I'd like to get involved in. You know how I like telling young folks how to dress," Mother Calloway said knowingly.

Angel knew all too well. It wasn't long ago when Mother Calloway was giving her magazines from which to order clothing.

"It would be an honor for you to serve on the ministry with me, but we'll have to work on your delivery, Mother. I'm not sure shoving a magazine in a young girl's face and telling her she dresses like a stripper will reach these women and young ladies."

"Oh, child, I wouldn't dare come at anybody like that. That was strictly for you. See, if you had put Vaseline on your face and had had your dukes up in round one, we could have long ago nipped this in the bud and got on to liking one another."

Angel chuckled. "Oh, Mother Calloway. You are too much."

"Better to be too much than not enough. You remember that." And with that, Mother Calloway walked toward Elder Paul.

"I will," Angel said with a smile, thinking to herself, *How could I ever forget?*

Part III

"California Angels"

Angel & Lady Arykah

Chapter 22

On the last Friday afternoon in July, First Lady Arykah Miles-Howell sat poolside at the Four Seasons Hotel in Beverly Hills, California. At 2:30 p.m. the sun was high in the sky and at its job full force. Though she could've done without the light sweat it was causing, the ninety-eight-degree weather felt good on her skin. It was her first time visiting the five-star resort, but it felt like home. After months of planning her first women's retreat and then having it go off without a hitch, it was time for some real rest and relaxation—for however long it would last, anyway.

Arykah rested comfortably on a cream-colored lounge chair that was layered with padding comparable to the heavenly mattress on the bed in her king-size suite. She sat and watched folks enjoy themselves in the massive oval-shaped pool. Thanks to the teal base of the pool and the jets that created waves, the water resembled the sea off a beach in Montego Bay, Jamaica, where

Arykah had married Bishop Lance Howell. She'd never forget the pure white sand and the turquoise salt water. The faux island in the middle of the pool looked like a piece of paradise all on its own. If Arykah had to guess, she'd say that there were well over two hundred folks splashing around in the water. She looked at most of the women, dressed in nearly nothing, entering and exiting the pool. Weighing approximately 270 pounds herself, Arykah was surprised to see some women with way more meat on their bones than she had on hers sashaying in itty-bitty swimwear.

Suddenly her breath caught in her throat. "Good gawd," Arykah said to herself when Rasputia strutted past her. Thank God Arykah's big, floppy hat and sunglasses hid her bulging eyes. Arykah was willing to bet her entire recent commission check from selling real estate that the character from the Eddie Murphy movie *Norbit* was five feet from her. There were no fat suits or camera tricks. This was the *real* thing.

Just like in the movie, the four-hundred-pound woman wore a light pink bikini. *She may as well be wearing a slingshot*, Arykah thought. There was no way on God's green earth the woman could have stuffed all that fat into a one-piece. She had no choice but to let it all spill out of the tiny bikini. And girlfriend was, indeed, letting it all hang out. *All* of it! *Everything*. Every dent, dimple, and dip.

Arykah shook her head. *Some folks have no shame*, she thought. It wasn't the swimsuit that Rasputia wore that stunned Arykah the most. It was the fact that no one else present at the pool seemed even to notice the sight that made her eyes sore. Granted, there were some thick *mamis* splishin' and a-splashin', and there was nothing wrong with that. Heck, Arykah herself was plus size. Being content with the skin a woman was in was her prerogative and an attitude every woman should possess. Who was to say it was acceptable for a size six to show any more skin than a size sixteen? But with the vision of the woman before her, who if she moved two feet more to the right would block the sun, causing real shade, perhaps there should be some sort of law on the books regarding size sixty.

"Ump, ump, ump," Arykah said to herself. She shook her head again as she watched Rasputia disappear inside the hotel. "Thank God she went to the left instead of the right," Arykah said under her breath. "Chick was about to mess up everybody's possibility of getting a tan."

Arykah pulled all her long blond strands over her left shoulder as she adjusted to the extreme heat. "This heat is not good for my weave," she mumbled to herself.

An extremely young and very attractive man, wearing black slacks and a starched, white, short-sleeved button-down shirt, approached Arykah. Arykah saw the hotel's logo stitched on the right side of his shirt. He balanced many drinks in small glasses on a tray on his right arm.

He smiled at Arykah, then knelt next to her while holding the tray. "May I offer you something to drink?"

Only having arrived at the hotel an hour or so ago, with all the California heat, Arykah was definitely thirsty. She smiled at the waiter and then saw the drink choices he held before her. They varied in color. Some were blue, some were red, and others were yellow or clear. They were all decorated with various fruits, such as lime wedges, strawberries, lemon wedges, orange slices, pineapple chunks, and maraschino cherries. "Do they all have alcohol in them?"

The young man pointed to two specific glasses. "The red drink is a virgin Bahama Mama, and the clear drink is plain 7UP."

Arykah eyed the other drinks. She recognized the piña colada, and her mouth watered at a frosty blue drink adorned with an umbrella. Had she been on vacation with her best friend,

Monique, Arykah would have helped herself to at least two alcoholic drinks. Back home in Chicago, she and Monique often got together for a girls' night out and indulged in appetizers and drinks. But Arykah was in California on first lady business. She was expecting company to join her at the pool, and she wanted to be coherent. Since she was here on official ministry duty, she didn't want her spirit to be drunk with wine if the Holy Spirit was to call on her without warning. She had to be ready to minister at all times, so she chose the virgin Bahama Mama and the 7-UP. "Thank you," she said to the waiter.

"No problem." He smiled and went to walk away.

Arykah nudged him with her elbow, stopping him before he left. She looked at the piña colada. "If I wrap things up a little early, I'm coming back for you." She looked up at the waiter. "Not you. The drink," she confirmed and then signaled for him to carry on. She watched him walk away. "Although with one too many piña coladas, I might come back for you too," Arykah whispered to herself, and then burst out laughing, knowing darn well no other man could ever make her do her hubby wrong.

Arykah had hit the jackpot when she met Bishop Lance Howell. His good looks and stature had impressed her the first moment she saw him.

Bishop Lance Howell was all that! Four of those waiters couldn't equal all the man she had waiting on her at home. Just the thought of her husband alone gave her a thirst that needed quenching.

Arykah took two sips from each of her drinks. She then set both glasses on the cream metal-trimmed table with a smoked glass tabletop that sat next to her. Next, she leaned back to enjoy the scenery. Her peripheral vision caught the figure of a woman exiting the pool about fifteen feet away from her. Arykah gave the woman her undivided attention, because Miss Thing demanded it. She had the body of a goddess. Arykah couldn't help but to admire the woman's figure-eight shape. She was drop-dead gorgeous in her metallic gold bandeau with deep cutouts on the sides. "I'm glad Lance isn't here," she mumbled to herself as she watched the woman sashay away. "I'd have to kill him. So a man thinketh."

Arykah wasn't a hater. Ole girl had it going on, but so did Arykah. She wore a size twenty-four and was very confident in her own skin. The pink and yellow one-piece swimsuit she wore was cute. It had an attached miniskirt that stopped a few inches down her thighs. The last time Arykah had worn a two-piece out in the open was when she was about twelve years old. That was when her foster mother had purchased her a set of Wonder Woman Underoos, a red and blue training bra with panties to match.

"I thought I'd find you out here." The pleasant and familiar voice tore Arykah's thoughts away from the could-be, should-be swimsuit model.

Arykah looked up and saw Angel standing over her. Without saying a word, Arykah scanned Angel's petite, size six frame, which was hugged by a black two-piece swimsuit. Her belly, arms, legs, and thighs were toned. Just enough muscle definition, so she did not appear manly.

"Turn around." Arykah took her index finger and spun it around, signaling to Angel that this was what she wanted her to do.

Not knowing if she had gum stuck to her or something, Angel began to do a spin, looking down at herself for anything that shouldn't be there. After chasing her tail in two full spins, she stopped and looked at Arykah. "What?"

Arykah eyeballed Angel up and down. She couldn't find one trace of cellulite anywhere on her body. Not one stretch mark was visible. No extra skin, flab, nada. She looked up into Angel's eyes and said, "I hate you!" then rolled her eyes. Okay, so maybe she was a hater in the infancy stage.

Angel laughed out loud, then sat down on a lounge chair next to her new friend. "Where did *that* come from? I never pegged you as a hater."

"Uh-huh. That's because I'd never seen you in your James Bond girl getup." Arykah scanned Angel's long, slender legs and flat belly again. "Walking up on me, looking like Halle Berry. All thin and pretty. The West Coast agrees with you. I'm gonna have to refer to you as California Angel." Arykah picked up one of her drinks. "How did you find me?" She took a sip.

"I'd know that hat anywhere," Angel said. "It screams out 'First lady!'"

Arykah's wide, multicolored, floppy sun hat matched her swimsuit perfectly.

"You look cute," Angel said, complimenting her.

"I do, don't I?" Arykah ran her hand down her body as far as she could reach. She then placed her drink back on the table.

"Yeah, I can't even front, Lady Arykah. You're looking kinda fly."

"Girl, I try," Arykah said. "Before you got here, I had to fight off three men. I swear, sometimes it's an inconvenience to be fat and sexy."

Angel laughed at her friend. Even though she knew Arykah had just fabricated a story, Angel gave her a high five. "I ain't even mad at ya."

The same young waiter came back, his tray replenished with fresh drinks. He knelt next to Angel and balanced the tray in front of her.

"Hello, ma'am. May I offer you something to drink?"

"Well, let's see here," Angel said as she scanned the glasses. Before she chose a drink, Angel looked at the table between her and Arykah and saw two glasses. She then looked up at Arykah and asked, "Are you sober?"

Arykah sighed. "Unfortunately."

Angel turned back to the waiter. "Which of these drinks will keep me out of trouble?"

He pointed to three separate glasses. "Coca-Cola, virgin Bahama Mama, and 7UP."

Angel chose the Coca-Cola and the 7Up. "Thank you," she said to the waiter before he walked away. Angel set her two drinks on the table, next to Arykah's drinks. "So, how was your flight from Chicago?"

"Uneventful," Arykah answered. "I spent the entire four and a half hours wondering exactly what Lady McKenzie's dilemma is. I really don't know why I'm here."

"She didn't tell you anything?"

Arykah shook her head.

"Humph," was all Angel said. She then picked up one of her drinks and took a sip.

Arykah looked over at Angel. "Do *you* know what's going on with her?"

"Well, uh, you know, like I said, we're on the prayer line together. She didn't really go in depth when discussing things, but you know." Angel took another sip of her drink, sure not to make eye contact with Arykah, whose eyes she could feel burning a hole right through her.

"No, I don't know," Arykah spat, turning her body toward Angel.

"Well, I don't want to speculate, and since First Lady McKenzie is the one who has you here, I think she should be the one to tell you what it is she wants you to know." Angel went to take another sip from her drink, but Arykah snatched it away from her. Some of the beverage spilled out and dripped down Angel's hand. "Hey!" Angel placed the drink back on the table.

"*Hey*, my big toe," Arykah said. "Angel, you better give me something. Please don't let me walk into that church blind as a bat."

Angel thought for a moment. She looked into the pleading and desperate eyes of her friend and then exhaled loudly. "Okay, okay." She shifted her body to face Arykah. "First Lady McKenzie has a serious problem."

"I gathered that much when she called me and begged me to come to California, but she refused to go into detail on why she needed me. Said she didn't want me coming into this with any preconceived notions. Since she's your friend, and since you gave her my number, I agreed to come. Well, dang it, I'm here, and somebody gotta let me know something." Arykah was trying to keep her composure.

Angel picked up her Coca-Cola. "May I?" She asked permission, just in case Arykah had any more thoughts of snatching her drink.

Arykah puckered her lips and shrugged.

Angel sipped through the straw. She placed the drink back on the table, leaned back in the lounge chair, and exhaled loudly.

It took everything in Arykah to remain calm. The patience of Job she did *not* have.

"There's a trick pushing up on her husband," Angel finally confessed.

Arykah's back came away from the chair. *"What?"*

Angel anticipated this type of reaction from Arykah. When it came to heifers trying to steal pastors from their wives, her friend was not having it. "Uh-huh. Apparently, some woman has been sending Pastor McKenzie gifts, cards, flowers, and candy. The woman sends them to the church, addressed to 'the reverend.'"

"What?" Arykah shrieked again. "Lady McKenzie ain't got a clue who the ho is?"

Angel shook her head. "Nope."

"All she gotta do," Arykah began, "is stare each woman in the eye, and the one who can't look directly in her eyes is the culprit. Cast your troubles to the Lord, but if you cast your eyes away from me, then I know you trying to screw my man."

Angel shook her head again. "Girl, you and your Bible references! It's too much."

"What's too much are these Holy Rollers rollin' up on the preachers like they're professional ballplayers or something. Dang. You almost can't half blame the mothers of the church for being suspicious of broads and going loco."

Angel was taken aback.

"Oh, not you," Arykah said apologetically. She didn't want Angel to think she was now condoning all the hell the Savior Manger church mother had put Angel through. "But damn. Taking back what the devil stole from us . . . First ladies gotta take back their husbands from the hussies always running up in the church, trying to tell our men, 'God told me you was my husband.'"

Arykah was snapping off for real. She had to remove her designer shades and wipe the sweat that was starting to form on her forehead and drip down her face. And the perspiration had nothing to do with the heat, either, at least, not the heat from the sun. Instead, the heat was rising out of her very being after she heard what Angel shared with her about First Lady McKenzie's troubles.

Angel was almost glad she'd gone ahead and told Arykah in advance about the situation she was there to deal with. She'd rather Arykah turn up at the hotel pool than in the house of the Lord. Besides, it would give her a little time to calm down and handle things decently and in order, under the direction of the Holy Spirit and not her flesh.

"I'm telling you," Arykah said, gripping each side of the padding on the lounge chair, "first ladies taking that verse about not looking at their faces too seriously. They betta get to eye-ballin' these women. You can see right through these floozies."

"You think it's that easy?" Angel inquired.

Arykah nodded her head. "Sometimes it is."

Angel wasn't 100 percent certain of that tactic and prayed she never had to find out. She felt sorry that another first lady was having to deal with it. "I really hope you can help her, Arykah," Angel said. "I knew First Lady McKenzie was troubled, and after what you did for me at Savior Manger, I felt led to give her your number. Not to mention what you did for your own situation when you found yourself in a similar predicament with your husband's ex." Angel cleared her throat. "Minus the fighting and going to jail part, of course."

"Girl, you got me down here, knowing darn well I'm about to catch another case," Arykah said, leaning back and adjusting her hat. "Heck, I'm still on probation from beating that broad down. This ain't no divine setup. This some Compton-ish setup." Arykah tightened her lips and began to mumble. "I'm going to jail again"— she looked down at herself—"this time in a bathing suit. Every fish in the joint gon' be trying to get some of this good-good."

"That's not going to happen," Angel declared. "After all, that's why you have me here, remember? I got you. I got your back, and I'll *hold* you back if I have to."

Arykah looked Angel up and down. "Girl, who are we kidding? You aren't even a buck two-five if you were to jump in that pool and come out soaking wet . . . with towels wrapped around you. You can't hold me back." Arykah rolled her eyes and looked ahead. "Lord, help me," she said.

"And He will. The Lord's got your back, and so do I."

Arykah turned and faced Angel. "Well, does Lady McKenzie at least have a team? Every first lady should have a team, you know."

Angel knew, all right. Arykah had made very clear to Angel herself the importance of a first lady having people in the position to have her back.

Back in Chicago, at Freedom Temple Church of God in Christ, Team Arykah consisted of five ladies whom Arykah trusted with her life. They were her eyes and ears. They kept the riffraff and craziness away from Arykah. Team Arykah had her back. The ladies had fought for her and gone to jail with her. Arykah knew, without a shadow of a doubt, that they'd cover her and protect her at all costs. Team Arykah was about that thug life, in a Christian kind of way.

Angel shrugged her shoulders. "I can't say for sure if First Lady McKenzie has a team."

"What about family?"

Angel nodded her head. "I remember her mentioning that her two sisters are members there."

Arykah leaned back against her chair. "Well, at least she has family to support her."

"Unlike myself," Angel noted. "I have no team or family at Savior Manger. If you hadn't flown to Ohio to rescue me, I don't know what I would've done. I was at my wit's end with Mother Calloway. I thank God for you. You set that old biddy straight."

"How have things been since I was there?" Arykah asked.

She hadn't liked having to go ham on Mother Calloway, not one bit, but the Holy Spirit had instructed her to meet the old woman right where she was at and to speak her language. Perhaps just a tiny bit of Arykah's flesh had managed to seep through, but overall, the mission had been accomplished. Mother Calloway had gotten the message. And it had taken less than a full day in Ohio for Arykah to complete her assignment. Yes, Arykah could have easily sat around Savior Manger for a week, observing and putting in her two cents here and there, but that wasn't how she'd been called to operate at that particular time. Swift. Sometimes God had to give His children a swift kick in the behind to get them straight. Arykah's encounter with Mother Calloway was one of those instances.

"Things have been absolutely perfect," Angel said. "At least with Mother Calloway, anyhow. I don't have any problems out of the woman. Mother Calloway stays in her place, and I stay in mine. She did try me a couple of times, but I handled it with class and finesse and just a pinch of Lady Arykah's style." Angel laughed, and Arykah joined in.

"What?" Arykah leaned to the side. "You got a li'l ratchet with it?"

"Well, I can't call you up every time somebody comes for me, can I? I love how you came and stood up for me, practically fought my battle for me, but I have to fight my own."

"True, true," Arykah agreed. "But that battle was not yours. It was all mine, and I loved all three minutes of all twelve rounds." Arykah made an uppercut gesture.

"Twelve rounds, my foot!" Angel said. "It was a TKO in the first round. Mother Calloway's face kissed the ground."

Again, the women shared a laugh. Arykah would have gotten an even bigger laugh out of the fact that Mother Calloway actually admired her as a first lady, but mum was the word. Angel had agreed, per Mother Calloway's request, not to make mention of it.

Arykah looked over at her friend. "But is Angel sitting on the front pew? That's what I *really* wanna know."

A huge grin swept over Angel's face. "Yes, I am," she answered with confidence. Arykah could sense the pride exuding from her friend's pores. "My husband escorts me to my seat in the sanctuary, and Mother Calloway no longer assists him in laying hands on the women. That's *my* job now."

"All right now," Arykah said. She held her hand up, and Angel high-fived her. "Order has been set in the church."

"Even my assistant, Carmen, can't do enough for me now."

"That's because I set her straight too," Arykah stated. "I don't know if she'll ever be armor bearer material, but I think Carmen knows what being your assistant entails now. Still, you need a team, Lady Angel. Carmen is a start, but let's continue to pray that God sends you a Team Angel."

"Yeah, I know I do. But I have no friends at Savior Manger, and I'm just beginning to let my guard down with Carmen."

"I think you and Carmen should fly to Chicago and visit my church. Both of you could benefit from watching Team Arykah at Freedom Temple. Carmen needs to see what it really means to support a first lady."

"I'd love that," Angel said.

"Then it's done," Arykah said. "So what's going on tonight?" She took a sip from one of her drinks now that she was back in a calm and relaxed state.

"It's Women's Week at God's Saints Chapel. They've had service, with women guest speakers, every night this week."

"Who's speaking tonight?" Arykah asked.

"I haven't a clue," Angel answered. "But it should be you."

All of a sudden both women were torn away from the conversation. In front of them they saw a man wearing swim trunks. He was cut up with muscles all the way down to his feet. He was in the pool, arranging the swimmers around him in preparation for water aerobics.

"Ooh, look. Looks like they are about to exercise." Angel stood. "I'm gonna join in." She looked down at Arykah, who hadn't moved a muscle. She continued sipping on her drink, as if Angel hadn't said a word. "Are you coming?"

Arykah looked from Angel to the swimmers. She looked hesitant but then gave a "Why not?" shrug, as if she was giving in and would participate.

Just then an announcement was made by a voice that blared through the four overhead speakers surrounding the pool area. "Guests, I'm happy to announce that the poolside buffet is now open."

Arykah stood. "You go your way, and I'll go mine."

Angel laughed. "Okay. How about we meet in the lobby at six-thirty? We can ride to God's Saints Chapel together. Service starts at seven."

"Sounds like a plan," Arykah said. "A car is supposed to be waiting for us."

"I'll see you then."

They waved their good-byes and went their separate ways. For the next hour Angel indulged in an intense but fun water workout. Arykah, on the other hand, indulged in all-you-can-eat jumbo cocktail shrimp on ice, traditional chicken wings, steamed parsley red potatoes, nachos, as well as some other delicacies.

"This is California livin' right here," Arykah said to herself as she dipped a large shrimp in cocktail sauce and savored the taste. "Here I was talking about Rasputia, when I'm just a couple more buffets from looking just like her." After she had stuffed herself, Arykah felt guilty. It had become normal for her to repent for overeating. Gluttony was the sin that so easily beset her. She lived to eat; she didn't eat to live. Arykah was so full that she had to waddle back to her room. She could get in a nice power nap before going to God's Saints Chapel. But as Arykah stepped on the elevator that would take her to her floor, she was already hoping that good food would be served at the church.

Once in her suite, Arykah went straight over to the bed and did a back flop onto it. She stared up at the ceiling. "Lord, why you let me eat all that food? Now I got the itis." She shook her head before closing her eyes. "Just don't let me sleep through this service tonight. You brought me here to use me, and now I ain't no good." Arykah let out a harrumph. She was so frustrated. Here she'd avoided those cocktails because she didn't want her spirit to be drunk on wine, so that the

Holy Ghost could use her. Now here she was, drunk on appetizers. Different product, same result. And all she could think was one thing. *Hell, I may as well have had the piña colada.*

Before Arykah drifted off to sleep, she remembered that she hadn't talked with her husband since she'd arrived in Los Angeles earlier that day. She rose from the bed and retrieved her cell phone from her purse, which sat on the nightstand. She sat back down on the bed and searched her list of contacts. When she had gotten to the names that started with the letter *H*, Arykah pressed HUSBAND.

After four rings she heard, "Hey, cheeks."

Arykah simply tingled inside when her husband called her by her nickname.

"How's California treating you?" he asked.

"A little too good, honey. I just got finished sinning."

Lance knew what that meant. "You ate too much, huh?"

Arykah chuckled. "I ate too much, and then I ate again. I just left the lunch buffet. I don't know how to behave myself when the food is unlimited. I need you to pray for your wife, Bishop."

Lance laughed out loud. "Cheeks, I ain't gonna even waste my time or God's time. Do you remember just last week, when you ate a whole half of caramel pound cake? You felt so bad that you got down on your knees and begged the Lord to give you control. As soon as you stood up, you went back into the kitchen and ate the other half of the cake."

"I didn't eat the whole cake, Lance. Stop lying."

"Cheeks, you ate the entire cake."

Lance wasn't exaggerating, but Arykah didn't want to confirm it. "Anyway," she sighed into the telephone, "you miss me?"

"More than you'll ever know," Lance said. "Are you ready for tonight?" He couldn't see Arykah nodding her head.

"Yes. Now that I know why Lady McKenzie flew me here. It seems that a woman is pushing up on her husband. Sending him gifts, cards, and candy. You know, Lance, if it's one thing I hate, it's a woman who can't get her own man. Tricks who try to steal married men should be put to death with stones, just like back in the Old Testament days."

Lance chuckled. "That's a little extreme, don't you think?"

"Nope. It's hard out here for married women, especially women who are married to preachers. I know you ain't forget what just happened at our own church with your ex."

When Bishop Lance's ex-girlfriend had approached Arykah and had said that she wanted her man back, Arykah and Monique had jumped the woman right in the fellowship hall. Arykah and her partner in crime had spent a whole day behind bars before making bail and had been served with restraining orders. Neither of them had been permitted to go within one hundred feet of the bishop's ex-girlfriend. But thankfully, Lance had had a trick up his sleeve, which he'd used to get his ex-girlfriend to drop all charges against Arykah and Monique.

"No, I haven't forgotten," Lance said. "And I don't wanna have to fly to Los Angeles and bail you out of jail. Why can't you let Lady McKenzie fight her own battles?"

"There won't be any fighting, Bishop." At least Arykah hoped there wouldn't be any need to fight. But if a tramp got in her face, she couldn't make any promises not to go Floyd Mayweather on her. Arykah had zero tolerance for husband stealers.

"There had better not be," Lance warned her. "You gotta clean up your reputation. Around Chi-Town you're known as the first lady who fights."

Arykah laughed. "Lance, stop lying."

"I'm serious, Arykah," he said sternly. "I don't want you to lose your cool. You have no filter and no patience." Lance knew his wife was a firecracker, always ready to explode.

Given the tone of Lance's voice, Arykah knew she had better heed what he was saying to her. Whenever he called her by her first name, Arykah knew Lance meant business. "Okay, honey. I promise not to get arrested."

"All right then," he said, not really believing her promise. He wasn't there to oversee her actions; he'd just have to trust her.

"What are you doing tonight?"

"I have a meeting with the deacons at the church."

"Okay, honey. I'll call you in the morning."

"When will you be home?"

Arykah exhaled. "Well, that all depends on whether I can identify the tramp that's pushing up on Pastor McKenzie. I hope she comes to the service tonight. Then I'll point her out to Lady McKenzie and be on a plane in the morning. If she doesn't show her face tonight, I'll have to wait until Saturday's program or Sunday morning service to whup her a . . . uh, I mean to point her out."

"Arykah!" Lance said her name as if he was scolding a three-year-old for stealing a cookie from the cookie jar.

Arykah laughed into the telephone. "I'm just joking with you, Bishop."

Lance was worried. "No, I don't think that you are."

Arykah knew she had better get serious and ease her husband's worries. If Lance demanded that she hop on the next plane out of Los Angeles, she'd have no choice but to obey him. "Babe, I was joking. Okay? I am here on an assignment from the Lord. I won't mess up. I know how serious this matter is. A marriage is at stake."

Lance didn't believe, for one second, Arykah's words. But she was there already. He had no choice but to brace himself for her phone call from a Los Angeles jailhouse.

When he didn't respond, Arykah knew he had reservations. "Don't worry, Bishop. I'll be on my best behavior. Promise." Lance couldn't see that Arykah's fingers were crossed. "When I get back home, I'm gonna do something real nasty to you."

Lance knew all too well what Arykah was doing. Every time she tried to distract him from a heated conversation, she'd change the subject to sex, and it almost always worked.

"That ain't working this time."

"I'm gonna have a stripper pole installed in our bedroom."

Lance was intrigued, but he didn't want to let Arykah know it. "It still ain't working."

"I'ma put my Mardi Gras mask on, then slide down that pole. Then I'ma slide all over you."

Lance became aroused at the visual Arykah was giving him.

"I really hope you find that husband stealer tonight."

Arykah laughed out loud. "I love you, Bishop," she said.

"Love you more."

"How's my baby doing?"

Arykah's teacup-size Yorkshire terrier, named Diva Chanel, was a gift from Monique and her husband, Adonis. Arykah had fallen in love with Diva Chanel's little wet nose the moment she saw her. They were joined at the hip. Not only did Diva Chanel accompany Arykah to work, but the little fur ball also attended church every Sunday morning.

One Sunday morning the only thing Lance had been able to do was shake his head when he saw Arykah and her mini me, dressed in matching pink and yellow outfits, coming down the steps. They'd been about to head out to church.

Oh my God, I have two of them, *he thought.*

Arykah kissed the tip of Diva Chanel's nose. "Isn't she cute, Lance?"

He exhaled. "Arykah, you're so extra."

"You're extra right, and I extra agree."

"I didn't think you were serious when you mentioned bringing her with us. You can't take Diva Chanel to church."

She looked Lance in the eyes. "Of course I can."

"Dogs do not belong in church."

"Shhh." Arykah silenced him. "Do not call her that. She has feelings."

Lance frowned. "Call her what? A dog? That's what she is. She has four legs, a snout, she's hairy all over, and she has a tail. Diva Chanel is a dog, Arykah, and she's not going to church."

Arykah glared at Lance. "She is going to church."

Time was of the essence. Lance couldn't spare another minute arguing with her. "You're gonna leave her upstairs in your office, right?"

"Lance, she fits right in my handbag. No one will even know she's there."

He exhaled. "So, what if someone else wants to bring their dog to church?"

"I'm the first lady of the church. Everybody can't do what I do."

With Arykah having spoiled the dog as if it really were a child, the answer to how the dog was doing was a no-brainer.

"Diva Chanel is just like her mom," Lance said through the phone receiver. "She doesn't listen to me."

Arykah nodded her head.

"She does whatever the heck she wants to do."

Arykah nodded her head again.

"And, I swear, sometimes that dog cusses me out when she barks at me."

Arykah nodded her head a third time. *That's my girl.* She had taught Diva Chanel well. "Make sure to give her a treat before bedtime, Lance."

"A treat for what?"

"For being a good girl."

"Didn't I just tell you that she doesn't obey and she does what she wants to do? She gets no treats, cheeks."

Arykah sighed into the telephone. "I wish I had brought my baby with me to California."

"You and me both."

They closed the conversation with more "I love yous," and Arykah disconnected the call and lay back on the bed and exhaled. She didn't know what was gonna happen at God's Saints Chapel that evening. Didn't know if she was gonna run across a tramp with a bad attitude. She thought about the promise she'd just made to Lance that she wouldn't get arrested. Arykah looked up at the ceiling and said, "Lord, please don't let what I just said to my husband be a lie."

Chapter 23

At approximately 6:30 p.m., Arykah stepped off the elevator at the Four Seasons Hotel and stopped the flow of traffic in the entire lobby. She was dressed in a deep purple paisley-print suit. The hem of the jacket and the skirt bottom were adorned with Swarovski crystals. The first lady wore a matching deep purple paisley-print hat with a twenty-four-inch brim that was also adorned with Swarovski crystals. Her gold tresses flowed past her shoulders. A diamond tennis bracelet blinged out each of her wrists, and the gems flirted with the lighting, causing a fiery spark with every movement she made. Her earlobes were completely hidden behind diamond studs. Her feet sported six-and-a-half-inch, dark purple, paisley-print peep-toe stilettos that she had had custom made to match her suit. Her makeup was flawless. Arykah represented royalty in every sense of the word. She was beautiful.

Every head turned in her direction. Talk about shifting the atmosphere. Just the mere presence of Arykah made the bellboys want to go grab some grapes fresh off the vine and feed them to her slowly, one by one. And watch her chew and wait for her to swallow. Ready to dangle the vine over her mouth again.

Curious onlookers wondered who Arykah was. She had to be a celebrity, A-list, at that. Some folks snapped a picture of her for general purposes. They weren't quite sure which movie she'd starred in, which popular series she was the creator of, or which song she'd sung to win a Grammy, but they weren't going to miss out on capturing a shot of her. They'd Google it and try to figure it all out later.

Arykah stood, allowing folks to get a still view of her. She wasn't doing it on purpose or to be arrogant. She was sweeping the room with her eyes, in search of Angel. "Ah, there you are," she said after spotting her friend on one of the couches in the lounging area of the lobby. Every soul watched Arykah make her way over to Angel, who had her eyes buried in a tour book and was highlighting things to do in the city.

"Hey, California Angel," Arykah said to her friend as she approached.

Recognizing Arykah's voice, Angel spoke first and then lifted her eyes from the pages of the book. "Hey. You rea—"

Angel's words got stuck in her throat at just the mere sight of Arykah. Her mouth remained wide open, as she was in awe of the vision before her. When Arykah had visited Angel at her church back in Ohio, she had dressed to the nines. Arykah had also taken Angel shopping and had picked her out a nice outfit. So Angel was well aware of Arykah's impeccable taste and ability to dress her rear end off. But tonight Arykah had done the darn thang in piecing together her attire.

Angel twisted her upper body to put the book on the contemporary block table next to her. It slid out of her hands and onto the table with a thump, all while Angel never once took her eyes off of Arykah. She rose to her feet in front of her friend.

"Oh . . . my . . . God," Angel said, spacing her words out. She circled her friend, scanning Arykah's entire being, from her extremely wide purple hat to the French manicured toenails that peeked out of her heels. "Lady Arykah, you are stunning. Oh . . . my . . . God," Angel said again. She looked around the lobby, at the folks staring at Arykah. They were whispering to one another. Angel assumed they were, indeed, trying to figure out exactly who this superstar was.

"All these people think you're a celebrity," Angel said.

Arykah simply smiled. In all honesty, she hadn't been fazed by those folks. As a matter of fact, she didn't even look around in order to confirm or acknowledge what Angel had just said to her. She took her word to be true. After all, Arykah had become quite used to people staring at her when she wore her Sunday best. Never mind that it was Friday. Nevertheless, she was heading to church, so she'd dressed accordingly.

"All right now, Lady A," Angel said once she'd finished giving Arykah the once-over. "I told you that you should be the keynote speaker. All eyes are going to be on you, anyhow."

Arykah gave Angel the side eye. "Girl, please. When they get finished looking at you . . ." She pointed at Angel's attire, moving her finger up and down in the air. "Look at you in that red, almost off-the-shoulder, partial-sleeve, three-quarter-length, ribbed, one or two inches from being a formfitting dress. Sookie sookie now."

Angel burst out laughing. "Really, Miss Fashion Queen? You gon' break it down like that?"

"Child, it's been broken, dead, and buried, 'cause you killed it. Especially with those nude patent leather stilettos. That's my girl!" Arykah held up her hand, and Angel gave her a high five. "And a fast learner." Arykah was very impressed.

"Of course," Angel said, then turned around to model her dress.

Arykah sang a line from one of Kenya Moore's song. "Now twirl, twirl, twirl, twirl."

The two shared a laugh as Angel finished spinning.

"It's easy to learn when you are taught by the best." Angel was referring to their shopping spree in Ohio, when Arykah was hell-bent on showing her how a first lady should dress. "I would have hemmed the dress a little shorter if I hadn't scarred up my legs while practicing walking in these stilts." She pointed down to her shoes.

Arykah chuckled. "But look at you now. Not only can you walk in them, but you can spin like Cinderella too. And the good thing about stilettos is that learning to walk in them is just like learning to ride a bike. Once you've got it down pat, you never forget how to do it."

"I hope so," Angel said. "Or the congregation is going to start questioning why I got all these rug burns on my knees."

Arykah stood there, confused, for a second.

"Wait for it," Angel said. And then *bam*! The lightbulb went off in Arykah's head.

"Ohhh." She put her hand over her mouth. "I get it." Arykah's cheeks turned crimson red.

"I knew you would eventually."

"You dirty girl, you. Child, I'm starting to rub off on you in more ways than one," Arykah said. "You ready? I'm sure our car is out there waiting." She nodded toward the exit doors.

"Ready like Freddy and two-ton Betty," Angel said.

Arykah paused and squinted her eyes. "Now, that corny stuff we still have to work on." She laughed and then looped her left arm through Angel's right arm. "Let's go get 'em, First Lady."

The two headed out of the hotel, where they immediately spotted a gentleman standing by a limousine, holding a sign that read MILES-HOW-ELL.

"That's us right there," Arykah said, pointing to the driver and approaching him. Angel was right behind her.

"Miles-Howell?" he asked, his eyes darting from Arykah to Angel.

"That's me," Arykah replied.

"Good evening," he said, placing the sign under his arm and shaking Arykah's hand. "I'm

Elroy. I'll be your driver for your entire stay here in Los Angeles."

"Thank you, Elroy," Arykah said. "I'm Lady Arykah." She turned to Angel. "And this is First Lady Angel."

"A city of angels, literally," Elroy said.

Arykah turned her attention back to the driver. "Whenever you see me, you'll see her. She's here to keep me out of trouble, so it's probably just a city of one angel."

The driver smiled at Arykah. "Oh, you don't look like trouble. You look like the epitome of class."

"Thank you, Elroy, but I'm still a work in progress." Arykah pointed up to the sky. "He ain't finished with me yet."

The driver tipped the black cap he was wearing and then went and opened the back door for them. "Ladies." He stood there, wearing a permanent grin on his face, as he extended his hand to Arykah to assist her into the limo.

"You're beautiful," he said to Arykah before he released her hand once she'd gotten inside the car.

Her smile got wide. "Thank you very much, Elroy."

His smile being contagious, Angel smiled back at him as she stepped up to the car. The driver reached for her hand. She placed her hand in his, and he helped her into the limousine.

"Another beautiful lady," he said. "God is good."

Arykah knew he was flirting with her and Angel, but she didn't entertain it. Her only reply was, "All the time," before he closed the door behind them. "You know he was saying that while staring at our derrieres while we bent over to get in."

Both women chuckled.

"But he's speaking the truth," Angel said. "Ain't nothing wrong with shaming the devil."

The driver got behind the wheel of the limousine and pulled away. Arykah looked over at Angel. "Does he know where we're going?"

Angel looked out the window like she would know whether they were headed in the right direction. "I'm sure Lady McKenzie gave him the itinerary when she hired him," Angel responded as she began to fidget in her purse. She pulled out her compact mirror to check her face. "If not, I'm sure as soon as he can get that mental image of our butts out of his head, he'll ask us for the address to God's Saints Chapel."

Arykah let out a harrumph and nodded. "You right about that. That man's got booty on the brain. I'm sure he ain't used to seeing no booty on these California size zero chicks."

"I know you right about that." Angel laughed and continued checking herself out in the mirror.

Arykah settled back in her seat. She gazed out the window at all the gorgeous palm trees. Every now and then she would let out a sigh.

"You okay?" Angel looked away from her mirror when she asked this question.

"Yeah, I'm good," Arykah said, not sounding so sure of herself.

Angel looked in her mirror again and began smoothing out her lipstick with her pinkie finger.

"All I know is that whatever I'm here to do for Lady McKenzie, I gotta do it quick, fast, and in a hurry."

Angel pulled her attention away from her reflection in the mirror. "And why is that?"

"Because I have on two pairs of Spanx. I am stuffed in these thangs like the creamy filling inside of a Hostess Twinkie."

Angel couldn't help but laugh out loud at her friend. "I know what you mean, girl."

Arykah snapped her head in Angel's direction. "You couldn't possibly know what I mean. The only thing you'd need a Spanx for is if you lost your slingshot and needed a backup."

"I'll have you know," Angel stated, "that I don't play with slingshots. Okay? And furthermore, I do know what you mean, because I just happen to have on a girdle myself." Angel did a little "So there" wiggle in her seat and went back to looking at herself in her compact mirror.

Arykah ran her eyes over Angel's dress. Angel was slim and trim. And Arykah would never forget Angel's toned body in her bikini earlier that afternoon. "Why?" Arykah asked, irritated. "For real, why you got on a girdle, Angel? Huh? Tell me, because I need a good laugh." Arykah sat there, serious as a heart attack, waiting on Angel to respond.

"Uh, because I need one, that's why."

That response wasn't good enough for Arykah. "If I told someone I was wearing Spanx or a girdle, the word 'why' would never settle on their tongue. But you, my friend, again, I ask you why." She began shaking her knee, urging Angel to hurry up and spit it out, and conveying that it better be good.

"Well," Angel explained, closing her compact, "believe it or not, I got a little extra skin here and there." Angel went to pinch something at her waist that wasn't there. "People see someone who looks skinny, but that doesn't mean we all together and tight."

"Girl, need I remind you that I just saw your ole itty-bitty self in a two-piece down at the pool? The only thing tighter than your body is a sixteen-year-old virgin's va—"

"Uh, uh, uh," Angel said, holding her hand up to halt Arykah's words. "We ain't even going there." Even though Angel was serious, she couldn't help but chuckle. Her friend was too much sometimes. Okay, most of the time. But she loved her all the same. "Believe me, I wouldn't waste my money on buying a girdle or risk a lack of oxygen if I didn't need one." Angel put her compact back in her purse and patted her belly, as if to insinuate that she had a gut.

Arykah frowned. "Are you crazy? You ain't got a gut. You ain't patting nothing but a bone."

"Humph," Angel said, this time patting her purse. "I know what my mirror shows me."

Arykah stared at Angel for a moment. Angel deliberately looked straight ahead, even though Arykah knew Angel could feel and see her staring at her through her peripheral vision. Arykah opened her mouth to say something else but then decided just to keep quiet and to look out the window and catch the picturesque scenery. Even though Arykah had consciously chosen to pick her battles, she felt that Angel was delusional in thinking she needed to wear a girdle. In Arykah's mind, Angel looked almost anorexic. She couldn't fathom why Angel needed to wear any kind of support. But every woman was different. Arykah guessed that Angel was probably insecure about certain parts of her body, just as many women were, no matter what their shape or size.

Feeling that Arykah had let the whole girdle and Spanx thing go, Angel decided it was safe to strike up another conversation. "You ready for tonight?"

Arykah shrugged her shoulders. "I'm as ready as I'll ever be. I really don't know what the atmosphere will be like when we get to God's Saints Chapel." Arykah ran her hand over her torso. The two pairs of Spanx were forcing her lower abdomen into her rib cage. She silently prayed. *Lord Jesus, give me strength to get through this evening.* Arykah loved her thickness. She wasn't doubled up on Spanx because she was trying to look slim. She was just a true believer that if she wanted people to take her seriously and see the God in her, her twins and muffins couldn't be jiggling all over the place, distracting folks.

She would never forget the one time she went to see one of her favorite Gospel artists perform. Arykah couldn't even half pay attention to the musical ministry for fear the woman's boobs were going to pop right out of the top of her blouse. Every time the artist 'bout caught the Holy Ghost . . . bounce, bounce, bounce and flap, flap, flap. Those boobs were like a backup instrument. When the artist was being still, Arykah had had the impression that the woman's nipples, belly button, and lower stomach patch were smiling at her. Together, they looked like a great big ole smiley face. *Say cheese!* Then, when she danced or strutted across the stage, that smiley face would make all kinds of expressions. That artist had given the scripture about being still in the Lord a whole other meaning. Arykah had sworn that from that point on, she'd wear however many Spanx it took to keep her body parts, skin, and meat in their proper place.

Arykah had had to recite a similar prayer to the one she'd just issued, though, when she'd worn a pair of shoes that kicked her butt by the end of the night. But tonight was just beginning, and she was already sending prayers up to the Lord. Arykah meant that request wholeheartedly too. She wanted God to grace her with the knowledge that she needed to aid Lady McKenzie, but she also needed grace to remain in the layers of Spandex around her belly and buttocks.

"As long as you're ready, all will be well. And that's all God asks of us, to at least be ready," Angel said.

Arykah nodded her agreement as she continued to stare out the window. After a moment she began fidgeting in her seat. She just couldn't seem to get comfortable.

"You okay?" Angel asked when she saw that Arykah couldn't keep still.

"Yeah, I'm all right," she lied. Arykah actually wished that she could click her heels together three times and fast-forward the evening by four hours. Then she'd be back at the Four Seasons Hotel, lying in her king-size bed, Spanx free, with an alcoholic drink in her hand. Nothing strong. Just a little something to take off the edge or the aftermath of the wedge, or should she say wedgie?

After the women had engaged in thirty-five minutes of small talk, with some moments of silence in between, the limousine turned into the parking lot of the church. The parking lot looked more like a driveway that might have been extended.

The ladies had a clear view of the building. Arykah saw that it was a small church, almost like a little gingerbread house. Just looking at the size of the building, she guessed that maybe it could house up to one hundred people comfortably on a Sunday morning. She couldn't help but wonder how such a small congregation could manage to keep the lights on, let alone flip the tab for her all-expense-paid trip to California. It was no secret how some church folks were when it came to paying tithes and offerings.

They wanted to get all dressed up, go enjoy a New York Strip dinner, but leave only enough to cover a meal of a hot dog and a bag of chips. Not to say that prayer and blessings cost money. Not that they were free, either. Only Jesus already paid the price for those. But electricity, heat, gas, air, water, and all that other stuff weren't free. Sports fans keep the lights on at the stadiums and arenas, but some folks didn't even want to keep them on at the church they worshipped at.

"It's cozy here, huh?" Arykah said to Angel, trying her best not to sound condescending. She really wasn't trying to be. She had just expected something different. She hadn't been exactly sure what to expect, just not this. "I see why they call it a chapel."

Angel nodded her head. "It looks very intimate." She hurried and thought of something that might sound complimentary. "I bet all the members know one another. I like those types of churches. I've attended a couple alongside Isaiah when he's had to go be a guest preacher. They're just like family at these smaller churches."

The two women looked at each other. Arykah was the first, of course, to speak up and keep it real. "Child, who are we kidding? This church so small, with all His perfect vision, God probably has a hard time finding it come Sunday morning."

"Stop it." Angel playfully smacked Arykah's knee and managed not even to crack a smile.

"What? You know I'm telling the truth." Arykah began to dig in her purse and pulled out her cell phone.

"Oh, yeah. That reminds me that I better turn mine off too." Angel dug her phone out of her purse.

"Oh, I'm going to turn my phone off, but not until I call the hotel and make sure my stay really is paid in full." Arykah began looking up the hotel number as she mumbled. "I think Lady McKenzie got her numbers mixed up. She's two numbers off."

"What do you mean?" Angel asked, confused, while she turned her phone off.

Arykah snatched her upper body back and looked at Angel like she was crazy. "Angel, she has me staying up in the Four Seasons, knowing dang well she should have booked me at the Motel 6. Four and six. Like I said, Lady McKenzie is two numbers off."

"Girl, give me that phone." Angel went to snatch Arykah's phone from her hand, but Arykah pulled it away too quickly.

The limousine came to a stop at the front entrance of the church building.

"Okay, okay. I'll at least wait and call after service." Arykah turned her phone off. "But be prepared to have a roommate in your suite if things ain't kosher."

Angel shook her head as the car door next to her opened. Elroy stood with his hand extended, prepared to help the ladies exit the car. One at a time they stepped out of the vehicle. The parking lot was pretty packed, and the women who were now entering the church for tonight's service were looking to see who the two women were who had arrived in a limousine.

"Ladies," Elroy said, "I'll be waiting here for you when it's over." He reached into his pocket and pulled out a business card. "This is my number. Hold on tight to it, just in case you need me. Enjoy yourselves."

"Thank you," the women said in unison, then turned to face the building.

Arykah just stood there and stared at it for a moment. "Now I know how Snow White felt. I don't even know if I can fit in this place."

Angel sucked her teeth. "Cut it out and let's go," she said as they walked up the three church steps that led to the door.

Angel might be able to relate to the whole small church thing, but Arykah couldn't relate to that at all. She wished that was the case at her home church. There Arykah sat in the midst of over five hundred members, and she saw new faces every Sunday. She thought back to just a couple of Sundays ago, when a husband and wife greeted her in the sanctuary.

"Good morning, Lady Arykah," the wife said as she stood holding hands with her husband.

Arykah hadn't seen either of them before and didn't know their names.

"Good morning, Sister," Arykah replied, greeting the wife with a smile. Her eyes then connected with the husband's. "Good morning, my brother. May God bless you both."

The couple smiled at Arykah and walked away.

Arykah had felt so awkward. There was nothing worse than someone walking up to her who knew exactly who she was, and yet she couldn't pick them out in a lineup on an episode of *Law & Order* to save her life. As the first lady of the church, everyone knew who she was, but Arykah longed for the day when she could address her members by their names. For that, she could say she envied Lady McKenzie.

Angel opened the door and then moved to the side so that Arykah could enter first.

"Well," Arykah said, "the good news is that because God's Saints Chapel is a small church, it shouldn't take me long to sniff out the trick who's pushing up on the pastor."

"That's if she's here tonight," Angel said.

"Humph. Trust me, honey, if a woman is trying to get at the pastor, she's gonna be at the church every time the doors open. And that's the truth."

"But it's a women's event," Angel said.

"Which means there's all the more reason for the husband stealer to be here. She wants to see the wife and study her as much as possible. Because remember, her ultimate goal is to *become* the wife. She wants to buddy up to Lady McKenzie so that she doesn't suspect anything. And besides, on occasion the pastor is known to show up at events like this that are taking place in the house he is the head of. If nothing else, just in the beginning of the service, to at least give his blessings and prayers to the service."

Angel hadn't planned any women's conference or events at her church, so she wasn't sure what usually took place. She shook her head in disbelief at Arykah's wisdom.

"What?" Arykah asked.

"For you to be dang near as new at this first lady thing as I am, you sure know a lot about it."

"Honey, like I told you, the person these tricks are, *I* used to be. Graduated cum laude and could go back and lecture." Arykah chuckled as they entered the church vestibule. The vaulted ceiling with a bubbled stain-glass window of Jesus on the cross made the space feel bigger than it actually was.

"There's Lady McKenzie right there," Angel said, pointing to a woman who stood just outside the sanctuary doors. She was shaking hands with, giving hugs to, and thanking the women who were entering.

"She's pretty," Arykah said. "The picture on their church Web site doesn't do her justice. I'm going to have to talk to her about that. Honey, as a first lady, you supposed to give the *bam* on that photo. Use a twenty-year-old picture if you have to, but you better be snatched and beat!"

Angel agreed. The picture of Lady McKenzie was nice, but to see her in person, this woman was astonishing.

Lady McKenzie's complexion was a mahogany brown with a bronze glow. Even though Arykah and Angel stood about ten feet away from where Lady McKenzie stood, they could see that her skin was flawless. Her short blond feathered haircut was impressive. Not a strand was out of place. Arykah appreciated when a first lady actually looked like a first lady. She felt that no one should ever have to guess what a woman's status in the church was. A pastor's wife should always exude elegance and grace, and she should not fit in but stand out. She should look like a leader instead of a follower. Even if Angel had not pointed out who Lady McKenzie was, Arykah would have known that she was the first lady of the church.

Lady McKenzie stood at that door with her head held high and her shoulders back. Her posture was strong but alluring. Arykah knew a confident woman when she saw one. So she couldn't help but wonder why Lady McKenzie couldn't handle this matter of business herself. Arykah couldn't tell everything about a person from just looking at them, but she could tell enough. And underneath Lady McKenzie's kind and genuine smile, that woman didn't play.

"First Lady Angel, my God!" Lady McKenzie gasped when she looked over and saw Angel, someone she wasn't expecting to talk to again until their next prayer on the morning prayer line. When she had called Angel a few weeks ago and told her about her situation in the church, Angel had given Lady McKenzie Arykah's contact information. Angel had shared with her how Arykah had helped her when she came to Savior Manger. She'd assured Lady McKenzie that Arykah, through the direction of the Holy Ghost, could help her as well.

Lady McKenzie hurried over to where Angel stood. "Honey, it's so good to meet you in person!" she exclaimed to Angel as she rocked her back and forth in her arms.

Angel felt like a rag doll. Lady McKenzie wasn't a big woman, a size ten at best. But she was five feet nine inches tall, and with the way she was swinging Angel's body back and forth, Angel might as well have changed her name to Raggedy Ann.

"Same here," Angel said. She placed her arms underneath Lady McKenzie's arms and gripped Lady McKenzie's shoulders with her hands. Looked like she was holding on for dear life.

"And Lady Arykah. Welcome!" Lady McKenzie released Angel and opened her arms wide as she moved toward Arykah.

Arykah stepped into the embrace.

"Oh, woman of God, I just thank you." Lady McKenzie held Arykah in the hug and rubbed her hands up and down her back.

Arykah could feel the tension in this woman's body. "It's all right, First Lady. Everything is going to be okay." Arykah squeezed the woman a little tighter, letting her know she was there for her.

It really did pain Arykah to see another first lady in the same distress she had found herself in at one time. She honestly hadn't seen the day coming when God would make attending to other first ladies her ministry, but first with Angel and now with Lady McKenzie, God had been setting this up all along.

"Thank you. Thank you. I know it is," Lady McKenzie said as she slipped out of the embrace and sniffled. She pulled out the handkerchief that was in the pocket of the soft mauve pantsuit she was wearing and wiped her nose. She then allowed a spirit of joy to cover her face. Her mother had definitely given her the right name, Joy, because she stood there, looking full of joy.

Lady McKenzie's smile was so big and sincere, Arykah felt that it could easily take the place of the sunshine. Before another word could be said, Lady McKenzie gave Arykah one more big hug. "Yes, Lord. I feel it in my spirit. She's the one. My help cometh from the Lord, and you sent the right one. Yes!" The more Lady McKenzie praised, the tighter her grip got on Arykah.

Arykah felt like Lady McKenzie was squeezing the life out of her. The bear hug combined with the two pairs of Spanx took her breath away. It wasn't until Lady McKenzie released Arykah that she was able to inhale, exhale, and then speak. "Thanks for inviting me. It's so wonderful to meet you, Lady McKenzie. Where God wants me to go, I'll go. So to God be the glory."

"Amen," Angel said.

Lady McKenzie looked at Angel. "And I'm so glad you could join her." She reached out and squeezed Angel's hand.

"Me too," Angel said.

Lady McKenzie was definitely the huggy-feely type, as she pulled Angel in for another hug. She gave her the same bear hug she had just given Arykah. "This is such an awesome surprise. God is so very good. I didn't know you were coming to California." She released Angel and looked into her eyes. "Why didn't you tell me you were coming?"

Angel shrugged her shoulders. "Then it wouldn't have been a surprise, now, would it?"

"You got me there, huh?" Lady McKenzie said. She then quickly turned to Arykah.

Upon instinct, Arykah hurried up and backed away. She got in a Karate Kid stance.

Both Angel and Lady McKenzie looked at her like she was crazy.

"I'm not trying to be funny, Lady McKenzie, but I got on two pairs of Spanx, and your tight hugs don't complement the feeling. So if you come at me with one more of them hugs, I'm going to have to Mr. Miyagi you and wax on, wax off." Arykah stood in her stance, just as serious as a heart attack.

Lady McKenzie's mouth dropped open.

Oh, Lord, Angel thought, not knowing how Lady McKenzie was going to react to Arykah. They hadn't been there five minutes and already Angel was about to have to intervene. The next thing Angel knew, she heard some cackling, then all-out laughter.

Lady McKenzie was holding her stomach, she was laughing so hard.

Arykah looked at Angel, and Angel shrugged. Arykah slowly came out of her karate stance.

Once Lady McKenzie got her laughter under control, she looked upward to the heavens and said, "God, you most *definitely* sent the right one." She put her arm around Arykah's shoulder and led her into the sanctuary, with Angel right beside them.

On one hand, Angel was glad that Arykah's actions hadn't turned Lady McKenzie off. But on the other hand, if Lady McKenzie was about that life, and Arykah was about that life, Angel was willing to bet the farm that before their time was up in California, some poor preacher-stealing heifer was going to lose her life.

Chapter 24

A female usher escorted the three first ladies down the center aisle. The journey wasn't but a hop, skip, and a jump, considering the sanctuary wasn't that large. There were about ten pews to the left and ten pews to the right of the center aisle. Each pew could comfortably sit about ten people.

"This church may be small," Angel whispered to Arykah, who was walking behind Lady McKenzie, "but the spirit of the Lord is larger than life."

Unlike in most churches that both Arykah and Angel had visited, the members weren't chattering, talking about last night's episode of a popular TV show, or bragging about a new car, house, or job and disguising it as a praise report. Yes, some members really did have genuine praise reports to share, but those with a spirit of discernment knew a show-off when they encountered one. Whether any of the folks at God's Saints Chapel were show-offs couldn't yet be determined, as everyone was in full prayer mode.

Arykah nodded to the words Angel had spoken. "You ain't never lied. Girl, do you feel the anointing up in this place?" Arykah whispered back to Angel.

Angel nodded as she observed the women, and some teen girls, standing in prayer with joined hands. Some sat on the pew with bowed heads, while a few women were already at the altar, on their knees in prayer.

The usher stopped at the first pew and extended her hand for the women to sit. Lady McKenzie stepped aside and allowed her guests to be seated first; then she sat on the end. Once they were seated, the usher extended programs to the ladies. All three either spoke or nodded their thanks.

Lady McKenzie stood, turned to face the pew on which only seconds ago she'd sat, and got down on her knees. She cupped her hands on the pew, closed her eyes, and then bowed her head in prayer.

Arykah and Angel began their prayer right where they sat. Arykah didn't know why Angel hadn't followed suit and gotten down on bended knee as Lady McKenzie had. But Arykah knew that if she herself had bent one knee, she'd be stuck in that positon forever. She'd learned long ago that plus-size women ain't got no business kneeling down. One time when Arykah saw her husband kneel to pray, she'd knelt next to him. But when the prayer was over, it had taken all the strength that Bishop Lance had to lift her from the floor. From that moment on, Arykah had either sat or lain down on the bed to pray.

The power of God in God's Saints Chapel rose like the aroma over a field of flowers. The sweet, sweet smell of the presence of the Lord became intoxicating as weeping could be heard.

"Yes, Lord," Angel mumbled as she shook her head in awe. It truly felt as though God was wrapping His arms around her and comforting her at that very moment, and she knew He was via the Holy Spirit. "Thank you, Jesus." The touch, the feeling became so overwhelming that tears began to flow down her cheeks. Her blood was running warm through her veins.

Arykah, too, began to get filled up with the Holy Ghost, who was navigating throughout the sanctuary, laying His hands on God's people. She was on her feet and couldn't even remember using her own strength to get up off the pew and stand on them.

With Lady McKenzie on her knees in prayer, Angel sitting on the pew and blessing the Lord, and Arykah standing on her feet with holy hands raised, they were merely falling in line with the atmosphere that had already been set up in that place. It went without saying that it was going to be a powerful program this evening.

As Arykah stood there with her hands lifted, she conversed with the Lord in prayer. There was no negative energy or thoughts flowing through her being. All was well in spirit and in truth. She couldn't fathom how the Jezebel spirit of whatever woman was trying to pull asunder the pastor and his wife could even survive up in that place. Even the spirit of the demon that wanted to let loose and cuss Arykah out for doubling up on the Spanx had been forced into submission and neutralized. It had no power up in that place.

"Thank you, God, for all the fasting and praying that have gone forth in this place to prepare not only for Women's Week, but even for my presence, God," Arykah said.

Lady McKenzie had not informed Arykah of what all had taken place in preparation for the week, but even a babe in Christ could detect that that place had been consecrated. No weapon formed was going to prosper over this program or Arykah being there to do what she had to do. This built up Arykah's confidence and courage to move forward in her assignment there in

California. It was just a reminder that yes, she had Angel there to have her back in the natural, but God would always have her back in the spirit.

Arykah had no idea how long she'd been in conversation with her Lord and Savior, but by the time she opened her eyes and was mentally out of the spirit realm and physically back in the church sanctuary, everyone was on their feet, clapping their hands to the three women at the altar leading praise and worship.

"Lord Jesus," Arykah said to herself as she looked around at everyone just clapping and singing along with the three women. She exhaled, not even realizing that it didn't hurt to breath anymore. She'd gone to another place, a dimension in the Lord where not even Spanx could stifle her praise. She turned to face the women who were singing. She felt so awakened and refreshed, like she'd taken a nap in the Lord's bosom. Once she was fully aware of her surroundings, she joined in with everyone else by clapping her hands. She didn't recognize the song, but when they hit the chorus, it was simple enough where she could sing unto the Lord, and so she did for the next ten minutes, along with everyone else.

By the end of the third song, which was a worship song, the Lord had moved so mighty up in that chapel that they could have ended service right then and there and everyone would have gone home satisfied and full. But when the praise and worship leader called up Lady McKenzie to introduce the speaker of the hour, it was clear that the show was still going to go on. But Arykah wasn't so convinced that it was all part of the Holy Spirit's agenda. This church didn't seem like the kind that would play around and try to put man's agenda above what God wanted. Arykah had no doubt that if the Holy Spirit had instructed Lady McKenzie to close out in prayer and call it a night, that was exactly what she have would have done. But when Lady McKenzie walked up to the podium, took the mic, and was well into her second sentence, it was clear that was not what the Holy Ghost had directed her to do. So perhaps it was the speaker who had been given the instructions to do so.

"I just want to thank everyone for coming out to tonight's service," Lady McKenzie began. "We have a phenomenal speaker here to share with you what thus sayeth the Lord."

The congregation gave a hand praise.

"But before I introduce tonight's speaker, I first want to give honor to the shepherd of this house, *your* pastor, *my* husband, Pastor McKenzie," Lady McKenzie said.

As Pastor McKenzie came through a door behind the pulpit, escorted by three armor bearers, the members of the congregation stood to their feet and began to clap.

Arykah stood and clapped as she nodded and looked at Angel while smiling. "Did you catch that?" she asked her.

Angel shrugged her shoulders. She didn't know what Arykah was talking about.

"Lady McKenzie said 'your' pastor, and she put special emphasis on the word 'my' in 'my husband.' She just sent a strong message to the trick who's chasing after Pastor McKenzie."

Angel nodded her head in agreement. "Ha," she said.

Arykah brought her attention back to Lady McKenzie. "I know that's right, First Lady. Tell 'em your man's role in their lives."

Angel laughed and, over the applause, said to her friend, "Arykah, you crazy."

"I'm real," Arykah replied, correcting her.

"That you are," Angel agreed.

While Pastor McKenzie said a few words, Arykah took note of how Lady McKenzie stood no less than two feet from her man. She kept her eyes on him, smiling and looking at him with such love and admiration. Her demeanor alone should have been the kryptonite for any floozy who even thought she could overpower the love Lady McKenzie had for her husband.

"Can everyone give a hand to my lovely wife?" Pastor McKenzie asked the congregation. "She worked endlessly to see that you women had a truly blessed week." He extended his hand to Lady McKenzie and then followed his hand with his eyes.

"Well," Arykah said to herself as the congregation now gave their first lady a hand praise. The way Pastor McKenzie was looking at his wife did not go unnoticed by Arykah. His blue eyes, indeed, held for her the same level of love and admiration that hers held for him, but he had a little something *extra* going on in his, and First Lady McKenzie didn't. It was the other *L* word. *Lust.*

Arykah almost had to fan herself just from watching the way the pastor was staring at his wife. His snowy-white cheeks were now flushed.

Lady McKenzie was too busy looking out at the congregation, thanking the congregants with a light head bow to take notice. And as Arykah looked around, smiling but deliberately checking out her surroundings, she saw that all the women out in the audience seemed to be gleaming and genuinely cheering on their first lady.

"Yes, you have blessed us for sure, First Lady," the woman behind Arykah even called out.

Arykah could get in only a quick sweep of the room before having to turn back around and face the pulpit. She didn't want the congregation becoming suspicious of her, wondering who the heck this woman was who was staring down their throats. But in that quick glance, she wasn't able to detect with the naked eye any woman who might be faking the funk, clapping for Lady McKenzie while gazing at the pastor. Her spirit wasn't able to discern any fakeness, either.

Arykah watched the pastor, with his spiky blond hair, thank everyone for coming out and supporting his wife's efforts. He then turned the mic back over to her. Lady McKenzie accepted the mic from her husband, who planted a kiss on her lips while staring her in the eyes.

"Well, dang," Arykah said to Angel as Arykah turned and pulled her lace church fan out of her purse.

"What?" Angel inquired

"Usually the only time I get wet in church is if I break a sweat doing the Holy Ghost dance or get baptized." Arykah opened the fan and vigorously began fanning herself. "But today I'm getting wet for a whole bunch of different reasons in a whole different place."

Angel stared at Arykah for a moment before it hit her what Arykah was alluding to. "You are going to hell in a handbasket with gasoline Spanx on," Angel said, dead serious, while shaking her head.

Angel turned to face the pastor and his wife in the pulpit. A cute chocolate and vanilla swirl couple they were. She had noticed how when Pastor McKenzie passed the mic to his wife and she accepted it, he had continued staring into her eyes, while ever so gently rubbing her hand with his fingers. Angel felt like she'd just seen several pages of a romance novel acted out between husband and wife. She stared at the couple, in a daze, watching as Pastor McKenzie looked out at the congregation, then threw his hand up to wave good-bye. Then he exited the pulpit the same way he had come in. Before disappearing, though, he shot one more sensual look at his wife.

Arykah leaned in and whispered to Angel, "Close your mouth and wipe the slobber."

Arykah's voice snapped Angel out of her gaze. She then looked at Arykah and said, "Girl, if you going to hell, then I am too." She snatched Arykah's fan and began fanning herself.

"Told ya," Arykah said.

"That man loves his wife."

"And he doesn't mind showing it," Arykah added.

Even though Arykah hadn't yet detected anything or anyone that raised a red flag, in her mind, the night was still young.

Chapter 25

The speaker of the hour was in the pulpit, whooping and hollering. What started off as a calm, gentle spirit in the atmosphere had been *bulldozed* by the lady preacher, who obviously wasn't in tune with the Holy Spirit. She might be giving a good Word, but her harsh delivery made it sound more like clamorous noise. Now if her spirit were lined up with the Holy Spirit, her delivery would have more of a teaching and conversational tone, or maybe she would have nixed the sermon she had planned altogether, said a few words of thanks, and then closed out.

It wouldn't have been the first time Arykah witnessed something like that happen. Back at her own church there had been a couple of occasions when Bishop Lance Howell spent all week getting a Word together, but come Sunday morning, God used something or someone else to minister to His children. God would put the Word away for another time if God so desired. But not this guest speaker. She wasn't going to miss this opportunity to be before a congregation, spitting out her message. She acted like she was mad at somebody. There was a possibility that she was mad at the devil, but heck, she should take it out on him, and not the poor congregation.

Neither Arykah nor Angel had a problem with those who delivered the Word in a powerful tone and did a little whooping and hollering here and there. Some services and Words from the Lord did, in fact, call for all that. But the messenger had to be clear that his or her usual way of doing things didn't conflict with how God wanted His people to receive His message. Sure, even Arykah herself had gotten caught up in the spirit a time or two and had leaped from her seat and given a shout. But she knew how to keep her spirit under submission when hollering just wasn't conducive to the atmosphere.

Arykah glanced at her watch and saw that it was 9:00 p.m. The speaker had been introduced at eight. Before delving into the Word, she had thanked her church and the people who came from her church to support her, had said a prayer, had read a scripture, and had even sung a song. And now, forty-five minutes into her actual message, from the sounds of it, she was nowhere near wrapping it up. Arykah wanted to go into the pulpit and pull the speaker's coattails. That was what Bishop Lance did at Freedom Temple when his guest speakers became long-winded. Bishop Lance's motto was "Get up, speak up, shut up, and then sit down."

The speaker was sweating, dancing, and yelling. She was preaching in this loud, singsongy type of voice. Arykah couldn't help but lean over to Angel and whisper, "Girl, why does this feel like entertainment? Like I'm at a Beyoncé concert or something?"

Angel shook her head. "Uh-uh. Even Beyoncé knows when it's time to shut it down." Angel looked at her watch and then looked at Arykah. She then nodded. "And look at her assistant over there, recording it all."

Arykah turned her attention to the woman who had carried the speaker's Bible and glasses to the podium for her. She now had her tablet in camera mode and wasn't missing a beat. "This is all a show," Arykah said. "It's probably going to be up on YouTube before the benediction."

"A darn shame too," Angel whispered. "God could really use her, if she stopped using Him."

"Ouch," Arykah said. "Talking about using God's name in vain." She shook her head and then turned her attention back to the speaker of the hour.

Everyone sat listening to the speaker go on and on about God's assignment in God's Saints Chapel. They were becoming restless. It was clear by the way folks kept looking at their watches or pulling their cell phones out to check the time. Some even yawned.

After another ten minutes Arykah leaned into Lady McKenzie's ear and said, "We did start at seven sharp, right?" Arykah was just making sure that she hadn't gotten caught up in the twilight zone and that at some point, time had not stood still, reversed, or something else.

Lady McKenzie cleared her throat and looked over at Arykah. There was a hint of embarrassment in her eyes. She knew that what was going on right now was a holy hot mess.

Arykah kept a sympathetic expression on her face. She wasn't holding any of this against Lady McKenzie. She was certain the first lady had been obedient in choosing all her speakers for the week. But after that, it was up to the speakers to be obedient to God. On the other side of someone's obedience was another person's blessing. Well, because the speaker had decided to showboat, instead of present the Word in the manner that God would have her give it based on His children in the room and the atmosphere, a whole bunch of folks would probably miss their blessing tonight.

Lady McKenzie nodded her head. "Service started at seven," she confirmed. She patted Lady Arykah's arm. "But it's okay. I'm sure she's going to wrap things up here shortly." At least she hoped so. Lady McKenzie would feel terrible if women began to leave the sanctuary while the speaker was still in the pulpit.

Arykah was no longer under submission and a spirit of peace and calmness, thanks to the breach in the atmosphere. With those Spanx cutting into Arykah the way she cut into her homemade 7Up pound cake, Lady Preacher better hope she said amen quick, fast, and in a hurry. Otherwise, Arykah didn't know how much longer she could keep quiet and stop herself from pulling the covers off this woman and shutting her down in the process. The Holy Ghost wasn't into embarrassing people, but Lady Arykah would step in to do the job, if necessary.

Arykah settled back on the pew and did her best to make peace with the two pairs of Spanx she wore. She'd always made it a point to be on time to every engagement she attended and to stay until the benediction. She never wanted anyone to think that her time was more import-ant than theirs. But, Lord, what she wouldn't give to put up her index finger and shuffle past Lady McKenzie, down the aisle, and out the door. She'd just have to get with Lady McKenzie another day, when she could breathe easier. If she did this, she would be that much closer to returning to her hotel and setting her abdomen free.

Arykah looked up at the speaker in the pulpit. She saw the woman pacing back and forth while screaming at the top of her lungs. She wiped her damp forehead with a terry-cloth towel that had been placed on the podium for her. Lady Arykah couldn't make out any words the preacheress was preaching, but the screaming rubbed her the wrong way. Arykah felt a sharp pain in both of her temples. The last time her head hurt like that was when she went to see Patti LaBelle in concert. Patti had screamed out those high notes and had held them for so long that Arykah had a migraine for three days straight. Arykah laughed inside at the comparison, because no sooner had she thought it than the speaker kicked her shoes right off, just like Patti did at all her concerts.

"Yikes!" Arykah hadn't meant to say it so loud. But when one of those shoes popped a church mother right upside the head, she couldn't help it. Arykah covered her mouth as the woman next to the mother began to care for her and then helped her out of the sanctuary.

Angel watched as the older woman held her head while being escorted out. "I'm going to have to invite this speaker to our church," Angel whispered in Arykah's ear.

Arykah snapped her neck back with the quickness and looked at Angel like she'd lost her mind. "What?"

"Yeah, girl," Angel said, nodding to the spot that the older woman had vacated. "'Cause you know that's about where Mother Calloway always sits."

At this point Arykah couldn't control herself. She burst out laughing. Angel was horrified. She immediately turned stiff and faced forward. She didn't want anyone to know she was with the woman who was laughing during service.

Arykah buried her face in her hands to muffle her laughter. Her shoulders heaved up and down.

"That's right. Let it out, baby!" the speaker hollered to Arykah, mistaking Arykah's laughter for crying. "Get your breakthrough."

Keeping her hands in position and her head down, her shoulders heaving, Arykah turned to face Angel. Still laughing, she said to her friend, "If this woman don't go on somewhere else, I'ma break through, all right. I'm a break through these Spanx like the Incredible Hulk and then break her neck for having me ruin two good pairs of Spanx."

At this point Angel was no good. All she could do to hide her own laughter was to pretend to comfort Arykah. She leaned into Arykah and began hugging her. Their two heads were resting against each other. The two women's shoulders heaved up and down while they laughed. From the outside looking in, it appeared as though they were sharing a spiritual moment.

This *really* gave the speaker something to preach about. Thinking her words had moved the two first ladies to tears, she raised her voice an octave higher and really began to go in. Even though not many of the other women had been moved, they wanted to celebrate the break-through of their first lady's guests.

All around the sanctuary the women were on their feet, applauding and shouting back at the preacheress. Lady McKenzie joined in. After managing to stop laughing and to gather her composure, Angel stood and joined in on the praising as well.

Arykah kept her seat. She took this moment to get her mind right and get herself together. She had to repent for allowing the speaker to entertain her. After apologizing to God for acting up, Arykah took a moment while all eyes were on the speaker to look around the sanctuary and size the women up. This was an opportune time that she couldn't let slip by her.

There was no doubt in Arykah's mind that the thorn in Lady McKenzie's side was present in that room. She had to be. Arykah couldn't imagine the Jezebel spirit not wanting to be there to try to manipulate her way into either Pastor's, Lady McKenzie's, or both their good graces. The skank would try her best to be slick, chameleonlike, and conniving. Arykah knew that try as this woman might, there was no way she would slither past her undetected.

Being that it was just a small group of women, no more than fifty, hopefully Arykah wouldn't have to work too hard to find who she was looking for. And if she couldn't spot her right off the bat, there was no need to worry, as Arykah had the nose of a bloodhound when it came to this kind of stuff. She was gifted in sniffing out folks who were living foul. The stench of the unrighteous would penetrate Arykah's nostrils and sting, as if someone had pressed smelling salts against her nose. But as she looked around the sanctuary and saw the women offering up praise to God, Arykah didn't detect anyone who was falsehearted.

The spirit in the room was genuine; the praise was real. Arykah took the time to study each woman's movements and facial expressions. Some women had holy hands raised. Others actually had tears running down their faces. Some women sat on the pew, weeping, while other sisters comforted them. There were even two women who were taking turns praying for each other.

Arykah turned back around, confused. What was she missing? Was the culprit she had come all the way to California to track down not in attendance tonight? Or was the heifer just that good at disguising herself and mixing in with the sisters who truly had Lady McKenzie's best interests at heart? Arykah did one last sweep of the room and came to the conclusion that the woman who was trying to steal the pastor from Lady McKenzie was not in the sanctuary that evening.

She was so very disappointed. Not only would it have been nice to uncover the woman's game and call her on the carpet about it, but things also would have gotten personal. Arykah would have dug into that woman so good, the same way her support garments were digging into her. Heck, somebody had to pay for Arykah's discomfort. Might as well be the holy hooka.

Arykah looked down and picked up the program the usher had given her. She gazed at the beautiful color photo of Pastor McKenzie and Lady McKenzie on the front. She couldn't deny that Pastor McKenzie was a handsome man. He had that Channing Tatum creamy vanilla skin. His ocean-blue eyes were hypnotizing. Arykah let out a harrumph. She could imagine that Pastor McKenzie had broken many a heart back in the day. He had gentle features. His smile was intoxicating. He had perfect teeth. Pastor McKenzie was beyond just regular handsome. He was a beautiful man. Not beautiful as a white man, just beautiful, period. Arykah in no way, shape, or form was condoning any woman going after another woman's man, but she sure could understand why any woman with good vision would be smitten with him.

One thing Arykah admired was the fact that even though it was a women's conference, so to speak, and Lady McKenzie was the overseer, she'd still included her husband right there on the program with her. Again, Lady McKenzie wasn't no punk when it came to letting the women know whose man Pastor McKenzie was, so Arykah couldn't understand for the life of her why any woman would still try her.

She opened the program and her breath caught when she saw that the very first thing inside was an encouraging word from the pastor. It looked as though it was a handwritten note that had been copied onto the program. It was just so personal and touching. This pastor and first lady were one indeed in every endeavor of ministry. She thought about how awesome that was as she read the pastor's note.

As God's Saints Chapel celebrates its ninth annual Women's Week, I pray that the spirit of the Lord be among you. As your head shepherds of this house, Lady McKenzie and I pray that God will touch you, heal you, comfort you, and guide you. As Romans 12:2 says, "And be not conformed to this world: but be ye transformed by the renewing of your mind, that ye may prove what is that good, and acceptable, and perfect, will of God."
—*Pastor Gregory J. McKenzie*

Excellent penmanship, Arykah thought to herself when she saw his signature.

The screaming and hollering brought Lady Arykah's attention back to the preacheress.

"Say 'Yeahhh,'" the speaker shouted.

The women shouted back at her, "Yeaahhh."

Arykah shook her head, thinking that she'd gone from being at a Beyoncé concert to a Patti LaBelle concert to one featuring a rapper. "Geesh!" Arykah said, not the least bit concerned that anyone would hear her voice over all the yelling.

The preacheress threw her head back and repeated, "Say 'Yeahhhh.'"

Arykah looked around as the women yelled, "Yeahhh." She noticed that some women looked uncomfortable shouting but tried to be obedient to the lady of the hour. This was so foreign to others that Arykah could tell they were repenting to God afterward for yelling in His house like Big Mama used to do when they were little.

The third time was the charm, as the women in the sanctuary were instructed to shout just one more time.

Arykah's migraine kicked into overdrive. She pressed her right hand against her right temple. Between the screaming and the pain caused by her support garments, she was fit to be tied.

"You all right?" Angel asked after she sat down and saw that her friend looked a little distressed.

"This is too much. My head is killing me." Arykah rubbed her temples. "But I'm telling you, if Flavor Flav come out, or some other kind of hype man posing as an armor bearer, I'm out of here. I will give Lady McKenzie back every dime she done spent on getting me here."

"I know. I know," Angel said sympathetically, patting Arykah on the knee. "I wish I had some aspirin for you."

"I wish I had a gun." Arykah put her hands in her lap and glared at the speaker.

"*Arykah*!" Angel gasped.

"Not to shoot her," Arykah was quick to say. "No, I'd give it to her so she could shoot her own self. I'm sure she'd love the YouTube hits, declaring that it was all in the name of Jesus."

All Angel could do was shake her head.

"Father, I'll triple my tithes when I get back home if you shut this woman up right now," Arykah pleaded, looking up to the heavens.

As if on cue, the preacheress laid the microphone on the podium and sat down in what looked to be the pastor's chair.

Lady Arykah exhaled. "Father, I love you."

Lady McKenzie got up from the pew and walked up to the podium. "Ladies, let's give the woman of God a hand praise."

The sanctuary erupted in thunderous applause—everyone was grateful to God that He'd finally shut this woman up.

"Ladies, before we give the benediction and head to the fellowship hall for the small reception, I have a couple of other women in the room

I'd like to acknowledge," Lady McKenzie said. She looked at Arykah and Angel. "Lady Arykah and First Lady Angel, can you two please stand?"

Angel and Arykah stood while Lady McKenzie made brief introductions, stating where each woman was from and the names of their churches.

"First Ladies, please come up and say a few words," Lady McKenzie insisted.

Angel and Arykah smiled at each other and then headed toward the mic.

"You know I'm not good at talking in front of people on the spot," Angel whispered to Arykah on their way up to the mic, "so you just say whatever."

Arykah nodded her okay as the two approached the podium. They both gave Lady McKenzie a hug. Lady McKenzie then extended the mic, which Arykah took. Then Lady McKenzie stepped to the side to give her guests the floor.

With the microphone in hand, Arykah looked out at the crowd. She quickly scanned the room. Not only did she want to make eye contact, acknowledging as many women as she could, but she was also still on the hunt for anyone who stood out. The women were all so graceful. But hidden in their eyes were desperate pleas: they were begging Arykah and Angel not to take this opportunity to preach a sermon.

"Don't worry, ladies," Arykah began. "I won't be long before you. I think enough has been said."

Angel cleared her throat, warning Arykah not to go there.

"Matter of fact, I think the woman of God here"—Arykah nodded to the speaker in the chair, who was wiping off her sweat—"has said everything God has ever wanted you women to hear."

A few women who had caught on to what Arykah was hinting at tucked in their lips to keep from laughing. The speaker took it as a compliment and nodded her thanks.

"So with that, First Lady Angel and I just want to thank your first lady for our invite and for you all welcoming us to worship and celebrate God with you. Thank you."

Arykah extended the mic to Lady McKenzie. The congregation clapped for Angel and Arykah as they took their places back on the pews.

Once they were seated, Lady McKenzie once again thanked all the women for coming out and then gave the benediction.

Needless to say, Arykah was elated. And it was apparent when she shouted amen louder than anyone in the sanctuary.

Chapter 26

As Lady McKenzie escorted Angel and Arykah to the fellowship hall, women stopped her to thank her for all her efforts over the week. Both Angel and Arykah pardoned themselves and made a beeline for the restroom, while Lady McKenzie stood out in the church vestibule, where her members were congregating before heading to the fellowship hall.

"So, did you see anyone who looked suspicious?" Angel asked Arykah as they headed to the restroom, which a parishioner had pointed out to them.

"I hate to say it, but I was wrong," Arykah confessed. "I honestly don't think Miss Thing is in the house tonight, after all."

"But you know your stuff, and you were certain she wouldn't miss this opportunity for the world," Angel noted.

"I know. I know," Arykah said, agitated that Angel was rubbing in the fact that she'd been wrong about the situation. "My support garments could be cutting off my discernment, as well as my circulation."

"I'm sure in the future one pair of Spanx will suffice," Angel said as they entered the restroom.

"Well, dang!" Arykah exclaimed, looking around the bathroom in awe.

A nice-size carpeted sitting area greeted them right when they walked in. To the left was a round coffee table with two high-back chairs. There was a queen bench against the wall. The wallpaper was a rich gold and purple, the epitome of royalty.

On the wall to the right was a long mirror with a freestanding shelf. On each end of the shelf were wicker baskets full of Bath & Body Works toiletries, including hair products, spray-on deodorant, and so on. When they walked past the carpeted area, their feet hit the gold, silver, and black marble sink area. The mirrors there had vanity lights above them. Four stalls stood there, all handicapped sized.

Both Angel and Arykah, still admiring the beautiful restroom, managed to bend down enough to see that all four stalls were empty and that they were the only ones in the restroom.

Each woman, silenced by awe, pushed open a stall door.

"Get the freak out of here!" Angel exclaimed.

The stalls had beautiful paintings hanging over the toilets. There was a shelf inside and hooks to hang up purses, Bible bags, and so on. A little shelf attached to the wall contained women's feminine items, including feminine wipes, free of charge.

"I can spin around in here," Arykah said. "And you know I'm a big girl, so that ain't always no easy feat in a public bathroom. But this joker right here!" Arykah exclaimed. "Now I'm gonna have to upgrade the women's bathroom at Freedom Temple. This is gorgeous."

Inside her own stall, Angel could hear the tapping of Arykah's shoes. "I know you ain't doing a *Gone with the Wind* fabulous twirl in the bathroom."

"The heck I ain't," Arykah said.

All Angel could do was what she usually did around Arykah, shake her head. So that was what she did, and then she handled her business. Arykah hadn't finished taking care of business in her stall when Angel emerged from her own stall. And so she washed her hands and sat down in the sitting area, waiting on Arykah to come out. Before long she heard the toilet flush, so she just knew that it would be only a matter of time before Arykah exited the stall. But a "matter of time" came and went.

After reading a couple of scriptures from the Bible that sat on the coffee table, Angel got up and went to check on Arykah. Just as she was about to knock on Arykah's stall door, Arykah came out.

"I thought something might have happened to you in there," Angel said. "I was coming to see about you."

"Oh, girl, I'm fine now," Arykah said as she stuffed something into her purse and made her way over to the sink. "Now that I got rid of one of these—"

Angel put her hand up to cut Arykah off. She did not want to hear Arykah say the name of the brand of support garments she wore one more time unless the maker of the product was going to pay her royalties.

"Let's just go," Angel said. "I'm starved."

"That's why you should have torn up that buffet back at the pool like I did," Arykah said as she began washing her hands. "You heard Lady McKenzie say it's going to be a *small* reception. Now I don't even feel bad that I ate for two—me and you. Ha!" She dried her hands on a paper towel.

"Oh, so you got jokes, and you're all happy again, now that you can breathe once more."

"Just like Toni Braxton. Come on, girl," Arykah said as she pranced out of the restroom, with Angel right behind her.

The two first ladies followed the lingering crowd to the reception.

"Oh, here they are," Lady McKenzie said, raising her hand and waving as they entered the hall. She walked over and met them. "Unfortunately, the speaker had to leave. She said she'd poured so much virtue out that she didn't have the strength to attend the reception."

"Oh, that's too bad," Arykah said, even though from the front pew she'd overheard the conversation about this as it took place in the pulpit. The speaker might have exerted herself too much to stay and fellowship, but another thing Arykah had taken note of was that the woman sure had had enough strength to lift her hand and kindly accept the love offering Lady McKenzie had prepared for her in an envelope, and she'd counted it right there in Lady McKenzie's face.

The speaker then had had the nerve to say, "Did you plan on taking up any other type of collection for me at the reception or anything?"

Arykah had cocked her head to the side and had thought, *You ungrateful, greedy heifer. Did you really just ask Lady McKenzie that?*

Angel had read Arykah's facial expression, and it was in that moment that Angel had thanked the Lord from heaven above that she worked out at home. Her repetitions with her hand weights had paid off, as she'd built the muscle and strength she needed to hold Arykah back and prevent her from charging into that pulpit.

"Just let Lady McKenzie handle it," Angel had begged her friend as she maintained a death grip on her arm. "Like my husband told me, sometimes a first lady has to find her own way of handling things."

Back when Mother Calloway was taking Angel through the wringer, Angel's husband had wanted Angel to find her own way and to be able to stand up for herself. It had worked for Angel, so she figured it would work for Lady McKenzie as well.

Lady McKenzie had handled the speaker diplomatically and gracefully. By the time Lady McKenzie got finished with the lady preacher, she'd sown the monetary seed that Lady McKenzie had given her in the envelope right there at God's Saints Chapel.

"See there," Angel had said to Arykah.

Arykah had had to admit that Angel was right about letting Lady McKenzie take care of the situation. "See? I knew I needed you here," Arykah had told Angel. "That would have been my case right there."

Angel had agreed. And now, as they stood before Lady McKenzie in the fellowship hall, she was glad the speaker hadn't been able to stay. Angel wouldn't have been able to concentrate, as she would have had to keep Arykah from laying holy hands on the woman, and maybe even a foot or two.

"Lady McKenzie, that women's restroom . . . ," was the first thing Arykah said. "I'm not trying to be funny, but that was like a sanctuary."

Lady McKenzie laughed. "You know, I grew up in the church. I can recall overhearing all sorts of things in the bathroom when I was a girl. It was like the go-to place women went to share their testimonies. When Klymaxx came out with that song 'Meeting in the Ladies' Room,' that's what came to mind. So many tears were shed in that women's restroom. So many prayers went forth. When I shared all this with Pastor McKenzie, he didn't even fight me on the renovation. So, yes, our women's restroom has had a better makeover than our fellowship hall." She laughed again, and the women joined in.

"And the spread we have laid out *is* beautiful too," Lady McKenzie noted and then walked the two women over to the table where the food was.

"My, my, my," Arykah said, putting her hand across her chest. Her mouth watered at the feast before her. Her eyes couldn't take it all in. "Is that potato salad with fine red onion chopped up in it? And is that over there turnip greens with a little bit of cabbage?" Arykah's eyes moved a little farther down the table. "Girlll, is that angel-hair pasta with steamed spinach and garlic?"

It was clear that Lady McKenzie had done her research to find out what Lady Arykah's favorite foods were. Of course, she'd had some of the guest speaker's favorite foods prepared as well. The monetary token of appreciation would have to suffice for the speaker, though.

"How did you know?" Arykah asked.

Lady McKenzie shared that the morning after Lady Arykah agreed to fly to California, she had called Freedom Temple and had introduced herself to Mother Myrtle Cortland, the church's secretary. She had explained to Myrtle that Arykah would be visiting God's Saints Chapel and that she'd like to plan a reception that included some of Arykah's favorites. That would be her little token of appreciation, her way of reminding Arykah how grateful she was for her coming out to California.

Myrtle had revealed to Lady McKenzie all of Lady Arykah's favorite foods. So when Arykah saw that the buffet consisted of potato salad, turnip greens, angel-hair pasta with spinach and garlic, sweet potatoes, hot water corn bread, baked honey ham, meatballs, wing dings, homemade macaroni and cheese, and her favorite dessert, banana pudding, her breath caught in her throat.

"Small reception, my foot," Arykah said to her hostess with a raised eyebrow.

"Oh my God," Angel said as she stood next to Arykah, looking over the delicacies on the table. "This is a feast for a king."

"In this case, a queen," Lady McKenzie said and looked at Lady Arykah.

Arykah's eyes couldn't behold all the food before her. "This is amazing. I love everything you have here." Arykah could have kicked herself for going through the poolside buffet earlier like she was Mrs. Pac-Man. She wanted to return to the ladies' room and take off the remaining Spanx she still wore. Keeping it on would restrict her from eating the way she wanted. But then again, Arykah didn't want to embarrass herself and show everyone her sin of gluttony. She decided that she would be a lady and behave herself properly. She would eat only one serving of everything Lady McKenzie had prepared for her, but she would make sure to leave with a doggie bag.

Lady McKenzie smiled broadly. "I know. I did my homework." Just then she looked up. "Haley, honey, you made it."

Arykah and Angel watched Lady McKenzie embrace the blond-haired, freckle-faced, green-eyed white woman who had approached the three of them at the buffet table.

"I told you that I understood your conflict and that you were excused from attending tonight's service." Lady McKenzie rubbed up and down the woman's back, as if she was comforting her. She pulled away from the woman she had called Haley. "How is he, sweetheart?"

Haley's eyes watered as her voice got caught in her throat.

"Oh, sweetie, it's okay." Lady McKenzie pulled her back into a hug.

"No, no. I'm okay, First Lady," Haley said, pulling away from Lady McKenzie, putting her index finger up under her nose, and sniffing.

Meanwhile, Arykah and Angel stood observing the interaction.

"Oh, I don't mean to be rude," Lady McKenzie said, remembering that Arykah and Angel were standing right there. "Ladies," she said to them, "this is my armor bearer, Haley." Next, Lady McKenzie told Haley the first ladies' names and where they were from.

"Pleased to meet you both," Haley said, wiping tears from her eyes. "I would shake your hands, but . . ." She looked down at her wet hands.

"It's okay. We do hugs," Angel said, then hugged the woman. Arykah followed suit.

"I'm going to go get a napkin to wipe my face," Haley said. "If you'll excuse me," she said to all three women, then walked to the other end of the table, where the paper products were.

"I told her not to come." Lady McKenzie was looking at Haley while talking to the ladies. "Poor thing's husband is in hospice. Found out he had prostate cancer, stage four, just a few months ago. It's all happening so quick." She shook her head. "Let me go tell her she doesn't have to stay." She patted Arykah on the shoulder. "If you'll excuse me, ladies."

Arykah and Angel watched as Lady McKenzie went after Haley. They then turned and looked at each other.

"Miss Haley has no inkling as to who I am and why I'm here," Arykah said.

"Means Lady McKenzie didn't mention your being here or why you're here."

"Means she don't trust her knowing," Arykah said. "That's smart of her. But at the same time, if she don't trust her, why should we?"

Angel nodded, deep in thought.

"You thinking what I'm thinking?" Arykah asked.

"Yeah. That you were right all along," Angel said. "The hussy trying to steal Pastor away from Lady McKenzie wasn't in that sanctuary."

"Uh-huh." Arykah nodded. "But she's darn sure here now."

Chapter 27

Lady McKenzie did her best at insisting Haley go and be with her husband, but Haley declined, stating that helping out at the reception would get her mind off of the inevitable.

Arykah hated to say it, to even think it, but Haley probably cared more about keeping her eye on the prize than being there for her dying husband. After all, and sadly enough, her husband was about to pass. She was already working on her rebound, who just happened to be the married pastor.

Realizing that she was not going to win the battle with her assistant, Lady McKenzie turned over the duties of the reception to Haley. Haley thanked everyone for coming, had one of the church members pray over the food, and then instructed the guests, all of whom were now seated at tables, that once Lady McKenzie, Arykah, and Angel were served, they would be permitted, one table at a time, to get their food.

As she always did, Arykah indulged in the banana pudding first. Whoever made the rule that dessert had to come last needed to repent. "Oh my God," she moaned. She looked at Lady McKenzie, then pointed to her dessert. "See, this right here is blessing my soul right now."

Lady McKenzie chuckled. "I'm so glad you like it. And guess what?"

Lady Arykah looked at her. "Tell me."

"There's another whole pan of banana pudding hidden in the fridge just for you."

Lady Arykah's eyes bulged, and her mouth began to drool. Just the thought of being back in her hotel room, sitting in the middle of her king-size bed with the pillows propped up behind her, intrigued Arykah. She was looking forward to being alone with just her television, her banana pudding, and the peace and quiet. "You're spoiling me," she said to Lady McKenzie. "Really, you are. I mean the wonderful flight, the five-star, all-inclusive resort. It's too much, Lady McKenzie."

Angel agreed with a nod, as her mouth was full of a juicy meatball she'd just popped in it.

"I'm very appreciative that you're here," Lady McKenzie said to Arykah. She then turned and looked at Angel. "Both of you." She smiled, and Angel smiled back.

A young woman who looked to be in her twenties approached the head table and set a red porcelain mug down in front of Lady McKenzie. "Here is some hot lemon tea for you, First Lady." The young woman looked like she could be biracial.

Lady McKenzie looked up at her and smiled. "Thanks, Bryeisha. You always know what I need."

"You're very welcome. Can I get you or your guests anything else?" Bryeisha asked, looking at all three ladies seated at the table.

Arykah quickly sized the young lady up. She seemed eager to please Lady McKenzie. It could be sincere, or she could be trying to play the sweet, innocent, and helpful role so that Lady McKenzie wouldn't suspect anything. Arykah would soon determine which it was.

Arykah had seen Bryeisha helping at the reception, but she hadn't noticed her in the sanctuary during service at all. She must have been helping prepare for the reception the entire time.

"Anything you ladies need," Bryeisha announced, "please don't hesitate to ask." She looked at Lady McKenzie and handed her a couple of extra napkins. "Especially you, First Lady." She then kissed Lady McKenzie on the cheek. That could have been the kiss of Judas, for all Arykah knew.

"Thank you, sweetness," Lady McKenzie replied.

On any other occasion, Arykah might not have thought there was anything out of the ordinary with their little interaction. But this young woman was trying too hard. Even if she were older, Arykah might not have thought much of it. Older saints knew proper etiquette toward a first lady, but young folks had to be taught. And usually it took years of training. This one looked way too young for all that. This new suspect didn't put Haley in the clear, but the PYT was at the top of Arykah's list. Young women these days thought that just because they had a few more miles left on them, a man would rather ride them than his old faithful. Just cocky like that. Well, needless to say, Bryeisha was now on the radar, and if she went too fast, Arykah would have to turn on her lights and sirens and pull her over.

Lady McKenzie leaned forward and looked over at her guests. "I don't think I properly introduced you all. This is Bryeisha, ladies. She's my husband's niece and the church secretary. She'll get you anything you need if you want more of anything."

Just then Arykah exhaled. Unless Pastor McKenzie was on some R. Kelly or Buddy Holly

freaky-deaky ish, there was no way Bryeisha
had a chance at being the secret admirer. And
as young and fine as Bryeisha was, it was safe to
say that she wouldn't be pursuing any man, and
an old one at that, who happened to be her uncle.
Men were probably pursuing her by the dozens.
Arykah didn't do it immediately, but she told
herself that before the night was over, she would
probably have to cross the church secretary off
her mental list of suspects. With Bryeisha looking mixed, it appeared as if Pastor McKenzie's
siblings enjoyed a little dip in the chocolate pool
every now and then as well.

This task might be more difficult than Arykah
had originally thought. She'd hate to have to give
Lady McKenzie her money back if she ended up
being of no help to the woman at all. Heck, she
was going to have to start drawing up a contract
or something. No refunds, exchanges, or returns
if she couldn't crack the case.

After a few minutes, Lady McKenzie asked
Bryeisha to bring her more fruit punch and
Angel requested another helping of macaroni
and cheese. Arykah denied herself something
at the moment. She watched Bryeisha serve
her first lady with a kind and genuine heart.
Bryeisha smiled with every effort she made. She
just looked like good people. But Arykah wasn't

a fool. She didn't go completely by looks. Looks sometimes didn't mean a thing. Prime example was putting Snoop Doggy Dogg next to Martha Stuart. Who was the felon?

But her spirit didn't detect anything foul with Pastor McKenzie's niece, so Arykah eventually decided that Bryeisha wasn't a low-down hussy and exonerated her. Then she had Bryeisha bring her another helping of wing dings. And Bryeisha even served Arykah with a smile as well.

As a matter of fact, all the women present in that room were gracious, kind, and couldn't do enough for their first lady or each other. None of the women had given another a smile in the face and a once-over behind the back, at least not that Arykah had noticed. And she had done her best to study each and every lady who was attending the conference. Not one of them gave Arykah bad vibes. Truth be told, even Haley's spirit seemed clean. Well, not at first, of course. It wasn't until after Arykah deliberately and accidentally bumped into her in the kitchen that she changed her opinion about Lady McKenzie's assistant.

At first it was like a red flag that Lady McKenzie had kept trying to get Haley to leave, yet Haley had insisted on staying. Now that was the spirit of a troll who wasn't going to miss sucking up to the first lady if life depended on it, even if it was her husband's. But then Haley had finally given in and had admitted that maybe she did need to remain by her husband's side, that she had been operating in fear. Haley agreed that she'd head out right after she finished tidying up a couple of things.

Arykah spotted Haley going to the kitchen area, which she had done a couple of times that evening, both she and Bryeisha. They would refill the food or take empty pans back to the kitchen.

"Ladies, please excuse me for a moment," Arykah said as she stood.

Lady McKenzie probably assumed that Arykah was going to the restroom again, but Angel knew better. Lady McKenzie's back was to the kitchen, but Angel was facing it, and she saw Arykah slip through the kitchen door.

In the kitchen Arykah found Haley standing over the sink. She walked over to her and saw that her shoulders were shaking, as if she was laughing. As Arykah got closer, she realized that Haley wasn't laughing at all.

"Haley?" Arykah said with concern.

Haley looked over her shoulder and saw Arykah standing very close to her. She quickly wiped the tears from her eyes with her hands and gathered her composure. "Yes, Lady Arykah? May I get something for you?"

"No. I don't need anything," Arykah said. "But I wanted to check on you. Are you okay?"

Haley forced a smile. "Yes, I'm fine."

"No, you're not," Arykah countered. "Lady McKenzie shared with me the news about your husband."

Haley's eyes bucked wide; then they retracted. Arykah knew she was upset that her first lady would share her personal information with a stranger.

"Please don't be angry with Lady McKenzie. She loves you, and she's concerned. I have an armor bearer who is actually my best friend. She and I have been through many trials together."

How quickly Arykah's feelings toward Haley had turned. Right now, she was truly concerned about the woman, rather than entertaining the thought that Haley could be responsible for making Lady McKenzie's life miserable. Arykah felt a pull toward Haley. She needed to comfort her. Bless her. Lift her up before God. At that moment, Arykah knew that she was in California not only for Lady McKenzie, but for Haley as well.

"Tell me more about your husband's condition," Arykah said. "I understand that he's suffering from cancer."

More tears spilled onto Haley's cheeks. Arykah stepped closer to her and wiped them away with her hand. Her heart broke for Haley. She was so young, yet she had been dealt a heavy blow. Arykah didn't know what she would do if she were in Haley's shoes. She couldn't even imagine the pain and agony she would go through if Lance were stricken with a terminal illness. She didn't think she could survive without him.

Haley did, in fact, want to open up to Arykah, but she was hesitant. At first she wondered why Arykah was so interested. Then she looked into Arykah's eyes and saw a woman with a sincere spirit. She could almost feel warmth coming from Arykah's body. "He has stage four prostate cancer."

Even though Arykah already knew this, she was still somewhat shocked. Haley didn't look to be more than thirty years old. Arykah assumed she'd married a man closer to Arykah's own age. Prostate cancer was normally a problem for middle-aged men.

"How old is your husband, and what is his name?"

"Joshua is thirty-seven."

"Oh my goodness," Arykah said. "Prostate cancer at his age? Are you sure? Have you gotten a second opinion?" The diagnosis couldn't be right.

Haley nodded her head. "We've gotten a second, a third, and even a fourth opinion. Each doctor was just as shocked at their findings."

Arykah's heart sank. Everyone who had been born had to die at some point. Arykah imagined the perfect death was when someone was one hundred years old and slipped away in his or her sleep. But to be given a death sentence at just thirty-seven seemed so unfair. "I am so sorry, Haley. I can't begin to imagine the pain that you and Joshua are going through. Is he a saved man?"

More tears dripped onto Haley's cheeks. She sniffed a couple of times before saying, "Yes, he is."

Arykah grabbed Haley's hands with her own and began to pray. She petitioned the throne of grace like never before. Some of Arykah's words Haley understood, and some she did not. Arykah spoke in an unknown tongue as she called out Joshua's name. She prayed for a divine healing in Jesus' name. The more Arykah prayed, the tighter her grip became on Haley's hands. At some point Haley's knees wobbled. It was like Arykah's prayer was draining the very strength from her body.

Bryeisha entered the kitchen, carrying two empty water pitchers. She stopped dead in her tracks when she saw the two women holding hands, with their heads bowed. Bryeisha saw tears pouring from Haley's eyes. She stood silently and listened to Arykah's prayer. Bryeisha thought Lady McKenzie's guest was a powerhouse as she spoke to God on Haley's behalf.

"We claim heeaaling, ha. In the name of Jeeesus, ha," Arykah sang. "Father, in the naaamme of Jesus, we need yoouu to do a miraculous thing for Brother Joshua, ha. No, we won't believe the doctor's report, ha. But we're gonna belieeeve the report of the Lorrrd, ha."

Bryeisha was moved at Arykah's words. She saw that Haley was having a hard time standing on her own two feet. It seemed that Haley was intoxicated. She was swaying from side to side as she held on to Arykah's hands. Bryeisha set the pitchers on a nearby table and came and stood directly behind Haley. She placed her hands on the left and right sides of Haley's waist.

"Open up the heavens, Lorrrd, ha, and pour out a blessing for Brother Joshua right now. I know you can, ha. And I know you will, ha. Now, Lorrrd, ha." Arykah stomped her left foot on the floor. "Now, Lorrrd, ha." She stomped her foot again. "The doctors have said no, but you can still say yehesss, ha."

"Glory to God," Bryeisha blurted out. She couldn't keep her silence any longer.

Suddenly, there were more hands on Haley. She felt someone place a hand on her forehead, while another person pressed a palm against her abdomen. Haley didn't open her eyes. She knew women were around her, probably others who had been helping with the reception, and they made her feel as though she was wrapped in a warm quilted blanket. They gave her a sense of security. Haley kept her hands tightly in Arykah's grip.

Arykah kept singing and praying. Sweat began to stream down both sides of her face. "Now unto Heeyimah, who is able to dohoo exceedingly abundantly above all that we could ever ask or even think, ha. According to the power that worketh in us, ha."

There were voices all around Haley. Encouraging words flowed throughout the kitchen. Arykah released Haley's hands and put pressure on her chest, which caused Haley to stumble backward.

"Cancer!" Arykah hollered out. "You gotsta leave Brother Joshua's body, ha. You done took up residence loonng enough, ha. You have worn out your stay, ha. *Get out!*" she screamed.

The voices surrounding Haley became louder, as the others began to pray for their sister.

"Keep the faith, Sister Haley," Arykah said to her. "God always has the last say-so." She stepped closer to Haley and blew in her face. In less than a second, Haley fell into Bryeisha's arms.

Arykah had gone boldly to the throne of grace. She had gotten somewhat boisterous, and she'd even broken out in a sweat. But unlike the evening's earlier speaker, Arykah had done it all in the mighty and most powerful name of Jesus. Amen.

Chapter 28

Back in the fellowship hall, after the deliverance that had just taken place in the kitchen and after Arykah had sent Haley to be with her husband, the three first ladies were seated and were eating again. Arykah drank from a glass of lemon iced tea that she had been served. Her throat was parched after she had gone hard for Haley's husband. But that was what Arykah was known for. She was a powerhouse when she got in the presence of the Lord.

Back in Chicago, at her home church, Arykah was often approached with special prayer requests from her members. There had been times when members walked directly past Bishop Lance Howell's office and knocked on Arykah's door for prayer. It wasn't that the members of Freedom Temple didn't trust that their pastor would pray for them and ask the Lord to fulfill their needs, but when Arykah prayed, she prayed. She got down and dirty with it. When Arykah finished praying for them, the members knew, without a shadow of a doubt, that God had heard her. They left her presence with the confidence that came from knowing that Jesus would indeed make everything all right.

Arykah had been putting off sharing her report about the night with Lady McKenzie. Unlike her visit to Ohio, it looked like finding the husband stealer was definitely going to take more than a day's work.

She swallowed a large gulp of the iced tea, then leaned into Lady McKenzie. "She's not here." Arykah had never been one to beat around the bush, play ring-around-the-rosy, sugarcoat things—none of that. She was not at God's Saints Chapel to waste anybody's time, especially her own. Unlike tonight's speaker, when Arykah was on assignment from God, she didn't even think about making it about herself and using God's time and name to benefit herself.

Lady McKenzie looked at Lady Arykah. "*Who's* not here?"

"The woman who's pushing up on your man. She's not here tonight."

Lady McKenzie looked all around the fellowship hall at the women, who were eating and chatting with one another. She then leaned into Arykah. "How can you be sure of that?"

"I have discerned each lady. No one is after the pastor. Everyone in this room has a genuine love and respect for you. The skank isn't here."

That was disappointing news for Lady McKenzie. She had hoped that Arykah would come to California and fix her problem, just as she had done for Angel back in Ohio. The way Angel had told it, it had taken Arykah less than twenty-four hours.

Lady McKenzie's situation was completely different, but secretly, her expectations had been the same. So maybe Arykah couldn't turn things around in only a day. She had thought, though, that she could at least get a good start on it and that she would have something more to report by now. Even if Arykah merely pointed her in the right direction in terms of who she should watch out for, Lady McKenzie could handle the rest. She had grown up in Compton and was no punk. She'd take it to the streets, like a gangsta, if she had to, but she didn't want things to go that far.

The last thing Lady McKenzie wanted was to bring any type of embarrassment to herself, her husband, or her church. That was why she was certain that God wanted to step in, use one of His own to address this situation for her. Lady McKenzie was a saint. She loved the Lord. She'd represented God's Saints Chapel with much love and integrity toward her fellow man. Those women loved her. She knew them all by name. Some were like sisters to her, and the younger women like daughters, especially since she and Pastor didn't have any children of their own. Both of them were in their late thirties, so in this day and age, it was definitely still possible for them to start a family outside of their church family. The two of them had always wanted children, but lately, with ministry taking priority, they'd been like two ships passing in the night. And now some little dinghy was trying to row up to Pastor McKenzie and sail off into the sunset with him.

Lady McKenzie hated to think that for one moment one of her sisters in Christ would disrespect her marriage in such a way. But who else could it be? All the items the secret admirer had left had been left at the church, so it had to be a member. If that was the case, though, then why couldn't she discern who it was on her own? After all, there wasn't but a handful of women there.

Lady McKenzie felt that her closeness to these women was what kept her from discerning who the culprit was. Her heart didn't want to believe that one of them could betray her in such a way, so her eyes wouldn't let her see who it was.

That was why she needed Arykah. She needed someone who wasn't biased in any form or fashion, someone who could call out the spirit of Jezebel. But now that Arykah had also failed at detecting a non-genuine heart, Lady McKenzie felt defeated.

"Will you excuse me?" Lady McKenzie said, her eyes watering. "I need to go to the ladies' room." She stood and hurriedly exited the fellowship hall.

Arykah and Angel looked at each other.

Arykah had witnessed the somber look on Lady McKenzie's face. She shook her head. "Child, I know what it's like not knowing, not knowing if the next woman who calls your husband up for prayer really just wants to get on her knees *just* to pray," Arykah stressed. "If you know what I mean."

"Oh, I *know* what you mean," Angel replied. "Those first few times Isaiah got phone calls at night because one of the sisters was in need, I'd be lying in bed, praying. At first I would truly be praying for the sister in need, her family, or whatever situation that was going on that required his spiritual guidance. But then my prayers would turn into selfish ones." Angel chuckled. "Me praying away any spirit of deceit, lust, and manipulation that one of these women might be hiding behind." She chuckled again.

Arykah pulled her neck back so far, it conjured up the image of a giraffe. "That is *no* laughing matter."

"What?" Angel asked. "My husband having to go out in the middle of the night to tend to some of his female members?"

"No, you *letting* him," Arykah said. "Girl, I don't care how tired you are, if you just stayed up all night rewatching every season of *Scandal* on Netflix, you get your behind up and go with your man," Arykah exhorted.

"But I trust that prayer works. Isaiah always prays before he leaves. I cover him in prayer the entire time. I just didn't think it was necessary for me to go along. And in addition to that, I don't want him to think that I don't trust him."

"I trust Lance wholeheartedly," Arykah said in a "Don't get it twisted" manner. "It's some of them so-called women of God that I don't trust."

"So you mean to tell me you get up out of bed *every* time your husband gets one of those calls? You get dressed and go with him?"

"Absolutely not." Arykah shook her head emphatically. "Sometimes I go with rollers in my hair, my big fuzzy slippers on, and my coat over my pajamas. I'm not playing with these folks or the devil." She looked at Angel. "And you shouldn't, either." Arykah let out a harrumph.

"And truth be told, Angel, the women at my church haven't called my home in the wee hours of the night in a long time. They know better. It took only one time for me to set them hussies straight."

"What do you mean?" Angel asked her.

"Two weeks after Bishop Lance and I were married, we got a call at two in the morning from a chick at the church, saying that she was in distress and she needed the bishop to come and lay hands on her. I didn't question Lance about it. I got my behind up out of that bed, brushed my teeth, then got in the car with my husband. He thought that I was just going to support him, but I had my own agenda."

Angel was intrigued. "Girl, what happened when y'all got there?"

"I told Lance to stay in the car and that I wanted to handle this request as the new first lady of Freedom Temple. Well, I rang the tramp's doorbell, and she answered it, wearing her birthday suit. She got the shock of her life when she saw me standing there with my robe and hair curlers on."

Angel's mouth fell open. "Wha . . . ha . . . you . . . err . . ." She couldn't get any proper words out of her mouth.

"When she saw that it was me and not the bishop, she tried to close the door shut, but I pushed it back open. I came at the door with all my two hundred and eighty pounds. That door didn't stand a chance."

"Oh my God, Arykah! Did you kill her?" Angel was genuinely worried. She really felt that Arykah would put someone in a body bag if she had to.

Arykah shook her head. "Nah. I prayed for her," she said nonchalantly.

"You *prayed* for her?" Angel shrieked. "What you mean, you prayed for her?"

Arykah looked at Angel. "Well, that's what she said she needed. I told that chick that she was to neva, eva, eva, eva ring my telephone again. I also told her that she needed to remove herself from the roll at Freedom Temple, 'cause if she stepped foot in the church again, I was gonna stomp a hole in her hind parts. I asked her if she understood, and she nodded her head. And after that, I simply bowed my head and said, 'Jesus wept,' and walked out the door. The following Sunday, right before the benediction, I stood before the church and told the congregation what happened."

Angel gasped. "You didn't!"

Arykah looked at Angel and turned up the sides of her mouth. "You *know* I did. I warned every chick in the house that I wasn't to be played with and that I am not the woman to try. My phone ain't rang in the wee hours of the morning since."

"You're a bully, Arykah," Angel said to her.

Arykah nodded her head and owned up to it. "I'm a beast too. And guess what?" she said to Angel. "I ain't got Lady McKenzie's problem, either."

Just then Bryeisha walked over to the table. "Is everything okay with First Lady?" she asked. "I saw her get up and leave a minute ago. I was helping Mother Jenkins out, so I couldn't immediately see about her. Is all well?"

Arykah paused for a moment. "You know what, honey? Why don't you finish helping the good people of God's Saints Chapel, and First Lady Angel and I will go see about Lady McKenzie." Arykah said all this as she stood, kindly letting the young lady know that it wasn't really a suggestion. "Okay?"

"Yes, ma'am." Bryeisha nodded, concern about Lady McKenzie filling her eyes.

Angel stood. She patted Bryeisha on the shoulder as she followed Arykah out of the fellowship hall and to the ladies' room.

They found Lady McKenzie sitting on a lounge chair in the ladies' room. She was surrounded by three other women, who were seated on the lounge chair with her. One woman patted Lady McKenzie's right hand and asked if she was okay. Another woman removed the cap from a bottle of drinking water and gave the bottle to her first lady. The third woman sat at Lady McKenzie's feet, with concern written all over her face.

Lady McKenzie wasn't crying, but all those who were present knew that she was upset. She swallowed two gulps of the water, then said, "I'm all right, ladies. No need for any of you to be concerned."

"But we are concerned, Lady McKenzie. We've never seen you this way before," said the woman who sat at her feet.

Arykah walked farther into the room, with Angel close on her heels. "Ladies," Arykah said, addressing the women who were supporting Lady McKenzie, "can First Lady Angel and I speak with Lady McKenzie privately please?"

None of the three women made a move to honor Arykah's request. They didn't know why their first lady was upset. And they didn't feel comfortable leaving her alone with complete strangers. For all they knew, Arykah and Angel could be the reason why Lady McKenzie was distressed.

"Why privately?" asked the lady who was seated the closest to Lady McKenzie. She had seen Arykah whisper words to her first lady before she stood from her chair and rushed out of the fellowship hall.

Arykah's posture shifted upon hearing the woman's inquiry. Her features changed.

Angel gently grabbed Arykah's elbow before she made a move. Arykah made eye contact with Angel, then brought her gaze back to the woman who had questioned her.

"It's fine," Lady McKenzie said to all the ladies. "It's okay to leave us alone."

"Are you sure?" asked the lady who was caressing her hand.

Arykah sucked her teeth loudly. She was about ten seconds from jumping on all three of the women at once. They were working her last nerve.

"How about we go into my office, Lady Arykah?" Lady McKenzie said as she stood from the lounge chair. "We'll have all the privacy we need."

Arykah and Angel followed her out of the ladies' room. Arykah knew the three women were going to talk about her behind her back, but she didn't give a darn. She had to pick her battles, and in her spirit she knew she had to save her strength for the all-out war to come.

Chapter 29

Lady McKenzie entered her office and plopped down in her chair. Arykah stepped into the office, and Angel followed her inside and shut the door behind them. Arykah saw the distraught look on Lady McKenzie's face. It broke her heart to see the first lady in such a downtrodden state. Even if Arykah had to flip the dime herself, she was not going to leave California with her sister in Christ broken down like this. So she mocked one of her favorite characters on a reality show when she thought to herself, *Jesus, fix it*. It might not have worked for Phaedra Parks and Apollo, but Arykah prayed it would work for the McKenzies.

"Don't you worry. I'll get to the bottom of what's going on," Arykah said to Lady McKenzie as she watched Angel grab a tissue from a box of Kleenex on top of the first lady's desk and give it to her. Arykah meant every word of it. She didn't believe in giving folks false hopes. She felt in her gut that the Holy Spirit was leading her to the truth, a truth that would set Lady McKenzie free from being bound. Arykah spoke with authority. She was done coddling the first lady. It was time to be a soldier in the army of the Lord and get back to work. "You told me that you and your husband have been keeping the items he receives from this wannabe mistress."

Lady McKenzie nodded.

"I need to see the cards, gifts, notes, candy, panties." Arykah threw her hands up. "And whatever else your husband has received from his secret admirer."

"Certainly," Lady McKenzie said. She stood from the chair and escorted the women out of her office. "We keep them in the storage closet upstairs, above our offices."

"This place has an upstairs?" Arykah asked.

"Yes," Lady McKenzie answered. "That's all that's up there, though. Just the storage room." She looked around as she walked down the small hallway and passed the fellowship hall. "This used to be a house before we turned it into a church." She nodded at the room where the reception was taking place. "That was the family dining room, which, of course, is now our fellowship hall," Lady McKenzie said. "The pastor's office to the left was the master bedroom. My office was another bedroom."

"That's how my husband's and my offices are set up," Angel said, chiming in. "Right across from one another."

"That's our private staff bathroom." Lady McKenzie pointed. "And next to it is where Bryeisha works. I think the family who once lived here used it as a small den or TV room or something."

"I take it the sanctuary was the living room," Arykah said.

"Yes, but we added five feet onto it," Lady McKenzie told her. She reached a door at the end of the hall, where she stopped and turned around to face the ladies. "Above here is the attic, which we use as our storage room." She opened the door. "I think one of the older children of the family who lived here used it as their bedroom." Lady McKenzie walked up the steps. Angel was right behind her, and Arykah went last. "As a matter of fact, I think it belonged to the older child, who had actually passed." Lady McKenzie continued to talk as she climbed the steps. "He committed suicide in this very house."

"That's awful," Angel gasped, still on Lady McKenzie's heels.

"The child didn't die immediately. He spent a couple of weeks in the hospital, brain dead, before the family decided to let him go on and be with the Lord." Lady McKenzie reached the top of the steps. She waited for Angel to arrive before she stood in front of her and continued. "Because it was a suicide, the insurance policy wouldn't pay. They were stuck with hospital bills, funeral expenses. They lost the house. It went into foreclosure, and we got it for a steal. It's unfortunate that their tragedy turned out to be a blessing to us, because God's Saints Chapel has been like a home to this little community. Everyone here knows each other."

Angel smiled. "Yes, Lady Arykah and I were saying that we bet everyone here was just like family. Weren't we, Arykah?" Angel said, staring at Lady McKenzie, waiting for Arykah to respond. When Angel didn't get a response, she asked again. "Weren't we, Arykah?" She turned to see that Arykah was not up in the attic with them.

Both Angel and Lady McKenzie looked down the steps to see that Arykah was still on the second step from the bottom—right where she had been when Lady McKenzie first mentioned something about a death taking place in that house.

"Lady Arykah," Lady McKenzie said with concern. "I'm sorry. Are the steps too much for you?" she asked.

"Or maybe you should lay off the Spanx altogether," Angel snapped at her in a hushed whisper.

Arykah threw her hands on her hips, tilted her head to the side, and shot Angel a look, as if to ask, "How you gon' throw me under the bus about my support situation in front of company?"

An apologetic look crossed Angel's face as she shrugged, then mouthed, "Sorry."

Arykah sucked her teeth and rolled her eyes. "But, anyway, it ain't the steps, and it ain't the Spanx," she told them.

"Then what is it?" Lady McKenzie asked, confused but eager to make right whatever was wrong.

Arykah looked from one first lady to the next. Both Angel and Lady McKenzie stood at the top of the steps, eager to resolve the situation so that they could do what they'd come up to the attic to do.

"Lady Arykah, please, what's wrong?" Lady McKenzie asked with much concern.

Arykah swept both ladies with her eyes just one more time for good measure. "You two are serious, aren't you?" Arykah looked at Lady McKenzie. "Now, you might be used to it by now, but, Angel . . ." She looked at her friend. "Angel, if you don't get your narrow behind down these steps," she said, pointing to the step beneath her, "you getting left right here with the bogeyman, because me and Elroy will be down the street, heading back to the hotel." Arykah pulled her phone out. "Matter of fact, let me call him now to come meet me out front." Arykah went to turn and walk back down the couple of steps she'd climbed. "Where's that card at?" she said in reference to the card their limo driver had given them.

"Girl, what are you talking about?" Angel asked as she stood at the top of the steps, with her hands on her hips. "Ain't no dang bogeyman, and you, as a Christian woman, should know better."

"And you, as a black woman, should know better," Arykah spat back before she turned around and got a chance to walk down the steps. "Now, Lady McKenzie"—she looked at the host first lady—"I mean no disrespect." Then she glanced back at Angel and, with a hand cupped around her mouth, said in a harsh whisper, "She's married to a white man. Some of their nonsense might have rubbed off on her. She don't know no better."

At this point it didn't matter how dark Angel's skin was. Her beet-red cheeks stood out like Rudolph's nose in the midst of all those other reindeer. "Arykah, you *do* know that if I can hear you, *she* can too?" Angel replied in the same harsh whisper. She had also placed her hand on the side of her mouth and was pointing to Lady McKenzie with her other hand.

Arykah leaned in sarcastically, as if she was going to whisper again. "And *you* know she can hear you too." She made the same pointing gesture at Lady McKenzie.

"Ladies, ladies," Lady McKenzie interrupted. "Please." She patted the thick air down with her hands, a signal for her guests to settle down. She did not want their little tiff to escalate. She looked at Arykah. "Please, Lady Arykah, share with me your concerns," she pleaded.

"I'm concerned that you two black women are up in the attic, where some kid committed suicide. Then he didn't die right away. His family lost everything, including the house in which he killed himself, a house that they had to sell for dirt cheap. They're probably homeless now, and his sisters are probably turning tricks just for a Happy Meal, yet we all up in their house, happy, praising the Lord, shouting hallelujah, and eating a feast. That poor boy probably real good and pissed off now, so I'm getting out of here before he gets to making lamps fly across the room and picture frames fall off the wall." She stepped down her last step, which placed her on the bottom landing.

"Arykah, girl, now cut it out," Angel said. "You know we are covered in the blood of Jesus."

"And that's the only blood I want to be covered in." She pointed to each lady. "Not yours and not yours. So I'm out."

Angel looked at Lady McKenzie, totally embarrassed by her friend's words. She wanted to apologize to her, but Arykah had turned to walk away, so Angel made the split-second decision to try to stop her. "I'll be right back, Lady McKenzie." Angel hurried back down the steps as quickly as she could in her stilettos. By the time she reached the bottom, Arykah was clear past the fellowship hall. "Arykah, wait up. Hold on," Angel called out, having to pick up speed to catch up with her.

Angel had never seen a woman of Arykah's size move so quickly, not even to get to a buffet. She was out of breath by the time she caught up with her friend. She could barely speak. "Arykah, please wait," she huffed.

"That's why we can't find the whore up here trying to steal Pastor McKenzie. There ain't one. It's a ghost. This joint is haunted, and like I said before, I'm out of here." Arykah went to walk off again. "Shoot, I got enough spirits to contend with back in the Midwest. I don't need to be bringing no new ones all the way from the West Coast," she fussed.

It took Angel only a couple of steps to catch up with Arykah this time. She grabbed her friend by the arm, stopping her in her tracks. "We are here to help Lady McKenzie, in spite of the history of this place." Angel looked around. "We do not operate in fear. God did not give us the spirit of fear."

"I'm not operating in fear," Arykah said, clarifying matters. "I'm using wisdom. And forgive me for saying it, but you acting just as stupid as some of them white folks in those horror movies we used to sneak in and see as youngins. Black people don't go to the light, Carol Ann. And when black people walk into a big, spooky-looking house and a voice whispers 'Get out,' we get the hell out. So bye!" Arykah turned to stomp off one last time.

"No. I will not let you leave." Angel had a death grip on Arykah's arm, but Arykah must have literally had the strength of Christ, because she was dragging poor Angel down the hall on her two stilettos like in a scene in a cartoon. "Stop it. Stop it," Angel commanded her.

Finally, Arykah did stop, but only to check Angel. "Look, sis, I love you. I brought you here with me, hoping you would be the voice of reason, but there ain't nothing reasonable about wanting to go sniffing around an attic after hearing the story Lady McKenzie just told us."

Arykah got nose to nose with Angel and said through gritted teeth, "I oughta make you turn in your black woman card right now." She pulled away from Angel and straightened herself out. "If you want to stay, that's fine. I'll look into getting Mary Mary or just one of the Marys to sing at your funeral. Depends if they still together or not, because you know Tina be tripping, but nonetheless, I'm taking myself back to that five-star resort, where the only spirits I'll be dealing with come with olives on a toothpick. Now in the words of Russell Simmons, 'God bless you. Good night.'"

Arykah turned on her heels and headed for the door.

"Fine," Angel shouted. "I'll tell Lady McKenzie that you decided to vacate your assignment." Then Angel said in a very convicting voice, "Now, what are *you* going to tell God?"

Chapter 30

Angel and Arykah were headed back to the attic, with Arykah still fussing at Angel under her breath.

"How you gon' bring God into it?" Arykah said.

"How you gon' leave Him out?" Angel replied in a huff.

"Oh, now you wanna jump bad," Arykah said. "You should have been jumping bad when Mother Calloway was 'bout to go upside your head, but no, you wanna jump bad with the person who saved you from Aunt Esther back in the ole days of *Sanford and Son.*"

Angel ignored Arykah's insults. "I know I came here on an assignment. That's to have your back and be the voice of reason. I'm not going to abandon my assignment by letting you abandon yours."

As far as Arykah was concerned, she'd been as good as out that door before Angel had to go and remind her that she was in California because that was where God would have her be. If she left the church, not only would she not be keeping her commitment to Lady McKenzie, but she wouldn't have been keeping it to God, either. Knowing there were consequences to pay for disobedience, she had turned her butt around and marched right back into that church, fuming.

"You can stop pouring salt on the wound," Arykah said. "I'm here. You've fulfilled your assignment. Now I'm gonna fulfill my assignment and get out of here."

Angel smiled and lightly elbowed her friend. "I knew you would come to your senses and come back."

"Yeah, you're right. I did come to my senses. I would have been a fool to walk out of here without my banana pudding."

"Jesus, fix it for real," Angel said under her breath as the two women reached the steps to the attic. She walked up the first two steps and realized that Arykah was still hesitant. She walked back down the steps, got behind Arykah, and then nudged her to go up the stairs.

"I'm going. I'm going," Arykah huffed and then continued huffing every step of the way until she reached the top, where Lady McKenzie was over at a table, with a large-size plastic bin in front of her.

Lady McKenzie didn't waste time by asking the two ladies questions about Arykah's temporary disappearing act. That was neither here nor there. Her help was back. She immediately began pulling items out of the box to show Arykah.

"At first it started off with little cards like this, which would be mixed in the basket with the tithes and offerings." Lady McKenzie held up a small manila stock card with the handwritten words *I offer myself to the Lord . . . and to you, Pastor.*

"Now, this some bold mess right here," Arykah said. "This chick didn't even care that whoever would count the money would see this." She then asked Lady McKenzie, "Who counts the money?"

"Sometimes the pastor and sometimes myself. But we usually have someone from treasury right there in the room with us."

"Do you remember who was counting the day this first note was received?" Arykah asked.

"It was me. When I saw it, I was shocked. But I simply put it to the side and addressed it with my husband later." After explaining, Lady McKenzie pulled a box of chocolates from the bin.

Arykah stood in disbelief. "She gave your husband those too?"

Lady McKenzie nodded, handing the box to Arykah. "Left them on his desk one evening, sometime during Bible study."

"Your husband found them?" Arykah asked.

Lady McKenzie shook her head. "No. Me again. My husband had sent me up to his office to grab his jacket. That's when I spotted them on his desk, wrapped in a ribbon."

"Was there a note attached?" Arykah asked, examining the box.

Lady McKenzie began digging around in the bin. "Yeah. I think I kept it." She continued looking and then pulled out a little card and handed it to Arykah as well.

Arykah read the card out loud. "Since I know you like chocolate, here's for your sweet tooth." Arykah looked up at Lady McKenzie. "Oh, so she got jokes too? She's playing on the fact that your husband is a white man married to a black woman."

"Hmm," Angel said. She had been silent up to this point, allowing Arykah to do her detective work. In her mind, it could be a woman with race issues. That note could have been her little dig at Pastor for not choosing someone of his own race. The woman could have been attempting to bring him back to their side. It was possible that she didn't have anything against black people. It was also possible that she did have something against black people being in a relationship with white people.

Arykah still stood there in disbelief, with the chocolates and note in her hands. "I can't believe this."

"I know, right?" Lady McKenzie said. "Heifer buying my husband chocolates." She crossed her arms and then rolled her eyes.

"Not that," Arykah said. "Unbelievable that these chocolates are all the way from Germany and y'all didn't eat not a one. What a waste."

"Uh, Lady McKenzie," Angel said, trying to keep things on track, "what else is in there?" She nodded at the bin.

Both Arykah's and Angel's jowls dropped when Lady McKenzie pulled out a pair of men's black silk boxers. Lady McKenzie laid them on the table and then stepped back.

Arykah went to pick them up but paused first. She looked at Lady McKenzie. "I'm figuring since he didn't eat the chocolate, he didn't wear these drawers, either."

"Oh, no, he didn't wear them," Lady McKenzie confirmed.

Arykah picked them up and examined them, looked at the tag. "What size does your husband wear?" she asked.

"That size." Lady McKenzie nodded toward the underwear Arykah held in her hands. "She was right on the money, which means she has literally been sizing my man up." She then pulled more cards, notes, and items out of the bin, then placed four of the cards on the table. "This is everything that arrived here at the church."

Angel's mouth was still hanging open after seeing the pair of boxers. She had no words for the disrespect. What kind of woman would do something so trifling and then think that a man wanted her?

Arykah placed the underwear and the chocolates on the table and then began examining the items that lay before her. She thought it was childish the way the secret admirer was stepping to the pastor. "These are games that kids play."

Angel looked at Arykah. "How do you mean?"

Arykah picked up the box of chocolates. "Although these are made in Germany, they can be picked up at any convenience store, just like those delicious gummy bears that are made in Germany that you can get at the dang dollar store now. So, clearly, the trick didn't spend any *real* money by springing for Fannie May chocolates."

In Arykah's mind, if a woman was trying to steal a man from his wife, she would go all out. The quality of these items indicated that hardly any thought had been put into them at all. Simply not the actions of a woman, period, let alone a man-stealing floozy.

Arykah set the chocolates on the table and picked up the boxers again. She rubbed the fabric between her thumb and index finger. "This cheap material." She shook her head and held the boxers up in the air. "These were purchased at Walmart all day long." She tossed them inside the bin and picked up the four cards that Lady McKenzie had placed on the table. She turned them over and looked at the back of each card. "Humph. The heifer couldn't even spring for Hallmark?"

Arykah shook her head. She opened a couple of the cards and then read them silently to herself. "Generic thoughts," she said out loud. The mystery woman hadn't put any thought into the messages inside the cards. Arykah herself had once stood in the card section of a store for over an hour, trying to find the perfect birthday card for Lance. Men might be able to go inside a store and randomly pick out a card, but women took it more seriously. The words had to be almost as if they'd written them themselves. They had to draw forth emotions, and the cards Arykah had read thus far completely lacked emotion.

She turned the cards over again. This time she wasn't looking at the name brand. "I'll tell you what. Whoever is behind this is a cheap ho, that's for sure," Arykah commented out loud. Once again, this mystery woman had opted to do her shopping at the dollar store.

Angel put her hand on her forehead due to how blunt Arykah was. She looked over at Lady McKenzie, who hadn't been affected by Arykah's words at all. She was just standing there, like an understudy to the world's greatest brain surgeon. She was watching Arykah closely and taking mental notes.

"A dollar each." Arykah flung the cards back on the table. One slid off the table and onto the floor. "This doesn't make sense to me."

"What doesn't?" Lady McKenzie asked, picking up the card that had fallen.

"Let me tell you something," Lady Arykah said, looking at Lady McKenzie dead in her eyes. "If I wanted to impress a man, especially a man of the cloth, I certainly wouldn't shop for gifts at Dollar General." Lady Arykah looked at the boxers and candy, then at the cards. She shrugged her shoulders. "This all looks suspect to me." She raised an eyebrow at Lady McKenzie.

"Suspect?" Lady McKenzie was confused. "What exactly do you mean by suspect? I can assure you that these things aren't fake. This entire situation is very much real and has had me losing sleep at nights. I myself pretty much found the majority of the items. It was just humiliating." Lady McKenzie's eyes filled with tears. "The boxers were in his private mailbox here at the church. I found them the time he asked me to stop up at the church and grab his mail for him. I pulled them from the mailbox myself. They weren't wrapped, packaged, or anything."

Arykah snapped her head back and let out a shriek. "*The mailbox?* They weren't delivered by U.S. mail, UPS, FedEx, or anything else?"

Lady McKenzie shook her head. "No. There wasn't even a postmark or a tracking number that I could use to even begin to research who they could have come from."

Arykah sighed. "This is all so juvenile. So tacky. Like a kid who's got a crush on another kid but doesn't want them to know it." She looked at Lady McKenzie and then at Angel. "I smell a rat."

"I do too," Lady McKenzie said to Arykah. "That's why I called on you. I need you to exterminate."

Arykah picked another one of the cards up and read it. This one had a hand-penned message, in addition to the standard one that was printed by machine inside the card. She read the handwritten message out loud.

"When I'm near you, I feel faint. I lose my breath at the very sight of you. She can't love you like I can."

Angel shook her head. "Humph, humph, humph. The nerve." She looked at Lady McKenzie sympathetically. She couldn't even imagine having to deal with something like this. She'd take Mother Calloway over a secret admirer any day.

"You see what I'm dealing with?" Lady McKenzie asked Arykah. "It's too much." She broke down in tears.

Neither Angel's nor Lady McKenzie's words had penetrated Arykah's brain. She was focused on the handwritten letters in the card. The cursive writing was familiar to her. The way the letters *l* and *k* looped. And the hook in the letter *y* wasn't complete. The way the letter *t* was crossed with a slanted line. She'd seen those particular letters written in that style before.

Arykah stared at the letters hard, like she was dissecting them. She was in a trance.

Angel stepped to her. "Arykah, you all right?"

Arykah put her hand up. "Yeah. Just give me a minute," she answered without removing her eyeballs from the familiar-looking letters.

Both Lady McKenzie and Angel stood still, quietly staring at Arykah. They watched her eyes bulge, then decrease in size. They saw her shake her head from side to side, then nod.

Arykah closed her eyes tight. She had to recall where she had seen those same letters. It took her a second, but she did ultimately recall it. Her eyes opened to the size of golf balls. "Well, pluck my chicken a thousand times, why don't ya?" Arykah said. How could she have forgotten just that quickly? Her mouth dropped open; then she closed it. She opened it again, staring down at the card, but then closed it once more.

"Dang it, Arykah. Unless you got TMJ and are trying to crack your jawbone, for crying out loud, *say* something," Angel spat.

Arykah looked at her, then at Lady McKenzie. "Can't be," she mumbled under her breath. "But why?" she asked no one in particular. She began shaking her head. "I just don't under . . ." Her words trailed off when yet another lightbulb went off in her head.

"What? What is it?" Lady McKenzie was getting somewhat agitated.

Arykah tossed the card back onto the table. She looked up at the ceiling. "I know good and doggone well that I ain't fly all the way to California for this. Is this some kind of prank? I mean, I know you got jokes, God, but *really?*" Arykah looked forward and just shook her head.

"What do you mean?" Lady McKenzie asked. Her eyes were filled with tears again. Arykah had figured something out. It was something too devastating for her to even speak about. Lady

McKenzie was sensing the worst as a tear slid out of her eye.

Angel hurried over to comfort Lady McKenzie by putting her arms around her.

"Go on and say it," Lady McKenzie urged Arykah. "I can handle whatever it is you have to say." She sniffed. Her legs wobbled just a little, and she was uncertain if she really did have the strength to handle it.

Lady McKenzie picked up the card Arykah had just read. She opened it and read it to herself while she spoke. "What is it about this card that has triggered something in you?" she asked Arykah. She was offended that Arykah would think that she'd fly her all the way to California for childish games. "I can assure you that this is not a prank, some lovesick puppy little girl playing games. It's real. There is a woman out there who is after my husband. Even if it was a prank by a child or something, I don't think they could take it this far."

Arykah looked at Lady McKenzie. "Lady McKenzie, I know beyond a doubt that you have me here because you feel someone is trying to trouble the waters in your marriage. I know that you believe it could be anyone, even the closest people to you, which is why not even your assistant knew who I was and why I was here. Deep down inside your heart, you didn't put it past any woman to be the culprit we are looking for."

"Oh no." Lady McKenzie began crying harder given what Arykah had just alluded to. "Haley has been my friend for years. I can't believe it's her."

"It's not," Arykah said. "Haley's got troubles of her own. She ain't got time to be pursuing another woman's husband."

Lady McKenzie immediately stopped sniffling and looked at Arykah with a tilted head. "It's not Haley?"

Arykah shook her head.

"Then who? I mean, what?" Lady McKenzie was getting fed up with the whole situation. It had been weighing her down enough already. Her spirit had been heavy. She'd been restless. Her husband would try to hold a conversation with her over dinner, and she'd be staring off, trying to play detective in her mind. By the time she got to bed, she'd be exhausted from all her Nancy Drew work. This mistress was actually winning, in an indirect way, by causing issues between the pastor and his wife.

"I don't play games, Lady Arykah." Lady McKenzie had a sternness to her tone. If she had to wait one more minute to find out who the hooka was who was trying to get at her man, she was going to lose her mind.

Arykah looked at her. She was both visibly upset and shaken. "You honestly haven't put two and two together, have you?"

Lady McKenzie couldn't even speak anymore. She just shook her head as tears fell.

"Can we go back to your office so I can sit you down?" Angel suggested to Lady McKenzie, who seemed to be getting weaker by the second. "Maybe get you some water?" Angel thought the poor woman was going to have an anxiety attack.

"Yes. That would be good," Lady McKenzie agreed, and Angel began the trek of leading her back down the steps.

Arykah just stood there for a moment. She stared at all the evidence and signs of another woman that Lady McKenzie had collected. She stood there, truly 100 percent baffled. What disturbed her the most was that Lady McKenzie hadn't figured this thing out on her own. Arykah had had to repeat tenth-grade math, and yet she'd been able to put two and two together in no time at all. How could Lady McKenzie not recognize the handwriting and the fact that it didn't even have a woman's touch to it? Clearly, Lady McKenzie was highly upset that Arykah would assume that she'd waste her time for foolishness. But Arykah wondered how Lady McKenzie would react when she revealed to her just who, in fact, was truly behind it all.

Chapter 31

Arykah stood in the attic for a few more seconds before it dawned on her that she was up there all alone. "Oh, heck, naw," she said, taking off toward the steps. "Shoot." She stopped in her tracks. If she was going to prove her case to Lady McKenzie, she needed to be able to point some things out. She ran back to the table and snatched up the cards. That was all she really needed, as the proof was inside the cards, as clear as day. With the evidence in hand, she headed down those steps and back to the hallway.

She saw Angel escorting Lady McKenzie into her office, which they'd passed on the way up to the attic. When Arykah walked into the office, Angel was helping Lady McKenzie take a seat behind her desk.

"I'll be right back," Angel said to the distraught woman once she was seated. "I'm going to go grab you a bottle of water from the fellowship hall."

Lady McKenzie simply nodded.

Before exiting the office, Angel grabbed a couple of tissues from the box on the credenza and handed them to her.

"Thank you." Lady McKenzie sniffed as she accepted the tissues.

Angel patted her on the shoulder and then hustled toward the door. Arykah was standing in the doorway. Angel connected eyes with Arykah and then nodded for her to go in and do her thing.

Arykah took a pause to ponder how she was going to do this. Lady McKenzie was all up in her emotions right now, so Arykah wanted to be as careful as possible with her words. When people were all up in their emotions, they didn't necessarily communicate or reason well with others. Lady McKenzie had a little fire to her, and Arykah certainly did. This could be an explosion waiting to happen if Arykah didn't proceed with caution. She spoke as she walked toward Lady McKenzie's desk.

"I can see that you are upset right now," Arykah began. "I know it's not just about the cards, the candy, the boxers, and all that stuff, but about my comment up in the attic as well. I didn't mean any offense to you when I questioned why I was here. I never meant to insinuate that you had me here under false pretenses. So I apologize if it came off like that."

"Thank you for that," Lady McKenzie said. "Apology accepted. I'm just feeling a certain kind of way right now, and I may have overreacted. You're not the one I'm mad at. So I apologize if you felt any disrespect." She looked into Arykah's eyes, her own now red and puffy. "But I assure you, I brought you here to help me. I know there are other things you could be doing, so I would never foolishly infringe upon your time."

Arykah nodded. "Lady McKenzie, I believe with my whole heart that you were on a mission when you called me. I heard desperation in your voice the day I received your call. I know that you truly believe that these cards, those chocolates, and those boxers were sent to your husband by a woman who wants to take your place."

"That's right," Lady McKenzie said while nodding her head. She was glad to see that she and Arykah might be ending up back on the same page.

"Well, I have some good news and some bad news," Arykah said.

Lady McKenzie just stared at her, waiting with bated breath for her to share either bit of news. She didn't care which; she just wanted to hear some news—*any* news. She'd flown this woman across the map and put her up in one of the best hotels in the area. This woman had to tell her something so that they could reach some type

of conclusion. Besides, she needed validation
for Arykah being there in the first place. She'd
already told her husband a half-truth about
Arykah's presence.

When she had to get approval from the board
to pay for Arykah's expenses, she'd presented
Arykah as someone who was going to be part of
Women's Week. In more ways than one, she was.
Lady McKenzie's spirit had felt a little convicted,
since she knew that she'd allowed her husband
just to assume that Arykah would be a featured
speaker when all Lady McKenzie had had her do
was stand and say a few words behind the real
guest speaker. Lady McKenzie felt she'd had no
other choice, though. What was she supposed
to tell her husband? "Honey, I'm paying this
woman to come investigate and find out who
your little hoochie secret admirer is"?

No way would she have done that, especially
when a deep-seated part of her didn't know if the
woman was somebody her husband had actually
messed around with and when this was her way
of trying to expose him. All kinds of thoughts
had gone through her mind. She wasn't putting
anything past anybody, so she'd had felt a little
touched when Arykah alluded to this being some
kind of joke, although Lady McKenzie would
have given anything for it to be just that.

"Are you ready to hear what I have to say?" Arykah asked kindly.

Just then, Angel walked into the office, carrying three bottles of water. She handed Arykah one as she passed her to get to Lady McKenzie. She then extended a bottle to Lady McKenzie and opened her own.

The women thanked her, and then Arykah continued.

"I'll take the liberty of giving you the bad news first," Arykah said. She took a swig of her water, cleared her throat, and then continued. "The bad news is that someone did send cards, letters, candy, and boxers to your husband."

"Oh, and I forgot about the flowers," Lady McKenzie said, remembering those. "They died, so I didn't keep them. As a matter of fact, I killed them when I threw them across his office."

Both Angel and Arykah looked at each other in shock.

"What?" Lady McKenzie said, clueless as to why they would be shocked by her reaction to the flowers. "I'm a woman first before I'm a first lady. The woman—the wife—walked into her husband's office and saw flowers from an admirer sitting on his desk, with a card talking about how the Lord said he was supposed to be her husband. What would you have done?"

"Thrown them flowers across the room," Arykah was quick to say, "then put on the tennis shoes I keep in my office and gone to find that skank."

"Exactly!" Lady McKenzie replied. "But instead of going to my office and getting my tennis shoes, I went to my office and called you."

"And you made a good decision," Angel told her.

"I know I did," Lady McKenzie said, still showing Arykah she had faith in her. "Now, what's the good news?"

"Well, I don't even know if I'd call it good news, but I know who the person is who sent those things to your husband."

Lady McKenzie sat up straight in her chair. "*Who is she*?" she shrieked. She'd been waiting desperately for this moment. The anticipation was killing her.

"But first," Arykah said, "I need to let you know that it's *not* a woman."

Lady McKenzie's mouth dropped to the floor. "Oh, Lord Jesus!" She jumped up from her seat and began speaking in tongues. She dropped to her knees and looked up to heaven with lifted hands. "No, no, no. Not the down low." Just then, as the thought settled into her brain that her husband might have something going on with another man, her emotions turned to anger.

She struggled to pull herself up off the carpet until Angel walked over and helped her up off the floor.

Once she was standing, Lady McKenzie reached under her desk and pulled out a pair of tennis shoes. She sat in her chair and began to put them on.

"Lady McKenzie, what are you doing?" Angel asked.

"Oh, it's tennis shoe time for real now." She pointed to her purse while she stuffed her foot into one of her tennis shoes. "Baby, look in my purse and get me that Vaseline," she ordered Angel.

Angel looked at Arykah, horrified. Arykah stood there with a slight smirk on her face and a look that said, "This is my kind of first lady."

"Arykah, aren't you going to do something?" Angel said in a pleading manner.

"Of course I am," Arykah replied. She then looked at Lady McKenzie. "Lady McKenzie, you need me to hold your earrings for you? I wouldn't want anything to happen to them. What are they? Two, three carats?"

"Arykah!" Angel gasped, her eyes nearly bucking out of her head.

"Oh, girl, I'm just messing with you." Arykah shooed her hand at Angel and laughed.

"This is not a time for jokes," Angel said, not finding a thing funny.

Arykah went and placed her hands on Lady McKenzie's shoulders both to calm her and to stop her from putting on her tennis shoes. "Lady McKenzie, Angel is right. It's not time for jokes. It's time for prayer." With that being said, Arykah took one of Lady McKenzie's hands in one of hers. She grabbed Angel's hand with her other one and then nodded for Angel to grab Lady McKenzie's other hand. Arykah led them in a prayer, asking that the Lord give strength to Lady McKenzie and that He open her heart and mind to receive and believe the truth.

"Amen," Angel said.

There was a moment of silence while they waited on Lady McKenzie to say the same. When she said nothing, Angel gave her hand a little squeeze.

"Oh," Lady McKenzie said. "Amen."

"Now, looky here," Arykah said as she showed Lady McKenzie one of the cards.

Lady McKenzie took the card and looked at it. "Yes. I've read this card," she said. "Over and over and over again."

"And you didn't find anything familiar about this card at all?"

Lady McKenzie read it once more, this time looking to see if anything stood out to her. "Well, no." She shook her head and handed the card back to Arykah.

"And how long did you say you've been married to Pastor McKenzie?" Arykah asked.

"We've been together for eight years, married six," Lady McKenzie answered.

Arykah shook her head. "Darn shame when a woman can't even recognize her own husband's handwriting. I guess we can thank technology for that. With all this texting and e-mailing and such, men don't write their wives little love notes anymore."

"What—what are you talking about?" Lady McKenzie asked, her emotions going from anger to confusion. She took the card out of Arykah's hand and read it again. Her mouth moved silently as she read the handwritten portion before a knowing look formed in her eyes. She looked up at Arykah. "Oh my God." She immediately snatched up the other cards and started examining the signatures.

As Lady McKenzie examined the cards, Angel looked at Arykah, her eyes begging her friend to tell her just what the heck was going on.

Arykah held up a finger, telling Angel to wait a minute. Her hope was that Lady McKenzie would figure it out on her own, without her having to spell it out. Every spouse knew his or her mate's handwriting. Either Lady McKenzie was acting dumb or she was mentally challenged.

Either way, Arykah wasn't going to procrastinate any longer. "Girl, your husband is behind all this. He sent these things to himself."

Angel gasped and sucked all the air out of Lady McKenzie's office. She covered her gaping mouth.

All the blood drained from Lady McKenzie's face. Had she heard clearly the woman she'd sent for to help solve the mystery of the secret admirer? Sure she had, but a part of her was going to prevent the words that had been uttered from penetrating her brain. She wasn't seeing right. She wasn't hearing right. A mistake had been made. Whether the mistake was inviting Arykah to California or Arykah trying to pin this mess on her husband, Lady McKenzie did not want to accept Arykah's findings. She couldn't. That would mean that her husband was crazy, weird, or even worse—psychopathic. It didn't make sense. And like Judge Judy—the woman whose show she'd been recording since the days of VCRs—said, if it didn't make sense, then it wasn't the truth.

Lady McKenzie shook her head as she read the first card yet another time. "No. I mean, the handwriting is close, but it can't be." She looked up at Arykah. "I mean, why in the world would he even do something like that?" The more Lady McKenzie tried to answer her own question herself, the more her head began to hurt. "I can't . . ." She put the cards down on her desk and buried her forehead in her hand.

Angel shook her head. "Why would her husband do something like that?" Angel asked, directed her question at Arykah.

"Well, he's the one we need to be asking," Arykah said. "But if I had to guess, maybe to make his wife jealous."

"But that doesn't make sense, either," Lady McKenzie said. "He knows I'm not the jealous type."

"Well, maybe he would like for you to be," Arykah replied. "Not jealous to the point that you would put on tennis shoes, Vaseline, and take your earrings off, but jealous to the point where he at least knows you care. Nothing feels good about thinking that your spouse feels that don't nobody else wants you. That says a lot."

"I don't feel that way," Lady McKenzie told her. "I know that I have a fine husband and that women from all walks of life and of all colors might be attracted to him. But I'm not going to spend all my time focusing on that."

"That's not hard for me to believe, considering you don't even focus enough to know your own husband's handwriting after all these years," Arykah said. She wasn't trying to be mean or nasty. She was just speaking the truth.

Arykah was laying it all out on the table as plain as day, but for the life her, Lady McKenzie still couldn't buy her husband going to such extremes. Seeing that Lady McKenzie still wasn't totally convinced, Arykah pressed on.

"Another reason why your husband might have done this is that he was maybe trying to get a little excitement out of you. Probably just wanted to rattle your cage a little to see if the tigress would come out of it."

Lady McKenzie's face got all torn up. "And just *what* exactly are you saying, Lady Arykah?" She was highly offended.

"I'm trying to be as diplomatic as possible, Lady McKenzie," Arykah said. "But if you want it straight, with no chaser, well, here it goes."

Angel braced herself for anything that might come out of Arykah's mouth.

"Perhaps your husband is bored in your marriage," Arykah said flat out. "And maybe even in the bed."

She might as well have slapped Lady McKenzie across her jaw. A yellow jacket's sting couldn't have hurt more than Arykah's words just had.

Lady McKenzie walked to the middle of her office, feeling a whole ball of emotions, which was creating a tornado inside of her mind. Here she had invited this woman to California, with all her expenses paid. This woman had come highly recommended by her prayer-line friend. Angel had told her that if anyone could figure out who the culprit was who was trying to interfere with her marriage, it would most certainly be Lady Arykah Miles-Howell from Chicago, Illinois.

When Angel had said that Arykah was gifted yet raw, soft-spoken yet brash, mild mannered but sometimes rough and tough, Lady McKenzie had wasted no time calling up Arykah to summon her to the West Coast. But Lady McKenzie would never have imagined in her wildest dreams that Arykah would flip the script and say that her husband was behind this mess. Truth be told, for Arykah even to suggest that Pastor McKenzie was bored and was looking for excitement in their marriage pissed her off royally.

She turned and glared at the woman she'd invited into her church, thinking it was fine time that Arykah herself knew what it felt like to be cut with a razor-sharp tongue. "You've got a lot of nerve," Lady McKenzie snarled, seething.

Just then Bryeisha approached the doorway. "First Lady McKenzie, you never came back to the fellowship hall. I was worried about you. Is everything okay?" she asked, her eyes darting around the room. She was looking for someone to confirm that everything was kosher.

"Not now, Bryeisha," Lady McKenzie snapped. She had been about to read her guest the riot act, and she didn't want the church secretary interrupting. "Go on. I'll be back down in a minute."

"Are you sure, First Lady?" Bryeisha said, sensing her first lady might need her to have her back.

"Bryeisha, trust me, your first lady has got this." Lady McKenzie spoke with complete assurance and authority.

Oh snap, Arykah thought, catching wind of Lady McKenzie's sharp tone. Where Arykah came from, folks didn't talk like that unless they were ready to do something. Arykah didn't know if she should start taking off her shoes, earrings, and rubbing Vaseline on her own face.

"Okay," Bryeisha said with a shaky voice. "I'll be right out here if you need me."

"Thank you, Bry," Lady McKenzie said as she watched the young woman walk away. "Now, where were we?" She turned and faced Arykah.

Before Lady McKenzie could even continue, Arykah spoke. "Lady McKenzie, I did not come here to offend you," she said sincerely.

Of course Lady McKenzie would take offense. After telling Lady McKenzie what she had to say, Lady Arykah so much as expected she would be offended. Any woman would be hot under the collar and would want to defend her husband.

Had the shoe been on the other foot and had someone suggested that Bishop Lance Howell was doing some dumb stuff like this, Arykah would certainly throw a punch or two. But when it came to her marriage, Arykah was on top of her game. Bishop Lance would never be bored with her. She had too many whips, chains, costumes, and feathers to let that ever happen. Arykah knew all too well how devious and sneaky broads could be. She made absolutely sure that Bishop Lance didn't have the time or the energy even to think about entertaining another woman's advances.

"I'm not your enemy," Lady Arykah said. "You invited me here."

Lady McKenzie let out a sarcastic chuckle and looked at Angel. "Is *this* your idea of a joke? I trusted you."

Angel didn't know what to say. She was caught in the middle. Yes, she had recommended that Lady McKenzie reach out to Arykah. But even she herself was shocked and flabbergasted that Arykah would suggest that the pastor was tormenting his own wife. She also knew that Arykah was always on point and didn't sugarcoat anything.

"And you trusted your husband as well, correct?" Arykah said after realizing that Angel wasn't going to respond to Lady McKenzie.

"Well . . ." Lady McKenzie's words trailed off.

"Don't you know your own husband's hand-writing?" Arykah said in a sympathetic tone. "I mean, how could you not know? Do y'all file taxes jointly? Sign the taxes together?"

"Well, yes, but—" Lady McKenzie began, but there was no *but*, so she cut her own words off.

Watching Lady Arykah interrogate the pastor's wife brought back memories to Angel. At the women's conference she remembered Arykah telling over three hundred women that some of their marriages were so dry that they didn't even know where their husband's birthmark was.

Lady McKenzie's eyes were blazing, but she still tried her best to keep it together to the very end. She lifted her head and puffed her chest out. "Of course I know my husband's handwriting, and I also know that he'd never do anything like this. We've been together for close to a decade. I know my husband. Do you know *yours*?"

Arykah snapped her neck back. "Honey, this is not about *my* husband. Things are just fine back in Chicago, where I'd rather be cuddled up under my husband, but instead, I'm here to see about you and yours. But to answer your question, I *absolutely* know my husband's hand-writing. I could sign his checks for him if need be. But back to you," Arykah said, feeling that she'd thoroughly read Miss First Lady and now needed to get back to the situation at hand. But why even waste her time? Things were going left, so she wanted to go right—right out that door. But God had not instructed her to do so. At the end of the day, she was not going to allow the devil to use Lady McKenzie to run her off before she completed her assignment. But, Holy Ghost, help her not to catch a case!

Arykah took in a deep breath and exhaled. She closed her eyes and did it again. And again. Feeling she was back in a good space mentally, she opened her eyes. "Where is your husband's birthmark?" Arykah asked in a cool, calm, and collected manner.

"Aw, shoot. Here we go," Angel said under her breath. She already knew that her friend was about to start preaching and teaching up in there. Yes, this was what they'd come for. Not to argue and throw digs at one another, but to help one another.

Lady McKenzie opened her mouth to speak, then closed it. She looked up at the ceiling. She was thinking.

"You don't know where it is, do you?" Arykah asked her.

"Of course I do," she spat back at Arykah.

Arykah knew that Lady McKenzie was way past pissed with her, but she didn't care. She pressed on. "Where is it, then?"

Lady McKenzie looked Arykah up and down. "That is *none* of your business."

"I don't want your husband," Arykah told her. "I'm just trying to help you keep him. Now, you spent a lot of money to get me here, Lady McKenzie, but like I said before, I'm not here to play games, which I'm starting to think is something both you and your husband like to do. But that being the case, seems like if y'all played more games with each other, you'd *know* where his birthmark was without even having to think about it."

Angel held up her index finger, walked away from the ladies, and took a seat. She was too weak even to stand after that one.

"I believe it's on his left knee," Lady McKenzie said matter-of-factly, trying her best to go tit for tat with Arykah.

Arykah raised her eyebrows. "You *believe*? You can't say for sure?"

Lady McKenzie pursed her lips. Clearly, she had exercised poor judgment by inviting Arykah to California, and in that moment, she vowed never to speak to Angel again for getting her mixed up with this ghetto heathen disguised as a saint.

"Let me tell you something, First Lady," Lady Arykah said. "I know my husband's signature, I know how many freckles he has on his face, and I can look into his eyes after we've been apart for hours and know what type of mood he's in. And I can point out his shaboinka in a lineup."

"Oh my," Angel said weakly. She'd thought she had heard the extent of Lady Arykah's raw tongue, but it looked like there was still more skin to peel off the onion, which could bring any set of eyes to tears.

Lady McKenzie had no words. She just didn't know how to react.

"You don't have to believe what I'm trying to tell you," Arykah said. "I know it's a hard pill to swallow that your husband is behind this, but he is. There is no mistress, secret admirer, or down-low brother. It's your husband."

Lady McKenzie refused to accept it. She shook her head. "Uh-uh. No way."

"The fact that you don't even recognize that the writing on the cards is your own husband's is proof that you are not paying as close attention to the man as you should be. I saw his handwriting only once, on tonight's program, and I recognized it. The last thing you want is for another woman to be doing what *you* should be doing."

Lady McKenzie gasped.

Angel closed her eyes and clenched her teeth together. She knew exactly what Arykah was trying to say, but she also knew that Lady McKenzie, in her state, wouldn't take it that way.

Lady McKenzie's eyes bulged. Her chest heaved up and down. She stepped to Arykah. "How dare you!"

Arykah removed her hat from her head and tossed it on top of Lady McKenzie's desk and quickly stepped out of her stilettos. Tempers were escalating, and Lady McKenzie had gotten in her personal space. Arykah knew what usually came after that. She wasn't about to get caught slipping.

Angel immediately got up from her seat to go separate the ladies.

"Don't walk up on me," Arykah warned Lady McKenzie as Angel now stood between the two of them. "Trust when I tell you, you don't want none of this. Now, I've tried to maintain my composure by not snapping off, but don't take me for no punk."

Lady McKenzie knew that she could get a little excited and heated, but this Arykah chick just had her appalled. She had come out of character enough and was not about to go to the point of no return by going to blows with another woman of God. God wasn't in this, not one bit, so it was time to terminate her business with Arykah.

"You know what? Get out of my church," Lady McKenzie said to Arykah. She then looked at Angel. "Both of you."

Deep inside, Lady McKenzie didn't really want Arykah to go, or Angel, for that matter. What she really wanted was for Arykah just to take the truth with her. Arykah was right. Hearing everything she had to say to Lady McKenzie was a hard pill for Lady McKenzie to swallow, one she'd rather choke on and die from rather than admit she'd been lacking in any area as a wife. But there was definitely a ring of truth to what Arykah was saying, and there was a strong possibility that her husband could have resorted to such measures to get her attention.

Arykah really didn't even need to be told to get out. Her flesh had long been ready to go. She had done what she came to do. If Lady McKenzie didn't want to accept the truth, it would be her problem. Besides, that lone pair of Spanx was having a tumultuous affair with her abdomen. "Humph, you ain't said nothing but a word." Arykah stepped into her heels and grabbed her hat. "Let's go, Angel," she said. She placed her hat back on her head. Yes, she wanted to do the Lord's work, but even though she hadn't clearly heard the voice of the Lord telling her to exit stage left, she did not trust her flesh to stay in that room a minute longer with Lady McKenzie.

"Wait a minute now," Angel said. "Both of you need to calm down." She looked at Arykah. "Arykah, you came here for a reason, and I don't think you'll be okay with leaving here this way."

"I've tried with her," Arykah said, "but I got on my good weave today, virgin silky. I can't anymore." Arykah headed to the door, but Angel grabbed her arm to stop her. Arykah looked at her. "Didn't we already go through this? Child, you a buck-oh-five. I can drag you all the way to the limo if I want, but you got on your good shoes, and I don't want to jack them up, no more than I'd want to jack my hair up. So as Spike Lee would say, do the right thing, and let go of my arm."

There was a look of fear in Angel's eyes, because she knew there was one thing Arykah did not do, and that was lie. Angel had a matter of seconds to release Arykah's arm before her heels got worn down. But Angel was not going to allow fear to deter her from her own assignment, either. She truly felt she was there not just because Arykah wanted her there, but because God did, to make sure Arykah completed her own assignment. "I won't let you go," Angel insisted. "We are sisters in Christ, and we are not going to end things this way."

Lady McKenzie looked at Angel. "I don't want you to take this personal, First Lady Angel.

You have been nothing but kind, sweet, gentle, understanding, and Christlike." Her tone went from butter soft to hard as a brick. "But this thing right here . . ." She gave Arykah the once-over. "She has insulted me and my husband."

"*Thing?*" Arykah repeated.

Angel could feel the muscles tightening in Arykah's arm, which she was still holding on to. All Angel could picture was Arykah knocking out Lady McKenzie the way they did poor ole Miss Sofia in *The Color Purple*. "On second thought, uh, yeah, Arykah, I think we *should* go." Angel looked back at Lady McKenzie as she began pushing Arykah toward the door. "Thank you for having us, Lady McKenzie. You have a lovely church. God bless you, and I'll talk to you on the prayer line." Angel continued trying to push Arykah out that door as quickly as she could, but now Arykah wouldn't budge.

Arykah stood there, staring at Lady McKenzie. Angel was surprised that it wasn't a mean, evil glare, but one of sympathy.

"I get it," Arykah said to Lady McKenzie. "I get it now." She looked up and said, "Thank you, Holy Ghost." She then turned her attention back to Lady McKenzie. "You're hurting. Hurt people hurt people. And you know what? I honestly do get that now."

Just moments ago, as Arykah watched Lady McKenzie snap at her, she'd realized that wasn't the kind, loving, touchy-feely woman they'd met earlier that evening. This was the hurt Lady McKenzie. Arykah had to understand that just like herself, Lady McKenzie was human. As a matter of fact, if she looked a little deeper, she'd see that Lady McKenzie had a lot in common with her. If most women just took the time to get to know each other, they'd find that their struggles were their common ground. The things that should bring them together they often let pull them apart.

"It was never my intention to hurt you, Lady McKenzie, to insult you or your husband in any way," Arykah said. "But you need to face reality."

Just when Lady McKenzie thought Arykah was going to come to her senses and lay off, she still insisted on coming at her. So without even allowing Arykah to finish what she had to say, Lady McKenzie pointed to the door. "Please leave my church."

Angel knew Arykah well enough to know that she was not about to come for Lady McKenzie. If only Lady McKenzie would just see this thing from a spiritual angle rather than staying in the natural, maybe they could get somewhere. "Lady McKenzie, please—"

Lady McKenzie held up her palm to silence Angel. "Just go. Now. Please." She spoke in a low tone, as if she was too drained even to try to get loud.

Arykah didn't need to be told a third time. She walked toward the office door.

"Arykah, wait a minute." Angel just couldn't allow herself, or Arykah, to give up. She wanted to fix the situation. She didn't want the trip to California to be in vain. She knew that if anyone would be the one to help Lady McKenzie, it would be Arykah. Angel was starting to see that maybe their being in California had nothing to do with helping Lady McKenzie figure out who was trying to sabotage her marriage, and perhaps everything to do with helping her grow her marriage. "Please, ladies. The Word says that we should not lean on our own understanding. I know none of this makes sense to us, but God doesn't make mistakes, and if we would just remove ourselves and let God be God and use us how He sees fit, then maybe we can get some type of resolution here."

Neither woman looked as though they were picking up what Angel was putting down. So Angel resorted to what she knew would work, because it always did.

"I just feel in my spirit that a prayer needs to go forth right now," Angel said. "Then, afterward, Lady McKenzie, if you want us to go, we'll go."

Arykah appreciated the fact that her friend refused to give up. But she needed to let go and let God. Arykah had exposed the truth. Perhaps that was all God had wanted her to do here. She was ready to return to her hotel and maybe to try to salvage this trip with a little sun in the morning and a poolside drink, this time with *plenty* of alcohol.

"Look, Angel," Arykah said, "she obviously can't see reason. Rather than submit to what God is trying to show her, she wants to fight like the devil. And if I have to strip and step out of these Spanx in this office, it won't be pretty. So with that being said, I think it's best, like Lady McKenzie said, to leave." Arykah walked out the door.

Angel stood there, feeling completely defeated. "What just happened here?"

"You recommended I bring that lunatic here to help me. *That's* what just happened!" Lady McKenzie answered hotly.

Angel turned to Lady McKenzie. "Listen, First Lady McKenzie," she said, starting to lose her cool herself, "Lady Arykah may be a lot of things. I will admit that she can be a bit brash and outspoken, but she isn't a lunatic. I have seen her in action, and I know she's good at what she does. I know she punched you in the gut when she stated that your husband was behind the shenanigans, but if you can't take a blow from her, then what makes you think you can take one from the devil?"

Lady McKenzie thought about Angel's words for a moment.

"I mean, seriously," Angel continued, "Jesus bled, died, and hung on the cross and didn't say a mumbling word. He was crucified, spat on, poked, and kicked. A sista say the wrong thing to us, and we ready to snap off. Tuh!" Angel rolled her eyes. "And we wanna be like Jesus. Even He's laughing at that." Lady Angel looked at her friend with pity in her eyes. "I'm sorry this didn't work out, Lady McKenzie. My friend and I really did mean well." With that, Angel exited the office. She hated to leave Lady McKenzie in dire straits, but it was clear that Lady McKenzie didn't want to be in her presence.

Lady McKenzie sat behind her desk and went over the events of the evening in her head. She had been so excited to see Arykah and welcome her into her church. She hadn't expected to be slapped in the face with absurd accusations. She thought about all the gifts that had been sent to her husband. When she thought about it, the boxers *were* cheap. The box of chocolates was far from Fannie May. She picked up one of the cards and studied the handwriting. She dug through her desk drawer and pulled out past Sunday programs in which Pastor McKenzie had included handwritten notes, like he'd done in tonight's program. Though she didn't want to admit it, Lady McKenzie saw that the cursive writing in the cards bore a striking resemblance to her husband's writing. The more she studied and compared the writing, the clearer it became that Arykah could be right. No, that Arykah *was* right. What was even worse was that Arykah's reasons behind why her husband might have engaged in such activities might be on point as well.

Lady McKenzie loved her husband, but she loved the Lord, the church, her ministry, and her church family too. It was no secret to herself that she had never really learned how to balance it all. Things had got so bad with her that once she planned a women's conference that would take place on her and her husband's anniversary weekend, and she didn't even realize it until after the fact. Then there had been the times when she was so worn out from doing ministry all day, that come nighttime, she had nothing left for her husband. As she sat at her desk, one instance and occasion after the next popped into her head, all reasons why her husband might feel slighted by his wife. All reasons why he might feel it would the extraordinary to achieve the ordinary out of his own marriage. And because Lady McKenzie had been so spiritually busy to be of any earthly good to her husband, she hadn't even been able to recognize it on her own. She'd called Arykah and asked her to come for one reason, but God had sent her for a whole other one.

"Jesus, what have I done?" she said to herself. She felt awful just thinking about how she'd treated her guests when all they'd tried to do was help. All they had done was help. Arykah had brought her the truth, but because she didn't understand it or want to hear it, she'd taken the pain she felt out on Arykah and Angel. Apologies for Arykah and Angel might be in order, but there was someone else she needed to apologize to first.

Chapter 32

In the limousine, as Arykah and Angel headed back to the Four Seasons Hotel, the mood was a solemn one.

"Girl, I can't get out of all my clothes soon enough," Arykah said, deciding to break up the monotony. "My belly is singing a song." Even though she chuckled, Angel sensed it was just a cover-up.

Angel looked at Arykah. "How do you feel about what just happened at God's Saints Chapel? Lady McKenzie is devastated."

"As any woman would be," Arykah said. "I can't fault her for feeling the way she does. It's gotta be embarrassing. But first ladies have to realize that the same way some of them feel their husband may be giving more to the church and the ministry than he's giving to them, it can be a two-way street."

Angel stared out the window. "I hated leaving her there like that. It just doesn't feel right. It doesn't feel complete."

"I hated leaving her there too, but she just wouldn't listen to reason—or grasp the fact that God was trying to tell her something." Arykah let out a chuckle.

Angel turned toward Arykah and asked, "What are you laughing at?"

"We both know that she may not have wanted to hear it from God's messenger, but just wait until she's alone with Him and can't avoid *His* voice." Arykah laughed again. "She won't be able to avoid the truth then."

"You're absolutely right about that," Angel declared with certainty. There had been plenty of times when she hadn't wanted to see the truth for what it was or hear anything anyone had to say about something. But when God spoke, it was bond. Who could argue with God? Still, a part of Angel felt as though God hadn't finished speaking through Arykah. "Arykah, are you absolutely sure this is how you want to end things with Lady McKenzie? Telling her that she should suspect her own husband is overwhelming for her. Don't take this the wrong way. I'm not trying to doubt you. I believe you hear clearly from the Lord. But do you think that's all He had to say concerning this matter?"

"Girl, look," Arykah replied. "I keep it one hunnid. The writing is on the wall. Well, in Lady McKenzie's case, the writing is on the cards.

Once she gets over the initial shock and looks at the evidence, she'll come to realize the truth of the matter."

"But why would a man do that to his wife?"

"They've been married for what? Six, eight years? Something like that. The honeymoon is over. He could be looking for a little more spark in the relationship. That is not uncommon, Angel."

"But why not just come out and tell her that? Why put her through such torment?"

"Can you imagine a man, after spending almost a decade with his wife, saying to her, 'Yo, babe, you don't do it for me anymore. I need for you to drop it like it's hot'? Now, let's keep it real. If it was a brotha, okay, maybe he would say something like that. Pastor McKenzie may not have the courage to be open and honest with his wife. Shoot, Kirk Franklin wasn't playing around with his wife. He broke out the pornos."

"Well, if we're comparing the two and I was on an episode of the game show *Jeopardy*, I'll take a fake secret admirer for two thousand, Alex," Angel said.

"I don't know, Angel. Maybe in Pastor McKenzie's mind, by sending those gifts to himself, he figured it would make Lady McKenzie think another woman wanted him and make her step her game up. Girl, I know when Lance and I step out and he's looking all good and smelling good and every woman in the room is eyeballing him, we barely make it home before I'm putting it on him. Not only does the other women being attracted to my man remind me what a gift and blessing I have, but it also reminds me that I ain't the only person who wants to take the bow off of the gift. So I gotta let him know he can always get that. *Pop, boom, pow.*" Arykah did a little back-and-forth move with her hips.

Angel sat back in her seat and exhaled. "Maybe you're right. I just hope that she and Pastor McKenzie can work this out."

"They can if he's honest, because don't think for a minute that she ain't on the phone with him right this second."

"You think?" Angel scrunched up her nose. "Seems like this would be more of a face-to-face talk."

"Child, you saw how feisty Lady McKenzie is," Arykah said. "Does she *look* like a woman who can wait to get home to pick that fight? Child, bye." Arykah flipped her hand. "But I'll tell you this much. If Pastor McKenzie doesn't man up and tell his wife what he wants and needs from her, Lady McKenzie will have another problem on her hands. When the real secret admirer comes along, temptation is going to be that much bigger of a battle."

"Well, I'm going to give her some time to cool off, and then I want to check on her," Angel said. "Perhaps give her a call."

"That's a good idea. Better you than me." Arykah let out a harrumph. "Besides, she's your friend. She's going to need you when the truth comes out. Make sure to stay in touch with her no matter how much she tries to push you away."

Angel nodded. "I wonder if she'll welcome us at tomorrow's service."

Arykah snapped her neck toward Angel. "I'm *not* staying for tomorrow's service. I'm flying back to Chicago tomorrow. I don't even think I could enjoy the California sun now even if I wanted to." Arykah sighed. "My work here is done, and I don't feel led to hang around. And you shouldn't, either. Just in case Lady McKenzie doesn't cool down, I won't be here to have your back." Arykah paused while she looked Angel up and down. "And personally, I don't think you can take her. Besides, she didn't throw just me out of the church. She threw you out too."

"I guess you're right," Angel agreed. "Then I'll change my flight too and head back to Ohio. I definitely don't want to stay here without you." Angel turned and stared out the window the rest of the way back to the hotel.

Once Elroy dropped them off, the two women parted ways and headed to their own suites. Although Arykah was hell-bent on heading out the next day and Angel had agreed that she would as well, Angel would have to pray on it. It didn't matter what she or Arykah said. God always had the last word.

Arykah stripped as soon as she stepped foot in her hotel suite. When she pulled off that final pair of Spanx, she said, "Lord Jesus, you know I bless your holy name." She went and slipped on her white, fluffy Egyptian cotton robe, supplied by the hotel. Unlike the Spanx, Arykah didn't mind the robe hugging her body. Next, she immediately went and grabbed her iPad. She logged on and wasted no time at all booking her return flight home on the open-ended ticket Lady McKenzie had purchased for her.

Arykah wasn't an early riser. She was still feeling jet-lagged and getting used to the time zone change. And truth be told, she wouldn't mind a couple more hours poolside at the Four Seasons Hotel. So she'd chosen a flight that departed tomorrow, at six in the evening. Next, she showered, slipped into a pair of palazzo pajamas, then stretched across her bed. She used the remote to power on the forty-two-inch flat-screen television and searched through the channels. She saw that the movie *Training Day*, starring Denzel Washington, had just come on. Arykah settled back on her pillow to enjoy the flick. She normally would have snacked while lying back and watching a flick, but she'd done enough snacking for the day. She would enjoy the movie without the sound of her chomping on potato chips or slurping on a soda.

An hour into the movie, Arykah heard a soft knock on the door. She frowned and checked the time on the digital clock on the nightstand. It was after midnight.

"Who can *that* be?" She rose from the bed, and before she could even make it over to the door, she figured out just who it was. Angel had probably come to her room to try one last time to get her to stay in California longer and go talk to Lady McKenzie. Angel had already sent her three texts since they'd returned to the hotel. Two were to ask Arykah if she was sure they should leave. The last was Angel letting Arykah know that she was about to hit the BOOK FLIGHT button on her computer screen and snag an early flight in the morning, so if Arykah wanted to change her mind and stay, this was her last shot. None of the texts had worked, so now the persistent little thing had come over for one last plea in person.

"Look, Angel," Arykah said, flinging open the door and starting her refusal spiel before Angel could even speak. "Oh my." Arykah grabbed her chest, startled by the figure standing outside her door.

Lady McKenzie stood in the hallway, holding a small aluminum pan covered with aluminum foil. She shrugged her shoulders, smiled, then said, "You forgot something."

Lady Arykah sniffed the pan and then returned the smile. "Is that my banana pudding?"

"Yes," Lady McKenzie answered. "And I've got five words for you."

"Oh, Lord," Arykah mumbled. She could only imagine what they were going to be now that Lady McKenzie was no longer in the house of the Lord, where Arykah was certain the first lady had bitten her tongue several times. Arykah knew she had.

"I'm sorry," Lady McKenzie said.

"That's two words." Arykah still braced herself.

"You were right."

Arykah paused, then stepped back and opened the door wider. Lady McKenzie had brought a peace offering, and she was smiling. Arykah figured it was safe to let her into her suite. "Come in."

Lady McKenzie entered the suite and set the aluminum pan on the wooden table just inside the door.

"What happened?" Lady Arykah asked. "You threw me out of your church, and now you bring me banana pudding? What gives?"

"Well, I—"

"Wait," Lady Arykah interrupted. "Let's discuss this over dessert." She went into the small kitchenette and retrieved two spoons from the drawer next to the sink. She washed them and returned to the living area. She gave a spoon to Lady McKenzie and invited her to have a seat at the dining table, then placed the banana pudding on the table and sat down.

"Shall we call First Lady Angel?" Lady McKenzie said. "I think I owe her an apology as well."

Arykah shook her head. "It's really late, and I know she has an early flight to Ohio in the morning."

"I thought you both were staying at least through Sunday."

Arykah pulled back the aluminum foil and dug in. "We were, until you threw us out of church. For all we knew, you'd probably have sharpshooters camped out on the roof of the church, ready to take us out when we got there."

Lady McKenzie laughed out loud. "I can understand why you feel that way. I was hot when y'all left. I've never dismissed guests from my church before. I was so out of character, and I deeply apologize for that."

Arykah moaned at the sweet taste of the banana pudding. She took another scoop from the pan and held it up. "This makes up for it." She inserted the spoon in her mouth and savored the taste. Arykah recalled the last time she'd shared banana pudding with Bishop Lance. They'd ended up eating the dessert from each other's bodies. But her thoughts shouldn't be about her and her own husband right now. This was still about Pastor and First Lady McKenzie. After all, as long as she was in California, she was still on business. "So, how did you come to the conclusion that I was right? I take it you had a conversation with your husband."

Lady McKenzie looked downward. Even though Arykah had accepted her apology, she was still embarrassed by the way she'd acted. "After you and First Lady Angel left my office, I reexamined the handwriting on the cards." She looked up at Arykah. "Then I examined myself. And since the room was quiet, I was finally able to hear from God." She chuckled. "I concluded that everything you said made sense."

Lady Arykah nodded her head and kept eating. "Told ya." There was no shame in her game. Arykah had no problem giving out a good ole-fashioned "I told you so." It beat the good old-fashioned butt whipping she'd wanted to give her just an hour ago.

"Yep, you did," Lady McKenzie said. "I went home and confronted that joker, but not before I'd called him up, fussing him out at the top of my lungs all the way home."

Arykah laughed. "Yeah, us black women are just so passionate, aren't we?"

Lady McKenzie nodded her agreement.

"Well, at least he didn't deny it," Arykah said. "You know a brotha would have pulled the Eddie Murphy all day long." Arykah began mocking one of the famous comedian's most notable stand-up comedy act lines. "Wasn't me."

Lady McKenzie shook her head and laughed. "No, he didn't deny it. He confessed. And was almost excited that I'd figured it all out." She looked at Arykah. "With a little help, of course." She winked. "Besides, I didn't give him a choice but to tell the truth. I started the conversation off by telling him that I was gonna ask him a question that I already knew the answer to. And that if he lied to me, there would be hell to pay."

"Ha!" Arykah yelled out. "You're my kind of chick." The two high-fived each other.

Lady McKenzie played around in the banana pudding with her spoon. She'd yet to take a bite. "It didn't feel good to sit and listen to my husband of so many years tell me what you had already figured out—that he was bored with me."

Arykah refrained from uttering the "I told you so" that was resting on the tip of her tongue. She figured she'd just wait and let out one big one when all was said and done. So she continued to listen to Lady McKenzie share her conversation with her husband.

"He felt that I would get jealous and think there was competition. As a result, he hoped that would urge me to spend more time with him and spice things up in our bedroom."

Arykah cleared her throat. She put her spoon down. "First ladies wear many hats. We gotta be the wife, the mother, the counselor, the teacher, and the minister all at the same doggone time. We are constantly being pulled in every direction."

Lady McKenzie finally inserted a spoonful of banana pudding into her mouth. "Uh-huh. Now you're preachin', 'cause that's sho' 'nuff the truth."

"We get so lost in the hustle and bustle of everyone else's lives and complications that we don't have the time to see about our own households. And you have only a handful of members at God's Saints Chapel. My church, Freedom Temple, has well over five hundred members on the roll. Humph. My phone never stops ringing. And on top of that, I sell real estate."

Lady McKenzie's eyes popped out of her head. "You work outside the church and the home?"

Arykah nodded. "Yes, ma'am. But I have no children, so that makes it a little easier. But even still, I have a huge church, so I guess my members are like my children. I get called because a married couple is fighting. I get called because a child has run away from home. I get called when my members have fallen ill. I get called when a member has left her husband. There's no end to it. But . . ." Arykah paused and looked Lady McKenzie in the eye. "I never neglect my husband and his needs. I take care of home first. How can I find the time to mend someone else's marriage and not tend to my own? My husband and I are newlyweds. We're in that honeymoon stage, where we can't get enough of each other. But you, on the other hand, have been married for what? Six, seven years?"

"Yes."

"Lady McKenzie, let me ask you something. And a warning. This may be more personal than the question about the birthmark."

"Go ahead," Lady McKenzie said.

"When was the last time you made love to your husband?"

Lady McKenzie didn't seem embarrassed at all by Arykah's question. "Girl, with preparing for Women's Week and getting everything in order, plus dealing with church folks and all their problems, I just don't have much time for intimacy. It's been probably about a month since I sexed him."

Arykah threw her shoulders back and screamed out, "*A month*?"

Lady McKenzie thought for a moment. "It may even be longer than that. Being a pastor's wife is tough."

"Girl, you're preaching to the choir, but a month is *waaay* too long. Heck, you gotta try to at least jump your man's bones three times a week. You're so busy with church stuff and fixing everybody else's marriages that you neglect your own. That ain't fair—to you or your man."

"You're right, Lady Arykah. You've been right about everything." Lady McKenzie stood up, exasperated. She turned her back to Arykah. "I didn't want to believe it, though, and I probably never would have, not on my own. Not without you painting the entire picture for me. That's why God sent you here. God could have easily had me figure all this out on my own. But if I had gone to my husband and he had told that he was responsible for sending himself the items, I wouldn't have believed him. If a man receives flowers, candy, and boxers, and says, 'Honey, I sent them to myself,' what woman in her right mind would believe him? I would have thought he'd had a one-night stand, and now the woman was obsessed or something, kind of like in that movie *Fatal Attraction*. It had to go down just like it did, and you had to break it down for me."

"I don't agree with the way Pastor McKenzie got your attention, but I understand why he did it. Most men would've just found themselves a side chick to do what their wives wouldn't do. And trust me, honey, there are plenty of shameless tricks that are more than willing to walk in your shoes."

"Humph," Lady McKenzie commented, turning back around to face Arykah. "You ain't gotta tell me. I've been in this game a long time. I know how it's played."

"So, you now know what you gotta do, right?"

"Yeah, I gotta get back on my honeymoon."

"And take a real one," Arykah advised. "Y'all need to go away, far away from the church and the members. 'Cause there will always be someone who needs you, but you gotta draw the line in the sand. Your marriage is suffering. Your husband has sent you the message that he is not happy."

"I hear you, Lady Arykah. I'll book a honeymoon getaway."

"And *stay* on the honeymoon," Arykah ordered. "When you return home and to the first lady duties, don't forget that you have a man at home, waiting on you. Do you work outside the church?"

"No, and my husband doesn't, either. We're both cooped up in the church all day, every day."

"Girl," Arykah sang, "you mean to tell me that you're around your husband twenty-four-seven and y'all ain't getting it in? Are you nuts?"

Lady McKenzie shrugged her shoulders. "He always has someone in his office, and I'm busy, as well, planning church activities, updating our Web site, or counseling women."

"Okay, listen, Joy. Can I call you Joy?"

"Absolutely."

"Joy, you ought to feel blessed that after all these years, you have a husband who still lusts after you. I noticed how your husband looked at you in that pulpit. But the sad thing about it,

Lady McKenzie, was that I don't even think *you* noticed it. There was no reciprocity whatsoever on your part. He was saying all sorts of things to his beloved with his eyes, but you didn't hear any of it."

Lady McKenzie replayed her brief interaction with her husband in the pulpit. Arykah was right. He'd been crying out for his wife to show that she lusted after him the same way he did her. She'd completely missed that opportunity to let him know that she did, with just a small look in her eyes.

"You gotta be spontaneous," Arykah continued. "Go into his office, lock that freakin' door, go over to his desk, take your hand, and in one sweep, throw all that paperwork on the floor and give your husband what he's been craving. Give him the shock of his life. Make his fantasy into a reality."

"In the *church*?" Lady McKenzie asked.

"Girl, heck, yeah. Wherever. Y'all are married. It's okay." The first month of Arykah and Bishop Lance's marriage, they had christened his office, her office, the fellowship hall, the library, all the Sunday school classrooms, *and* the choir room. "Go out and buy some sexy lingerie," Arykah advised. "Bringing toys into your bedroom works wonders too."

Lady McKenzie's cheeks turned crimson red. *"Toys?"*

"Don't knock it till you try it," Arykah asserted. She figured that if Lady McKenzie saw the gadgets in the treasure chest that she kept hidden in the rear of her closet, she would have a heart attack. She and Lance were total freaks. "You better give that man what he wants. He's looking for some spice. Try new things. Seduce *him* for a change. Get yourself some crotchless panties."

Lady McKenzie opened her mouth wide, then quickly covered it. "Girl, *what*?"

"Do you wanna be your husband's freak, or do you want someone else to be it? You better drop that holier-than-thou attitude and blow his mind. Yes, he is a pastor, but he's a man first. All pastors have the same desire. They want an angel on the front pew and a dirty devil in the bedroom."

Both Arykah and Lady McKenzie laughed so loud, they wouldn't have been surprised if hotel security came to kick them out.

"Oh, Lady Arykah, you are *too* much," Lady McKenzie said. "How can I ever thank you enough? You've helped me so much."

Arykah waved her hand to dismiss the question. "No thanks is necessary. Just heed my advice and you'll be all right. By the way, I taught on this very subject not too long ago at the First Lady Conference Angel and I met at. There is a YouTube link. I'll make sure I send it to you."

"Thank you. I'd appreciate that." Lady McKenzie looked around. "Well, I guess I better head on out."

Arykah stood.

"I really wish you and First Lady Angel would reconsider staying in California and would attend the conclusion of Women's Week."

"We've already made our flight arrangements. Besides, I'm really anxious to get to my bishop. He has no idea that I'm coming home this soon, and I can't wait to surprise him." Arykah shimmied her shoulders and winked.

"I know that's right." Lady McKenzie smiled. "I totally understand. But I don't want you to be a stranger. Please come back and visit." She took Arykah's hands into her own.

"I promise I will," Arykah said. "And I'm extending to you an invitation to Chicago, to be my special guest at Freedom Temple."

Lady McKenzie smiled again. "And I accept." She pulled Arykah in for a hug and thanked her again before exiting the hotel room.

Arykah put her dessert in the mini-fridge and then rushed back over to her bed to get back to the movie. "Man, I hope I ain't missed my favorite line." She got back to the television just in time for her favorite part. "Come on and give it to me, Denzel." Arykah began beating on her chest while saying, "King Kong ain't got nothin' on me."

Fortunately, Arykah hadn't missed her part. But she couldn't even keep her eyes open five minutes before she was snoring and slobbering. It was the sound of her phone beeping and buzzing to alert her that she had a text that woke her. She grabbed her phone, which was lying next to her on the bed. She noticed the time before reading the text. It was 6:35 a.m., and the text was from Angel.

> Boarding the plane. Wish our trip had had a wonderful ending. Have a safe flight back to Chicago. Talk to ya soon.

Arykah rolled onto her back and stared up at the ceiling. She'd be sure to call Angel when she got home and tell her about Lady McKenzie's visit to her hotel room the night before. It had turned out to be a wonderful ending, after all.

"Lord," Arykah said aloud in prayer, "I thank you for choosing me and using me. I thank you even more that this mission is over. And although it truly is an honor to be called upon,

I think I'm done solving other folks' problems for a while. In Jesus' name, amen." Deep down inside, Arykah couldn't lie; after going to Ohio to help Angel and then to California to help Lady McKenzie, she'd more than likely found her true calling as a speaker *and* mentor to other first ladies. But she still wanted a breather.

Arykah rolled back over to get in a few more hours of shut-eye before she concluded her stay in California with breakfast and a dip in the pool. Her eyes hadn't been closed for five minutes before she was alerted that another text had come through. Again, she picked up the phone. It was yet another message from Angel.

She read the text message to herself. First Lady SOS!

Arykah then threw the phone back on the bed. All she could do was shake her head while staring up to the heavens. "Lord, I may have spoken too soon."

About BLESSEDselling Author

E. N. Joy (**E**verybody **N**eeds Joy)

BLESSEDselling Author E. N. Joy is the author behind the New Day Divas, Still Divas, Always Divas, and Forever Divas series, all of which have been coined "Soap Operas in Print." She is an *Essence* magazine best-selling author and has written secular books under the names Joylynn M. Jossel and JOY. Her title *If I Ruled the World* earned her a book blurb from Grammy Award–winning artist Erykah Badu. *An All Night Man*, an anthology she penned with *New York Times* bestselling author Brenda Jackson, earned the Borders best-selling African American romance award. Her urban fiction title *Dollar Bill* (Triple Crown Publications) was mentioned in *Newsweek* and has been translated into Japanese.

After thirteen years as a paralegal in the insurance industry, E. N. Joy divorced her career and married her mistress and her passion:

writing. In 2000 she formed her own publishing company, where she published her books until landing a book deal with St. Martin's Press. This award-winning author has been sharing her literary expertise on conference panels in her hometown of Columbus, Ohio, as well as in cities across the country. She also conducts publishing/writing workshops for aspiring writers.

Her children's book *The Secret Olivia Told Me*, written under the name N. Joy, received a Coretta Scott King Honor from the American Library Association. The book was also acquired by Scholastic Books and has sold almost one hundred thousand copies. Elementary and middle school children have fallen in love with reading and creative writing as a result of the readings and workshops E. N. Joy gives in schools nationwide. In addition, she is the artistic developer for a young girls' group called DJHK Gurls. She pens original songs, drama skits, and monologues for the group that deal with issues that affect today's youth, such as bullying.

E. N. Joy served as the first content development editor for Triple Crown Publications and as the acquisitions editor for Carl Weber's Urban Christian imprint for ten years. Now she does freelance editing, ghostwriting, write behinds, and literary consulting. Her clients have included *New York Times* best-selling authors, entertainers, aspiring authors, as well as first-time authors. Her notable literary consulting clients include actor Christian Keyes, singer Olivia Longott, and reality television star Shereé M. Whitfield.

You can visit BLESSEDselling author E. N. Joy at www.enjoywrites.com, or e-mail her at enjoywrites@aol.com.

OTHER BOOKS BY E. N. JOY:

Me, Myself and Him
She Who Finds a Husband
Been There, Prayed That
Love, Honor or Stray
Trying to Stay Saved
I Can Do Better All By Myself
And You Call Yourself a Christian
The Perfect Christian
The Sunday Only Christian
I Ain't Me No More
More Than I Can Bear
You Get What You Pray For
When All Is Said and Prayed
One Sunday at a Time
Lady of the House
Ordained by the Streets
"A Woman's Revenge" (Anthology: *Best Served Cold*)
Behind Every Good Woman
Flower in My Hair

Even Sinners Have Souls (Edited by E. N. Joy)
Even Sinners Have Souls Too (Edited by E. N. Joy)
Even Sinners Still Have Souls (Edited by E. N. Joy)
The Secret Olivia Told Me (N. Joy)
Operation Get Rid of Mom's New Boyfriend (N. Joy)
Sabella and the Castle Belonging to the Troll (N. Joy)

About Nikita Lynnette Nichols

Nikita Lynnette Nichols, a Chicago native, was born in 1970. She attended Fort Dearborn Elementary School and graduated from the Academy of Our Lady High School in 1988.

In 2007 Miss Nichols signed a two-book deal with Urban Books. Her debut novel, titled *A Man's Worth*, was released in 2008, and it was followed by the release of *Amaryllis* in 2009. Miss Nichols signed a second two-book deal with Urban Books and released her third novel, *A Woman's Worth*, in 2010, followed by *Crossroads* in 2011. Miss Nichols was then offered a third book deal with Urban Books, and this led to the publication of her novel *Lady Elect* in 2012. Each of these titles made it to the best-sellers list at Black Expressions.

In 2012 *Lady Elect* was nominated for "Best Christian Fiction Book of the Year," an African American Literary Awards honor. That same year Miss Nichols partnered with movie director/producer Zelie Dember-Slack to cowrite the screenplay *Lady Elect*, which was based on her latest book release. Miss Nichols became an award-winning screenplay writer in 2013, when *Lady Elect* was a finalist in the Beverly Hills International Film Festival and was among the finalists in the screenplay category at the Moondance International Festival. The year 2014 saw the release of her *Damsels in Distress*. Miss Nichols's latest books, *Lady Elect 2* and *The Ugly Side of Me*, were published in 2015.

Other Books

by Nikita Lynnette Nichols:

None But the Righteous
A Man's Worth
Amaryllis
Crossroads
A Woman's Worth
Lady Elect
Damsels in Distress
Lady Elect 2

31901060963453